BROKEN FOR YOU

BROKEN FOR YOU

Stephanie Kallos

Grove Press
New York

Printed in the United States of America

Lyric permissions for Broken for You *by Stephanie Kallos:*

"The Nearness of You," words by Ned Washington, music by Hoagy Carmichael.
Copyright © 1937, 1940 (Renewed 1964, 1967) by Famous Music Corporation,
International Copyright Secured; All Rights Reserved. Used by Permission.

"Shall We Dance?" Copyright © 1951 by Richard Rodgers and Oscar Hammerstein II,
Copyright Renewed; Williamson Music owner of publication and allied rights throughout
the World; International Copyright Secured; All Rights Reserved. Used by Permission.

"April in Paris," by Vernon Duke and E. Y. Harburg, Copyright © 1932 Kay Duke Music
(ASCAP)/Universal Polygram International Publishing, Inc. All rights for the U.S. on
behalf of Kay Duke Music (ASCAP) administered by BMG Songs, Inc. (ASCAP).
Published by Glocca Morra Music (ASCAP), Administered by Next Decade Entertain-
ment, Inc. All Rights Reserved. Used by Permission.

"Blues in the Night" by Harold Arlen and Johnny Mercer. Copyright © 1941 (Renewed)
WB Music Corp. All Rights Reserved. Used by Permission. Warner Bros. Publications
U.S. Inc., Miami, Flordia 33014.

ISBN 0-7394-5299-1

Grove Press
841 Broadway
New York, NY 10003

For my children,
Noah Gregory Johns and Samuel Liam Johns

They're so much more than objects. They're living things, crafted and used by people like us. They reach out to us and through them we forge a link with the past.

—Guendolen Plestcheeff, decorative arts collector (1892–1994)

. . . He took Bread; and when He had given thanks, He brake it, and gave it to his disciples, saying, Take, eat, this is my Body, which is given for you.

—From the Prayer of Consecration, Holy Communion

BROKEN FOR YOU

Prologue

While the woman sleeps and dreams of all that breaks, come into this house of many rooms. Once your eyes adjust to the darkness, beginning to take in what is visible, you may notice a silence that is not quite silent. There is another language being spoken here, a tongue that emanates from white clay, fire, the oils of many skins, the fusion of rent spirits and matter. The woman hears this language always, even in her sleep, because she is guilty, and because those who speak to her are never silent. But for you, the innocent, there may only be a humming, a distant drone.

You might wander the rooms, wondering at its source. If you touch something, even lightly—that small figurine on her writing desk, say; the plump porcelain leprechaun from Belleek—you will perhaps become aware of a subtle change, a quickening that animates the molecules around you and sends them skittering across your skin. Pick up the figurine, trace its cool, silky contours with your fingers, and this feeling intensifies. The distant drone becomes louder, less indistinct, giving you the vague impression of an evolving language, heard from far away. Something in your awareness might start to take shape, something vaguely unsettling. Perhaps you shouldn't touch anything. You put the figurine down, possessed by the sudden certainty that you are being watched.

But no. Somewhere, the woman still sleeps—she is weeping now. There is only her and you, and whatever else this house contains. Moonlight, streetlights, headlights, starlights . . . All find a way inside and refract off thousands of glazed and polished surfaces. The light does not beautify what is already beautiful. It does not caress. No, it is sharp, random, erratic. Everything looks panicked. In this shooting light, even the stolid, bulbous soup tureens seem fearful.

Leave now. Come back later, when the house is not bereft and its inhabitants are not desperate. There will be employment for you then. You'll feel more at home. Your hands will have a purpose, your relationship to these objects and their guardian will be clear and comfortable. Come back when you're ready. You'll find what you've been looking for.

PART

ONE

One

❧

Margaret

When Margaret Hughes found out she had a brain tumor, she stared at the black-and-white images illuminated on the screen behind her physician's desk—"slices," he called them. She was surprised to see that her brain looked like two halves of a desiccated walnut.

Her physician spoke of cisterns, vessels, ventricles, a star. Of cells that had forgotten how to die. It was so complicated, so difficult to understand, but in all fairness she had no one to blame but herself. She was the one who'd insisted on seeing the images, made him promise that he'd be straightforward, tell her the *names* of things, explain why she'd been experiencing these headaches, these slips of the tongue, errors in cognition, apparitions. The fact that he continually referred to the images as "slices" only made matters worse; Margaret had already been so flustered before her appointment that she'd left home without finishing breakfast.

Dr. Leising pointed out the mass effect of the enhancing something-or-other as seen on Coronal Slice #16. Margaret's stomach rumbled.

I can't believe it, she thought. *I forgot to eat my jelly toast.*

Her physician concluded his speech and asked Margaret how she wished to proceed, what interventional options she wanted to pursue, and was there anyone she'd like to call. "Stephen perhaps?" he suggested, rather too lightly. "Mightn't he want to know?"

Well, of *course* her ex-husband would want to know. Couples don't go through what she and Stephen had without forging some kind of enduring connection—even (although few people understood this) a complicated, battle-comrade kind of love.

But there was something irritating in Dr. Leising's tone—as if he didn't think she should hear his prognosis in the absence of a male shoulder to weep on. As if she couldn't handle things without the benefit of counsel by some father-by-proxy. Margaret had managed her own affairs nicely for most of her life. She wouldn't be railroaded, pitied, or bamboozled now. *I might look like a nice, diffident old lady,* she thought, *but I'm not about to be treated like one.*

She asked a few pointed questions. Dr. Leising gave answers which she considered unacceptable, evasive, patronizing, and then launched into yet another discussion of her "slices." Would it never end?

Margaret couldn't listen anymore, so she excused herself to the rest room, took the elevator down to the street, and walked until she came upon a café with the words "Desserts, Etcetera" painted on the windows. She deliberated. On the rare occasions when she had to leave the house, she made sure to have as little contact as possible with other people; on the other hand, she was so hungry that she felt nauseous. Peeking through the window, Margaret saw that the café was open but empty of customers. This was satisfactory, so she went in.

Inside was a display case filled with artfully presented pies, cakes, cookies, and an assortment of French pastries. Margaret whispered their names: *Génoise à l'orange. Mousse au chocolat. Crème Brûlée. Roulade à la confiture.* She felt better already. Hanging over the counter was a menu written on a large chalkboard which included sandwiches and soups as well as desserts.

An anorexic-looking girl with short blue-black hair and black lipstick was talking into a telephone behind the counter. "I don't give a shit, Jimmy," she was saying, her voice tense and hissing, "You CANNOT use the juicer at three o'clock in the morning, I don't care HOW aggravated your 'vata' is!" Margaret waved to get the girl's attention. "Gotta go. Bye."

The girl hung up and loped to the counter. "Yes," she enunciated through clenched teeth. "What can I get for you?"

"It all looks so good," Margaret said. On closer inspection of the girl's face, Margaret was alarmed to see that she was wearing a gold ring through her right nostril. She tried not to stare at it. "What is your soup of the day?"

"Split pea," the girl said, and sniffed.

God, Margaret thought, *I hope she doesn't have a cold.*

"Well, in that case . . . I'll take a slice of raspberry cheesecake, a slice of pear ganache, the crème brûlée, and the caramel flan."

"For here?"

"Yes, please."

Nose Ring began punching the buttons of a small calculator. Her fingernails were painted dark blue and sprinkled with glitter. They looked like miniature galaxies. "Do you want whipped cream on your flan?"

"Excuse me?" Margaret said. "Whipped what?"

"Cream. On the flan."

"No, thank you," Margaret said without thinking, but then, "I mean yes! Why not? Whipped cream!"

"Will that be all?"

"Tea, perhaps. Do you have peppermint tea?"

"Have a seat," Nose Ring said. "I'll bring it out when it's ready."

Margaret awaited her desserts. On the café walls there were several black-and-white photographs of empty buildings, streets, docks, parks. Margaret didn't much care for them. There were no people in the photographs, and something about the time of day the photographer chose or the angle at which he took the photos gave even the most benign landmarks—the Seattle-to-Bainbridge ferry, the pergola in Pioneer Square, the Smith Tower—a menacing, doomsday appearance. They made Seattle look like a ghost town, and they reminded Margaret of an old movie. . . . What was it? It took place in New York City; it was about the end of the world. . . . She had found the movie very disturbing, although she couldn't say why. She couldn't for the life of her remember the name of it.

"*The World, the Flesh, and the Devil,*" said Nose Ring as she arrived at Margaret's table.

"What?"

"That old black-and-white movie about the end of the world. You were saying that you couldn't remember the name of it."

"I was?"

"Uh-huh." Nose Ring began unloading dishes and tea things from a large tray. "Harry Belafonte, Inger Stevens, and Mel Ferrer. *The World, the Flesh, and the Devil.*"

"Oh. Yes."

"Unless you mean *On the Beach*."

"I don't think so."

"Gregory Peck, Ava Gardner, and Fred Astaire? Directed by Stanley Kramer."

"No . . . I would've remembered Fred Astaire."

"Or you could be thinking of *Fail Safe*. With Henry Fonda as the president."

"I think you were right the first time."

Nose Ring stood up straight and announced, "I'm a film student."

"I see." Margaret smiled and nodded. She made another effort not to look at Nose Ring's nose ring. "Well, that must be very interesting!"

Nose Ring sighed. "Do you have everything you need?"

"Yes! Thank you! It looks lovely."

Nose Ring resumed her place behind the counter.

Margaret took a small, yellowed photograph out of her wallet; it was a school picture of Daniel, taken when he was eight. She stared at it.

The whole thing was quite simple, really.

According to Robert Leising, MD, and the various other neurology, oncology, and so-on-colleagues with whom he had consulted, Margaret had a very common type of malignant brain tumor: an "astrocytoma." A slow-growing star. The traditional treatment was surgery followed by radiation.

"What's the prognosis?" she had asked.

"Well," and here Dr. Leising had pulled one of six sheets of film off the light board and scrutinized it, "your age is—?"

As if he doesn't know, Margaret thought. "Seventy-five."

"Seventy-five." Dr. Leising nodded thoughtfully. He glanced at Margaret before resuming his study of the film. "Depending on the characteristics of the tumor—which we can't clearly define without getting in there and removing as much of it as possible—with treatment you have a chance of living as long as several years or as little as two."

"How much of a chance?"

Dr. Leising didn't look up. "Twenty-five percent."

"That's with treatment?"

"Yes."

"What happens if we don't do anything?"

"Excuse me?"

"I mean, if I only have a twenty-five percent chance of surviving this anyway, why don't we just leave it alone?"

"Maybe I haven't made myself clear, Margaret," Dr. Leising said, as if he were speaking to a nincompoop. That was when he resumed his discussion of Margaret's slices in a way that clearly constituted the American Medical Association's form of filibustering.

So, this was her choice: She could either undergo a *lot* of treatment and die, sooner or later, or she could undergo no treatment at all and die, sooner or later.

"Is something wrong?" Nose Ring had returned. "You haven't tried anything."

Margaret swallowed hard. Now that all of this lovely food was in front of her, she found that she wasn't hungry after all. She took a sip of tea, just to be polite.

"Is that your grandson?" Nose Ring asked, leaning closer. "Cute."

She's quite a young girl beneath all that makeup, Margaret realized. *And much too thin.* "Do you mind if I ask you a personal question?"

Nose Ring shrugged. "What is it?"

"Well, it's a rather trite question, I suppose, but if you found out that you had only a short while to live, maybe a year or two, how would you spend your time?"

The girl frowned. She picked absentmindedly at her fingernails, and showers of silver glitter flaked off and fell toward the floor. Margaret tried to follow the trajectory of the glitter, but it seemed to vanish into thin air.

"I suppose I'd think about whatever it is that scares me the most— relationshipwise, I mean—and then do it. Do the opposite of what I've always done."

Margaret studied Nose Ring. She'd always assumed that people who embraced dramatic vogues in fashion were actually compensating for an innate dullness of character or chronic insecurity. She'd expected someone who looked like Nose Ring to offer a superficial answer to her rather trite question: "Take up hang-gliding! Sail around the world! Race hot-air balloons!" Something along those lines.

"It would be a last chance, wouldn't it?" the girl went on. "To break all your old bad habits?" She caught herself worrying her hands and promptly stopped. "Well anyway, here's your bill. Pay whenever you're ready." She made her way back to the counter, looking pensive.

Margaret contemplated her own habits. She stared at Daniel's photo. He had been at that age when most children are self-conscious in front of a camera. But in this picture his expression was relaxed, serious, and sage. "You can see exactly what he's going to look like when he's twenty!" Margaret remembered saying to Stephen all those years ago, when the package they'd ordered came home from school: one 8x10, two 5x7s, four 3x5s, and many, many billfolds.

But Daniel would never be twenty. The 8x10 remained unframed. The billfolds were never passed out to school friends and teachers. Margaret wondered if Stephen still kept a photograph of their son in his wallet, along with pictures he surely carried of the children he had with his second wife. His living children.

"Jimbo?" Nose Ring was on the telephone, speaking gently. "I'm sorry I yelled before. . . . Yeah, I know. . . . I love you, too. You want me to pick up some Häagen-Dazs on the way home? . . . No, I'm not kidding."

Maybe it was time for a change. A commuted sentence. Margaret had no difficulty knowing what was required. Daniel stared back at her, without forgiveness, but without condemnation, either, his eyes alight with the detached, loving wisdom of a little monk. Margaret tucked the photograph back into her pocketbook, sipped her tea, and waited until Nose Ring hung up the telephone.

"Excuse me, dear," she called across the room. "Have you a pen I might borrow?"

"Sure. Are you a writer?"

"Oh, no," Margaret said automatically. "I'm . . ." *I'm anything I want to be,* she thought. *Anything at all.* "I'm the woman who invented the garlic press!"

"Ah." Nose Ring handed over her pen. "I'll get more hot water for your tea."

"Thank you, dear. That's very kind."

Margaret turned over the bill and began writing. "Room for rent in large Capitol Hill home. $250. All utilities included. Month-to-month.

Private bath . . ." By the time she was satisfied with the ad, her appetite was back. She started with the crème brûlée.

Magnifique! she thought, not minding that the café had begun to fill up with customers and she was no longer alone. *C'est parfait.*

Before she actually placed the ad she would have to ask permission. Of course she would. She couldn't just willy-nilly start taking in boarders without consulting her housemates. After all, they'd lived together practically forever. She'd tended their needs, kept them pristine and perfect, sheltered them. With the exception of those few intervening years when Stephen and Daniel had shared the house, they'd had her completely to themselves. Her devotion was unquestionable. Still, she knew they'd feel threatened. They'd never stand for a unilateral decision. It would take finesse, skill, and diplomacy to pull this off. What she intended would be a hard sell.

Of course, they'd want to know what was in it for them. They'd have a point. She'd have to come up with something.

Praise? Admiration? That might be an incentive. They'd be in contact with another set of human eyes. What could be the harm in that? They'd be ogled and applauded by someone besides her. That should be enough for the vast majority. Most of them were a bit shallow anyway. Fools for flattery. Yes, that could work. And she'd never take on anyone clumsy or bullish, that was certain. The more diffident among them could be reassured about that. They'd be in no danger.

So there. That was settled.

The next question was, how would she broach the subject? And who would she speak to first? Who would be the most receptive to change?

Not the soup tureens; as a group, they were consistently unimaginative and stodgy. The game pie dishes at least had a sense of humor, but they were cowardly, and always took sides with anything lidded. Which eliminated the teapots and casseroles and so on. It was very tricky, as the lot of them were quite cliquish. All of the figurines were out; in spite of her best efforts, she could never manage to address them without sounding condescending, and they resented her for it. One or two of the teacups might be sympathetic. She also considered the gold-encrusted inkstands, who, for all their decorative excess, had always struck her as fair-minded and sensible.

But, no. The others would never be convinced by anything so diminutive as an inkstand. She'd need an ally that was at the very least physically impressive. Objects responded to things like size and blunt speech. Margaret roamed the rooms of the house in her mind's eye: the Aviary Suite, Bonbon Dish Room, Smoke and Snuff Room . . .

Aha! She had it. The pair of Qing Dynasty garden seats. They'd be perfect. Large and commanding, with their sea-green celadon glaze, they were not only elegant but wise and plain-speaking. The fact that they once sat in the open air had given them more free-thinking views. And if all that weren't enough, there was the added prestige of their appraised value: eight thousand dollars each. The other garden seats were worth five thousand or less. If she could win over the Qing twins, Margaret knew, they'd get everyone to give her a fair hearing.

Margaret reviewed her defense. She headed out to the sunny atrium (also known as the Chinese Garden Seat Room), cleaning flannel in hand. She'd surprise all of them with a thorough polishing first to get in their good graces. Then she would plead her case to the Qings.

Two

❧

The First Respondent

"I came to him like a pilgrim," the young woman said, and held out her hands, palms up, like she was waiting to be given something: a stack of books, a platter of sweet potatoes, an armful of clean, folded linens. She was telling Margaret why it was she had no furniture, hardly any possessions at all, really, except for her clothes and her French press coffeemaker; that was why this was the perfect arrangement for her. They'd met maybe fifteen minutes ago, and Margaret was about to give her a tour of the house. They were still on the first floor. In fact, they hadn't moved since they'd met.

Her name was Wanda. That was how she'd introduced herself on the phone, and how she'd introduced herself when she showed up—two hours before she said she would—at the front door. "Hello, Mrs. Hughes. I'm Wanda. I'm here about the newspaper ad. We just spoke on the phone."

Margaret had trouble seeing Wanda clearly. The sun was setting, and the accumulating shadows slanted across her face in a way which gave it an odd, fragmented look. She was quite small, though, and her eyes were very large and dark.

"I've been doing affirmations about this, and I hope it's not inconvenient for you that I'm here now—I decided to splurge and take a taxi instead of the bus—but it just sounded like the answer to my prayers, and I really believe in following your impulses. I think it's so crucial."

Affirmations. Margaret knew that this word had a new and different meaning nowadays, but she didn't know what that meaning was.

"Is it all right for me to be here now?"

"Yes. It's fine. Come in."

But Wanda stayed outside, and right away started telling Margaret about her life: how she was deeply in love with a man named Peter; how Peter was troubled but brilliant, a furniture restorer by trade, an artist by passion who sculpted bigger-than-life-sized angels playing tenor saxophones; how he and Wanda had lived together in a New York loft they'd renovated themselves.

Margaret was very uncomfortable—less so with what Wanda was saying than with the fact that she was saying it while standing on the front steps. It was as if the paperboy had come to collect and then suddenly started describing the intimate details of his personal life.

"We built bookcases together, I tell you," Wanda went on. "We refinished an entire Victorian bedroom set. We had dishes. Coffee mugs. Wineglasses. We bought major home appliances. On credit!"

Margaret nodded sympathetically. She came from a generation of people for whom these events—the sharing of environments, worldly goods, and beds—automatically meant "marriage," but she understood that times had changed. She was pleased with herself for not feeling shocked at the fact that Wanda was a person who had been "living in sin," as the nuns would have said, with mouths as shriveled and briny as gherkins.

Then, Wanda went on, out of the blue Peter told her that he needed to simplify his life. His life was becoming too complicated, too cluttered, too full. "How can a life be too full?" Wanda appealed to Margaret, but she rushed on before Margaret had a chance to respond. Peter wanted to quit his job and get out of Manhattan. He wanted to travel, see open spaces, move west. He wanted, Wanda said bitterly, to be free. Find himself. Use Laundromats.

Wanda said, "I thought, Okay. I'll give it all up. My New York connections, my career, all of it. I love him that much. I can do this."

So, one weekend when Peter went on a camping trip to the Adirondacks, Wanda sold everything. Not just the things she and Peter had together, either, but everything. Things she'd bought with her own money. Things she'd acquired long before she met Peter and which had stories he never knew about or guessed at. Whatever she couldn't sell she gave away, threw away, or burned in secret ceremonies. And then when Peter got back and she told him about this extraordinary thing she'd done and said, "I'm ready," he stared at her with a blank look on his face and said, "I'm sorry. I thought you understood. I want to be alone."

How awful for her, Margaret thought. She was feeling less uncomfortable; as Wanda went on with her story, Margaret had moved one of the foyer chairs away from the wall and into the center of the hallway. She was sitting there now. Wanda didn't seem to mind; Margaret wasn't even sure she'd noticed. *How awful—after this young woman came to him with her empty hands, having divested herself of everything.*

That was when Wanda said, "I came to him like a pilgrim," and did that peculiar gesture.

When Margaret heard that word—and it was so startling; she hadn't heard it for years—her first thought was not automatically of the kind of pilgrim Wanda meant. When Margaret heard the word "pilgrim," all she could think of were those cardboard cutouts that elementary school teachers used to put up around Thanksgiving. *Maybe they still do,* Margaret thought. *Maybe times haven't changed all that much.* In November—after the black cats, benign ghosts, and witches on broomsticks, and before the Christmas trees and mangers and Wise Men and Santas and reindeer and holly and mistletoe and Dickensian carolers—teachers would explain for the thousandth time the meaning of the word "maize" and dutifully staple up a few pilgrims in those severe-looking black-and-white outfits. They might also put up some Indians. Turkeys. A horn of plenty or two.

Margaret learned early on in life that Thanksgiving was the time of year when even the best-mannered people ate and drank too much, and men—*especially* men: men you thought you knew, men you used to think loved you and would protect you—abandoned their higher selves and the postmeal society of womenfolk for baser pursuits; men like her father and his European colleagues went off to smoke various forms of malodorous tobacco and tell disreputable jokes behind closed doors, and, much later, men like Stephen and his friends not only thought nothing of leaving their wives to clean up the kitchen, but ended up falling asleep in undignified poses in front of the television set, while on the screen younger men—boys, really, who should have been home eating candied yams and chestnut stuffing and pumpkin pie—were hurtling against each other like senseless bulls. As far as Margaret was concerned, whatever dim hope had remained for the Thanksgiving holiday had vanished completely with the advent of televised football.

She couldn't for the life of her imagine why Wanda had chosen to come to her Peter like a "pilgrim"—unless she meant that, as some form of penance or self-denial, she'd adopted the colorless style of dress that made pilgrims resemble Cubist penguins. She *was* dressed rather plainly.

"You have beautiful things," Wanda said, sounding a little congested. Margaret was startled by this abrupt segue into normal conversational tone and content. Maybe the girl was less distraught than she appeared.

Margaret got up. Her legs felt stiff. "Why don't you come in."

Apparently Wanda was through talking about Peter; she showed all the symptoms of a down-winding music box. She plodded across the threshold, around the chair, and into the hallway. She sighed. She sniffled. She no longer looked like a person who believed that her affirmations—whatever they were—had been affirmed. Margaret found her sudden silence disconcerting.

"I'll show you the main floor first—unless you'd like to see the room right away?" Margaret waited, but Wanda made no reply. "It's on the second floor," Margaret continued. Her voice sounded strange, unfamiliar, hollow. She tried to remember the last time she had spoken this many words to anyone inside the house.

Wanda pressed her lips together, looked down at her feet, and sighed again.

To Margaret's left was a large, walnut-inlaid, glass-fronted cabinet crammed with eighteenth-century Bow figurines. She could feel them squinting at her through their excessive vegetal surroundings, their pouty little doll-like mouths wary. Nonetheless, they were intrigued.

"All right then!" Margaret proclaimed. "To the kitchen!"

She closed the front door but decided to leave the chair where it was; she didn't want to draw any more attention to the fact that she'd been sitting down while Wanda had been languishing on the front steps.

They moved toward the kitchen: through the foyer, down the hall-way, past the grand staircase, the living room, the library, the powder room, and the first-floor guest suite.

"Yes, your things are really beautiful," Wanda repeated, almost as if she too was aware of them staring at her. If Margaret hadn't known bet-ter, she'd have thought Wanda was buttering them up.

When they arrived in the kitchen, Margaret began explaining how whoever took the room would have full use of the appliances, pots and pans, everyday dishes, cutlery, and so forth, but not the china, crystal, or silver from the dining room étagère.

This policy had seemed reasonable enough to Margaret when she'd first designed it, but she suddenly felt self-conscious and miserly repeat-ing it to her first potential boarder. Besides that, she could not get used to the feeling of directing her voice to another living entity within these walls. It wasn't that her vocal cords went unexercised: For years she'd sung along with television commercials (those for Charmin bathroom tissue and Sominex were her favorites); occasionally she put on old re-cordings of her favorite musicals (*Gigi, My Fair Lady, South Pacific, The King and I*) and crooned along while she cleaned; she often practiced her French aloud; and of course she conversed with her things and their ghosts. But when there was a need to speak with real people—postmen, electricians, roofers, and so on—Margaret used her voice as little as possible. It had been years since she'd allowed herself unrestricted con-versation with another living person.

Margaret opened the large kitchen cupboard with the everyday dishes. It was a remarkably well-ordered cupboard by anyone's stan-dards and she was pleased to show it off. There were a dozen plates with a simple blue and white floral pattern, upended, evenly spaced, and held in place by a ridge near the back. There were twelve cups suspended at regular, measured intervals. Twelve cereal bowl-soup bowl-salad dishes. Salt-and-pepper shakers. A soup tureen. Gravy boat. Water pitcher. "These are the dishes you can use," she said. Wanda hummed appreciatively, but asked no questions. "They're Pfalzgraff, actually," Margaret elaborated. "They're very sturdy. We've had them for years."

In the dim light of the cupboard, hung there in their orderly fashion on specially rubberized hooks, the cups resembled a natural history display and made Margaret think of dinosaur bones. Then she noticed that something was wrong with one of the cups. "Well, look at this," she said, taking it down. There was a hairline fracture where the handle met the cup, and as she grabbed the handle she heard a gritty, unstable sound.

Then Wanda made a kind of pained exhalation, as if she'd been slapped. As Margaret turned around to see her running down the hall (was she leaving?), the cup fell away to the tile floor, breaking into several pieces, and Margaret was left holding the chunky, rounded handle.

She walked down the hallway, following the sound of short, muffled intakes of breath that sounded like crying—although she supposed it could have been laughing. She hoped it was laughing. She stopped at a respectful distance in front of the closed powder room door.

Wanda was definitely crying, and in a gasping sort of way that made Margaret wonder if the girl was asthmatic. "Uh . . . hello?"

The crying ceased.

"Excuse me? Wanda? Are you in there?" It was strange not knowing the girl's last name. Margaret would have much preferred to say, "Miss So-and-So, are you all right?"

There was a long, silent pause, and then Wanda blurted, "I'm wondering, do you have a pipe wrench?"

"Sorry?"

"I just noticed a small leak in here. Under the sink."

"Oh!"

"I think I could fix it. I mean, I *know* I could fix it. If you have a wrench, that is."

"I have a small tool kit for minor home repairs, yes."

"Great! I'm sure there's something in there I could use. I'll have this taken care of in no time."

"No need to rush."

"This bathroom is just beautiful," Wanda went on. "Is this a Limoges hand mirror? . . ." Her voice trailed off and she began whimpering quietly.

Margaret tried to think of something comforting to say. "You know, the room upstairs has its very own bathroom!"

"That's wonderful!" Wanda blubbered. "I'll check the pipes up there, too, if you'd like."

"How very kind of you." Margaret looked down and realized she was still grasping the cup handle; she examined it from various angles, wondering if it could be put to any practical use. "The tool kit's in the kitchen. I think I'll fix some tea while I'm at it. Do you drink tea?" From inside the bathroom, Wanda continued to make sounds very like those of a shamed puppy. Margaret waited a while longer, but when no further human utterance seemed forthcoming, she headed to the kitchen pantry.

She placed the cup handle on a jar of brandied peaches; the jar was well over a decade old, its contents certainly inedible, but because it bore a Christmassy label which read "Happy Holidays! With love from our home to yours," Margaret had been unable to throw it away. It mattered not a bit that she no longer remembered who'd given her the peaches. "That's typical," Margaret muttered aloud, with mild self-disgust. She fetched the small metal toolbox and scanned the pantry. *I'll have to remember to clear some shelves in here for whoever takes the room,* she thought. On her way out, she grabbed a fresh box of tissues.

From behind the powder room door, and much to Margaret's relief, came the sound of pipes squeaking as water was turned off and on. No whimpering. Having a plumbing project must have made the girl feel better.

To each her own, Margaret thought. After placing the box of tissues and the tool kit on the floor, she cleared her throat energetically and then retraced her steps to the kitchen.

Margaret was slicing lemons and waiting for the teapot to whistle when she remembered about the other kind of pilgrim. The kind that makes a long journey on foot, carrying little or nothing, to see someone, or something. Like a roadside shrine. Or a miracle: Jesus' face in a billboard ad for SpaghettiOs, the Virgin Mary etched in a cracked windshield, a statue crying blood . . . Or a relic: the Shroud of Turin. *Do they let ordinary people see that?* Margaret wondered. *Or just scientists?* The Vietnam War Memorial—*That's a kind of shrine, isn't it?*—or John Kennedy's grave, or the Tomb of the Unknown Soldier . . . Of course. The kind of pilgrim that Wanda meant traveled to places where saints were enshrined, or where miracles had occurred. Margaret herself had never gone on a pilgrimage. She had never allowed herself a journey of any kind, for that matter.

Margaret heard Wanda coming out of the bathroom and down the hall. She realized by the sound of the steps that Wanda must be very light indeed.

The girl offered up the tool kit with both hands as she approached. Her eyes were red and puffy from crying, but when she spoke her voice was completely composed.

"I'm sorry I disappeared, Mrs. Hughes. It's not like me to be so emotional. You must think I'm a loon."

No need to worry, Margaret thought, stifling a laugh. *I talk to eighteenth-century chamber pots.*

"Anyway," Wanda continued, "I took care of that leak." She couldn't seem to look at Margaret directly; her eyes roamed the kitchen, randomly at first, and then settling on the cup, which had rolled underneath the kitchen table. "Oh, no!" she said, getting down on the floor. "Did I do this?"

"Not at all. Just leave it." Margaret waved dismissively. "What kind of tea do you like?"

"Anything herbal is fine," Wanda replied, still kneeling, turning the pieces over in her thin-boned, freckled hands. Her nails were short and unadorned. Her hair was cropped close too—clean, but unkempt; its style reminded Margaret of the way Audrey Hepburn looked at the end of *The Nun's Story,* right before she left the convent. From this perspective, looking down on her, Margaret could also see that Wanda was not a natural blonde.

"I've just *got* to get off the caffeine. It's so toxic to your immune system. I've been thinking of doing one of those barley grass detox fasts."

"I beg your pardon?"

"You know, this isn't bad." Wanda was still scrutinizing the cup. "We could fix this *easy.* Do you have any epoxy?"

"In the pantry. But really, just leave it, dear."

Wanda got up suddenly and strode into the pantry with breathtaking authority. "Found it!" she called out triumphantly. "The handle, too!" She came out cradling the glue and the cup tenderly, as if she had a handful of newly hatched chicks.

"Really, it's not necessary."

"Let me do this," Wanda insisted. "I'm good at fixing things."

They sat at the kitchen table for half an hour. They drank a pot of tea. Wanda repaired the cup while Margaret studied her references; these consisted of a recent copy of her bank statement (Wanda may have abandoned all her earthly goods, but she'd had the good sense to hang on to her savings—which were quite impressive), a resumé (Wanda told Margaret that she was an "Equity stage manager," and whatever that was Margaret could see that she'd had extensive experience at it), and a list of job interviews she'd scheduled over the next month.

Wanda also volunteered a few other bits of personal information: Separated from her mother and father at an early age—she did not say how early, nor what had happened to her parents—she had been raised by an aunt and uncle and had grown up in Chicago. Her uncle was a plumber. Her last name was Schultz.

After they finished touring the house, Wanda went back into the kitchen. She carefully transported the mended cup across the room and set it on the counter in an out-of-the-way location. "Don't touch this for several days, okay? The epoxy has to dry thoroughly—I mean *absolutely thoroughly*. I think it's going to take. I think you might even be able to use it again."

"Thank you. It was really unnecessary."

"Well, don't thank me till you test it." Wanda began to help Margaret clear the tea things. "Do you know how soon you'll be making your decision?"

"By the end of the week. I'll call you either way."

"Thank you, Mrs. Hughes." Wanda clasped Margaret's hand. Again, Margaret was struck by the lightness and delicacy of this girl's bones— like a bird's, like something meant for flight. "I hope it works out. I think I could be really happy here. And useful, too, you know?"

Margaret interviewed several other respondents over the next few days: Deirdre, a would-be writer wearing a gray moth-eaten sweater and smelling of BO and French cigarettes; Sarah, a born-again Christian who looked exactly like Squeaky Fromm and who informed Margaret that she'd be leading weekly Bible study sessions; Candy, a newly divorced ad executive whose husband had custody of the children; and Eunice, a large-breasted woman who pretended to be surprised about the "no pets" part of the ad. She was covered in cat hair, and stomped off the porch. Margaret was afraid she might spray the front steps before she left.

Margaret sat at her writing desk and, setting aside the Belleek leprechaun, laid the applicant files out in front of her. Obviously, Eunice was a no-go. As far as the other candidates were concerned, Margaret tried to make herself see them objectively, give them all fair and equal consideration, but she couldn't get over the fact that Wanda was the only one who came into the house and cried. *Cried!* Nor did any of the others express an interest in plumbing—or in any of the other unseen workings of the house for that matter. No one else had asked the kinds of questions she'd asked. And—Margaret was certain she hadn't imagined it—there was an unusual curiosity radiating from her things when Wanda was in the house. Something about her had intrigued them. The young woman might be a bit emotionally unbalanced, but she had been tuned to the house and its occupants in a way the others hadn't. Yes, she was the one.

Margaret called and left a message at the YWCA switchboard. Wanda called back ten minutes later.

"The room is yours if you want it," Margaret said.

"Oh, that's wonderful!" Wanda exclaimed. "I'm thrilled, Mrs. Hughes, just thrilled! Thank you so much! I'll be there as soon as I can get my stuff together and catch a bus."

The girl's voice was brassier in tone and more exigent than Margaret remembered. It induced in her a sudden nervousness. "Please," Margaret said evenly, "call me Margaret."

"Margaret." Wanda rushed on. "I got a job today too, so everything is going just great! The power of affirmations, you know? Well, bye now! See you soon!"

Margaret hung up and closed her eyes, letting the residual buzz of Wanda's voice fade, waiting until its unsettling effect diminished. *What have I done?* she thought wryly. *I may live to regret this. Or not.*

The house hummed and creaked in its quiet, familiar way; it was like a crewless freighter, far out on a placid, pristine sea, carrying all the cargo of Margaret's life. Very little of this cargo was lawful. *Making it more like a pirate ship, I suppose,* Margaret thought, and then she recalled Daniel's pirate phase—*All children probably have them*—when, for days

on end, he'd donned a huge bushy black beard, tricorn hat, and eye patch
and hobbled about the house doing his impression of Long John Silver
in *Treasure Island:* "Them that die'll be the lucky ones!"

In her mind, Margaret floated from room to room through the entire house—all fifteen thousand square feet of it. Everything was in its
place. Nothing was undusted, or untended, or unremarked upon, or
without meaning. Every piece sat quietly for once, as if in agreement
with Margaret's choice—all secure in their places of honor throughout
the house. They sat, knowing their own stories and trusting that Margaret would keep those stories for them—as she had for years and years,
at no little cost.

Soon, she would have to make a decision about the fate of these things.
Not yet, but soon. She trusted them to make their wishes known when
the time was right.

Three

❧

Wanda

Wanda hung up the pay phone in the YWCA lounge. It was decorated in acrimonious shades of pink, orange, and brown, and smelled of ammonia and acetone. Not surprisingly, no one ever seemed to do any lounging there.

Hearing from Mrs. Hughes should have lifted her spirits, but she felt suddenly deflated. She trudged up three flights of dingy linoleum-covered stairs to her room. She retrieved a city map and several Metro bus pamphlets from her backpack. After unfolding the maps and pamphlets on her bed, she knelt, surrendering to the compression of cartilage and bone against bare floor. Nearby, on a wobbly table, was the morning *Post-Intelligencer* and a paper cup containing the lukewarm remnants of a triple espresso. Wanda sipped the coffee—pleasantly bitter and sludgy with cinnamon. Peter had taught her to put cinnamon in her coffee. She imagined the heavy brown liquid leaching into her teeth, saturating them with something far more preservative and strengthening than fluoride.

"Here we go," she said quietly. The words echoed against the room's hard, chilly surfaces.

The space had the anonymity of an uninhabited college dormitory. In addition to the bed and bedside table, there was a cheap pressboard bookcase, a chest of drawers, a dented metal trash can, a plastic molded chair, and a beat-up desk which listed so severely (one of its legs was shorter than the others) that unsupervised pens and pencils pitched off its surface and catapulted into the corner. Several of them had accumulated there over the past two weeks. Wanda felt no need to retrieve them; she had lots of pens and pencils.

She'd also made no effort to make the room homey in any way; her single affect had been to cover the mirror (which was bolted to the concrete wall) with a Mickey and Minnie Mouse beach towel. It was a souvenir from a trip she and Peter had taken to the ocean. She liked to imagine that it infused the air with the smell of seawater and sex.

Wanda looked at the wall above her bed. Taped to the wall was a piece of paper. At the top was written "Peter Hartzell"—directory assistance for the Seattle area listed no one of that name—and beneath that, "Rhett Pearllze," "Halle Zepettre," "Treat Phellerz," and "Teller Heart-Pez." There were no listings in the Seattle area for any of these names either.

"Shit," Wanda said. As bare as this room was, as empty as she had tried to keep it, it told the whole story. It couldn't keep its damn mouth shut.

She wandered to the gimpy desk, on which rested a "Rooms for Rent" section she'd torn from the *P-I* several days ago. A few other entries were highlighted in yellow—Wanda had lots of highlighters, too—but Mrs. Hughes's ad was notable because the rental price, an unbelievable two hundred and fifty dollars, had been aggressively circled and surrounded with question marks and exclamation points.

Margaret, Wanda remembered suddenly. *She wants me to call her Margaret.* That would take some getting used to; Wanda had been brought up to address her elders as "Mister" or "Missus."

She felt intensely grateful to be moving into a place that was noisy with someone else's history. Margaret herself was not noisy, and she was grateful for that, too, since her work as a stage manager required her for the most part to be around noisy people: actors.

Actors were, in fact, manageable, once you made peace with the fact that they had never really evolved into adulthood—not even the oldest and most cantankerous ones, the ones she addressed as "Mister": the Scrooges and Tartuffes and Captain Hooks and King Lears. They were "players," in the truest sense of the word—at least the best ones were, in Wanda's opinion; and once you understood their love of play and recognized that they were exactly like children—children needing enormous amounts of attention and reassurance and, of course, limits—you could manage them quite nicely. Actors could also provide a nice, succulent, dessert-course variety of sexual diversion.

Wanda had a lot of experience in this arena; she'd been sleeping with actors ever since she was fifteen, when she and Brian McConnell had surrendered their virginities to one another on closing night of *The Music Man*. Brian was the sixteen-year-old star, and Wanda, having found her vocation early in life, was the stage manager.

Closing nights had already become something of an emotional hazard for Wanda; they left her feeling uncharacteristically mournful and clingy. So when she and Brian discovered that the rest of the cast and crew had left for the party and the drama teacher had accidentally locked them in the catacombs of the costume shop—where, bogged down by mutual closing night melancholia, they'd taken forever to box up the mounds of rented turn-of-the-century costumes that had to be shipped back to New York—Wanda suggested that they make the most of a lucky situation. They were friends, they were equally inexperienced, the floor was a feather bed of petticoats and band uniforms, and—having both recently completed a semester of health ed—they knew the importance of being prepared; between them, they had twenty-four condoms.

It was an hour and forty-five minutes before the night janitor noticed the light under the costume shop door and started jangling his keys. All in all, Wanda's first sexual experience had turned out just fine. Not only that: She'd found a surefire way to banish closing night blues.

She slept exclusively with actors after that—right up to the moment when she met Peter. Always on the go, always leaving, always looking ahead to the next big part, they had a flighty but infectious spirit. They made her laugh. She got to watch their spotlit hammy antics from the obscurity of the sidelines; she liked that, too. And as she learned early on from Brian McConnell, good actors have a knack for improvisation, making them naturally gifted when it comes to sex—which is, of course, under the best of conditions a highly improvisatory event. But all that playfulness and self-absorption had a downside; eventually Wanda's thespian paramours started to resemble the Lost Boys of Never-Never Land, and since she had no desire to be anyone's mother, invariably the time would come for them to part. She was very careful to manage her personal dealings with actors as well as her professional ones, so that her affairs always ended amicably. This was important. Among stage folk, it is said that there are only thirty-three people in the theatre. To Wanda's colleagues, this expression has a generalized, benign meaning: "Everyone is connected, part of a family. Everyone knows someone you know." But to Wanda, it meant, "Don't burn any bridges, and don't screw and tell." She had never left bad feelings in the wake of a breakup.

Of course, she also had to interact closely with many other kinds of theatre professionals—directors and designers and light board operators and theatre technicians—and she strictly forbade herself from becoming romantically involved with any of them. She had to write cues, record blocking, attend production meetings, run rehearsals, oversee the running crews, command the proceedings of tech and dress rehearsals, maintain the quality and consistency of the show throughout its run. And she was good, very good, at all of it. But it was her ability to deal with actors—her skills as a peacemaker and go-between, her ability to smooth ruffled feathers, soothe bruised egos, and, when required, lay down the law—that made her a first-rate stage manager, one who could, based on word of mouth, her experience, and her qualifications, get work anywhere. She'd already secured a job at the biggest theatre in town, and she was confident that other jobs would follow. *That* part of her life, at least—the work part, where she was functional, extremely competent, and sane—would settle into a familiar routine.

This move into Margaret's house, however, was something entirely new, and she was mildly nervous about it. She had never in her adult life shared a living space with anyone but Peter. She had *certainly* never lived in a mansion with a woman of Margaret's age and apparent social standing.

Good thing I was able to get my shit together before she threw me out of the house, she thought, remembering how she'd rattled on about Peter and all but swooned in front of a total stranger. '*I came to him like a pilgrim?*' *Where the hell did THAT come from?*

Wanda walked over to Mickey and Minnie, pulled them toward her face, and inhaled. Nothing there but extra-strength Tide and fabric softener. She yanked the towel down and kicked it out of the way. Drawing close to the mirror, she stared at her face for the first time in two weeks.

She looked like hell. She reached up and gave a few firm, quick tugs to her right eyebrow, then her left; several weak-looking, dark, curving hairs stuck to her finger and thumb. She flicked them onto the floor.

"Thank God I'm getting out of here," she said out loud. "Thank God for Mrs. Hughes."

By cab, Wanda's first trip to Margaret's had been an easy twenty-minute ride, culminating in an ascent up a winding street so dark and densely wooded that, even encased in the safety of a taxi, Wanda had felt like an endangered character in a Grimm fairy tale. But the woods cleared at the top of the hill, and there was the Hughes mansion.

"Are you sure this is the right place?" Wanda had asked the cabdriver.

He looked down at the piece of paper she'd handed him when she got in the cab. "Yeah. This is it. You're gonna rent a room *here*?"

"Maybe." Wanda kept her eyes on the house as she gathered her things.

The Hughes residence—which sat on a huge lot in a neighborhood where *all* the houses were mansions—was astonishing: towering ornate pillars, tiered and cantilevered porches, multipeaked roof, leaded and stained glass windows. There was even an adjacent carriage house. But beneath all this grandeur, Wanda sensed something tired and sad. An art historian would have described the Hughes mansion as a splendid example of early-nineteenth-century Neoclassic/Romantic hybridism; but to Wanda, the house looked like a big neglected wedding cake.

"Geez. How much rent are they gonna be chargin' you?"

Wanda paid the cabbie and got out of the car. "Not nearly enough." Then she started up the steps toward the massive front porch.

She'd be a perfect Mother Abbess, Wanda thought when Margaret opened the door. Solid and androgynous, she looked nothing like her voice—which on the phone had been oddly high-pitched and squeaky. Margaret's eyes, though, were the real surprise. They were shimmering, reflective. The turquoise of a glacial lake on the fairest day of summer. It was her eyes, Wanda decided later, that had disarmed her so completely. Why else would she have launched into her long confessional about Peter and come so utterly undone? Stupid. She'd nearly ruined her chance to win what had to be the best rental bargain in the city.

The inside of the house was as remarkable as the outside. It had been built in 1909, Margaret explained, at a time when wealth from the Alaskan gold rush and the accompanying timber and shipping industries had begun transforming Seattle into a boomtown. Her father had been an investor in these growing industries. "He was good at making money," she said dryly.

The house was fifteen thousand square feet—the floor space of an average three-bedroom home, Wanda calculated, multiplied by ten—and it contained one amazing architectural feature after another: parquet floors, gilded canvas murals, carved oak columns and capitals, ornate plaster ceilings, brass fixtures, marbled and tiled fireplaces. Just this side of rococo, all of it was glistening and pristine and impeccably maintained. The outside of the house and its grounds may have been suffering from neglect, but on the inside, it could have been brand new.

And then there were Margaret's things. They were kept in glass-fronted built-in and freestanding cabinets which lined the walls of virtually every room in the house. The dining room alone contained what had to be thousands of pieces of functional dinnerware, coffee and tea sets, and serving pieces. Margaret identified a few of these, listing their names with detachment, as if she were reading from an insurance schedule. "Sherbet pails, 1781. Pigeon pie tureen, 1851. Chocolate service, 1815. Cheese bell, 1870. Tête-à-tête, 1775. Oyster stand, 1862. Strawberry dish, 1868. Ewer and basin, 1790. Coffeepot, 1730 . . ."

As they moved through the rest of the house, Wanda discovered that there were even more pieces that were purely decorative. In the small downstairs parlor, one cabinet contained animals in general—cats, foxes, sheep, squirrels, horses, lions, elephants, camels, cows—while another was devoted to various breeds of porcelain dogs. The large parlor was populated with grouped figures: hunting parties, mothers and children, cupids, courting peasants, boccie players, Greek gods. And on and on . . .

"Are all of these porcelain?" Wanda had asked.

"Not all, but many."

"Where did they come from?"

"My father. He owned an antique shop in addition to his investments. Here's the library."

The walls were lined with floor-to-ceiling bookcases. One of these had been appropriated for Margaret's collection of single human figures (dancers, soldiers, circus performers, map sellers, slaves, kings, musicians, and two entire commedia dell'arte troupes); the other cases were full of books. Most of them were related to art and art history, antiques, ceramics and porcelain, fine furniture. There were classic works of fiction as well (Dickens, the Brontë girls, Thomas Hardy) and another large nonfiction section was devoted mostly to World War II, religion, and European history.

"I hope you like to read," Margaret had said, completely without irony. "I would want whoever takes the room to feel free to borrow anything from the library, anytime."

The downstairs guest quarters, which Margaret referred to as "the Aviary Suite," housed porcelain birds: swans, peacocks, geese, quail, pheasant, parakeets, falcons, ducks, and a single golden eagle. Each of the upstairs bedrooms, too, were identified by their contents: the Bonbon Dish Room, the Smoke and Snuff Room, the Game Pie Tureen Room, and so on. Margaret's room was full of porcelain children. The room that would be Wanda's displayed glossy pyramids of vividly colored food.

What struck Wanda as even stranger than the *volume* of Margaret's possessions was the laconic way in which she described them, the obvious lack of pleasure she took in being their owner. Wanda noticed that certain names (*Factory names, maybe? Manufacturers?*) came up again and again: Capodimonte, Meissen, Popov, Sevres, Vincennes. She memorized bits of new terminology: soft-paste, hard-paste, biscuit-ware, majolica.

"Maybe you can tell me," Wanda ventured. "I've never really known what porcelain *is* exactly, what makes it prized."

Margaret answered in her odd, emotionless manner. "It's won where found."

"What does that mean?"

"There are two general categories of clay. Primary or residual clay is 'won'—retrieved—from the same place on earth where it was formed, thousands of years ago."

"And that's an advantage?"

"Primary clay—like china, from which porcelain is made—has never been transported from its original site, so it's very pure. Some people value that sort of thing."

They had arrived at the end of the tour and were on the third-floor ballroom, where a vast collection of ornate candleholders was exhibited.

"What's the other category?" Wanda was less interested in clay at this point than in Margaret's manner of response. How could she know so much about this stuff and care so little?

"Secondary or sedimentary clays. They travel." Finally Margaret stopped sounding like a bad recording of a boring textbook. "For centuries, they travel. Carried along by wind, rain, ice. They're won thousands of miles from where they were initially formed."

"So they're less pure."

"Yes. But because they've been buffeted about for such a long time, they're composed of smaller particles."

"And that's good because—?"

"Smaller particle size means greater plasticity. On the other hand, china clay—being composed of large particles—is more rigid, harder to work with."

"Ah. It suffers no fools." Wanda meant it as a joke, but Margaret looked so startled and tense that she feared she'd offended her.

Margaret turned away. "That's it, then. That's the whole house." She began moving through the ballroom, turning off the chandeliers and wall sconces. Her footsteps were heavy on the oak planks of the ballroom floor, their returning echoes even heavier. "Let's go downstairs."

Wanda asked no further questions, certainly not the one which had been at the forefront of her mind: *Fifteen thousand square feet? Eleven bedrooms? And you live here alone?*

Wanda took another sip of cold coffee and studied her city map and bus schedules. Getting to Margaret's by bus was not going to be easy or quick; she'd have to walk several blocks to catch the first of two buses, transfer to the second bus, and hike another quarter of a mile to the top of the hill. It would take at least forty-five minutes to get there. She had just enough time to pack her small inventory of possessions, settle her account with the good people of the Young Women's Christian Association, and be on her way. She grabbed her backpack and a small cardboard box from under her cot.

Into the backpack went:

1. Clothes: functional, tasteful, casual; a stage manager's wardrobe, which meant nothing too feminine or suggestive—Wanda had learned long ago that women of a small build, if they want to command any kind of authority, can't look too girly—but nothing too slouchy either. Pants and shirts, slightly tailored. Jeans, tees, and sweats for Mondays off. A black dress for opening nights. No jewelry.

2. Shoes: a pair of hiking boots, a pair of tennis shoes, and a pair of really brazen, really expensive fuck-me pumps to go with the opening night dress. Once in a while it was okay to look girly.

Into the cardboard box went:

1. Papers: Wanda's resumés, the city map, the bus schedules, legal papers, bank statements, letters of recommendation, old journals,

2. The French press coffeemaker and two pounds of French roast,

3. A small framed black-and-white photograph of a woman bowling, and

4. A postcard featuring a sunset view of Mount Rainier and the Seattle skyline—"As seen from Kerry Park on Queen Anne Hill, Seattle is always beautiful."—that had been mailed a little over two months ago. It was addressed to Wanda in care of her Chicago relatives and had been forwarded to Wanda's New York address by her aunt Maureen. Wanda had received the postcard one month after Peter left.

Aunt Maureen routinely forwarded Wanda's mail. There was no special mention of the postcard in Maureen's accompanying letter, and Wanda almost didn't find it; it was squeezed between a credit card solicitation and Wanda's Northwestern University alumnae magazine.

Even though the postcard bore no message or return address, and the sender had obviously made an effort to disguise his handwriting, Wanda knew it was from Peter.

Within two days, she had given up the loft and located someone who needed a New York-to-Seattle drive-away—a nice Manhattan programmer who'd been hired by Microsoft. She loaded her backpack and cardboard box into the backseat. She clipped the postcard to the visor and consulted her cross-country map: I-80 west and turn right at Cheyenne. What could be simpler?

At first, she was confident. It was so like Peter—to tell her in this indirect way where he was, even though he said he wanted to be alone. To express his need for her without words. To make no overt demands.

He might not even know why he sent the postcard, Wanda thought, serenely navigating Interstate 80 as it caressed the Appalachian Mountains. *He might not realize how much he needs me. He probably still thinks he wants to be alone. He's probably that delusional.*

She inched through traffic jams and construction slowdowns in Illinois, not stopping in Chicago to see her relatives. They weren't expecting her; and besides, there wasn't enough time.

Maybe he thinks he's doing me a favor by leaving me. Maybe he worries that loving him is too hard. Doesn't he think I know he's troubled? Doesn't he think I've taken that into consideration? I've had my eyes open. I'm no fool. I can take it.

She drove the length of the Nebraska panhandle without seeing another living soul. She started chewing her fingernails and developed a hair-pulling habit.

On the other hand, maybe he really does want to be alone. Maybe he doesn't want to be found.

She drank truck stop coffee. She listened to CDs of Thelonious Monk, Charlie Parker, Earl Hines, Rassan Roland Kirk.

Fuck, she thought by the time she crossed the Rockies, *I have no idea what he's thinking.*

But it was too late to turn back. After Wanda merged onto I-90, she drove the last twenty-four hours nonstop, making the trip from New York to Seattle in only five days.

Wanda stuffed the morning paper and the now-empty coffee cup into the trash can. She left Mickey and Minnie where they lay. She pulled Peter's name off the wall, crushed it into a ball, and then tucked it into her jeans pocket. She was almost done.

Under Wanda's pillow were the last two things to go into the box:

1. A small red and black journal.
2. The Book: a dog-eared, repeatedly highlighted paperback called *Creative Visualization.* She'd bought it shortly before chasing Peter to Seattle.

The Book put forth the theory that what a person envisions is what a person attracts, so that if you envision loss, despair, loneliness, etc., that is indeed what will befall you. The Book also claimed that all of us lie to ourselves all the time, so why not tell *positive* lies—known as "affirmations"—instead of negative ones?

For example, if Wanda felt like writing, "Nobody will ever love me again," which, according to the book's author, was a lie, she wrote instead, "A loving relationship awaits me." If Wanda felt like writing, "All men are fucked-up dickwads who deserve to die," she forced her hand into a steady calmness and wrote instead, "There are good men in the world, somewhere." If she felt like writing, "Fuck the survival of the species. The world would be better off if humans became extinct," she wrote, "Save the whales." And if she felt her spooks coming on, those familiar voices that said, "You're going to die alone. People started leaving you when you were six years old and they're going to keep on leaving you, so why bother?" she would print, as if she were competing for a penmanship prize, "I love myself. I. Love. Myself. I do not need another person's love to make me whole"; and she would think, *What a load of bullshit,* and watch the clear, precise lines of her script blur and melt into unrecognizable watery blobs.

If all else failed, she would copy the affirmation that was supposed to be the be-all and end-all of all affirmations: "This, or something better, will manifest for me for the highest good of the universe."

She called this affirmation the New Age Hail Mary. Lately, she'd had to use it a lot.

Wanda checked out of the YWCA, strode to the bus stop, and made the next bus with time to spare. Putting the cardboard box under her seat and the backpack in her lap, she settled in and began studying the other passengers, row by row, face by face, looking for Peter. One couldn't be too careful; he probably knew Wanda had come looking for him and would avoid her if he could. Furthermore, he was probably wearing a disguise.

After the first few stops, Wanda noticed a large woman getting on the bus. Her hairdo was suspicious; it looked like a Gabor sisters wig. Her broad hands were gloved. She wore dark glasses. Wanda thought she could detect a faint, smudgy shadow over her upper lip.

True, she seemed to have expansive, unmistakably feminine hips, and her pendulous breasts responded naturally to the swaying motion of the bus, but so what? Wanda had once stage-managed a play where one of the actresses thought her character ought to have big tits; the costumer had engineered a beautiful, natural-looking, 38D chest out of muslin and filled it with birdseed. Peter knew how to sew. And he was a sculptor, for God's sake. Anything was possible.

Wanda placed a hand on the center of her 30A chest and tried to quiet her heart. She would have to be tricky if she was going to find him. But maybe she could beat him at his own game. She knew about disguises too, after all. She had plenty of experience watching actors disappear into other characters, become unrecognizable behind layers of padding and clothes and wigs and makeup.

What kind of character would be most unlike her? What kind of person would Peter least expect? She wiggled her face around and tried out a few new expressions. She imagined speaking with a lower, more resonant voice. She hummed an old Peggy Lee song. She arched an eyebrow. She cocked her head.

Yeah, sure. She could do this. He'd never even see her coming.

If you'd asked her, Wanda would not have been able to tell you why Peter's departure had driven her to these extremes of emotion and action. Before he left, she had no idea that she was capable of such a dramatic, Old Testament style of grieving. Not that she'd ever read the Old Testament; she hadn't. But the point is, no one was more surprised by these excesses of behavior than Wanda herself.

They met when Wanda was stage-managing *Uncle Vanya* and the theatre borrowed a sideboard from the store where Peter did restorations. Refusing help from Wanda and her crew, he steered the massive piece onstage himself; once it was in place, he smoothed his big boxer's hands over it with a palpable and sensual reverence that gave Wanda an unusual empathy for Victorian furnishings. His pores released a hot yeasty smell that was tinged with citrus. Who knew why—a person can't explain these things—but in that moment, Wanda was finally arrow-struck by the mythical purblind boy.

Peter was older than the actors she'd bedded, and heavier, both in body and spirit. The bloom was off this rose, that was sure. But he had breadth and depth of experience, he'd struggled with depression, and—

what a relief!—he could talk about something besides his resumé: jazz, God, poetry. Instead of investing his energies in the transitory rewards of applause, good press, and self-promotion, he *restored* things, *made* things, brought forth the pentimento hidden deep in ancient wood. His sculptures were stationed around the loft where he lived and worked. After Wanda moved in, she felt protected by them, assured by their weight. Peter's angels may have had wings, but they weren't going anywhere. Yes, he was troubled, he drank too much, he was certifiably bipolar, but he was such a gentle drunk, so sweet in bed when he was soused. After years of improvising with volatile children, his slowness and steadiness was a balm, his somnolence after they made love a haven.

But he didn't love you enough, Wanda reminded herself. *He left you. He went away. Does he really warrant this kind of behavior? Is it worth going nuts over the man?*

The answer didn't really matter. Affirmations couldn't save her. Wanda had faced the fact that she would have to keep cracking up, little by little, like a windshield, until she found him. She just didn't seem to have a choice.

The woman on the bus turned out to be exactly who she seemed—a horsy matron with a postmenopausal mustache. So did the six other people Wanda felt bore certain suspicious resemblances to Peter, either in build or in manner, or in, well, aura.

Wanda wasn't stupid. She knew there was about a million-to-one chance that she'd find Peter riding the bus. But the enormity of the quest she'd undertaken began to sink in, and by the time she arrived at her final stop, she was deeply depressed.

She sat down on the sidewalk. She cried for ten minutes: the exact length of a union break. She got up and began picking up cigarette butts, Burger King wrappers, banana peels, 7-Eleven Big Gulp cups, anything she could find. She used them to construct a sidewalk collage of Peter's face. People came and went. They gave her odd looks, but they didn't intrude, didn't ask what she was doing. *It's amazing how much privacy you have,* Wanda thought, *when people think you're crazy.* After a while, she tenderly dismantled Peter's face and deposited it in the trash can that was chained to the Metro bus shelter. She opened her cardboard box, pulled out her red and black book, sat down next to the trash can, and began to write. She wrote the same affirmation, over and over again.

I am going to find him, Wanda wrote.

I am going to find him.

I am going to find him.

Then, feeling definitely cheered—*Maybe there's something to this creative visualization shit after all*—she gathered her things and began the arduous trek up the hill to the Hughes mansion, her new temporary residence.

Four

❧

Breakfast at the Schultzes', 1969

The last time Wanda had felt grief of this magnitude was twenty-eight years ago, when her mother, Virginia Maria Lorenzini O'Casey, disappeared without a trace. That had been bad enough. But then a few days later, Wanda's father, Michael Francis Joseph O'Casey, also left the scene. So, at the age of six, Wanda became an orphan.

Which is not to say that she was abandoned on the doorstep of St. Patrick's Cathedral and given up to the care and company of the Roman Catholic Church—Michael O'Casey had *that* much concern for his daughter, anyway. Wanda's father was a devoted atheist who'd started proselytizing against the church at his daughter's cribside, and even if he didn't plan to participate in Wanda's upbringing, he told her outright that he'd be damned if he'd let the priests and the nuns—*especially* the nuns—get ahold of her. No, Wanda was left on the doorstep of Maureen Schultz, Michael O'Casey's older married sister. Aunt Maureen and Uncle Artie already had eight children of their own, ranging in age from two to fourteen, and Wanda would later deduce another probable reason for her father's decision: He must have figured that adding another kid to the pile wouldn't make much of a difference.

On the morning Wanda's father told her he'd be leaving Chicago for a while and she'd be going to live somewhere else—he was fixing her a hot breakfast of scrambled eggs, sausage, and pancakes, which was very unusual, highly suspect, but at the same time, very nice—he explained his reasoning in the lilting cadence of his Dublin brogue: "You're goin' to be stayin' with my sister and her family. Your aunt Maureen will take good care of you. They'll be lots of other kids there for you to play with too—not like here, where it's just you and me and your mother." He'd paused to brush at his eyes. Then he fixed Wanda's plate and set it in front of her. There was enough food on it for a lumberjack.

Michael O'Casey sat down and sipped on his coffee. "And don't worry, darlin'," he had concluded, as if this were the best inducement of all: "You won't have to go to church."

He'd gone on to tell Wanda that her aunt Maureen hadn't been to Mass or to Confession since she'd married Artie—not that she wasn't a good woman with so-called Christian values; she was. But Michael O'Casey reassured his daughter that the only time she was likely to hear the word "God" was twice a year, on the two major Christian holidays, when the Schultz *mère* and *père* arose before dawn, fortified themselves with an entire pot of Maxwell House coffee, roused, rallied, and assembled the troops, and—after finding eight pairs of matching socks and good shoes, knotting seven ties and one bow, and seeing that eight sets of teeth were brushed, eight bladders and bowels were emptied, eight heads were combed, and eight coats were buttoned—walked in, usually during the processional, to the Good Shepherd German Lutheran Church in the neighborhood where Artie grew up.

"But *you* won't have to go," Wanda's father said, emphatically. "I'll make sure your aunt Maureen is clear on that point." Michael O'Casey sniffed and cleared his throat. "Now eat your pancakes. There's a good girl. I'll just pack a few things for you."

Wanda didn't remember much of the actual leave-taking. Her next clearest memory was of arriving in the Schultz family kitchen. Her entrance was at first scarcely noticed. The Schultz children—James, John, Jacob, Jesse, Jordan, Joshua, Jeremiah, and Jacqueline—were eating breakfast when their mother ushered Wanda into the kitchen.

"All right, now," Aunt Maureen began. "I need everyone's attention." At first, Wanda didn't know who Aunt Maureen was talking to; the kitchen table contained at least fifteen different boxes of cereal, two cartons of milk, and a large pitcher of orange juice, but there were no children that Wanda could see.

Aunt Maureen walked over to the table, which was very long; there was an empty chair at each end for Uncle Artie and Aunt Maureen, but there were no chairs on the side closest to Wanda. The reason for this arrangement became clear when Aunt Maureen picked up a pitcher and, moving smoothly from right to left, transformed herself into a well-oiled, perfectly calibrated Human Juice Dispenser.

Wanda—who would have many occasions over the next seventeen years to observe, and, over time, emulate Aunt Maureen's physical efficiency—was awed. She'd never seen her own mother pour anything at breakfast time besides shots of scotch.

"You boys remember your cousin Wanda, right?" Aunt Maureen went on, without spilling a drop.

Gradually, seven sets of steely, unmistakably male eyes peered over the cereal boxes, and Wanda was suddenly aware of the sounds of cornflakes and puffed rice being crunched into a mushy oblivion between seven sets of teeth.

"Why would we remember her?" said one surly voice, cracking slightly. "We've never met her."

"I know that, James Finnegan Schultz, and don't you be giving me that kind of smart mouth this morning if you please."

"Mine! Mine! MINE!" screamed another, much younger voice, and the kitchen tablecloth billowed violently.

"SHUT UP!" came a voice from behind the Kix box. Wanda heard an aspirate, hissing sound, its exact location indiscernible. She began to wonder if the Schultz family kept a pet snake.

"Do NOT talk to your sister like that, Jacob. Would you like me to talk to *you* like that?" Aunt Maureen barked. She put a comradely arm on Wanda's shoulder, and resumed in a more even tone. "I just meant that you've heard me talk about your cousin Wanda, who is my brother Michael's only child."

"Lucky kid," muttered James Finnegan Schultz, the oldest. Wanda could now pinpoint his position as directly behind the box of Cheerios.

"James . . ." Aunt Maureen spoke in the up-inflected "This-is-my-last-warning-buster" tone that all children recognize. James sank down behind his box.

"MINE!" came the shrill, under-the-table voice again, followed by a loud screech and more hissing.

"Are you being gentle to the kitty, sweetheart?" Aunt Maureen crooned to the tablecloth, and then continued in a stern, schoolmarmish tone. "Listen up now, guys. Your cousin Wanda will be staying with us for a while."

All the cereal boxes began to speak at once.

"For how long?!" shouted one.

"Where's she gonna sleep?" said another.

"Not in *my* room!" answered another.

"You've got to be kidding!"

"Another GIRL? That's GREAT! Just GRRRRRREAT!"

"Does Dad know about this?!"

"Girls have COOTIES! Girls are GROSS!"

"NO! NO! NO! MINE! MINE! MINE! I *WANT* IT!" screeched the demon under the table, and five pink, sausagelike fingers appeared from under the tablecloth, grasped its edges, and pulled.

Cereal boxes, bowls, spoons, butter knives, plates of toast and jars of jam, jelly juice glasses, and milk cups were all flung to the kitchen floor.

There was a stunned silence. The scene above the tabletop resembled *The Last Supper* gone horribly awry. Discovered beneath the table was a sweet-faced, pudgy, blonde child of about two, wearing a pink and yellow bunny suit.

"I ate mine all," said Jacqueline Kennedy Schultz, clutching an empty Mary Poppins bowl in one hand and an orange-striped kitten by the tail in the other. "I'm a GOOD girl." She smiled with an aggressive sweetness that made her look like Shirley Temple on amphetamines. Then she spotted Wanda.

Instantly, her baby face contracted into a scowl. She squeezed the kitten's tail harder, and it gave a pathetic, truncated squeak. "MAMA!" she yelled. "Who DAT?! WHO DAT LITTLE *GIRL*?!"

Aunt Maureen began to stammer. "It's nothing, darlin', don't worry, everything's fine. . . ." She knelt by the table and said in a voice that was desperately placating, "It's nothing."

Wanda noticed that all of the boys, even the big one called James, had taken a step backward; they seemed to be physically bracing themselves for another act of mass destruction.

Jacqueline went on, in escalating fury. "WHO DAT? DON'T WANT HER HERE! DON'T WANT DAT GIRL! DAT GIRL GO AWAY NOW! GO AWAY GO AWAY GO AWAY!"

Aunt Maureen and the seven Schultz boys looked on, clearly frightened and completely passive—as if this two-year-old, cranberry-faced tyrant were a force of nature, or an act of God. It became clear to Wanda, if somewhat puzzling, that no one in the room had any intention of doing anything.

It was at this moment that Wanda exerted a heretofore undiscovered gift—a gift that would not only serve her well during her seventeen-year tenure as a member of the Schultz household, but would also pre-determine her future choice of profession.

Ignoring Jacqueline's shrieks, and walking slowly and deliberately, Wanda unloaded her small suitcase onto the kitchen table. It should be noted that Wanda's focus and calm under these circumstances was impressive; by this time, Jacqueline's screams were causing extreme consternation among the Schultzes' human neighbors and a widespread attack of nervous dementia among the neighborhood pets.

Wanda picked a butter knife and a plate off the floor and wiped them clean with a napkin. Then with a full-volumed and commanding voice, she said, "DOES ANYBODY HERE LIKE *CANDY*?"

Instantly, Jacqueline shut up. The rest of the Schultz clan drew a collective breath and focused their full attention on Wanda. Extracting a king-sized Three Musketeers from her suitcase, she sliced off a gen-erous piece and held it out to Jacqueline, who pounced on it with both hands. The orange kitten, free at last, performed a textbook-perfect demonstration of "a bat out of hell" and skittered madly from the kitchen, never to be seen again.

Wanda placed the remaining chunk of candy on the plate and cut it neatly into eight pieces. After serving her male cousins (she made sure that James got his piece first), she walked over to Aunt Maureen. "You don't have to love me," she said, holding out the last piece of chocolate with the solemnity of an altar boy, "but I'm not nothing."

"Oh, sweetheart!" Aunt Maureen cried. "I'm so sorry!" She burst into tears, fell to her knees, and drew Wanda into a hug with such force that it took her breath away and sent the plate and remaining choco-late flying.

Wanda looked over Aunt Maureen's shoulder to gauge the effect of this overtly maternal and dramatic scene. There was no need to worry. All eight of the Schultz children were blissfully united in the happy consumption of sugar. Jacqueline had stuffed the entire piece of candy into her mouth; there was something especially satisfying to Wanda about the way it distended her cheeks. The little girl was eyeing the last piece of chocolate, which had landed under the table among the minefield of breakfast dishes and puddles of milk and juice. She looked at Wanda. A nonverbal but perfectly clear exchange passed between them. Jacqueline snatched the chocolate from the floor and popped it into her mouth. One of the boys started to protest, but Wanda shot him a look and he fell silent.

Wanda was then able to close her eyes and—knowing that a moment like this one would probably not come again soon, or often—allow herself to be lost in Aunt Maureen's embrace. It didn't matter that Aunt Maureen wasn't her own mother. It didn't even matter that it wasn't a real hug; Wanda knew that she had purchased this show of affection in the most shameful way imaginable. She didn't care. These were the facts, as Wanda perceived them: Her mother had disappeared, and Da was so sad about it that he had to go away, and stay away, until he found her and brought her back. Wanda was a bright child, and Michael O'Casey had been just vague enough in his parting words (*"I'll see you around sometime, darlin'."*) to give her the reasonable assumption that he wouldn't be coming back anytime soon.

Another child might have cried—and Wanda felt like it. But she didn't. Her instincts told her that crying would not endear her to the members of this family, where she'd be lucky to be noticed at all. She wisely recognized she'd be far more likely to secure a place of standing with these people as a peacekeeper, even if that meant giving up certain things.

So it was that Wanda O'Casey, aged six (she did not become Wanda Schultz for another ten years, when everyone finally accepted the fact that Michael O'Casey would not be coming back, and Uncle Artie and Aunt Maureen legally adopted her), abandoned her own childhood to take on the oversight and management of her cousins'—becoming, one might add, a godsend to her aunt Maureen. In this way, she took her initial step toward the first of her illustrious careers, as a highly successful and much sought after professional stage manager—a job which, in Wanda's mind at least, essentially paid her to continue doing what she'd done for most of her life: guide and negotiate truces between children. Big ones, to be sure, and card-carrying members of Actors Equity Association. But still: children.

The next morning, when Aunt Maureen arose at five A.M. as usual, a surprise awaited her. Her niece was asleep on the kitchen floor, surrounded by plates and bowls which she had apparently been trying all night to repair; there was a bottle of family-sized Elmer's glue still clasped in her hand.

It would be another thirty years before Wanda would revisit this memory and recognize that it contained all the elements that would compel her to discover her second career—the career that would eventually make her famous.

Five

❧

A Sacristan's Life

If Margaret had been inclined to talk about her childhood, she would have said that it lasted far too long—until 1946 to be exact, when an old man came into her father's shop and put a curse on her family. Until then her life had been a fairy tale that did not end with "happily ever after," but rather, began with it.

She lived in a young city at the top of a great hill in a palatial house with a view of mountains and lakes. A castle, really. The castle of the great King Oscar, her father.

"Papa O!" she called him, and truly there was a roundness to every aspect of her world then, a plump bounty that was everywhere: in the fat upholstered settees and ottomans in her bedroom; in the popovers bursting with jam that Cook brought still warm to the breakfast table each morning; in the perfect, spacious dome that graced Holy Names Academy, where she went to school; and of course in the suitcases and trunks Papa brought home whenever he returned from the land across the ocean, bulging with marzipan and marionettes and costumes like kimonos and always, always a new porcelain figurine to add to her collection. To be encircled by Papa O's arms was to know love and generosity.

Oh yes. He was a generous man. Everyone knew that. And everyone in his kingdom, save one, was happy: butlers, maids, gardeners, cooks;

the private tutors who gave Margaret lessons in singing and French; the partygoers who danced in the grand ballroom all night and waved gaily from their porches and automobiles during the day; even the doctors who made house calls, sometimes summoned from their beds in the middle of the night to tend sudden fevers, rattling coughs, or the bewildering, chronic ailments that plagued the mistress of the house.

King Oscar could make everyone smile. Everyone except Margaret's mother, who was composed of the darkness and mystery which fairy tales require. It is perhaps no wonder that she would reappear in Margaret's life sixty-three years after her death—not as a ghost exactly, but as a symptom, a noisy headache. As the chief manifestation of Margaret's pain.

She was beautiful. Famously beautiful in the way of long-legged, athletic girls in the 1920s and '30s, daughters of the new class of wealthy Americans who'd been blessed with an abundance of refrigerated milk and meat, good lineage, a private school education, fresh fruit and vegetables. And she was young—much younger than King Oscar.

In life, she was glimpsed rarely, and even then, only in the confines of her home. When she appeared, she was not dressed like other at-home mothers of the era, who wore belted shirtdresses with prim, up-the-front buttons that met the crisp half-moons of Peter Pan collars. No, Margaret's mother spent her days draped in transparent, diaphanous peignoir ensembles that showed off her fashion model figure and played up her resemblance to Greta Garbo. She had many peignoirs, all in complicated colors that could not be easily named.

Margaret's mother spoke little. When she did speak, it usually presaged events that were incomprehensible, dire, or both. Mostly, she lurked: on the other side of doors, in shadowy corners, against walls. She watched and listened, her exquisite face rarely reflecting any sign of emotion. Only occasionally did Margaret notice her mother's mouth contract, giving it a taut, wrinkled look that was like the smocking on Cook's starched cotton nightgowns.

Sometimes Margaret rummaged through a smelly box of photographs of her mother which she'd found while playing in the attic, photographs which predated marriage and maternity and showed her mother in the open air, in the light, dressed in tennis skirts, skiing ensembles, swimsuits. In all the pictures, she was wearing smiling expressions that Margaret had never seen; incredibly, her mother must have once been happy.

In other photos, she was in the company of other laughing and athletic-looking young people; even harder to believe was the possibility that her mother had once had friends.

Margaret concluded that something terrible had happened to make her mother the way she was; being a child, and an only child at that, she naturally assumed that *she* was that something. Luckily, though, this assumption did not engender a loss of self-esteem; Margaret was a happy child, loved in all the right and good ways that children need to be loved. Papa O and Cook petted and kissed and hugged her; she was disciplined when such measures were required, praised and rewarded for her successes; the rooms of the house were always teeming with people, so she never suffered from loneliness or neglect.

Her relationship with her mother was one a curious child might have with a rarely glimpsed neighbor living behind shuttered windows. And just as it is the absent guest who excites the most conversation, so it was that Margaret's mother became a great stimulant to her creative powers. She spent much of her young life imagining what was going on in her mother's head, giving voice to her stony silence.

It was not uncommon for Margaret to overhear grown-ups remark what a shame it was that the child looked so much like the father. But she didn't mind. She was proud to be allied with her father, in both her pudgy physique and her sunny disposition. Over time, she came to think of her mother as an ice-hearted queen, a sourpuss with whom no one kept counsel. She was fascinating, but only from a great distance, and only as a tantalizing fiction.

Margaret had two distinct memories involving her mother, two stories that she could have told. Like so many family stories, they had one meaning when viewed through the eyes of a child, but quite another after the veil of childhood was lifted.

In the first memory, Margaret is seven years old and dressed in an ornate shepherdess costume: linen blouse, rose-patterned brocade skirt, maroon bodice with a lace-up front, a bright shawl, a headpiece of silk flowers. Papa O had the costume made for her in Europe, just for her, there is no other like it anywhere in the world, and she is modeling it for him. He is applauding and laughing. He pops a sweet into her mouth, a rum truffle. He holds out a package. She unwraps it, carefully; she knows there will be something very fragile inside.

It is a small statue of a shepherdess. And look! She is wearing a costume exactly like Margaret's!

"Oh, Papa O!" Margaret cries. "It's beautiful! Thank you!"

She is about to hug him when he stops her.

"But wait, darling. This time when I am gone, I hear from the Sisters and the staff you are such a good girl that I have brought for you *two* figurines. Here."

She opens the second box and brings out a figurine which is an exact duplicate of the first, with one striking difference.

"Isn't it glorious?" Papa O's voice is so soft and low, he sounds like he's at Confession.

"But, Papa. It's all white. There are no colors on this one."

"Ah! That is because the kaolin, the clay in this one, is so pure, so rare, so magnificent, that it requires nothing else. Just form and light. Here. Let us put them both together on this table."

He sets the figurines side by side and then sits down in the armchair again and takes her hands. "Margaret, dear one, I know how much you love your gaudy colors, but here, close you eyes now. Touch them, one with each hand, Can you feel the difference? Can you?"

"Yes," Margaret lies. "I feel the difference."

"Now open your eyes and look. Which one is the original, and which is the copy?"

It is never hard to guess what Papa O wants her to say. And she does so love pleasing him. Margaret points. "This one. And this is the copy."

"Yes, Margaret, yes! So you see," Papa O explains, pulling her into his arms, "they both have value, of course they do. But this one . . . ah! This one comes from the purest clay and the finest factory in all the world: Meissen, darling. 1748. Now say it."

"Meissen," Margaret repeats. "1748."

"And this one is from Chelsea, 1753."

"Chelsea."

"Good girl. Remember always, my love, how important it is to recognize purity. Recognize it, and *prize* it. Papa O will not always be here to tell you what is the pure and what is the copy, do you understand?"

Margaret becomes aware of her mother, leaning against the door frame, looking on with her empty expression. "I see you're training the child early," she says.

Margaret's father looks up briefly, smiles, squeezes her even tighter. "She makes a beautiful shepherdess, don't you think, Cassandra?"

"Come see the figurines Papa brought me," Margaret says to her mother. "They are from Meissen and—"

"No thank you, Margaret. I've seen enough of your father's treasures. I'm going to bed."

Years later, many elements of this memory took on a new meaning for Margaret. But what struck her as the most obvious and important thing was the way her father had costumed her—not as the original, but as the object of lesser worth.

The other memory takes place a few years later, early one morning in 1934.

Margaret is dressed for school and eating her breakfast in the sunny atrium. She is waiting for Papa O to join her when she hears her mother's voice. It is hoarse and ragged.

"Margaret! Margaret! Where are you?"

Margaret's mother bursts through the French doors. She must have come from outside, Margaret realizes, incredulous, because the edges of her peignoir are grass-stained and soaked with dew, and because she is clutching the morning newspaper to her chest. Her feet are bare and muddy, and as she steps into the atrium she slips wildly on the tiled floor. Margaret is sure she will fall, but she somehow makes it to the table and stops herself by crashing into it. Behind her is Vidkun, the head butler. He is very pale and frightened.

Cook waddles in with the hot pastries and then stops, her mouth gaping "Missus?"

"Clara," Vidkun says, "Get one of the girls to summon Mr. Hauptmann."

"Where –?"

"He's taking his exercise in the ballroom. Tell him he's needed right away. And call the doctor."

"Yes, sir," Clara says. "Begging your pardon, missus. Here's hot pop-overs, in case you're wanting breakfast today."

"Thank you, Clara." Margaret's mother is tearing frantically through the newspaper, panting. The ink rubs off on her elegant fingers and they start to become smudged and gray. It's as if she is sickening with an insidious and fast-moving plague that turns human skin the color of ash.

Vikdun starts to approach her from behind; she senses him, snatches a butter knife, whirls around, and points the knife in his direction. She stares for a few seconds and slows her breath; when she speaks again, her voice is calm.

"Vidkun. I'd like some toast, please. Brown toast with no butter. I would also very much like some time alone with my daughter."

Margaret is astonished. She cannot remember her mother ever ex-pressing such a desire.

"Very well, madame." He walks backward into the kitchen, his re-ceding face the color of flour paste.

"Here it is." She slams the opened newspaper on top of Margaret's eggs and sausages. "Your father is always showing you, teaching you, and now I have something to show you too. Something to teach. You won't find it on the front page, no no no, you'll only find it here, right down here. Look, Margaret, look! In very small print, buried at the bottom of this page. Read it. Read! That expensive education your fa-ther is providing should be good for something!"

Margaret hears Papa O's footsteps thundering down the stairs, com-ing closer. She has never known her father to move this quickly.

"Please, Margaret, please." There are tears in her mother's eyes. "Read, darling."

Margaret isn't able to read much, and what she does read makes little sense. The article is about shops in places whose names are unfamiliar. Breslau, Munich. It is about men with beards. Judges, lawyers. There are other things in the story she does not understand. Storm troopers? Boy cots? And some people it says are tearing the beards of the men. What does that mean?

Papa O arrives. Vidkun and Clara emerge from the kitchen. Mar-garet's mother sits down at Papa O's place at the table and, with a per-fectly composed attitude of decorum, shakes the linen napkin onto her lap.

"Has your mother been troubling you, Margaret?" It is the only time Margaret has ever seen her father angry. She knows he is angry, even though he is not yelling, because his face is purplish red and his voice has sharp edges. "Look what she's done to your lovely breakfast." He removes the newspaper from Margaret's plate and pummels it into a ball. "Mother is sorry. Mother is not feeling well."

"Actually, I'm feeling very well," Margaret's mother says. "I just ordered toast."

Papa O moves across the room. His footfalls are so heavy that the china and fine crystal quiver against one another and make timid ringing sounds. "Mother has one of her headaches and will be going to bed."

"No," Margaret's mother says. "I'm hungry."

"Clara, put this newspaper out with the trash, and please see that Margaret gets a new plate. Come with me, Cassandra."

Margaret's mother and Papa O stare at one another, like a pair of stone lions. And then, without warning, Margaret's mother slowly plucks her linen napkin from her lap and starts stuffing it down her throat.

Papa O rushes toward her. His bulky body blocks her from Margaret's view, but Margaret hears gagging, grunting. Her mother's pale thin arms encircle her father and flail against his massive torso. The shape they make is like a gigantic beetle at war with itself. Vidkun rushes in and is absorbed into the creature. The table jumps up and down, the crystal glasses tip, roll, shatter. Clara hoists Margaret out of her chair and bulldozes her from room to room until she is out the front door and on her way to school.

Margaret's mother did not appear at dinner that night, nor at any meal ever again. Shortly afterward, Margaret arrived home from school to find Papa O's Mercedes-Benz and the doctor's Oldsmobile outside the house and a gathering of somber faces within. Cook put her arms around her and led her to the kitchen. She set her down before a cup of warm milk and ginger snaps, and then gently informed her that the maid who regularly awakened Madame Hauptmann to deliver afternoon tea had found the mistress dead.

"But what happened?" Margaret asked again and again, never satisfied with the answers.

"The mistress died in her sleep," Cook cooed, nestling Margaret in her dumpling arms and stroking her hair. "We should all wish for such a peaceful death."

But what if it wasn't peaceful? Margaret wondered. *What if she was having a nightmare?*

"She had a kind of explosion in her brain," the doctor explained. "You see, Margaret dear, the body cannot survive such an explosion, any more than a building can."

My mother wasn't a building! Margaret wanted to shout. *Is that the best you can do?*

Her school friends hinted that perhaps Margaret's mother, like Catherine in *Wuthering Heights,* had been pining for a lost love and died of nothing more complicated (or less romantic) than a broken heart.

"There was nothing wrong with her heart," Margaret griped. "Whatever killed her was in her *brain.*"

It wasn't sadness she felt, not exactly; it was frustration. Margaret had been following her mother's bread crumb trail of mystifying behavior, quietly and diligently gathering information and extrapolating on it. She'd expected to follow this trail for years and then one day catch up to her mother and confront her: *See?* she would say. *I understand now! I know what made you the way you are!* But in dying so suddenly her mother had become a riddle at the gate instead of the road you walked to get there—a too-brief, too-clever construction of memories, impressions, a few facts, and little else.

Of course, Margaret could make a guess. She could answer the riddle in any of a hundred ways, probably. But what if her answer wasn't the right one?

Ultimately it was her father's words that gave her some relief. "Mother had thoughts in her mind that hurt her," he said, in that straightforward way she loved. He never lied to her, never made her feel stupid or babyish. "She put a poison in herself by thinking. Remember this, dear one: Thoughts can be like a sickness. Wrong thoughts in the mind can be as hurtful to the body as bullets."

And so at twelve—the age when Margaret's friends were beginning the social odyssey which would carry them from debutante teas to coming-out balls to engagement parties to weddings—Margaret became the mistress of her father's house. It was she who greeted the partygoers, sat at the head of the table, accompanied her father to social and civic events. Under Papa O's tutelage, she became completely assured among the society of the middle-aged.

Young men were never invited to the house; it was just as well. Margaret was awkward with boys to begin with, and her years in a Catholic girls' school had done nothing to enhance her confidence. She knew she was plain and wouldn't be sought out in a room as other young women would be. The few older unmarried men she met suffered from inevitable comparisons to her father—none were half as intelligent or charming. So eventually, both the opportunity and the inclination for romance dwindled. Margaret was Papa O's girl, and content to be so. All things pointed to a splendid spinsterhood.

Papa O had planned to take her to Europe as a present after graduation—she had been such a good student, such a good girl, and she had worked so hard at her French—but then the war broke out, and it was not the time to go. The antique business did not suffer, though, and Margaret stayed home and learned everything there was to learn about porcelain. Papa O was so proud. They would go, he promised, as soon as all this nonsense overseas was over. He would take her with him and they would tour the great factories, visit the great cities she had heard about for so long. They would stay for months, maybe even years. He would show her everything.

And then he died, in his sleep. It was 1946. He was sixty-six years old. Margaret was twenty-four and still a stupid, stupid child.

She grew up soon enough. The fairy tale was finally over.

Twelve years later, she met Stephen Hughes.

She still went out of the house in those days; she had not yet exiled herself to the kind of life she would take up after Daniel died, the solitary life of the sacristan, with its grave and lonely responsibility of caring for sacred objects. She had not gone into hiding, not exactly. She kept a small staff at the house, made contributions to worthy causes, supported the arts, went to museums and the cinema, that sort of thing.

And then one day, she walked to the art museum to see the new Kandinsky. She sat down in front of the painting and let herself be tugged into its swirling, singing confection of pinks and greens, and after some time a young man with a sketchbook sat down next to her, and there they were in the room together, looking at art, and that was how it began. Who knew why he fell in love with her—a spinster! An old maid! That was what a woman like Margaret was called in those days. He wasn't interested in her money or where it came from, so there was no reason to tell him; he simply found the house and its contents beautiful. Even more miraculously, he found Margaret beautiful, and he loved to make her laugh. He would paint, he would teach, they would love each other, all would be well.

A few months later, Stephen proposed, and she accepted. He wanted to pay for the honeymoon himself. Knowing how much Margaret loved France, he took her to a hotel in Seattle where everyone spoke French and the balconies were hung with lavender. When they weren't making love, Stephen drew. He even drew a sketch inside their Gideon Bible, a sketch of Margaret in bed. Stephen thought she had beautiful breasts. Perhaps she did. He sketched her into the pages of the Song of Solomon.

"I have no words, Maggie," Stephen had said when he finished. He handed her the Bible, opened to the chapter titled "The Bridegroom Praises the Bride."

The drawing did not flatter; the face was Margaret's face. And yet it held something else: a radiance that she must have had—or at least, a radiance that Stephen perceived.

Yes, Margaret would remember, *it was a kind of light I had then. Stephen did too. We were young and we loved each other and we were full of light.*

Stephen had drawn a woman who was not beautiful, but who *was* beautiful, and Margaret read the words that her body contained, words that moved in and through and around her, like air, like breath, like water: "A garden locked is my bride. A rock garden locked, a spring sealed up. You are a garden spring, a well of fresh water, and streams flowing from Lebanon. . . ."

It had all been so very sweet.

Slowly, though, something else crept into their lives. Stephen's work as an artist was not well-received. He grew discouraged. He spent less time and passion on his painting. He wanted to contribute, to earn; he chafed at the idea that his wife's wealth supported them, but he hated teaching art. Money began to matter. He started to ask questions: Why was there so much? Couldn't they sell some of these things? They were questions that Margaret had to answer, of course, and after that, everything began to change.

Stephen went back to school. He painted no more symphonies of color and form. No. He would draw buildings instead. He would embrace straight lines and work with some promise of financial reward. *Money of our own!* he'd shouted. *Don't you understand?* He cared less about making Margaret laugh. He started drinking too much, too often, and Margaret found herself thinking more and more about the hollow-cheeked old man and his curse.

And then came the day she learned she was pregnant. A miracle, surely, a good omen, a sign of blessings for them. She couldn't wait for Stephen to come home from school, so she decided to walk to the university and find him.

After a few blocks, she came upon a neatly dressed man standing on a corner, studying a rumpled city map. Next to him was a little boy of about four or five, wearing short pants and a red blazer. He was holding two half-eaten jelly doughnuts over his head. His face was smeared with powdered sugar and raspberry filling. The doughnuts were engaged in a battle of epic proportions. "Crash! Crash! Crash!!" he shouted as the doughnuts collided against one another.

I'd best get used to that sort of thing, she thought happily, *especially if the baby's a boy.*

As she started to pass them, the man looked up. "Excuse me," he said.

"CRASH!"

"Jack! A bit less noise, please."

The doughnuts dropped in altitude. "Crash," Jack said softly, and took an enormous bite out of one of his aircraft.

"Do you know, are we anywhere near the cemetery?"

Jack looked up at Margaret, chewing in that openmouthed way that children have. The explosion of raspberry jelly inside his mouth made it look as if he were bleeding. It disturbed Margaret for some reason, and she tried to look away.

"There is a cemetery near here, yes."

"My mum's great-aunt is buried there. I promised her if I ever got to the States I'd visit her grave," the man went on.

"We're BRITISH!" Jack bellowed. He smiled expansively. His teeth were bright pink. He began screeching out a melody that resembled—just barely—"God Save the Queen."

"Jack! Quiet!!"

Jack fell silent and bit into his other UFO.

Margaret gave the man directions. The cemetery was not far. They would find it easily.

Her eyes kept wandering back to the child. He was chewing slowly, staring up at her with large, glassy, chestnut-colored eyes, the jam on his face starting to congeal. Margaret began to feel uneasy, nauseous, frightened.

"I'm sorry," she blurted. "I really must go."

She'd turned around and raced back to the house. She could hear Jack's bell-like voice for several more blocks; the air had been so clear that morning. "*CRASH!* CRASH! Crash . . . crash."

She recalled this memory many times after Daniel's death. She should have known then that the curse laid on her, and on anyone she dared to love, was real.

If she could bring herself to speak of it, this is the story Margaret would have told:

Things had grown very bad with her and Stephen. They had not talked of divorce. Like many people of their generation, the word itself—with its lip-biting, sibilant physicality—represented a kind of verbal apocalypse, never to be mentioned lightly. And in those days, of course, warring couples stayed together (they told themselves) for the good of the children.

One day, pining for the verisimilitude of happy family life, Margaret had suggested they venture out of the city for a Saturday outing. Stephen was amenable, Daniel was excited, and after a flurry of planning and packing they set out in Stephen's MG, the top down and the car loaded with a picnic lunch and drawing supplies. They were northwest-bound, for Skagit Valley, where the barley fields were greening and the tulips were in bloom.

On the way, she and Stephen had argued. He brought wine, even though Margaret specifically asked him not to. *Just for once!* she'd carped through clenched teeth. *Can't you be with us without feeling the need to get drunk?*

I can be with Daniel, he'd shot back under his breath, *but I cannot be with you, Margaret, if you want to know the absolute truth, no, I cannot be with you.*

At the end of this exchange, they shared a panicked look. Had Daniel overheard them? In the small backseat of the sports car, staring at the countryside and drinking his bottle of soda as the March wind rushed past and ruffled his hair, he didn't seem to have heard a thing. Still, out of their desire to shield him from rancor and make the day special, Stephen and Margaret fell silent. There was no more conversation between them after that.

They found a picnic site. Stephen drank wine and drew in his sketchbook. Margaret and Daniel ate lunch and wandered the tulip fields. With the dramatic, shifting sky and the intensity of color, it was like being inside an Impressionist painting. She laughed at the sight of Daniel among the flowers. Wearing a yellow and green striped shirt, his beanpole body just beginning to sprout, he was shorter than an average eight-year-old but exceptionally tall for a tulip.

"I'm going to the convenience store!" Stephen shouted from the picnic table.

"What?" Margaret was furious with him. He'd made no effort to be a part of this day, part of *them.* He wasn't even here.

"I'll be right back!" he called, and then started toward the car.

"I'll come with you, Dad!" Daniel yelled from across the field. "Okay, Mom?"

He so loves his father, she thought, reminding herself why she and Stephen must never separate. "See you soon, sweetheart!" she called back, but he was already a varicolored blur running toward his father, the tulip heads tossing in his wake as if they were clamoring to speak.

"Bye, Mom!" He waved from the car. "See you soon!"

She strolled the fields for a while, checked her watch—how far away was that convenience store anyway?—and then walked back to the picnic table, where the remains of their lunch had started to attract fruit flies and yellow jackets. She shooed them away and began packing up. Then she noticed Stephen's sketchbook and flipped it open.

He had been drawing Daniel, and her, on page after page. She'd forgotten how masterful he was, how perfectly he could describe something with a few simple lines and shadings. There were quick charcoal sketches—their faces in close-up, Daniel's creased and cast-off tennis shoes, Margaret's hands—and the beginnings of more detailed colored renderings of the two of them, in the field. There was so much love in the way he saw them that day.

She heard sirens, far away—a sound she'd grown inured to in the city, it was notable in this setting. She looked up from Stephen's sketchbook, toward the steady stream of city cars and their passengers as they raced along the highway.

Everyone had the same idea, she thought. *A weekend in the country.*

Children waved to her from backseats as they passed. So many styles of greeting, too: some were shy or impish, some grandly monarchial, others pulled goofy faces, one boy gave a solemn salute. Feeling like the sole spectator at a spontaneous parade, she waved back, trying to match each child in tone and form.

The sirens were coming closer. And then the parade began slowing down, drivers were braking, horns were being honked. The children turned away from her; they reached for the shoulders of their parents and pulled themselves forward in their seats. "What's going on, Daddy?" she imagined them saying. "Why is everyone going so slow?" And then Margaret realized how close the sirens were.

Where are they? she thought, her heart clenching now, her lungs rent. When the traffic came to a standstill and the crescendo of sirens was unbearable, she dropped Stephen's sketchbook and started running down the highway, toward the nightmare of flashing lights and crumpled metal and blood.

A line of officers blocked her way as if they were overgrown children in that game she'd watched Daniel play.

It's a bad intersection, they had said—

—red rover red rover send Daniel on over—

—*your husband probably didn't see the stop sign.*

Stephen had been critically injured. Daniel was already dead. His small chest was crushed. And the heart within it . . . Daniel's heart . . .

There had never been time for anger; grief—and the fact that Stephen himself had almost died—dulled that knife. There was a brief time after he was discharged from the hospital and came home (hardly whole, hardly recovered, but well enough, the doctors said) when the two of them made a sad attempt to find one another. But by then, of course, any value they had was compulsory. They looked for each other as if they were house keys.

And then at some point they stopped looking. They let themselves be lost, and invisible. Even on the few occasions they managed to inhabit the same room, it was as if they were made of watercolor, as if the molecules—or whatever it is that gives us a graspable substance—had come disjoined, and were floating in a fragile connectedness that was easy to sever. All Margaret had to do was sigh, send a soundless puff of air Stephen's way, and then sit back and watch as he came apart and dispersed harmlessly through the house: a pale, multicolored dust; a shower of glitter; wood smoke; or snow in one of those charming crystal globes. Nothing substantive. Nothing that could suffer pain or guilt or unbearable grief.

She wanted him gone, for his own sake. It was the only way he'd escape the curse.

Two years after Daniel was killed, Stephen left. And then everything was as it should be. The staff was let go and Margaret was alone, tending the sacraments, doing penance for the sins of her blood.

Six

Yin/Yang

Wanda's day off was Monday.

"That's when the theatre is dark," she explained.

Margaret assumed that turning off the electricity one day a week was a way for nonprofit organizations to save money. "That's very smart of them," she said.

Wanda gave her a puzzled look, and then went on to explain that she'd be working from Tuesday through Sunday, from nine until seven.

So in the beginning, Margaret didn't see much of her. The whole arrangement was far less life-altering than she'd imagined. Wanda left the house early—helmetless, Margaret noticed with concern, on a Peugeot bicycle she'd apparently found at a yard sale—and came home after Margaret had eaten dinner. Sometimes she came home even later, after Margaret had read, or watched a bit of television, and gone to bed. Their exchanges were pleasant, cursory, and formal—the kind of interactions one would have with an exemplary salesperson at Frederick & Nelson's. There was no trace of the battered, vulnerable person who had confided to Margaret the story of her pilgrimage and hidden in the powder room. The girl had lost her fragility and gone steely and businesslike.

She's not a girl! Margaret was constantly reminding herself. *She's a young woman.*

Wanda also had an uncanny ability to make herself evaporate—that was really the best way to describe it. It wasn't that Margaret expected to hear stomping or loud music; she knew, or at least hoped, that Wanda was a sensitive and courteous person. But she had expected to feel more of a presence, a shift in the air currents passing through the house. She'd lived alone for so long; surely the presence of another person would cause some kind of agitation, a ripple, *something*. But Margaret felt no such stirrings. On the few occasions when they were both home and in different rooms, it was hard to believe that Wanda was really on the premises. The girl was that quiet. Margaret had to admit that perhaps she'd hoped for someone more intrusive.

How absurd, she thought. *I've managed through sheer luck to take in the perfect boarder. Why on earth would I want anyone else?*

And then the answer came to her: What she desired deep down was someone who could whip up the stagnant currents in the house so thoroughly that they would never completely still. And only little boys could do that.

The first Monday after she moved in, Wanda offered to fix dinner.

"Sit," she said, pointing to the kitchen table. "Don't do anything."

Margaret obeyed instantly, feeling like one of those small, pink-eyed poodles that are always shaking with fear and/or infirmity. *She can certainly be bossy for someone so small.*

"I bought this today," Wanda said, handing Margaret a large cookbook. She began gathering ingredients and equipment. "I need to learn to eat better, and I thought this would be a good place to start."

"This is remarkable," Margaret said, thumbing through the beautiful pages. This particular cookbook had been written, and *illustrated,* Wanda pointed out, by the actor who'd played Henry VIII on that marvelous PBS series that aired several years ago. *There are so many wonderfully talented people in the world,* Margaret thought. *So many truly gifted people.*

Wanda retrieved the cookbook and shrugged. "Actors," she said with authority, "—all actors—are obsessed with food."

The kitchen counter rapidly became a mess of exotic-looking boxes, bottles, herbs, and produce that Wanda had brought home from the International District.

While Wanda cooked, Margaret sat as commanded and did nothing except sip tea and pretend to read the most recent issue of *Art & Antiques*. She was remembering the last time anyone had cooked for her: Mother's Day, 1968. Daniel had made her chocolate chip pancakes, burnt toast, and watery scrambled eggs. The kitchen had looked a great deal like it did at this moment.

The telephone rang.

Margaret had only one phone, and it rang often now; that was the one tangible way in which life had changed since Wanda's arrival. It cheered her to have her telephone ringing so frequently. Although she still had little idea of the nature of Wanda's work, or why it required so many phone conversations, Margaret felt that her home had suddenly become vastly important. Phrases like "communication network," "center of operations," "transmission center," and "central hub" came into her mind when she thought about her house; she felt inexplicably, happily attached to the outside world in a new and significant way.

Of course, the phone sometimes did ring for Margaret; it was invariably her doctor's office. "Wrong number," she would lie, and hang up, her heart pounding. Lately, she'd stopped answering the phone during the day altogether.

Wanda picked up, snuggling the phone between her shoulder and her ear. "Hello. Hughes residence." She continued to slice uniformly wide ribbons from something that looked like a sheet of petrified pond scum.

"Just a minute please." Wanda walked the phone across the vast kitchen floor. "It's for you."

"Thank you." Margaret noticed that Wanda's shoulder continued to linger next to her ear, maintaining a kind of half-shrugging tension even after she handed off the phone. Margaret had a sudden, uncharacteristic impulse to lay hands on the girl.

Wanda resumed her efforts at the counter. She still looked tense. Margaret couldn't remember ever having seen anyone cook with such fierce concentration.

"Hello," Margaret said.

"Margaret? Who was that?"

"Oh. Hello, Marita. That was Wanda."

"Who?" Marita's voice rose in pitch. Margaret flinched.

"My new boarder."

"What are you talking about?" Marita emphasized words with a combination of overarticulation and volume, in much the same way that many misguided people speak to the profoundly deaf. Margaret held the phone several more inches away from her ear.

"I've taken in a boarder, Marita, and her name is Wanda."

"What's she doing there?"

"Well, right now she's cooking dinner."

Wanda looked up briefly.

"Why would you do such a thing? Does Stephen know about this?"

"It's nothing to do with Stephen."

"You've got a stranger living in the house? Cooking for you?"

"She's not a stranger. She's been here a whole week." Wanda looked up; Margaret glanced at her and smiled. "She works for the Seattle Repertory Theatre."

"Stephen should hear about this, Margaret. You know how much we both care—and worry—about you."

Marita paused. Margaret knew that she was expected to make generic noises of the polite and grateful variety. She maintained an obstinate silence.

"Are you still there?"

Margaret sipped on her tea.

"Margaret!"

"Yes, Marita," Margaret said, "I'm still here." Margaret conjured a glossy color picture of Marita in her mind—she was wearing size-6 designer jeans and a hand-knit silk sweater with big hearts and flowers on it—and then, calmly and slowly, she began mentally tearing the picture into canapé-sized pieces. "Where *is* Stephen?"

"He's in Boston on a business trip. I'm calling him as soon as I hang up."

"It will be rather late there, won't it?"

"It doesn't matter, Margaret. He'll want to know."

"Fine, Marita. Always nice talking with you."

"I can't believe you've got a stranger living there." Margaret had finished tearing up Marita's picture and was jettisoning the pieces to a very large, very remote landfill. "What's she cooking, by the way?"

Margaret hung up. She looked at Wanda, who was applying herself vigorously to chopping a brown, shriveled-looking tuber. "I've always wanted to hang up on that woman."

Wanda gave a small, commiserating hum, but didn't look up.

"That was my husband's wife." Margaret continued. "She calls twice a month."

"Oh?" Wanda kept on chopping the mysterious tuber.

"His second wife, I mean, of course. Her name is Marita Kopplemeyer."

"I see." Wanda threw whatever-it-was into one of several pots on the stove and gave it a stir.

"She kept her maiden name." Margaret couldn't figure out if Wanda's terse responses came from a genuine disinterest or a desire to be polite. *Or maybe this kind of thing,* Margaret reasoned—*discussing one's husband's second wife—is de rigueur among theatre people.* "Her first name used to be Rita. She changed that, obviously."

Wanda hummed again, noncommittally, and then added, "Sometimes people need to reinvent themselves."

"Well, yes, I understand that. But why wouldn't she change her last name as well. Especially a name like Kopplemeyer." *Why am I talking so much?* Margaret wondered. *And about Marita, of all people.*

"She's quite . . . loud, isn't she?"

"She was Stephen's secretary," Margaret continued, and then surprised herself by adding, "They had an affair for about two years before we divorced."

Wanda whirled around; her expression was no longer noncommittal. "And you actually *talk* to her?"

She really is young, Margaret thought. "Oh yes. It's all fairly amicable."

Wanda picked up a head of garlic and began pulling apart the cloves. "That's very brave—and good—of you."

"Not really. I just decided, what's the point? Of being angry, I mean."

"Anger is human."

"Oh, I know. But staying angry forever—what good does it do?"

"I could never be that charitable to someone who hurt me."

Margaret wondered who besides Peter had cleft this girl's heart. "You might surprise yourself."

"I doubt it." Wanda began smashing the garlic cloves with a meat tenderizer. It was a technique Margaret had not seen before. "When I was a little girl, I got so mad at a doll for getting lost" (smash) "that when I found her again" (smash) "I took her legs and arms off" (Smash) "threw the legs away" (Smash!) "and put the arms" (SMASH!) "in the leg holes." (SMASH! *SMASH!*) Wanda paused. She was a little out of breath. She spoke to the pulverized garlic cloves. "I figured she couldn't get too far if she had to walk on her hands." She peeled the garlic cloves and then threw them into the largest pot. She stared intently into its depths. She was perfectly still—so still that, after a few minutes had gone by, Margaret began to wonder if she'd had a petit mal.

I never thought to ask any of the applicants about their health, Margaret realized. She was just about to get up and see if Wanda was all right when the oven timer went off; Wanda startled slightly and turned it off.

"Dinner's ready," she said gloomily.

"I'll set the table, shall I?" Margaret offered.

Wanda turned to Margaret, blinking and rubbing her eyes as if she'd just been roused from a refreshing sleep. Suddenly her whole body perked up, coming back to life like a newly rewound toy, and she began to gather plates, bowls, and silverware. "Absolutely not! No way! Sit!"

The meal—which consisted of bonito soup, barley and burdock stew, millet and cauliflower mash ("I decided to do two vegetable courses," Wanda said proudly), boiled dulse salad, turkey croquettes with tofu sauce tartar, and carob-rice pudding—was terrible.

Margaret would never have said this, of course. She remained deeply touched by the fact that this relative stranger (Marita had been right about that) had spent hours laboring over this unusual cuisine.

At the start of the meal, Wanda happily identified the names of the dishes and their ingredients as she served them. As the dinner progressed, however, she grew quiet, and it became more and more difficult to engage her in any sort of conversation. *We haven't spent much time together since we met,* Margaret thought. *Maybe she's feeling shy. I know I am.*

"How is your work going at the theatre?" Margaret asked.

"Okay." Wanda pushed her food around. "Good cast, good director . . ."

"And the play you're working on—what's it called?"

"*A Touch of the Poet.*"

"Is it a good play?"

"Well, it's O'Neill," Wanda said heavily, by way of explanation. "Would you like to see it?"

"I'd love to!" *She's disappearing again,* Margaret thought. *Right before my eyes, like Tinker Bell.* She fought the impulse to clap her hands together wildly and shout, "I believe in fairies! I do! I do!" Instead she said, "I haven't been to the theatre for years."

"You're welcome to use my comps," Wanda continued. "I get two for opening night. Someone should use them." She gazed into the depths of her millet mash.

"Thank you. That's very thoughtful."

"If you want to bring a friend, just be sure you warn them: It's O'Neill." Wanda scowled at a grayish piece of cauliflower. "This isn't very good, is it?" she said, finally.

"Au contraire!" Margaret lied. "I think it's delicious."

After dinner, Wanda tried to explain to Margaret the principles of macrobiotic cooking while she did the dishes; Margaret was not allowed to help with this, either. Wanda spoke with such earnestness and conviction it was as if she were detailing the events of a religious conversion. "yin attracts yang: yang attracts yin. . . . Yin repels yin: yang repels yang. . . ." Margaret found it all quite incomprehensible, and, in spite of Wanda's serious tone, somewhat ludicrous. Whenever Wanda said the words "yin" and "yang," Margaret pictured two tiny, red-faced Chinamen enacting a kind of Punch and Judy food fight, hurling seaweed and tofu pies into one another's faces. "Nothing is completely yin or completely yang. . . ." The Chinamen were apoplectic with rage—but not in a dangerous kind of way; now they were Laurel and Hardy wearing chef's hats. "Large yin attracts small yin"—and now they were Laurel and Hardy naked, except for their chef's hats—"Large yang attracts small yang." Margaret giggled. Wanda looked at her and frowned.

Margaret pressed her lips together. "Why can't they just say 'masculine' and 'feminine' if that's what they mean?" she asked.

Wanda shook her head. "Too many bad associations."

"Well, it certainly is . . . interesting," Margaret said, trying to keep from laughing. Naked Laurel (and his yin) and naked Hardy (and his yang) were now dancing the cancan. They were still wearing their chef's hats. "What attracted you to this kind of cooking?"

"Balance." Wanda said simply. "I'm interested in balance."

"Ahhh," Margaret said, nodding her head knowingly, as if she understood what Wanda meant. She didn't, not really. But it was obvious that the girl was having some kind of personal difficulty. *If she wants to tell me about it,* Margaret reasoned, *she will.*

The phone rang. It was still sitting on the table next to Margaret.

"That'll be Stephen," she said, letting three more rings go by.

"Shall I get it?" Wanda offered, but Margaret shook her head.

She added steaming water to her teacup, squeezed a bit of lemon and a generous amount of honey into it, stirred it, took a breath, and picked up the receiver. "Hello, Stephen."

"What's going on, Margaret? Marita just called, and she's frantic with worry."

His voice still surprised her, the worn voice of a sixty-eight-year-old man who used to drink and smoke heavily. In her mind she still saw him as young. "How are you? What are you doing in Boston?"

"She says you've got someone living there. Is that true?"

"Yes, Stephen. I'm sorry Marita troubled you about it."

"What on earth enticed you to take in a boarder? Now, of all times, when you might be—"

"How are the children?"

"They're fine. Stop avoiding the question, Margaret."

"It's a large house, Stephen, as you remember. I thought it was time I shared it with someone again."

There was a pause on Stephen's end. Margaret could hear the sound of a pencil moving restlessly across paper. It both pained and comforted her to know that Stephen still made little sketches when he was on the phone. She wondered what he was drawing. A vase of flowers, perhaps. A tree outside his hotel window. His own hand. Something living, she hoped.

"Is this person—what's her name, anyway?"

"It's none of your concern, Stephen."

"It *is* my concern, dammit. Is she trustworthy?"

"What are you implying, Stephen? What is it you're really worried about?"

"I'm worried about you, Maggie."

"Bullshit," Margaret said, more loudly than she meant to. She picked up the teapot and began to refill her cup.

Stephen continued in a determinedly even tone. "Do you really think this is a good time to be doing this sort of thing?"

"Yes, Stephen, I do." Margaret felt her voice rebelling. "As a matter of fact, I think it's the perfect time to be doing this sort of thing. I think it's the very best possible time."

Margaret heard a noise. She looked down. Her hands were shaking violently, and the tabletop looked like a battleground. Shards of porcelain lay in a pool of steaming liquid. The receiver was on the floor, looking dead as a stone; its cord quivered for a few seconds and then was still. Rivulets of hot water were starting to run toward the table edge.

Suddenly, Wanda was there. She pressed a handful of paper towels onto the table in front of Margaret and then took her firmly by both wrists. "Are you hurt?" she asked.

Margaret stared at her, stunned. She had completely forgotten that Wanda was in the room.

Stephen's voice came faintly from the floor. "Maggie? Are you all right?"

"You're okay," Wanda said. She picked up the receiver, wiped it dry, and handed it off. Then she was on her hands and knees again, underneath the table, at Margaret's feet.

"I'm fine, Stephen," Margaret said distractedly. She was watching Wanda mop up the spill and clear away the tea things. "I'm perfectly fine."

She's acting like a servant, Margaret realized. *She has the kind of polite invisibility that misses nothing and sees everything.*

"Have you heard anything from Dr. Leising?" Stephen asked.

She lied. "No, I haven't heard anything."

"You'll let me know when you get the test results, won't you? You'll let me know right away?"

"I will, Stephen." *I don't want people to be invisible. I want to see them, and I want them to see me. Come out, come out, wherever you are.* "What are you drawing?"

Stephen chuckled. "Your gold-digging boarder."

"Yes, and . . . ?"

"Does she look like a morbidly obese, mustachioed version of the Queen of Hearts?"

Margaret laughed. "No. Nothing like it."

"Glad to hear it." Margaret noticed a halting quality in his voice. *Has that always been there?* A transcription of his speech would contain little dashes and blanks, as if words were missing. "I'm sorry I blew up like that," he went on. "Just please let me know if you need me."

"I will, Stephen. I have to go now. Good-bye."

Wanda was leaving the kitchen with an expert unobtrusiveness. "Thank you so much for the meal," Margaret called out. "It was wonderful!"

Wanda turned. She looked surprised. "You're welcome." She started to go, and then said, "The teapot, and the cup . . . I'm sorry. I saved the pieces. They're over there in a bowl by the sink."

"Why should you be sorry?" Margaret asked. "I'm the one who broke them."

"Still . . ." Wanda hesitated. "They were lovely things."

"It doesn't matter. It's not important, really."

"I'm sorry about dinner, too. No one ever taught me how to cook."

Margaret laughed. "We have that in common then. Sandwiches and canned soup are the extent of my expertise."

"Well, good night."

"Good night. See you in the morning light."

Margaret sat at the table, listening to the diminishing sound of footsteps as Wanda moved down the hallway and up the stairs. At the end of a day, Margaret noticed, Wanda often moved with a heavy, funereal cadence to her steps. As if she were very, very old. As if she carried the weight of the world on her shoulders. *Daniel's footsteps sounded like that,* Margaret thought, *when the doors began slamming. He knew so much more than he ever let on.* Margaret drew in a sudden, knifelike breath that was almost the beginning of a sob.

She got up and moved to the kitchen counter, where the pieces of the saucer, teacup, and teapot mingled in the bottom of an aluminum mixing bowl. She reached into the bowl and began to turn the pieces over. *This teapot,* she remembered, *and this teacup . . . They were gifts from the mother of one of Daniel's friends. . . . What was her name? Gay, that was it. Gay Paxton. We used to take the children to the park, when they were little. And then, later, we used to have lunch together sometimes. We used to be close. Close enough for her to have given me this. It was for my birthday, I think. Yes, that was it. A birthday gift from Gay Paxton. And what was her*

child's name? I don't even remember if it was a boy or a girl, isn't that ter-
rible? Timmy! That was it. Or was it Tina? Tina Paxton? So many things
fell away after Daniel died. So many relationships withered. Especially the
ones with the mothers. That makes sense, Margaret reasoned, nodding her
head at a thick, rounded fragment from the teapot's midsection. *That*
makes perfect sense.

She sang in a quavering voice, "I'm a little teapot, short and stout.
Here is my handle, here is my spout. When I get all steamed up then I
shout . . ." Margaret stopped singing. She could hear the high, loud, clear
notes of Daniel's voice pick up the last line: "TIP me over and POUR
ME *OUT*!" She could hear his laughter. She could see his body, one thin
arm angled down to his hip, the other up to his forehead.

Margaret dropped the shard of porcelain back into the bowl. It made
a dull, tuneless ting as it hit the side and slid to the bottom. *Now I have*
relationships with things, she thought.

She opened the cupboard under the sink and tilted the bowl. Its contents rattled out into the garbage can. She stared for a moment, and then
thought, *That was stupid. They'll shred the plastic bag. They'll puncture it*
and I'll have to deal with this mess all over again.

"Not now," she said out loud. "In the morning." And she left the
kitchen and went upstairs without turning off the light.

Seven

※

Margaret's Dream, Part One

The dream has many variations, and several constants. For example, it always begins with a journey, but the form of conveyance might be anything: a B-52, a dirigible, a handcar on a railroad track. One time it was the Batmobile.

Of course, many times the dream takes place in an ordinary car, and in that case, it is always the same car: Stephen's MG.

In the beginning, there is a calm, weightless feeling—the kind of feeling one ought to have at the start of a journey, once the preparations are made and everything is in order. No encumberments. No impediments. The heavy burden of baggage is temporarily relieved; the tyranny of clocks is overthrown. The body feels lighter, emptier. The travelers are on their way, needing merely to drift, to be carried and upheld, like the bows on a kite string.

Ahead lies a stopping place, of course, and a cessation of movement. Arrival. Gravity will reassert its dominion, and the dreamer will step with her full, arrived weight onto Point B: the dot on the map toward which she is moving. That inexorable dot.

But at the beginning of the dream, there is divinity and peace and weightlessness. The journey begins. Her breathing alters, slows, deepens. A new quality of air fills her lungs and buoys her. All three of them. Yes: At the beginning, they're like a balloon bouquet.

* * *

This time, they're in a flying saucer—not the stuff of science fiction, but a porcelain saucer from Margaret and Stephen's wedding set. It's big enough to accommodate all of them, about the size of a large braided area rug. It is not equipped with seats, but it does have seat belts, and the passengers have buckled up for safety.

In the center, Daniel sits comfortably cross-legged, nestled in the saucer's circular indentation. It's as if he's in a small, shallow wading pool that's been drained of water. Margaret and Stephen kneel on either side of him, on the saucer's rim. Underneath them is the china pattern: a bold, complex collision of geometrical shapes in black and white and maroon, accented here and there with gold leaf. It rolls around the edge of the saucer like a carpet runner. All three of them wear togas fashioned from white cotton bedsheets.

Although there is no steering mechanism, it is understood that by some invisible means, some mental mastery—*Like a wizard, perhaps,* Margaret thinks, *or a sorcerer*—Stephen is the one who is directing their course.

In this version of the dream, Daniel is eight—the age he was when he was killed. Margaret and Stephen, however, are very old, maybe as old as a hundred. But they are not at all infirm; they are extremely fit and vital. A pair of ancient health gurus, like Jack LaLanne and his wife.

Daniel is drinking a bottle of Orange Crush and eating Bugles. Margaret and Stephen watch him with a smiling, indulgent benevolence while they sip beet juice from primitive earthenware bowls.

They are flying over a rural landscape that is infinitely and variously bountiful: There are fields of barley, milo, soybeans, and wheat; rice paddies; fruit trees; a field of cauliflower—the heads are huge, the size of inflated beach balls, and colored, too, in the same bright shades of red, blue, yellow, and orange.

The next phase of the dream begins with a weather change. At other times it's been snow. Hail. A plague of frogs. This time, it starts to mist. Mottled, bruised-looking clouds crowd around them, obscuring their view of the landscape below. Stephen scowls, the way some people do in an effort to improve their vision. Margaret shivers.

"Are you cold, Danny?" Margaret asks.

Daniel looks at her and laughs. "Hey, Mom! You have a mustache!"

"What? I do?" Margaret asks, wiping her hand across her upper lip. She looks down to see a smear of bright magenta staining her skin from the forearm to the index finger. She looks up at Daniel. "Did I get it?"

"No. Not quite."

Margaret swipes her other hand across her face.

"How about now?"

Daniel laughs again. It is a musical sound, a cascading parade of notes that reminds Margaret of a xylophone. "You're a mess!"

Margaret laughs. "I am?" She looks over the top of Daniel's head to Stephen. "Stephen! Look at me! I'm a mess!"

"We're out of juice," Stephen says, still staring straight ahead. Margaret notices that he's now holding a lit cigarette.

"Here, Mom." Daniel offers Margaret his empty box of Bugles and the Orange Crush bottle. "I'm done."

Margaret reaches out. A sudden gust of wind tears the box from Daniel's hand and sends it somersaulting violently into the clouds. As Margaret makes to grab the bottle, she fumbles it; there is a loud, dull thwack as it drops, still intact, to the saucer floor. Before Margaret can retrieve the bottle, it scuttles off the edge of the saucer. Margaret looks over the rim. Below them is a swirling cauldron of clouds; they are dense now, and vividly green. *HA!* Margaret thinks giddily, *Pea soup!* It is several seconds before she hears the faint crash of the bottle breaking far beneath them.

"It certainly is a long way down," she remarks, sagely. "I'd say about fifteen thousand square feet."

When Margaret looks up again, she notices a small crack in the saucer where the bottle hit. As she watches, the crack begins to lengthen in two directions, snaking its way across the saucer in a jagged line that separates her from Daniel and Stephen.

"I'm still thirsty," Daniel says. "Can I have some of that, Mom?"

"Sure, honey," Margaret says, and hands Daniel her bowl of beet juice. "Are you sure you don't want a sweater? I'm cold."

The crack has made its way to the outer edges of the saucer. Margaret watches, vaguely alarmed now, as the saucer breaks in two and Daniel and Stephen's section of the saucer begins to float away.

The mist turns to rain.

"Hey!" Margaret calls. "Where are you guys going? Can I come too?" She reaches down to undo her seat belt, but there doesn't seem to be a clasp anywhere.

"To the gas station, Margaret," Stephen answers. The distance between them is growing, and a fierce, steady wind begins to kick up. Stephen has to shout. "WE'RE ALL OUT OF JUICE!"

The wind smells odd, Margaret notices. Vaguely medicinal, like bourbon. The rain is being driven down hard and fast now; the raindrops feel like pinpricks. *This must be what it feels like to get a tattoo,* Margaret thinks. She continues to try and free herself from the seat belt; it seems to be tightening.

"I'll get you a sweater, honey! Wait!" she calls out, but the wind is whipping with such intensity that she can't be sure Daniel hears her. Daniel turns and waves at her.

"See you soon, Mom," he shouts. "I'll bring something back for you."

Daniel takes a sip from the bowl of beet juice. When he looks up again, his face, still smiling, is covered in blood. His mouth begins to move; he is trying to say something.

"WHAT, HONEY?" Margaret screams, frantic and terrified now. She thrashes wildly against the grip of the seat belt. "WHAT IS IT, DANNY? *WHAT?!*" As he drifts away, Margaret can see Daniel's mouth still moving, but his voice is drowned out by the roaring wind.

Stephen takes a long drag on his cigarette and then puts it out on the saucer floor. He looks up and—exhaling a gray, fetid cloud of smoke—blows Margaret a kiss.

Suddenly, Stephen and Daniel's part of the saucer explodes into a thousand pieces.

Margaret screams. There is blackness. The dream is over.

There is one other thing about the dream that never changes: When it is over and Margaret wakes up, she is always sobbing.

Down the hall, Wanda is dreaming about making love with Peter. They are in their loft apartment in Manhattan. Outside, beneath their window, a winged Charlie Parker stands under a lit street lamp and plays "'Round Midnight" on an Irish tin whistle.

And several miles northwest of the Hughes mansion in the Olympic View Apartments (B-101), a man with an extensive collection of Hawaiian shirts is wide awake. Insomniac by nature, he resists sleep because he fears the iconography of his dreams: When peopled, they feature characters from his past; when he is alone, he roams the rooms of a huge house in which, somewhere, a woman is crying. He can never find her.

He is trying to read a Dashiell Hammett novel on loan from the Central Branch of the Seattle Public Library. But his eyes keep straying to a framed black-and-white photograph which rests on the table next to his bed.

Usually, when he looks at this photograph—which is quite often—he pays scant attention to the other people in it. They are out of focus, and have a ghostlike, slightly dematerialized look that doesn't command visual attention. Their only purpose is to provide background interest for the central subject of the photograph—a woman bowling—in the same way that a chorus line of nondescript, leggy dancers provide decoration for a Broadway star.

Tonight, though, the man's eyes keep catching on one of the background figures: a little girl, barely visible over the top of the scorekeeper's table.

Goddammit, the man is thinking. *Her eyes.*

And then he does something he's never done before. He turns the picture facedown on the bedside table and refocuses his attention on his book, which is, after all, a helluva good one.

Her eyes—*goddammit*—are as big as saucers.

Eight

Going into Tex

Wanda was lounging against the kitchen counter, already reading the morning paper. Margaret immediately noticed an airiness, an ease in Wanda's body that she had not seen before.

She certainly looks like she slept well, Margaret thought.

She looks like she got laid, said Margaret's mother.

It was nearly eight-thirty, and Margaret was still in her bathrobe. She felt achy and disoriented, as if she'd been beaten. The dream had that effect on her, always.

"Good morning," Margaret mumbled, bleary-eyed.

Wanda startled. "I didn't hear you come in. Good morning." She put the paper down and filled her coffeemaker with hot water.

Oh good, Margaret thought. *I'm not too late for The Ritual.*

Since Wanda's arrival, Margaret had had many opportunities to watch her make coffee. She did not use the Mr. Coffee that was kept in one of the more remote kitchen cupboards. Instead, she measured several table-spoons of grounds and two teaspoons of cinnamon into a large glass carafe, filled it with not-quite-boiling water, stirred it with a wooden spoon, and let the concoction steep for exactly four minutes. Then she affixed an odd-looking lid to the carafe; it had a small hole in the center with a steel rod running through it. The rod was part of a plungerlike gizmo which had a black plastic attachment at one end—it was the approximate size and shape of a Mallomar cookie—and a larger steel-mesh circle at the other. Wanda applied the flat of her palm to the cookie and pressed it downward, quite slowly, till the steel circle met the floor of the carafe.

This process—which was conducted with great solemnity—had a calming, mesmerizing effect on Margaret. It was like watching the slow, graceful descent of a hotel elevator, from the mezzanine to the lobby, through one of those glass-walled tubes. Margaret populated the elevator with partygoing coffee beans wearing formal evening dress. They resembled the singing raisins in those television commercials. Once arrived, the Bean Creatures passed magically through the glass and proceeded to mill around the kitchen counter with great élan, engaging in sparkling conversation, drinking champagne, and dancing the tango.

Wanda's process of coffeemaking, or The Ritual as Margaret had come to call it, produced a beverage that was black and murky-looking. "French press," it was called. Margaret had never been to France, not even to French-speaking Canada—even though she spoke French fluently. Maybe the French really did prefer their coffee this way. Maybe drinking something as sedimented as river water was their way of paying homage to the Seine. Still—although she tremendously enjoyed watching Wanda make her special coffee—Margaret couldn't imagine how anyone, of *any* nationality, could drink something that looked, and surely tasted, like a petroleum by-product. The smell was nice, though.

"Can I pour you some?" Wanda made this offer every morning.

"No, thank you."

Wanda filled her cup and took a sip. Closing her eyes and holding the liquid on her tongue for a lingering moment, she looked exactly like a connoisseur savoring a vintage wine. "Mmmm," she purred. "That's good. That's really good."

Margaret shuffled into the pantry. There were sparklers of light in the periphery of her vision—unmistakable heralds of both an incipient headache and a visitation from her mother.

Wanda continued, "I won't be here much this week. My show is going into techs."

"Texas?" Margaret pulled a box of cereal from the pantry. "I didn't realize it was a touring play. Will you be gone long?"

"What?" Wanda said, and then gave a revelatory, "OOOH!" and laughed. Margaret couldn't remember hearing Wanda laugh before; it was a soft, resonant, thrumming sound, and for some reason it made her think of the small wooden building blocks that children play with. "I like that. That's funny." Wanda bit into a slice of jelly toast and went on, "No, not Texas. Techs. We're going into techs."

"Into Tex?" Margaret was still baffled. Her mind was rapidly projecting a series of rugged, outdoorsy images: cowboys, horses, boots, campfires, cattle, sides of beef. . . . She could almost smell the singed meat and the barbecue sauce. She felt slightly nauseous and had to grip the counter edge momentarily.

Wanda gave her a concentrated, level look and enunciated: "Technical rehearsals."

"Ah," Margaret said, and then reached for a bowl and began shaking cereal into it. She felt stupid again, and embarrassed. *Am I going deaf, too, on top of everything else?*

Wanda went to the fridge, pulled out a carton of milk, and started filling Margaret's bowl. "It's when we work out all the technical elements—lights, costumes, set changes, and so on. It can be stressful, but usually it's pretty fun. It's one time when stage managers get to play God."

"Oh." Margaret seemed incapable of anything more than monosyllabic speech. *It's so hard to break habits,* she thought. *Why is that? I wonder. Why can't I just talk?*

"Anyway, I just wanted to let you know that I won't be around much. Most nights I'll be getting home pretty late. Especially Thursday and Friday: I'll be gone from around nine until two in the morning."

"My."

"Okay then. I'm gonna brush my teeth and head out. Have a good day."

"Would you like to borrow my car?" Margaret heard herself say.

Wanda turned around. "Sorry. What was that?"

Are you insane? Margaret's mother spoke up. *What are you thinking?*

"Would you like to borrow my car?" Margaret repeated, emphatically.

"Oh, no, Margaret, that's very kind of you, but really . . ."

What in God's name are you doing, Margaret?

I'm breaking a habit, Mother. Be quiet.

Margaret had noticed that lately her mother was not only making herself heard but had started to materialize, just faintly, at the edges of her vision. It was troubling. "Do you have a driver's license?" she continued.

"Yes," Wanda replied, "It's from out of state, but —"

"Do you have a good driving record?" Margaret asked, and then felt immediately ashamed because it wasn't her question, it was someone else's. "I'm so sorry. What a presumptuous thing to ask. It doesn't matter."

Now Margaret seemed incapable of shutting up, and as she began to sprinkle sugar onto her cereal, she went on in a voice that was unfamiliar to her, a crisply enunciated voice that was both friendly and commanding. "You're a reliable person," she stated, gaining speed, "I know that, I can see that. You don't have to prove a thing. And don't worry about inconveniencing me, because you won't be. I don't need the car much. It just sits in the garage most days. I might have to use it once in a while—" She looked up at Wanda, who had come to a complete, openmouthed standstill. *I'm being loquacious!* she realized, gleefully. Then she went back to sprinkling sugar on her cereal—the physical action pleased and supported her somehow. "I'll make a call to my insurance agent today and get you on my policy right away. It shouldn't be any trouble at all."

She paused and looked at her Special K. It was blanketed by a thick layer of sugar.

"I don't know what to say, Margaret. It's a very generous offer, but—"

"Well, think about it," Margaret said. "I'd certainly sleep better knowing you weren't riding a bicycle home at that time of night."

"All right. I'll think about it."

"Good! *Très bien! Au revoir* then!" Margaret waved her napkin gaily at Wanda, and then took an enormous mouthful of cereal. It tasted wonderful, like Christmas.

By the time the kettle whistled, Wanda was out the door, and Margaret had forgotten that her teapot lay in pieces in the bottom of the kitchen garbage bag. *I suppose I could use the Clarice Cliff Orange Capri set circa 1930 from the dining room,* Margaret thought. *Or one of the Minton Majolica teapots. The Monkey with the tail handle, or the Fish-eating Fish. But really, how ridiculous. I've never used any of them, not in fifty years; why start now? Then again, isn't that what they're for?*

The phone rang. Without thinking, Margaret picked up.

"Mrs. Hughes, this is Pam, the receptionist at Dr. Leising's office."

Margaret's heart raced, as if she'd been running. "I'm fine," she said breathlessly.

"We've certainly had a hard time getting ahold of you, Mrs. Hughes." Margaret detected a certain amount of strain underpinning Pam's professionally cheery voice. "Dr. Leising would very much like to get you in for another appointment."

"Oh?" Margaret tried to sound blasé.

"Yeh-sssssss . . ." Pam lengthened the word in a way that made her sound as though she were talking to a very dim-witted foreigner. "Would eight forty-five tomorrow morning work for you?"

Margaret clenched her teeth and pressed down, hard. Her molars seemed to yield and compress slightly, as if they were made of wet mortar.

"I don't want to schedule an appointment," Margaret said. "Put Dr. Leising on the phone."

"Dr. Leising is with a patient right now, Mrs. Hughes. Can't we just go ahead and—"

"No. I want to talk to him in person."

Margaret was put on hold, and a heavily orchestrated arrangement of "Puff the Magic Dragon" came through the headset. She felt very large and very small at the same time, and she thought suddenly of Alice in Wonderland. *Eat this. Drink this.*

Her physician came on the line. "Good morning, Margaret. My receptionist tells me you want to speak with me before you come in." His voice—overly gentle, overly solicitous—annoyed Margaret tremendously. They were practically the same age, for goodness' sake. He'd been to her house for cocktails, about a hundred years ago.

"We've known each other a long time, Robert. Don't talk to me like a doctor. Talk to me like a friend."

"All right," he began. "As your friend, it would be irresponsible of me not to insist that you allow yourself to be treated for this tumor in an aggressive manner."

"There are things I need to do. I cannot be incapacitated."

"Margaret—"

"I don't want surgery. I don't want radiation therapy. There has to be some other way."

She heard his cell phone go off—it played that famous galloping snippet from the "William Tell Overture"—and then someone spoke in the background.

"All right, Margaret. I have to go now, and we shouldn't have this conversation on the phone anyway. Let's get you in the office so we can talk about how to proceed."

"That's fine."

"I'll give you back to my receptionist and she'll take care of you, all right?"

Margaret spoke with the receptionist and then hung up.

It's too damn bad, sweetie. Her mother was materializing on one of the kitchen chairs, wearing a white peignoir, looking very much like the character in that old movie—*what was it?*—about the beautiful dead wife who wouldn't leave the living alone.

It's a pisser. But look on the bright side: I'll see you soon.

"Are you sure about that, Mother?" Margaret said out loud. "Are you really sure?"

Margaret couldn't tell with certainty, but she had the impression that her mother had produced a deck of cards and was playing a game of solitaire. And cheating.

Margaret opened the cupboard under the sink. She pulled out the garbage container and inspected its insides. There, at the very bottom, were the remains of her tea things. She sat down on the kitchen floor. She began pulling the pieces out, one by one, and laying them down. Without exactly knowing why, she found herself laying the pieces in a circle, with herself at the center.

They stayed that way for a while, each silent, each busy in her own way: Margaret, on the floor, laying out a circle of porcelain; Margaret's mother, at the table, laying out her cards. And then Margaret heard a different voice. It was very faint, but very clear.

See you soon, the voice said.

Margaret froze. Someone else was materializing at the kitchen table, next to her mother. Someone smaller, more transparent, and wearing a cowboy hat. Margaret stayed on the floor, in the circle of porcelain, waiting, trying to will the pain in her head to go away.

It wouldn't. They wouldn't. She sat there for a long time.

Nine

❧

Living Arrangements, 1972

When Wanda got home that night it was nearly nine o'clock. She went into the kitchen to get something to eat and found a personalized note card—"From the desk of Margaret Isadora Hughes"—on the kitchen table. The note card read:

"Dear Wanda, I have taken care of the insurance matter, and you will be able to use the car beginning on Thursday, if you wish. As I said, it is absolutely no inconvenience for me, so don't give it a second thought if you are hesitant on that account. Also, if you would like a ride into work tomorrow morning, let me know. I have an 8:45 appointment downtown and would be happy to give you a lift. Sincerely, Margaret. P.S. I hope you had a wonderful day of technical rehearsals. M."

Wanda stood at the table and held Margaret's note limply. She read it several more times.

She unloaded her backpack onto the table and went into the pantry. She came back with a jar of peanut butter, a box of toothpicks, and a cup of banana rice pudding. Sitting down, she unscrewed the lid from the peanut butter, peeled the top off the rice pudding, and then, using the end of one of the toothpicks as if it were a very tiny spoon, she began to scoop out minuscule bits of food—first peanut butter, then pudding, then peanut butter, and so on—which she transferred methodically to her tongue.

The house was very still.

She'd be happy to give me a lift, Wanda thought. *That's nice. I could use one.*

From the time she was six years old until she was twenty-two, Wanda lived in a house that originally had one bathroom. A second bathroom was installed by Uncle Artie in the 1970s, when Jacqueline Kennedy Schultz turned seven and began entering beauty pageants. This bathroom, located in the basement, was designed to accommodate Jacqueline's ever-expanding artillery of cosmetics, hair accessories, and costumes. The bathroom was also intended to accommodate Jacqueline herself—who was, to downplay the obvious, a big presence in the Schultz household from her earliest infancy. The additional bathroom did not impact the other members of the Schultz clan; excepting only the most severe personal hygiene emergencies, it remained Jacqueline's private domain, and Wanda, Aunt Maureen, and the eight male Schultzes continued to make do in the single upstairs bathroom.

Sleeping arrangements at the Schultzes' were another matter.

The Schultz home had three bedrooms. Before the arrival of their youngest, Y chromosome–challenged sibling, the seven Schultz boys had occupied two of those three bedrooms in a setup that was fairly amenable to all concerned: The three oldest boys (James, John, and Jacob) shared one room, and the four youngest Schultz males (Jesse, Jordan, Joshua, and Jeremiah) shared the other. However, once Artie Schultz finally made his long-awaited X chromosome contribution, this arrangement underwent a radical change; shortly after Aunt Maureen was fully recovered from Jacqueline's birth (followed soon after by a tubal ligation), she announced to the male members of her tribe that baby Jacqueline would require a bedroom ALL TO HERSELF, and the boys' sleeping arrangement would be accordingly reconfigured so that the seven of them would now be housed together.

Imagine the resentment! Imagine the disbelief! Imagine the boys' confusion as their heretofore sensible, no-frills mother went daft chasing down curtains, pillows, wallpaper, bedclothes, and sheets in every conceivable shade of pink.

In an effort to mitigate the shock of these new circumstances, Aunt Maureen and Uncle Artie purchased four new bunk beds for their male offspring. This provided the seven Schultz boys with one bed too many, but the furniture dealer had given Uncle Artie an exceptionally good deal. "You'll WANT an extra bed," the salesman had said, jovially. "For overnight guests!" Uncle Artie and Aunt Maureen laughed so hysterically that they fell over in the middle of the storeroom.

But even though the bunk beds provided a certain fleeting fascination for James-John-Jacob-Jesse-Jordan-Joshua-and-Jeremiah, it soon wore off. All the boys, especially the eldest ones, grew surly and bitter; quite understandably, they did not thrill to the sight of their baby sister, who, on a nightly basis, blew kisses to the lemminglike masses as she paraded down the hall and retired into her palatial quarters.

One can thus easily understand the male Schultzes' uncharitable reaction to Wanda's arrival a mere two years after Jacqueline was born: She'd been abandoned by her parents? She was like an honest-to-God *orphan?* BIG DEAL! To the Schultz boys, Wanda was just another pain-in-the-ass girl.

As such, when Wanda first arrived, she was naturally installed in Jacqueline's room. This was just fine with the boys; it was *not* fine with Jacqueline. Wanda endured Jacqueline's rancor and the Pepto-Bismol excesses of her room for several months, but finally she couldn't stand it any longer. Wanda began longing to occupy that empty eighth bed in the boys' quarters.

She knew the boys would never acquiesce to this unless she could prove two things:

1. She wasn't really a girl, and
2. She had something of value to offer them.

Wanda set about deleting from her behavior and dress anything that was overtly feminine. She eschewed all things pink. She learned to make a variety of farting noises on her forearms and palms. She mastered on-cue belching. She attempted Apache war cries, rocket ships, El Train collisions, Italian race cars, and atomic blasts with less success—but no one could fault her enthusiasm.

Wanda began studying the social structure of the male Schultz tribe. She learned who was fighting with whom, and why. She noticed that the boys' squabbles often continued throughout the day, and so—when the warring factions were confined to their cramped bunkhouse bedroom for the night——made a hell of bedtime.

After extended research and considerable thought, Wanda developed an idea which she thought might accomplish her goals. She proposed this idea to Aunt Maureen one night while they were doing the dishes. Wanda was the only child in the Schultz household who routinely volunteered to help with this chore; it was the one activity that guaranteed a lengthy amount of time alone with Aunt Maureen.

Aunt Maureen washed; Wanda dried. The steam from the sink rose in milky, diaphanous sheets. Hands moved in and out of the water. Soapsuds drifted and regrouped themselves in subtly changing permutations. To Wanda, the soapsuds represented rare, biologically complex lifeforms that were unique to the Schultz kitchen, visible only to herself and to Aunt Maureen.

"I call it 'Musical Beds,'" Wanda said as she wiped a dish. Most of the Schultz family dishes bore chips and cracks. Wanda assumed these were acquired on the day her father left her. She believed that, before her arrival, Aunt Maureen's dishes had been perfect. And even though Wanda knew that Jacqueline had been the instrument of destruction, she believed that her presence had been the catalyst, and she never got over the feeling that the damage to Aunt Maureen's dishes was her fault. So, Wanda was very careful. In all the years she lived at the Schultz home, she never, ever, dropped anything.

As Wanda detailed her plan, Aunt Maureen listened intently. She was impressed. In essence, Wanda proposed to broker a sleeping arrangement on a nightly basis that would accommodate the alliances and feuds of the moment. "That way," Wanda said, "if you're not getting along with someone, you don't have to sleep close to them."

"What about compromise?" Aunt Maureen said. "Shouldn't they learn to compromise?" Even though at this point Wanda herself was only in second grade, Aunt Maureen was used to consulting with her on the challenges of child-rearing.

"Not at bedtime," Wanda answered. "At bedtime, it's too hard for boys to compromise."

"Good point." Aunt Maureen always treated Wanda with respect;

their relationship was an excellent model of joint mid-level management at its most effective. "But what about the boys that *aren't* fighting? They shouldn't be punished by having to move."

"I don't think it will feel like punishment," Wanda replied. "The way I've got it figured out, I think it'll feel like an adventure."

"Maybe," Aunt Maureen said, dubiously. She began drying her hands on a dishcloth. She looked out toward the dining room, where Jeremiah was sitting on the floor, ferociously chewing his toenails, and Jordan and Jesse were playing Oreo see-food. She leaned close to Wanda and whispered, "What about cooties?"

Wanda whispered back, "They can sleep in their sleeping bags."

After hearing a few more particulars, and agreeing to Wanda's last proviso—that there be no other family members present when Wanda talked to the boys—Aunt Maureen agreed to let Wanda attempt to implement Operation Musical Beds, then apprised Uncle Artie of the situation.

"Sounds terrific!" said Uncle Artie. "Just great!" Uncle Artie always sounded exclamatory.

Aunt Maureen assembled the boys in the living room, and then announced that Wanda had something of importance to talk about. "Your father and sister and I are going for a little drive."

"I know!" yelled Uncle Artie. "Let's go to Baskin-Robbins!!"

Uncle Artie weighed two hundred pounds. He spent his days beating on ancient rusted pipes with large steel wrenches. He was not a man naturally inclined to appreciate the subtle maneuverings of interpersonal diplomacy.

The boys rioted.

"Sorry," Aunt Maureen whispered to Wanda.

"It's okay," Wanda replied. "I can handle it."

"Settle down now, guys!" Uncle Artie bellowed happily. He had a habit of jingling his car keys in a way that made Wanda expect to see Dasher, Dancer, Comet, and Blitzen standing outside the front door. "We'll bring back ice cream for everyone! Come on, princess!"

"I WANT BUBBLE GUN! I WANT BUBBLE GUN! I WANT BUBBLE GUN! I WANT BUBBLE GUN!" screamed Jacqueline.

And they were gone.

Initially, there was some resistance to Wanda's plan.

"What a DUMB idea! Leave it to a girl to be so DUMB!"

"You mean we'll sleep in a different bed every NIGHT?"

"You won't *have* to," Wanda answered.

"That's CRAZY!"

"That's STUPID!"

"I want ice cream!"

"Hey! Who CUT ONE?!!"

"So how will we know where to go?" This question came from James, the oldest.

Wanda brought out a large chart. "You'll have a 'home bed,' kind of like a home*room,*" Wanda said. She looked pointedly at James; he was in junior high and understood the concept. "That's the bed you sleep in most of the time. But if you're having a fight with someone who sleeps close to you, you get to move somewhere else."

"You mean anywhere we want?"

"No. Not exactly anywhere. I'll help you decide where to sleep."

"Yeah," said James. "But what's the catch? What do YOU get out of it?"

"I get to sleep in the leftover bed."

"In OUR room?!"

"NO WAY!"

"*NO WAY!*"

"Girls have COOTIES! Girls are GROSS!"

"Not every night," Wanda said reasonably. "Just once in a while."

"Why?" asked James. "Why would you wanna sleep in our room?"

"Yeah. Jerkie Jackie's room is WAY bigger."

"Can you guys keep a secret?"

This got their attention.

"I hate pink. Pink stinks."

The boys snickered; Wanda was making progress.

Wanda brought out art supplies, poster board, and string. She asked the boys to give nonproprietary names to their home beds and design portable signs for them; they came up with "Starship of Doom," "Count Vlad's Sarcoffagus," "Sorcerer's Lair," "Bull Pen," "Booger Palace," "Cowboy Donut Store," and "Fort Farts-o-Plenty."

By the time Aunt Maureen, Uncle Artie, and Jacqueline returned—

with three gallons of ice cream—they were astonished to find the seven Schultz boys seated at the kitchen table, happily engaged in, of all things, an *art* project. "Well! I'll be darned!" said Uncle Artie.

Naturally, Jacqueline wanted to make a sign for her own bed, and insisted that her parents do the same.

So, Wanda dished up and served ten enormous bowls of ice cream, and then stood at the sink, looking on as the Schultzes laughed and ate and finished making their signs. Jackie's sign was "Queen Barbie's Beauty Palace." Aunt Maureen and Uncle Artie's sign was "National Headquarters: Zero Population Growth." It was hung not on their bed, but on their bedroom door. It hung there for the next thirteen years; as far as Wanda knew, it was hanging there still.

When everyone was done and had presented their artwork to the family, Wanda announced the sleeping assignments. The boys stampeded up the stairs to hang their signs and get ready for bed.

From that point on, bedtime was rarely accompanied by arguments, pummeling, or pouting; instead, there was a certain level of excitement as Wanda read off the sleeping assignments. There were hardly ever any disputes; when there were, Wanda managed them.

Peace reigned in the Schultz household—at least from seven o'clock until eight-thirty each evening—and Wanda got the one small thing she wanted: She'd become an indispensable member of the Schultz home. Furthermore, there was always that single empty bed, and Wanda always knew which one it was.

On many nights, when she couldn't sleep, and when the frilly excesses of Jacqueline's room reminded her of her outcast state, Wanda would take a pillow and a quilt, tiptoe into the boys' room, and crawl into that last empty bed.

Comforted by the tangy smells of her cousins' stale socks and male sweat, their even breathing, and their tamed tribal presence, Wanda was finally able to fall asleep. On those nights, she dreamed that her cousins would never leave her. She dreamed that they were adoring, protective, and loyal. She dreamed that they were the seven dwarfs, and she was Snow White.

And so, Wanda made a place for herself in Schultz society. To the boys, she became a kind of club mascot: not too bad, for a girl. To Jacqueline, she became a tolerated annoyance. And to Aunt Maureen and Uncle Artie, who would often remark in private about Wanda's amazing maturity, self-sufficiency, easygoing manner, and skills at negotiation, she became a blessing.

Wanda O'Casey was as happy as she could be, given the fact that her heart was broken.

Wanda went upstairs. Margaret had left a hall light on for her. She passed through her bedroom and went into the bathroom. She washed her face. She thought about how little had really changed, how much she still felt like a guest in someone else's life.

The bathroom was huge. And although it was situated between two bedrooms, there was no one with whom Wanda had to share it. Still, it was tiled—floor to ceiling—in an aggressively feminine Queen Barbie's Beauty Palace shade of pink.

Ten

The Hotel Orléans

When Margaret got up the next morning, she found a sheet of yellow legal paper under her bedroom door: "Dear Margaret," it read, "Thank you for the offer to use your car. I am still thinking about it. My hesitation is not just about inconveniencing you. It also has to do with some personal stuff that I'm dealing with. I'm trying to learn to do without a lot of things right now. In a weird way, it has to do with that guy I told you about. Peter. Anyway—sorry to ramble on like this!—you can understand why I'm reluctant to borrow your car, even though it's an extremely kind and generous gesture. I'll give it some more thought and let you know what I decide. Thanks again, Wanda. P.S. About tomorrow morning: If you're really sure it's no trouble, I'd love to get a lift."

Margaret was flattered that Wanda had decided to open up a little bit, and she felt suddenly energized—even cheerful. She checked her nightstand clock; it was a quarter of seven, and Wanda would be asleep for exactly forty-five more minutes. Margaret bathed quickly and dressed, lingering over her choice of clothes and taking special care with her hair. She brushed and flossed her teeth meticulously. Anointing her right index finger with a single drop of Chanel No. 5, she pressed it firmly behind each earlobe and into the hollow at her throat. She even applied some lipstick and—taking off her bifocals to do so—a bit of mascara; it came from a bright pink and lime-green tube she found rolling around in the back of one of the bathroom cabinet drawers. It occurred to her that anyone watching these personal preparations might conclude that she was getting ready for some kind of social event.

Well, she reasoned, *to me, giving someone a ride to work and going to the doctor's office is a social event.*

And the party's almost over, Chickie! said Margaret's mother, calling up from the kitchen with the enthusiasm of a high school cheerleader. *O! V! E! R!* Margaret was surprised—and slightly disturbed—to find that her mother was expanding her vocal range.

After taking some extra-strength ibuprofen, she went into the walk-in closet to regard herself in the full-length mirror. She wore a trimly cut, beige wool flannel skirt; a cream-colored silk blouse; a beige, cream, and pale yellow mohair cardigan; tan support hose (*without* tummy top control, she noted, with a quiet measure of pride); and tan suede Hush Puppies.

Pursing her lips, Margaret considered her reflection. *No one would think I was going to a very special social event,* she had to admit. *Nothing like dinner. Or the opera. Or tango dancing.*

You look like you're going to play bingo! called out Margaret's mother, alarmingly close now. The sound of her voice made Margaret literally jump. Margaret wasn't sure where her mother was calling from, but she sounded as if she'd reached the upstairs landing.

For chrissakes, Margaret, put on a little color!

Margaret glanced sideways, toward her bedroom door, which was still closed; she had the feeling that her mother had moved even closer, and was now positioned just on the other side of the door. Margaret pictured her lounging against the wall and buffing her fingernails.

Margaret rummaged around obediently in one of her dresser drawers. *There's nothing wrong with looking like a bingo player, Mother,* she countered. *It's what people my age do.*

Yes, but you don't, do you? You don't play bingo, or pinochle, or mah-jongg, or poker, or—

Get to the point, Mother.

You don't do anything except rumble around this old house.

Margaret stopped rifling through the dresser drawer; she turned and addressed the bedroom door directly. *Well, I might.*

Ticktock, Margaret. Ticktock.

I might *do something, Mother. You never know.*

HA!

I might do anything! Margaret found a small navy-blue and yellow polka-dot scarf, which she knotted neatly at her neck. She returned to the mirror to gauge its effect. It was not overly impressive. "Now I look like a Camp Fire Girl on my way to play bingo," she said aloud.

Margaret's mother heaved a sigh. *Life is wasted on the living!* she barked bitterly. Margaret pictured her flouncing off to another part of the house in search of someone with a more exciting wardrobe.

It was already a quarter past seven. Soon, Wanda would be getting up; she was an extremely punctual person. Margaret gave her reflection a parting glance. Sighing, she patted her hair, straightened her cardigan, opened her bedroom door, and proceeded cautiously down the stairs. She hoped the kitchen would be empty.

Wanda arrived in the kitchen, as usual, at precisely eight o'clock.

"Good morning!" Margaret said.

"Hi." Wanda busied herself with her backpack; it contained a number of books, writing implements, a ruler, a water bottle, an extra pair of shoes, and a large three-ring notebook.

That must be terribly heavy, Margaret thought. *No wonder she's tired so much of the time.*

"I got your note this morning."

"My note." Wanda gave Margaret a worried look and then began speaking very quickly. "I wrote it late last night, obviously, when I was feeling a little . . . grim, I guess you'd say. Yesterday was hard—it's tech week and everything—and I don't seem to be up to my usual level of . . . competence. Confidence. Anyway, I just hope my note didn't sound ungrateful or crazy or anything." Wanda clamped her mouth shut and studied a floor vent.

Having become familiar with the roiling landscape of Wanda's emotional life, Margaret recognized that the girl was barely holding herself together. There were so many things she wanted to say to her, but this was not the time to say them.

"Your note made perfect sense, actually," Margaret said, speaking gently to the top of Wanda's bowed head. "There are some things I'm trying to change about my life too. Loaning you the car has something to do with that."

Wanda looked up and blinked. Her eyes were glistening. "I see."

"You think about it some more and let me know what you decide."

"All right." Wanda began to buckle the straps of her backpack. "You look nice this morning. Where are you off to, looking so dressed up?"

Margaret paused to sip her tea. "I . . . I'm going to play . . . That is, I'm joining a . . . group of . . ." She faltered. "I have an appointment."

"Oh." Wanda poured herself a small glass of juice. "Well, you look very nice. Are you sure it's no trouble giving me a ride?"

"No trouble at all."

"We should get on the road pretty soon, shouldn't we? So you won't be late?"

"I suppose so. . . ." Margaret's body felt like a block of granite. "Don't you want coffee before we go?"

"I'll get something at the Uptown Café."

Margaret gathered up her pocketbook, coat, and gloves. Her head had started throbbing.

"It's only a couple of blocks from the Rep," Wanda continued. "Maybe we could meet there sometime. Maybe on one of my matinee days?"

Margaret tried to focus her attention by putting on her gloves. "That would be nice."

"Their lattes look like works of art," Wanda went on in a chipper voice as she hoisted her backpack. "It's by far the best coffee in town!"

Margaret was a very good driver, Wanda noted—not one of those abysmally clueless old ladies who squint over the tops of their steering wheels as if they're engaged in bunker warfare, rely on telepathy instead of turn signals to communicate intent, and never let the speedometer get above 15 mph. Erect, sharp-eyed, focused, and absolutely by-the-book in terms of traffic protocol, Margaret clearly took her job as the operator of a motorized vehicle seriously.

They had a limited conversation when they first set out—the kind of polite, semiconscious exchange that people have when they either don't know each other or there's something else on their minds: "How is work going?" "Isn't it a nice day?" "It's been a lovely spring. So little rain for March." "Are the winters here really that terrible?" "Oh, not so bad. A bit dreary, but . . ." And so on. But as they headed into heavier traffic, Margaret's solemn expression made it clear that a vigilant regard for the rules of traffic safety overrode any further participation in social niceties. Soon, they both fell silent.

"Just take Roy Street till it runs into Queen Anne," Wanda had said after they'd passed several minutes without speaking. "Then turn left."

"Oh, yes," Margaret replied, distractedly. "I remember this neighborhood."

Wanda was struck again by how little she knew of her landlady. This was the first time she had seen Margaret outside the confines of her house. Maybe that wasn't too remarkable; after all, Wanda kept unusual work hours. Margaret might do all kinds of exciting things during the day. She probably had a very full life.

"Bye! Thanks again!" Wanda called. She watched Margaret pilot the aged Volvo—signaling, maneuvering, and merging with the oncoming traffic so gracefully that Wanda imagined an accompanying piano playing ballet barre music.

It was early; the Uptown wasn't crowded yet. Wanda secured one of the window-side corner tables she preferred and then stepped up to the counter. She ordered a hazelnut espresso scone and a triple Americano, no room for cream. She settled into her chair. From this vantage point, she had a good view of the entire café, as well as the sidewalk and street. She could blend in. Observe without being observed. For the next several minutes, she studied the faces of each and every person in the Uptown Café.

Then she got out her little red and black book and began to write her affirmation.

Dr. Leising was indeed able to offer Margaret several acceptable treatment options: prescription medications, biofeedback techniques, dietary and vitamin supplement advice, and chiefly, regularly scheduled visits to the Radiology Department for CT scans to monitor her condition. He also lobbied convincingly for the engagement of a live-in nurse. Margaret agreed with special enthusiasm to this last suggestion, augmenting Dr. Leising's well-stated arguments with an unvoiced one of her own: Wanda might enjoy the company of another woman, one closer to her own age. Maybe she'd be willing to confide her troubles to someone who was more like a sister.

Rebounding from the dread which had characterized the beginning of her day—a dread, she realized, that had been an insidious, anchoring force for all the unknowing months before Dr. Leising confirmed the presence of the tumor—Margaret left the office feeling weightless as a swallowtail.

She should probably call Stephen as soon as she got home and tell him the whole story. After all, she promised to let him know about the test results, keep him informed. Marita was fond of her too, Margaret knew—hard as that was to admit—and the news that she'd be dead in a year or two would upset them, to say the least. She was not looking forward to the conversation. It was so difficult to face the *fact* of them sometimes: Stephen and Marita, Marita and Stephen, Stephen and Marita and their three young children. In a sense, Stephen was very much at the beginning of his life. *It's nice for men that they can start over like that,* she thought without bitterness, but without exultation either.

I'll call later, she decided finally. *There's no hurry, after all, and it's such a lovely day.*

Leaving her car in the lot next to the medical building, she set out on a walk. At first she was uneasy. Downtown Seattle seemed as exotic as another country—so noisy and unfamiliar. It had been a long time since she'd spent any time downtown. *Years, probably,* she realized. *I used to come down here quite a lot. I guess there was a time when it didn't seem like so much trouble. And of course, when I had Daniel, there were other reasons to get out of the house. Visits to Santa Claus, the art museum, the Four Seasons Tea Room, Pike Place Market, and so on. Special outings.* Margaret's eyes swept across the moving crowds of shoppers and office workers and tourists. *And all of this . . . activity,* she thought, wonderingly, *it's been here, all this time. It all goes on, even when I'm somewhere else.*

There were confetti-like splashes of color from early blooming daffodils, tulips, hyacinths, jonquils, and crocuses. Even though the air was damp and cool—Margaret was quite comfortable in her wool cardigan—many people were without coats. Some even wore shorts and sandals.

She stopped to regard the window displays at The Bon. They featured mannequin families, artfully arranged on AstroTurf landscapes and engaged in various springtime activities: Easter egg hunts, gardening, tea parties. Chalky-skinned mothers and fathers lounged near picnic baskets stuffed with petrified baguettes and croissants, wedges of Brie, purple grapes, and gourmet sandwiches. Their well-mannered, pale, cherubic-faced mannequin children wore unscuffed shoes and carried baskets laden with designer eggs, Godiva chocolates, and complacent fake bunnies. *I guess that's somebody's idea of Heaven,* she thought.

She walked on—past enormous bookstores and Thai restaurants and banks with unfamiliar names, past computer outlets and software retailers and shoe emporiums. She was astounded by the number of people in Seattle who were just sitting around drinking coffee. Starbucks. Seattle's Best Coffee. Tully's Coffee. And the espresso carts! There seemed to be one or two of these on every block.

Tattoo parlors. Movie complexes. Copy stores. Video arcades. So many things had changed.

Margaret decided to take a chance that at least one thing in downtown Seattle had stayed constant. She started walking in the direction of the Hotel Orléans. She was fairly sure she remembered how to get there. It was several blocks north of the main shopping district—*Yes! There it is!*—on a quiet cross street that was lined with mature cherry trees in full bloom.

As she approached the hotel, a slight breeze stirred, and a few cherry blossoms shook loose onto her shoulders.

From across the street, she looked up at the hotel's curving facade, its delicate, filigreed, wrought-iron balconies set with pots of lavender, and the curved, intersecting slopes of its mansard roof. The noisiness and bustle she'd found so disorienting just a few moments ago seemed to fade, so that all she could hear was the steadying, hypnotic sound of the front courtyard fountain.

Drawing closer, Margaret saw a woman appear at the front entrance—she seemed neither young nor old—wearing a fine straw cloche hat and a full-skirted floral dress. The fabric of the dress moved gracefully, responding in a light, easy, playful way to the woman's body as she set off, full of purpose, toward some other part of the city. *I could wear a dress like that,* Margaret thought, *and not look too ridiculous.*

Breathing in the early spring air, she was filled with a vast, complicated, unspecific sense of the past—of many other springs long gone—and she felt a small, tentative unfolding sensation in her chest. *No wonder they talk about heartache,* she thought. *That's exactly where one feels it.*

One of the hotel valets approached her. "Madame," he said, using the French pronunciation of the word, "may I help you?" He was in his late fifties perhaps, and his face—round and benevolent as a full moon—looked concerned.

"No, thank you," Margaret replied brightly, pressing a hand against her cheek. "I'm just admiring the hotel."

"She's a grand old beauty, isn't she?"

"Yes, indeed." They stood silently for a moment, gazing at the fountain just outside the hotel entrance. It was a small-scale replica of the Tuilleries in Paris. "I was here many years ago," Margaret said, almost to herself. "On my honeymoon."

"Really?" The valet smiled expansively, revealing two sets of brilliant, white, perfectly even teeth. He could've been a spokesperson for Pepsodent.

"It was in 1958. Around this time of year."

"Aaaah," the valet replied. "That was just a bit before I came to The Orléans." Suddenly, he clapped his hand to his chest. Margaret was sure he was going to recite the Pledge of Allegiance. "Mr. MacPherson, at your service!" he announced, still holding his hand over his heart. The gold name tag that brushed the tips of his fingers read, "M. MacPherson, Senior Staff," and beneath that, "Valet Supervisor." He continued, "I've been here for over thirty years."

"My goodness!"

"If you don't mind my asking, did you have the Honeymoon Suite?"

This question, which might have struck Margaret as prurient coming from any other stranger, was offered with such warmth and innocence that she felt perfectly comfortable answering. "No, we didn't. My husband . . . we couldn't afford it, but we had a lovely little room, all the same. It was on the third floor, I believe. We were able to look out at the fountain."

"I see," Mr. MacPherson responded, narrowing his eyes and placing a manicured finger lightly against his lips. He looked positively judicial. "315, maybe. Or 317. Do you, by any chance—" and this was the first time he seemed reluctant to speak—"if you don't mind my asking, do you remember the colors of the room?"

"Oh." Margaret paused again. "Well . . . I'm fairly certain that the walls were done in a kind of rose color. Wallpapered, I believe?"

"Oh, yes," Mr. MacPherson replied, gently authoritative, "all the rooms in the hotel are wallpapered."

"And the bedspread . . ." Margaret had a sudden memory of the bed-spread—a happy, rumpled mess on the floor, at the foot of the bed—and of Stephen, laughing, naked, on top of it. She felt her cheeks go warm and wondered if she was blushing. "It was rose too."

"Not pink?" Mr. MacPherson asked, regarding Margaret with a piercing, urgent look. "You're quite sure it wasn't pink?" Margaret had a strong impulse to call him Sherlock.

"Oh, no. Definitely not pink. More of a mauve, I think. It had a fleur-de-lis pattern—"

"*AHA!*"

"—with soft moss green and gold as well."

"*Definitely* Room 317 then, if it was fleur-de-lis in rose and gold. Room 315 was paisley in lavender and pink."

Margaret was impressed. "How remarkable!"

"And you enjoyed your stay at the hotel, did you?" he went on. "In Room 317?"

"Oh, yes. They were three of the happiest days of my life."

"You know," he said, his voice lowered to a conspiratorial whisper, "you didn't miss a thing by not staying in the Honeymoon Suite. In truth, there's no better room in the entire hotel than Room 317."

"However are you able to remember such details—about the rooms and so on—after all these years?"

"Well, it wouldn't be so easy now," he replied. "Ever since 1970, all the rooms except for the suites have been decorated in much the same way. So these days, it's much more difficult to tell them apart." He glanced quickly around the courtyard, stole a look at his wristwatch, and then continued, without missing a beat. "I have to admit, I think that's a shame. I understand the reasoning, from a financial point of view, but I do think the hotel lost something when management made that decision." Mr. MacPherson turned slightly as another, much younger valet sauntered outside and slouched against one of the topiary trees flanking the hotel's front entrance. "Please, would you excuse me for just a moment?"

"Of course."

Reaching up to touch the brim of his gold-braided hat, he gave Margaret a deferential nod and then walked briskly to where the young valet was standing.

Margaret watched as he spoke to his subordinate. Although the older man's face never lost its kind expression and his voice never rose in volume or in pitch, the young valet—who was several inches taller than Mr. MacPherson—began to look visibly chastened. His whole body sagged. His thumbs went into hiding. His chin seemed about to quiver.

Then, Mr. MacPherson reached up and placed a firm, comradely hand on the young valet's shoulders and spoke again. The young valet rallied suddenly, straightening himself to his full height. *Why, he's enormous!* Margaret thought, aghast. Then she had another thought. *Or, perhaps . . . is Mr. MacPherson really that small?* The two men exchanged a smile, and then Mr. MacPherson strode back to where Margaret was standing.

"Sorry about that," he said, tipping his hat again.

"That's quite all right," Margaret replied. *Why, it's him!* she realized, looking down into Mr. MacPherson's eyes, which she now noticed were a startling, clear, aquamarine blue. *He can't be more than five feet two!* "You were telling me about the hotel rooms?" she prompted.

Mr. MacPherson beamed. "I know every room in the hotel, you see. The suites, too. I made a point of that. It took a long time, but over the years I've been able to memorize the different layouts, decor, and so on. I tell the young valets, 'You have to know all of the hotel—not just the outside, the part that everybody sees. You might think it doesn't have anything to do with your job, but it does.'" Mr. MacPherson paused. "Say," he said, looking suddenly chagrined. "I'm certainly talking like there's no tomorrow. Forgive me."

"Oh, please," Margaret said. "Go on."

He looked at the hotel. "I adore this old place. But it's not just her. Imagine if she'd sat empty all these years. She wouldn't be the same at all, now, would she?"

Beneath its elegance and formality, the hotel did seem to possess a certain friendly animation of expression, its gleaming window-eyes open and lined with thick wands of lavender, fluttering in the breeze like flirtatious eyelashes. The Hotel Orléans had the face of a kind and knowing courtesan who's had many lovers and aged well.

Mr. MacPherson plucked a tuft of lint from his uniform. "Where are you and your husband from, Mrs . . . ?"

"Hughes. I've lived in Seattle my whole life." She didn't add, *In a sad-eyed house.*

"And still, you spent your honeymoon here?"

"Yes," she answered, faintly.

"Many people who stay at The Orléans say they feel as if they've taken a trip to France."

Margaret was still staring at the hotel, wondering what Wanda's impression of her father's house had been the first time she saw it—and Stephen's. What had he thought? Had she ever asked? "We're no longer together," she muttered, half to herself. "*Nous avons cassé.*"

"I'm sorry." Mr. MacPherson looked genuinely distraught.

"What?" Margaret said. "What did I say?"

He reached out and cupped a supporting hand beneath her elbow. "Why don't you come inside for a while, madame. I'm afraid we're not quite set up for luncheon, but the restaurant is still serving continental breakfast. . . ."

"That sounds marvelous," Margaret said, allowing Mr. MacPherson to escort her past the sounds of falling water and into the hotel.

By the time she finished her croissant and fruit, it was nearly lunchtime. She wondered how Wanda's technical rehearsal was going, and whether the girl had eaten anything. She was so very tiny. She asked the waiter if the restaurant offered any special dessert pastries.

"*Bien sûr,* madame," he replied. "I'll bring out the cart."

Margaret selected a slice of Chocolate Amaretto Espresso Torte and had it boxed to go. She paid her bill and walked into the foyer. Mr. MacPherson was hovering at the hotel entrance and opened the door as soon as she approached. She had the surprising idea that he'd been waiting to speak with her again.

"It was such a pleasure meeting you," she said. "Thank you for your kindness."

"*Enchanté,* Madame Hughes." He bowed, as if it were the most natural thing in the world. "I do hope you'll come back for another visit."

She felt terribly reluctant to leave. As she walked away she kept wanting to turn around, go back, listen to more of his perfect French. *Silly,* she chided herself. *He has other things to do.*

She was halfway down the block when she heard his voice. "Mrs. Hughes!" he called.

He was running toward her. He looked very young. His long uniform coat was undone at the bottom; it made a gentle flapping sound as he ran; she thought of flags and circus tents and sailboats. He stopped a few feet away and said, "If you should come back—" He gave a quick backward glance, and then came a few paces closer and clasped Margaret's hands. It was not a rough gesture, but it took Margaret unawares. And although he had a very trim physique, Margaret was further surprised to find that his hands were plump, very soft, and warm, like newly risen bread dough. Then he went on in a slightly hushed voice. "The hotel likes us to address each other by our last names, but . . ." He tilted his head suddenly, making him look like a Scottish terrier hoping to entice his owner into a game of fetch. "My friends call me Gus."

"Okay, everybody, we're on break," Wanda said into her microphone. Her voice reverberated through the semidarkened theatre. "You're due back in an hour and a half, and then we'll pick up where we left off, with the end of Nora's speech, and keep going cue to cue. Good work, guys; see you at two. Houselights up please."

Wanda turned off her microphone. Clumps of people in the audience seats started moving sluggishly: the director and his assistant, the costumer and her assistant, the production manager, the lighting designer, the set designer, assorted theatre staffers. They finished scribbling on their clipboards and then started getting up, stretching, and making their way toward her en masse with glum looks. *Why does everyone get so pessimistic during techs?* she wondered. *Everything always falls apart before it comes back together.* Of course, the mood during these techs was bleaker than usual. It wasn't a Noël Coward soufflé they were whipping up, after all; it was Eugene O'Neill. Heavy as a beef brisket.

She took a deep breath and prepared for another requisite round of feather-smoothing and fire-extinguishing—tasks requiring an almost superhuman sensitivity to the various artistic dispositions involved. But this was why she was here.

Don't worry, she'd have to say, *the set changes will go more smoothly, the crew just needs to rehearse, the soundboard operator will get the levels, the actors will act, they'll button the right buttons, they'll find their light. We'll pick things up! We'll tighten those transitions! The show won't run over three hours, I promise. I promise, I promise . . . I'm hungry.*

Where was Troy? She massaged her neck. She had a couple of notes for him, not many. He was probably on the loading dock, having a smoke.

At least she'd scored a winner with her assistant. He'd been a dream during rehearsals, completely professional, easy to work with, more than competent for someone so young and inexperienced, and he'd kept his sense of humor as they slogged through techs. On the personal side, he was twenty-seven, had a Montana driver's license, a Taurus birthday, and an undergrad degree in philosophy. She'd sneaked a look at his personnel file. She just wished he'd wear long-sleeved shirts more often. He had really great arms. They were distracting.

Wanda felt a hand on her shoulder and registered a dense warmth seeping into her muscles, undoing tension she didn't even know was there and making her body temp rise.

It was Troy. "Hi," he said. "How you holdin' up?"

She shifted her body, putting more space between them. "Hi. I'm okay."

He held out a flat, white, rectangular box.

"What's that?"

"Your mother brought it over. She sat in the back for a while, house left."

"What?"

"She didn't want to bother you, she just asked me to give this to you and tell you she'd be waiting outside the reception desk door tonight to give you a ride home."

"What did she look like?"

"Blue eyes, gray hair, nice smile. You know . . . motherly."

"Did she *say* she was my mother?" Wanda felt irritated, without knowing exactly why.

"No, but—"

"Of course she didn't." Wanda opened the box and peeked inside. Cake. Really scrumptious-looking cake. "How do you know she was my mother?" she went on. "She might have been anybody. She might have been some crazy person out to get me. She might be an assassin. Maybe this is laced with arsenic." She lowered her face close to the box and sniffed.

"I just assumed—"

"Well, don't. Please." Wanda plucked an espresso bean from the top of the cake and popped it into her mouth. "She wasn't my mother."

"Got it."

"I don't have a mother."

"Right. Sorry."

With the tip of her index finger, Wanda made a quick apostrophe in the top of the cake and tasted the frosting. A rich, buttery concoction of coffee and amaretto and cream slid across her tongue like edible silk. "Oh. My. God." She let her fingers dive into the icing then, scooping off a thick swath.

When she lifted her hand to her mouth, she caught Troy staring at her. "You want some of this?" she offered. "Help yourself. It's incredible. There's a fork—," she started to say, but Troy was taking hold of her hand. He gave it his undivided attention, and then—in violation of the unspoken protocols governing stage manager/assistant stage manager relations—began defrosting her fingers with slow, skillful maneuverings of his mouth and tongue.

"Thanks," he said when he was done, looking up at her and smiling cordially. "I was really hungry." He was still holding her now-naked hand. There was a lot of heat being generated at that intersection, as well as at other physiologic locations that had been in deep freeze. He leaned closer—*Jesus Christ, has he always smelled this good?*—looked past her shoulder, and whispered, "Here they come. It's going a lot better than you think, so don't let 'em give you any shit. I'll be on the loading dock having a smoke if you need me." He turned around and headed backstage.

She stared after him, oblivious to the crowd of people who had gathered around her worktable, all talking at once, jockeying for attention, trying to give their notes. Troy's moving parts had an assured and well-oiled looseness which she hadn't noticed before, and which stirred in her an odd, petulant envy.

A prank, Wanda concluded, that's what it was. A brotherly, well-timed tease meant to distract her from teching a play by Eugene-effing-O'Neill, and damn if it hadn't worked, too—although how her underling knew she was inwardly stressed was something she preferred not to think about.

After he was well out of sight, Wanda caught her breath, got a grip on her chemistry, and cleared her mind. She ran the rest of the day with an iron hand and a poker face. No one, including her assistant, gave her any shit.

Eleven

❧

Wanda Gets Wings

When Wanda came downstairs the next morning and heard Margaret talking on the phone, she assumed that the caller was someone from the theatre. But as she approached the kitchen, it became clear that the call was for Margaret. Furthermore, this was no ordinary caller: not some vinyl siding salesman with a bullshit Lifetime Warranty, certainly not that Marita woman (*Who talks with their cheating ex-husband's second wife? Wanda still wondered. What kind of person does that?*) but someone unexpected. Margaret sounded positively giddy.

When Wanda got to the bottom of the stairs, she sat down on the love seat in the foyer and began thumbing through a copy of *Antique Interiors International*. From this vantage point, Margaret was perfectly framed by the kitchen doorway.

"That would be lovely! It's so kind of you to call. . . ." Margaret was absentmindedly playing with her hair. "You know," she went on, "if you don't think we'd be overdoing it, I have two complimentary tickets to a theatre performance. Do you like the theatre?"

Why, she's talking to a BOY! Wanda realized. *Good for you, Margaret.*

Margaret went on. "The Seattle Repertory Theatre . . . Yes, I believe they're quite a good group. . . . You're sure it's no trouble picking me up? . . . Well, the play starts at seven-thirty, so . . . Six o'clock for dinner will be fine. . . . Oh, anything . . . That sounds perfect!"

Margaret's caller said something that made her laugh. Wanda would not have believed that such a normally sedate person would be capable of such a laugh. It was an utterly goofy, ungainly, out-of-control laugh that combined honking and snorting in equal measure—the sort of laugh that leaves people either staring with detached disbelief or reveling in its wacky nonconformity.

"All right, then," Margaret said, when she regained her composure. "I'm looking forward to it! Au revoir!"

After hanging up, Margaret pulled a phonebook out of one of the kitchen drawers and began flipping through it. When she landed on the page she was looking for, she leaned close and scrutinized it for several seconds. "Good heavens," she said quietly. A coupon for Ben & Jerry's ice cream was affixed to the refrigerator door with a heart-shaped magnet. Margaret pulled off the coupon and began fanning her face with it.

"Good morning," Wanda said, coming into the kitchen.

"Oh!" Margaret startled. Her face was flushed.

Realizing that Margaret needed time to compose herself, Wanda got out coffee and cinnamon and put water in the kettle.

"How many listings would you guess there to be for the name 'Hughes' in the Seattle directory?" Margaret asked.

"I would have no idea."

"Come and look!" Margaret gestured Wanda to the counter and trailed her index finger along the pages of the phonebook as she spoke. "One, two, three, four . . . almost *five whole columns*! There are *fifteen* for the initial 'M' alone! Can you imagine?!" She grimaced suddenly and pressed the fingers of her right hand to the center of her forehead.

"Margaret," Wanda said, "are you—?"

Then Margaret flopped the phonebook shut decisively and spun around. "*Bonjour, ma petite!*" She bestowed minty kisses on each of Wanda's cheeks and then reached into the pocket of her housedress. "I have something for you," she said in the voice of a parent about to reward a child with an unexpected sweet or toy. She produced a set of car keys. "*Les voilà!*"

"This is awfully kind," Wanda said, accepting the keys. "Do you really want to do this?"

"*Mais oui!*" Margaret was completely transformed when she spoke even a few syllables of French: Her face became animated—her lips rounding and protruding in a way that made her look years younger—her voice grew extravagantly musical, and her eyes shone with a liquid, glimmering light.

She proceeded into the pantry. The air around her seemed to shimmer, and Wanda thought she could smell lavender.

"But are you sure?" Wanda called.

"*Bien sûr! Sans doute! Absolument!*" Margaret sang out.

"Well, thank you again. It's very generous."

Margaret reappeared in the archway separating the kitchen from the pantry wearing a white apron and rubber gloves. She carried a plastic caddy that was full of cleaning supplies in one hand, and an impressively large feather duster in the other.

"But it's nothing, *chérie! Rien du tout!*" She exited in the direction of the living room humming a tune; Wanda wasn't sure, but thought it might have been a song from *Gigi*.

"Now, this is just for the next few days, right?" Wanda asked as she followed Margaret. "Just until the show opens."

"*Non non non!*" Margaret called out adamantly. Wanda found her posed next to a glass-fronted étagère that was filled with Art Deco dancing girls. "You must use the car all the time!" Margaret chirped, punctuating her speech with flourishes of the feather duster. "*Tous les temps!*"

Margaret opened the étagère and took out one of the figurines; she wore a scanty, pimento-red costume with unusual sleeves—with her arms extended, they had the appearance of diminutive wings—and her hair was cropped in a flapper-style hairdo.

Of course! Wanda realized, as she watched Margaret wiping the figurine with a fine cloth. *The house—all of it—it's always immaculate, not a speck of dust or dirt anywhere, and there's never anyone else around. . . . That's what she does with her days: She cleans!*

"The car just sits in the garage," Margaret continued. "*C'est si ridicule,* when someone could be getting good use out of it! It's yours, whenever you want to use it," Margaret proclaimed. "For as long as you live!"

She stopped, gave Wanda a quick look, and then added, "Here, I mean: as long as you live here."

That night, by the time the director finished giving notes—first to the actors and then to the production staff—it was well after two in the morning before Wanda got the theatre battened down for the night. Troy stayed on to help; as her assistant, this was part of his job description. However, he insisted afterward on walking her to the car—a duty which was not within the parameters of their professional relationship.

Wanda protested. Ever since the frosting incident, she'd been on her guard. Prank or no prank, she did not want him getting the wrong idea. He was her assistant; she was in mourning. "I'm a big girl, Troy," she said in older sister tones. "I've lived in cities my whole life."

"Which way are you parked?" he asked, lighting up a Camel, clearly not willing to brook discussion on the subject. His smoking had lessened considerably since rehearsals began, Wanda noted. In fact—and the thought somehow both intrigued and troubled her—he might have cut down to one cigarette a day: this one.

"Up the hill," she said, and they set off.

Street parking at the base of Queen Anne Hill was hard to come by—there were several other theatres in the neighborhood, the ballet, the opera, restaurants, sports venues. And of course, that most famous of all Seattle's tourist attractions, the slim-waisted souvenir of the World's Fair that once upon a time symbolized the future: the Space Needle.

When Wanda had come to work earlier in the day—driving Margaret's car for the first time—she'd decided it was a waste of time to look for spaces that were close to the Rep, so she'd parked about two-thirds of the way up Queen Anne Avenue. She agreed to let Troy accompany her now because she figured that the effort of scaling a forty-five-degree uphill grade at two-thirty in the morning would make polite chitchat (never mind flirtation) superfluous, and prevent him from making the offer again.

His strides were long and slow. She kept up a brisk, determined clip and expected to outpace him; after all, he was a smoker. But it didn't seem to cost him anything to keep up.

"Nice night," he said in a smooth, well-supported voice. They were about halfway to the car. "I like the city when people are all tucked in."

"Yeah," Wanda gasped raggedly. "Nice."

This went on through techs, through dress rehearsals, through preview performances. Every day Wanda parked farther up the hill; every night Troy made the journey with her.

"Ever been to Montana?" he asked one night

Wanda huffed and shook her head. "Just . . . I . . . 90."

He looked at the night sky. His stride lengthened briefly, but he slowed as soon as he realized she was trailing him and puffing like an asthmatic.

"How'd you end up in Seattle?" she asked another night. Her lung capacity was improving.

He took a drag on his cigarette. "Followed someone," he said.

She nodded, relieved. "Ah!" she exhaled extravagantly.

"An actress." He paused, regarded his cigarette, then added. "We broke up last year."

The wind went out of her. "Why . . . did . . . you . . . stay?"

He looked at her. "Figured there's another reason I'm supposed to be here. Things have a way of working out the way they're supposed to. That's how I see it, anyway."

Wanda dragged her eyes away from his. She stared fiercely at the summit and asked no more personal questions after that.

Each night he'd stand by as she unlocked the door, got in, buckled her seat belt, and started the engine.

"Do you need a ride home?" she always asked. Having typed the production staff contact information herself—and taken special note of Troy's Queen Anne address and phone prefix—she knew he lived in the neighborhood, but it seemed impolite not to offer.

"No thanks. Good night." Then he'd put out his cigarette with the heel of his boot, turn around, and walk into the night.

Wanda would wait a moment or two before driving off. She couldn't help herself: She loved to watch him leave.

Twelve

❧

Opening Night

"What a coincidence!" Margaret was saying. "You knowing Wanda. It certainly is a small world!" She glanced at her wristwatch. *I can't imagine what's keeping her,* she thought. She bit into another forkful of angel hair pasta. It was scrumptious.

She was standing in the crowded lobby of the Seattle Repertory Theatre, where a lavishly catered party was well under way. The play had been over for some time, and although the actors had emerged from their dressing rooms half an hour ago and were all stationed near the food tables and engaged in a nonstop orgy of eating, Wanda was nowhere to be seen. In addition, Margaret had lost sight of Gus, who'd offered to get her another glass of sparking cider.

Since she didn't know anyone else, she'd struck up a conversation with one of the caterers—a chubby, moribund fellow dressed in a white chef's hat and jacket who looked exactly like the sad doppelganger of the Pillsbury Doughboy. He had been very forthcoming, much like Wanda the first time they'd met. And the similarities didn't end there: Like Wanda, he had recently broken up with his boyfriend (*You mean girlfriend?* Margaret had wanted to say, but thought better of it; she was quickly learning that a certain degree of open-mindedness was required when speaking with young people) and he was newly transplanted from New York ("I wanted to get as far away from that SOB—pardon my

French—as possible," he said. "I could've gone to Alaska, I guess, but nobody hates snow more than a Southern boy. I only lived in Manhattan as long as I did because of you-know-who"). His ex, an actor, had done a play with Wanda, so they were acquainted. Within ten minutes, Margaret knew almost everything about the caterer except his name. She was about to rectify this state of affairs when the actors launched another blitzkrieg on the food tables.

She spotted Gus. He was across the room, standing in a long line. He looked very nice in his tuxedo. The red and green plaid cummerbund was especially festive. Margaret was reminded of those lovely tins of Scottish shortbread one sees in delicatessens.

She had learned a great deal about him, too, in the past few hours. For one thing, he was older than she—by five years! Yoga, he told her, was what had kept him young. He taught a class for seniors every day at the downtown YMCA. He had a busy social life—attending lectures, concerts, art exhibits. He took classes at the community college. He sang with a barbershop quartet. "In our minds," he said, "we need never 'grow old.' It's the wrong expression, isn't it, if you think about it: When we stop growing, we are old!" Although he didn't say so— he was far too gentlemanly to tell tales out of school—Margaret suspected that going on dates with lady friends was a regular event in his life. And understandably so. One would be hard pressed to find many eighty-year-old gentlemen who were ambulatory, much less charming and attractive. Margaret hoped he didn't find her looks lackluster or her company tiresome; her life experience, compared with his, was really quite small.

She caught his eye and waved. He smiled broadly and waved back.

"Hello, ma'am." Margaret turned around to find a handsome young man standing beside her. He looked somehow familiar. "I'm the one you gave the box to the other day," he said, registering her confusion. "You know, for Wanda?"

"Well, of course you are! You took the cake!"

"I'm Wanda's assistant, Troy."

"I'm Margaret Hughes."

"I'm wondering, Mrs. Hughes, do you have any idea where she might be?"

"No I don't. It certainly is puzzling. I thought I was supposed to meet her here in the lobby after the play, but perhaps I was mistaken."

She scanned the room again. There was Gus, still standing in line, chatting congenially with a theatre patron behind him. She wondered what he'd look like wearing a kilt.

"You know," Troy continued, "when I first saw you, I thought you were Wanda's mother."

It was a bittersweet thing to hear. "You did?"

Troy nodded. Margaret saw something behind his eyes, a compassionate, assessing wisdom. *Old soul,* she thought. *Still water.* "No. Wanda just lives with me. We're housemates."

"She told me that she doesn't have a mother," he continued.

"That's right, as far as I understand it."

"She was really firm about it—the way she said it, I mean. She seemed . . . angry."

"It's probably a difficult subject."

"I keep wondering what she meant," he said, almost as if he were talking to himself.

"Well, she didn't mean it literally, of course. I think she was just saying that her mother is dead. Her father, too, I believe."

"She's an orphan?"

"Well, yes," Margaret went on. "I believe it happened a long time ago, when Wanda was quite small. Still, it's a terrible thing."

"I can't imagine growing up without your folks."

Why, he's in love with her! Margaret realized.

"She's an orphan," Troy reiterated disbelievingly. He stared at a solitary dollop of hummus and an empty pocket bread on his plate. "How do you ever get over that?"

"Well, you don't, of course." Margaret suddenly felt ashamed of herself for not having recognized the single thing about Wanda that should have been obvious, something this young man had seen instantly. "Some things one isn't meant to get over."

He narrowed his eyes—they were kind and intelligent and there was a great deal of thinking going on behind them—and nodded. "Would you please excuse me, ma'am? I'll find out where she is and tell her you've been looking for her."

"That's very kind."

"It's been a pleasure talking with you, Mrs. Hughes."

Margaret offered her hand. "You as well, dear." She watched him go. *I must remember to tell Wanda that it's perfectly fine for her to have houseguests,* she thought.

There were still five people ahead of Gus. Margaret noticed that he was now standing on one leg. His other leg was bent at the knee; it crossed over his standing leg in a way that allowed his foot to rest high up against his thigh. His eyes were closed. His smile was beatific. His balance was perfect. *He looks as if he's having a pleasant dream,* Margaret thought. *About butterflies, maybe. Or Campbell's Cream of Mushroom Soup.*

Gus opened his eyes and caught Margaret staring at him. Flustered and embarrassed, she extemporized a broad, lengthy pantomime—occasionally enlisting the aid of her empty paper plate as a prop—indicating her plans to go upstairs to the ladies' lounge, powder her nose, conduct another search for the mysteriously missing Wanda, and then reunite with him back in the lobby.

At the end of this performance, which garnered not only Gus's fascination but that of several theatre patrons in the immediate vicinity as well, Gus nodded robustly and lifted his glass and Margaret's in an expansive toasting gesture. She made a small curtsy and hurried upstairs.

It was nearly midnight. Margaret had hoped to find Wanda and thank her for the tickets before she asked Gus to take her home, but since the girl was nowhere to be found, Margaret wasn't sure what to do.

She walked through the ladies' lounge, where two pale, silent young women stood at opposite ends of a very long mirror; they were both applying lipstick that seemed, in Margaret's opinion anyway, several shades too dark.

Entering the vast tiled bathroom—which appeared to be completely empty—Margaret went into a stall. After a few moments, she heard someone crying quietly.

She bent over and looked under the wall to her left. At the end of the long row of stalls, she spied two tiny, fine-boned feet huddled close together; they were wearing black evening shoes with stiletto heels and small rhinestone accents on the ankle straps. Next to the feet was an overstuffed backpack.

"Wanda?"

There was more muffled snuffling. Margaret spoke louder. "Hello!"

The feet came to attention. "Hello?" replied a congested, glueysounding voice. "Are you talking to me?"

"Wanda?"

"Margaret?"

"Yes. Are you all right?"

"Of course! Fine and dandy! I just—" She erupted in a fresh round of sobs.

Margaret felt a need to express a sense of sympathy and connection—even though Wanda couldn't see her, of course—so she continued to study Wanda's feet in hopes of gaining further clues as to her state of mind.

A pair of wooden clogs, a pair of Reeboks, a pair of Rockports, and a pair of turquoise cowboy boots came into the bathroom. *People certainly attend the theatre wearing all kinds of clothing these days,* Margaret thought, regarding her own shoes—modest, dark blue Naturalizer pumps in a style called Beryl which she'd polished earlier in the day.

Margaret and Wanda stayed in their stalls. Wanda's crying did not, as one might have expected, abate; instead, it seemed to intensify. Toilets flushed. Stall doors banged open. The shoes made their exits—rather more quickly, Margaret noticed, than they had entered.

"Your shoes are very elegant!" Margaret called, once the bathroom was again empty.

"Thank you!" Wanda bawled.

Margaret emerged from her stall and washed her hands. She peeled the flaking silver foil from a roll of breath mints and placed one on her tongue. She patted her hair. She freshened her powder and her lipstick. She looked down the long row of stalls. Wanda's door was still closed, and behind it, Wanda kept on crying. *This certainly is familiar,* she thought.

Someone was coming into the ladies' room lounge.

"I saw Jason Robards do it, you know," a voice said.

"No. Really?"

"Years ago, of course. On Broadway."

"That must have been quite something."

Margaret took a step away from the sink and looked over her left shoulder. Two women—Margaret guessed them to be somewhere in their sixties—were slowly making their way through the lounge toward the bathroom.

One of the women was strikingly tall and wore a bulky woolen cape. Two emaciated, support-stockinged legs and a wooden cane protruded from the bottom; the woman's head emerged from the top, its near-perfect roundness accentuated by the fact that it was nearly completely bald. The overall effect was of a perambulatory floor lamp, with the bald head providing a small, globular finial.

The other woman was shorter, and the shape and size of her torso suggested that it had been formed by adhering together five large, adipose spheres: two for the breasts, one for the stomach, and two for the buttocks. She was wearing a multicolored peasant getup—long full skirt and billowy blouse—accessorized with massive amounts of gold jewelry. This seemed to provide the wearer with a constant source of irritation; she pulled, grasped, rearranged, straightened, and twisted her numerous necklaces, bracelets, and earrings relentlessly—exactly, Margaret thought, the way people attempt to physically command unruly pets or children who won't go where they're told.

Why doesn't she just take them off? Margaret thought, annoyed.

The woman began to leaf through her program with one hand as she reprimanded her unruly necklaces with the other. "The fellow tonight was quite good, of course. . . ." Her jewelry clanged in protestation. "But he couldn't possibly compare with Jason Robards."

"Well, of course not. How could he?"

"He was an alcoholic, you know."

"Who?"

"Jason Robards, of course. Most truly brilliant artists are. I suppose it's the price one pays." She dropped her program and shoulder bag on a lounge table, bounced over to the mirror, and began fiddling with the backs of her earrings; from what Margaret could see, they consisted of multiple doodads affixed to numerous small chains—like miniature charm bracelets suspended vertically from her earlobes. *They'd be the perfect earrings,* Margaret thought, *for the ghost of Jacob Marley.* Casting a stern look at her own reflection in the mirror, Margaret intoned quietly, in her best effort at a voice from beyond the pale, "I wear a *ponderous* chain. . . ."

"These earrings are killing me!" the woman exclaimed. Her bald friend, who had sunk into one of the lounge chairs, gave her a disapproving look.

From behind her stall door, Wanda started sobbing again.

Seeing both women cast puzzled glances in her direction, Margaret faked several explosive sneezes and began vigorously pulling sheets of paper toweling from the dispenser. It made rhythmic, thwacking noise.

"And then the girl," the woman continued over the racket, retrieving her purse and program. "The one playing the daughter."

"Yes." With a great effort, her friend pushed herself out of the lounge chair and once again began inching toward the bathroom on her thin legs and her wooden cane.

"I found her a bit . . ."

"What?"

"Brittle!"

"Brittle."

"Yes! That's what I thought too! She was much too brittle. No softness. No sense of transformation, you know. At the end of the play, I mean. When one needs that."

"At the end, yes," the bald woman said.

"She lacked nuance! She hadn't enough colors!"

Just as the women were about to enter the bathroom, Margaret stepped in front of them and blocked their further progress. "Excuse me ladies," she said, "but the bathroom is out of order."

"What do you mean?" demanded the fat woman.

"Nothing in here is working. It's out of order."

"All of it?" the bald one asked.

"Yes. Something broke. A pipe." Margaret cleared her throat. "That's it!" she announced heartily. "An important main conduit! A significant main pipeline to the facility! Broken!"

Margaret paused, noting that the bathroom was suddenly, eerily silent. She turned around and bent over to see whether Wanda's feet were still in her stall. They were. Margaret was relieved to see one of the feet move slightly, as if it were sighing.

"Everything is stable for the time being," Margaret continued, straightening herself into what she hoped was an authoritative posture, "but we're expecting a flood at any moment."

"But, what are we supposed to DO?" the fat woman whined. "I have to pee so bad my teeth are floating!"

"The theatre apologizes for any inconvenience." Margaret placed herself between the two women and began to usher them toward the door. "Under these special circumstances, you are of course welcome to use the men's room."

"The MEN'S room?"

"Yes. It's quite all right. Just call out before you enter. You know: 'Hello there! Women present! Plumbing emergency!'"

The fat woman eyed Margaret's unadorned suit jacket suspiciously. "And you would be?"

"The facilities manager," Margaret replied. "Mrs. Marley."

"Is it near?" the bald woman asked, wearily. She reached out from beneath her cape and touched Margaret's hand; Margaret felt as if she'd been dusted with a light, dry snow.

"It's just around the corner," she replied. "You can't miss it. Good luck."

The bald woman started off. "Come along now, Golda. It's very late."

"Use the MEN'S ROOM?!" Golda griped. "I've never HEARD of such a thing!"

She grabbed the wad of necklaces around her throat and tried to pitch them over her shoulder. They flew back at her with a loud, jangling hostility; one of them smacked her in the chin. "SHIT!" she hissed, and waddled away.

As soon as Margaret closed the outer ladies' room door, Wanda began keening again, louder and more uncontrollably than ever. Margaret walked quickly through the lounge and into the bathroom to stand in front of Wanda's stall.

"Have you any writing paper?" she asked.

There was no change in the volume or intensity of Wanda's lamentation, but her backpack slid out from beneath the stall door and then lay in a morose heap at Margaret's feet. She unbuckled the straps and opened it; among the many things she found inside were:

1. A yellow legal pad on a clipboard, the top page of which contained a mysterious list with items like: "#16A—s/b 5 ct. fade instead of 4" (the word "GODDAMMIT!!" was also scrawled across the bottom of the page and underlined numerous times). Other pages were filled with sketches—very good ones, too—of figures, hands, faces, one of which was Troy's.

2. An assortment of pens, sharpened pencils, and Magic Markers, rubber-banded together,

3. A package of gum (Margaret unwrapped a piece and popped it into her mouth),

4. A small, unmarked red and black book,

5. An empty box of chocolate-covered espresso beans, and

6. A small framed black-and-white photograph of a child watching a woman bowling. The child was peeking over a Styrofoam cup. She was very small, and her eyes were very wide.

Margaret tore off a clean sheet of paper, and using one of the Magic Markers wrote: "Out of Order. Please Use the Men's Room. Your Cooperation Is Especially Appreciated. Thank You. The Facilities Manager." Extracting the chewing gum from her mouth, Margaret divided it into four dime-sized wads, which she affixed to the corners of the paper. She walked back into the lounge, opened the outer door a crack—there was no one outside—and posted the paper. Then she barricaded herself and Wanda inside with one of the lounge room love seats.

She was out of breath. Her forehead was clammy; her skull was starting to constrict. Lowering herself onto the love seat, she closed her eyes and listened.

Wanda's cries were rhythmic now, harshly percussive. They had the inexorable force of a drum, but one that was playing itself. The poor drummer had lost all control.

I suppose it's also me in there, isn't it? Margaret thought. *That's familiar too. The memory of me, crying behind a closed door. But then there was Daniel, and the doors were open for a time. All the doors: open and close, open and close . . . One of the first things children delight in, isn't it? One of the first concepts they grasp: "Door open! Door closed! Door open! Door closed! Watch your fingers, sweetheart!" It's also one of the first ways they hurt themselves. Dresser drawers and cupboards, and the inner doors of houses: old ones, especially, so huge and heavy, the dreaded fear of crushed fingers, fractured bones, it comes so soon after they're born, before they're walking even, they find the doors, fascinated with the way they can move something so big, fascinated with that treacherous sliver of space that extends from the top to the bottom, that place where their fingers shouldn't go. "No, NO, sweetie! Not there! Hurt baby! Hurt!"*

And then, later still, no one outside the door: a small room, with the door closed, inside a bigger room, with the door closed, inside a house, with the entrance locked. A door within a door within a door.

Margaret opened her eyes. She glimpsed a pale green haze hovering on one of the upholstered chairs in a corner of the lounge. *What are you doing here?* she asked.

You got out, Margaret's mother answered petulantly. *Why shouldn't I? I haven't been to the theatre in years. I thought it would be pleasant. But my God! Doesn't anyone dress anymore?*

Different times, different fashions.

And the play! So grim!

What did you expect, Mother? After all, it is O'Neill.

Margaret sensed her mother slide off the chair and glide toward the bathroom door. She wasn't wearing one of her peignoirs this evening; instead, she modeled a classic, two-piece suit from the 1930s, with a pert, flouncy peplum and padded shoulders. It was the color of key lime pie, and had a little pearl-trimmed hat and veil to match. Standing just outside the bathroom, Margaret's mother looked coolly in the direction of Wanda's stall and began slipping off her gloves.

What is it she does, exactly?

She sits in a little booth, Margaret replied, vaguely, *and . . . manages things.*

That's hardly impressive.

She's very important, Mother. They couldn't do it without her.

That may well be, missy—and you needn't get so huffy about it with me!—but you can't convince me that she's doing anything creative. She's not an artist!

Margaret's mother paused, then executed an elegant spiraling motion with her spine that allowed her to examine the backs of her seamed stockings.

She has to watch the wretched thing every night? Margaret's mother went on. *No wonder she's depressed.*

Margaret's mother sighed, then settled on the love seat next to her daughter.

You look nice, she said.

Thank you, Mother. So do you.

Are you going to stay out here, or are you going to go in there and make yourself useful?

I'm going in.

Good. I'll see you at home. Wait a minute. . . . Margaret felt her mother lean closer. *I remember those earrings. I've been looking for them. Have you been into my things, Margaret?*

They're all my *things now, Mother. Remember? You're dead.*

Margaret's mother got up and slipped her gloves back on. *No need to gloat, Margaret. Ticktock, ticktock.*

And she was gone.

Back in the bathroom, Margaret heard restless foraging noises and sniffles; she pictured Wanda within her stall as a mournful, undernourished chipmunk at an abandoned campsite.

Margaret slid a box of tissues under the stall door and waited while Wanda blew her nose several times.

"You lied about your name," Wanda said, finally—but in her congested, overwrought, and weakened condition, it came out sounding like, "Ooh eyed a bower dame."

"I beg your pardon?"

"*Barley,*" Wanda tried to enunciate. "Ooh toed dim urn Amos *barley.*"

"Excuse me?"

"I taught id was honey. You sub-eyed me."

"I'm so sorry!" Margaret replied.

"Israelite," Wanda said quietly—her most baffling utterance yet. "Dank ooh. Dank ooh forte aching guerre ami."

Wanda fell silent, and Margaret could tell that whatever had just transpired had been somehow comforting. Still, she felt uneasy about initiating any further conversation.

Wanda gave her nose a final, robust honk, and then asked, in comprehensible English, "Have you been waiting in the lobby?"

"Yes!" Margaret chirped, thrilled by the return to mucus-free conversation. "I've been worried about you. So has that nice young man."

"Who?"

"I think he said his name was Troy."

"Oh. Him. My assistant."

"Yes! He seems very considerate."

"Huh," Wanda grunted, and the conversation sputtered.

"I enjoyed the show," Margaret offered.

"You did?"

"Very much. Mr. MacPherson enjoyed it too. Thank you again for the tickets."

"It's a good production, I think. But . . ." Wanda's voice began to quaver. "I messed up three cues, the sound levels in Act Four were way off, and the characters . . . They're so . . . damaged!"

The backpack landed next to Wanda's feet with a dull phalumpf! The stall door swung open, and Wanda—as if borne on the wave of a miniature tsunami—flew out and fell sobbing into Margaret's arms.

Oh dear, Margaret thought as she petted Wanda's hair. *I bet she doesn't weigh ninety pounds soaking wet.*

Wanda's face was tear-streaked and blotchy, her upper lip was sheeny with snot, and her eyelids had the white, puffy look of a dead fish's underbelly. Margaret was reminded of the way that very young children cry: fearlessly, shamelessly, with a total, noisy, self-centered commitment to grief that makes no apologies nor any effort whatsoever to contain the natural outflow of bodily fluids. The fact that Wanda was able to cry this way made Margaret feel sure that she had not cried much as a child. It was as if she were making up for lost time. *She's an orphan,* Troy had wisely observed, which summed up everything and explained a great deal.

Wanda's sobs were starting to subside, and Margaret sensed an arising discomfort in her birdlike body.

Margaret gently extricated herself and started dabbing at the smudges of mascara under Wanda's eyes. "Why don't you take some time to freshen up," she said. "I'll wait for you at the top of the stairs."

Wanda sniffed. "You really liked the play?"

"I really did." Margaret took a few steps toward the lounge and then stopped herself. "Oh! I almost forgot." Pulling off her pearl earrings, she placed them in the saucerlike curve of Wanda's small hand. "Wear these, dear. They'll look beautiful on you."

When Wanda emerged from the ladies' room a few minutes later, sans backpack, Margaret noticed for the first time what she was wearing: a floor-length, sleek black dress with long fitted sleeves and a neckline that draped from one shoulder to the other in a soft, hammocklike curve. The dress was slit high up on each side to reveal beautifully shaped, athletic legs, as well as the high-fashion shoes that had languished so pitifully in the bathroom only minutes earlier. Wanda looked stunning. Margaret was certain that if she hadn't come across her in the bathroom, she wouldn't have recognized her.

"I'm sorry about all that." Wanda smiled weakly. "Opening night jitters."

"No need to explain. You'll feel better once you have something to eat."

The lobby was starting to empty; aside from one actor who was still hovering at the food tables devouring the last of the buffet, the few other people who remained were getting ready to leave.

Gus and Troy had found each other, Margaret was happy to see, and had been joined by Wanda's acquaintance, the caterer Margaret had spoken to earlier. They formed an agitated trio at the foot of the stairs.

Margaret waved to get their attention. "Hello everyone!" she sang out. "We're back!" They looked at her with lost puppy eyes. *Poor dears,* she thought. *So helpless without leadership.* "Is there any of that marvelous food left? This girl could use some nourishment."

The men snapped into action. Introductions were made, hands were shaken. The caterer bustled back to his station—his name, Margaret finally learned, was Bruce; Gus set a chair for Wanda at the end of the catering table; Troy brought her a fresh napkin, silverware, and a glass of water.

"Gus and I will be leaving now," Margaret said. "Thank you again for the tickets."

"I'll see you at home." Wanda waved as Bruce set a feast before her: hazelnut Gorgonzola angel hair pasta, arugula salad with caramelized pears, rosemary bread, lemon bars.

Wanda tucked into this cuisine with a surprising amount of zeal, Margaret observed, and she wondered if the caterer might be interested in permanent employment. On the way out, she picked up one of his business cards (the heading read, "Kosher Katz: I cook, you eat") and slipped it into her pocket.

"When you get to be my age," Gus was saying, "there's no point in goin' round the barn. You're a delightful lass, Margaret Hughes, and I'd be honored if you'd consent to spend more time with me."

They were home from the theatre. They'd taken a walk through the neighborhood—it was a cool and starry night—and were now standing on the porch.

"I'm practically retired," Gus continued. "I stay on at the hotel mainly to train the youngsters. It's important to the administrators that the valet staff maintain a certain tradition of service and style."

"I see." Margaret was trying to buy some time. She hadn't reckoned on this, on feelings of . . . attraction. Not at her age.

"What I mean to say is, I have a good deal of free time during the days and so forth."

Margaret felt her eyes widen. *What could he possibly have in mind?* "Yoga," she blurted. "I'd like to learn more about yoga." It seemed like a safe response, and the best one she could come up with.

He beamed. "You would be welcome to attend my class, anytime. I could show you some breathing techniques. They'll add years to your life, I guarantee."

That would be nice, Margaret mused.

"And sun salutes," Gus went on, excitedly. "They're marvelous, just marvelous. The kind of yoga I practice is called *vinyassa,* or flow yoga, and sun salutations are a key component. Tremendously important. And beautiful! You wouldn't believe it. Like a dance."

She so enjoyed listening to him.

"*Vinyassa* is much more than a form of exercise," he went on. "It's a meditation. A metaphor for life."

His passion—for the Hotel Orléans, for French language and culture, for books and ideas, for yoga, for art, for staying young—was infectious.

But more than that: It was fortifying—in the way of weight lifting, she supposed, or running a marathon. "How so?" she asked.

"The intention," Gus said, "is to move as if everything is transition. As if nothing ends."

That was it, she concluded. Spending time with him was the spiritual equivalent of building bone mineral density. With a companion like Gus, it would be difficult—maybe even impossible—to give up on anything.

"You'll see," he concluded. "When you come to class."

"I can't wait."

He was moving closer now, taking her hands. Margaret could smell his aftershave. "I'm sorry," he said. "I'm talking far too much. I do that when I'm nervous."

There was a sweet warmth accumulating in Margaret's belly. *Oh, Lord,* she thought. *I thought I was all through with this.* "I had a wonderful time," she said.

He gave her a serious, considering look. "You know," he said, "ever since I saw this house of yours, there's been something I've wanted to say."

"What is it?"

Inclining his face close to hers, he whispered urgently, "Rapunzel, Rapunzel, let down your long hair!"

His words broke all the spells that had been cast upon her, so that by the time they kissed for the first time, Margaret was full of light, and laughing.

Margaret went to the kitchen and put on water for tea. It was very late—she hadn't found herself awake at this time of night for years—but she knew she'd never be able to sleep if she couldn't quiet her mind. Wanda had told her about this aspect of a theatre person's life—how difficult it is after a performance to wind down and relax. Margaret had half-expected to find Wanda still awake, perhaps even in the kitchen.

But the house was quiet, and Margaret figured she must already be in bed and asleep. She'd beaten Margaret home; the Volvo was parked in the driveway when she and Gus had pulled up, and the lights in her room were off. *Poor dear,* Margaret thought. *She had such an emotional night. I hope she sleeps late tomorrow.*

While the tea brewed, Margaret walked the main floor rooms, turning off lights, bidding good night sleep tight to her things.

So much was happening, and so suddenly, too. She'd opened the door of her house to one person, just one, and now there were others who wanted to come in. Never mind that none of them had made overt requests; she heard their beseeching cries as clearly as she heard the prayers of the gravy boats. It was as if she'd been playing poker with the house and its contents and they'd called her bluff. *"Be careful what you wish for"—Isn't that what they say?*

And what had she wished for? Company, yes; not necessarily intimacy, but shared experience; laughter; conversation. She must have wished for danger, too, in a sense, since she and her valuables had been tucked into this house, untouched by other human hands, for decades. Preserved from discovery and natural disaster. Now *they* had wishes. They wanted something too. "Once the door is open," they seemed to be saying, "you can't shut it again, impose limits, set degrees of openness. There are no half-measures now. And you can't invite danger without accepting it in all its forms."

Wanda—this unhappy young woman who wore her heart on her sleeve—had been the first to answer Margaret's invitation. Out of all the others who could have come, who *did* come, but weren't chosen, she was the one who'd been set down firmly and squarely in the center of Margaret's world. Who knew why. It didn't matter. Margaret had been given the privilege of bearing witness to Wanda's life and the very particular color of her heartache. And now Wanda was pulling other energies in her wake. Of course. It couldn't be avoided. Not everyone was an island; Wanda was connected to other people, and now those people were connected to Margaret.

"We don't 'grow old,'" Gus had said. "It's the wrong expression. When we stop growing, we *are* old."

Margaret had almost finished her rounds on the main floor; she stood in front of one of the glass-fronted étagères in the dining room, the one housing her wedding china. Reaching into her pocket for a tissue, she pulled out two theatre ticket stubs, Bruce's business card, a gum wrapper, bread crumbs. She gazed at these commonplace bits of debris; they all had meaning. She studied her wedding china; it was exquisite, and utterly false.

After saying a last good-night to what had once seemed flawless, Margaret turned out the light in the étagère and started making her way back to the kitchen. The tea would be ready. She hoped it would help her sleep.

Thirteen

❧

The First Breaking

When she was sure Wanda was awake—it was mid-morning—Margaret went upstairs and knocked quietly on her bedroom door.

"Come in."

Margaret found her lying on her bed. It was littered with crumpled tissues. A box of Kleenex was on the bedside table, next to a large bouquet of daffodils. Buttery yellow and optimistic, the flowers were incongruous with Wanda's pale, tired face.

In front of her on the bed was the small red and black book that Margaret had noticed last night. From the way Wanda shoved it aside—rapidly; one might even say *furtively*—and placed a protective hand over it, Margaret guessed that it must be some kind of diary.

She's a bit old for that sort of thing, isn't she?

Mind your own business, Mother, Margaret countered, crossly. *Diaries are lovely.*

"How are you feeling?"

"I'm okay." Wanda glanced up at Margaret with eyes that were red-rimmed and glassy. Sitting up briskly, she shoved the red and black book into a bedside table drawer. Then, with a single, efficient gesture, she swept the tissues to the edge of the bed and deposited them in the wastebasket.

"I kept a diary when I was young too," Margaret offered.

You did? asked Margaret's mother. *I never knew that.*

Wanda pressed her lips into an unenthusiastic grin. She pulled at her left eyebrow. "What's up?"

"I'm sorry to trouble you," Margaret said. "Is this is a bad time?"

"No. I wasn't doing anything important."

Margaret stood in the doorway and glanced around the room. It had been weeks since she had seen Wanda in this setting, and she was struck by how out of place Wanda seemed, how much her human presence was subjugated by the room's decor: the heavy Victorian bedroom suite; chair, ottoman, and chaise lounge, all upholstered in worn black, pink, yellow, and turquoise floral chintz; matching floor-length curtains topped with limp, ruffled valances; and walls so insistently pink that they looked as if they were flushed with a life-threatening reaction to shellfish. "Who decorated this room?!" she exclaimed, as if seeing it for the first time.

"Excuse me?" asked Wanda.

"However can you stand it? It's smothering!"

You liked it well enough when you were a little girl, said Margaret's mother.

"No I didn't," Margaret said. "I never liked it." She actually felt her lungs constricting, and had to fight off the impulse to rush into the room, tear down the heavy curtains, and throw open the windows. "Don't you find it smothering?"

"I hadn't really thought about it. . . ."

See? She likes it, anyway. Margaret's mother swept in and and took up residence on the settee, arranging her limbs, robe, and facial features in a way suggesting that John Singer Sargent was about to paint her portrait. *It's a charming room! A perfectly lovely room!*

"Well," Margaret went on, frowning. "If you're sure this isn't a bad time—"

Where exactly did you keep this so-called diary?

"——I have a *project,*" Margaret enunciated, "that I could use some help with."

"Uh-huh," Wanda said dully.

What project? asked Margaret's mother, sitting up so quickly that the hem of her robe caught on one of the settee legs and tore slightly.

"There are some things that I'd like to clear out of the house."

What things? demanded Margaret's mother, springing off the settee and crossing the room with urgency. She and Margaret stood face-to-face.

"Ah," said Wanda. "Well, I'm good at packing." She got up wearily and raked a hand through her hair. "Are they going to the Goodwill?"

"They're downstairs. Are you sure you don't mind doing this now?" *Doing what?*

"No. Not at all. This is a good time. Let's do it."

What are you up to, Margaret?

Why don't you check the attic, Mother? There's a loose floorboard just under the east window. I believe you'll find one of my diaries hidden there.

You had more than one? Margaret's mother squeezed past her. *Why didn't I know this?*

Margaret's mother scuttled toward the attic staircase. The flimsy, torn robe of her peignoir ruffled crazily behind her, like a hopelessly insubstantial mainsail.

As Wanda followed down the stairs, Margaret said, "You should feel free to change your room in any way you'd like. So that it suits your personality. It's *your* room now. I hope you know that. I might not have made that clear when you moved in."

Of course *you didn't make it clear, you ninny,* Margaret chided herself. *You made the poor girl feel anxious about using the Tupperware, for goodness' sake. Why would she think it was all right to redecorate?*

"You should also know," Margaret continued, "that it's perfectly fine for you to have houseguests. At any time. Day or night." She waved her hand airily. "Girl friends. Gentlemen friends. Assistants. Whatever."

"That's very nice of you," Wanda replied.

"I occasionally might have guests myself."

Wanda stopped, mid-step. "You might?"

"Occasionally, yes." Margaret continued her brisk, capering descent and spoke with exaggerated nonchalance. "The gentleman you met last night, for example."

"Mr. MacPherson?"

"Yes! Mr. MacPherson! You might possibly be seeing more of him!" Margaret reached the bottom of the stairs and turned to look up at Wanda. "He's offered to give me breathing lessons." Margaret did a half-pirouette and walked through the foyer until she was out of sight.

"Wow," Wanda said to herself, and then chased after her.

By the time Wanda arrived in the dining room, Margaret was already standing in front of a freestanding cabinet containing a set of china. Using a delicate brass key, Margaret opened the cabinet doors. She stood back and hugged her arms close, as if she suddenly felt a chill.

"Here it is."

Wanda didn't know much about fine china, but she knew enough to recognize that this—like everything else in the house—had probably cost a small fortune. The pattern featured orange, yellow, and black geometric shapes decorated in gold leaf.

"You're getting rid of this?"

"That's right."

"All of it?"

"Every bit."

"How come?"

Margaret reached into the cabinet and picked up a dinner plate. "I don't do a lot of entertaining anymore. Never did, actually." She held the plate with two hands—steadily, firmly, as she had always done. "My father was the great entertainer. My husband, too, to some extent."

Margaret was regarding the plate with an expression Wanda hadn't seen on her face before. It was a funny look to give a plate, nothing at all like the look women used to give plates in those old dishwashing liquid commercials. Nothing at all like the radiant, transcendent look that accompanied their exclamations of "I can *see* myself!" If Margaret *could* see herself in this plate—and it's quite possible that she could; it was gloriously, scrupulously shiny—she certainly didn't like what she saw.

"It's my wedding china," Margaret continued. "We were registered at Frederick & Nelson's." She began turning the plate over in her hands.

"It's very . . . ornate."

"It's gaudy. Self-centered. Desperate. Preening. I've never liked it." Margaret's hands were gaining courage now; one of them left the plate and fell limply to her side. *It's just a plate, after all,* she thought, at the same time knowing full well that it was much, much more than a plate.

"It also happens to be the only set of china in the house that actually belongs to me."

"I don't understand."

"The point is, no one ever uses it."

"But are you sure you want to give all this away? Couldn't you sell it?"

"I don't want to give it away. Or sell it," Margaret announced, as much to herself as anyone. "I want to break it."

With that, she let go.

For a while, it was as if gravity ceased to exist, and the plate made its way to the hardwood floor with the dreamy languor of a snowflake. A great deal of time seemed to go by, and as Margaret watched the slow, unreal descent of the plate, she thought, *I could still catch it if I wanted to, change history, interrupt this tragedy. It's not too late.* She heard Wanda gasp and saw her make an involuntary lunge for the doomed plate. *How funny,* she puzzled. *No one likes to see something break— even if that thing has no relationship to them whatsoever. Even if they're completely unattached to it. Why is that? I wonder. It is, after all, the inevitable fate of a plate, isn't it? If it's not shut away, that is. If it's put to its intended purpose—as a vessel, something useful, something human hands are meant to handle and interact with. The natural fate of a plate—and therefore the appropriate one—is that it be chipped or cracked or broken. Why should that decrease its value?*

The plate arrived. The sound it made was not nearly as loud as Margaret had anticipated, nor did it shatter dramatically as she had secretly hoped. Actually, the damage was probably not irreparable. But Margaret was in charge of this plate's future, for the time being anyway, and she did not want to see it repaired.

Both women stared, speechless, at the plate's remains. The house, too—and whatever entities it harbored—maintained a shocked silence. Without knowing exactly why, Margaret giggled abruptly, and then, just as abruptly, stopped.

"Crash," she said.

Wanda looked up from the ruined plate. "Margaret?" she said, putting a hand on her shoulder. She didn't seem to realize that she had begun to weep. "Margaret?" Wanda repeated. "Are you—?"

"It's all right, dear. Really. It's what I want to do."

Margaret patted Wanda's hand and smiled radiantly. The tears gave her face a dewy, glistening look. And then she was on the move, yanking dishes out of the cabinet with an energetic carelessness.

"Let's get these out to the back patio, shall we?"

As Wanda watched her haul the first armload of dishes outside and heard the clamor that followed a few seconds after her exit—in the theatre this would have been accomplished with something called a "crash box"—she suddenly knew that she had found a home with someone who was as deeply aggrieved and crazy as she was.

It was tremendously comforting.

It took them a bit under an hour to do the whole job.

It would've taken much less time had they simply boxed up the entire set of china and dumped it all at once. That would have been the quick, efficient way to do it. But when Margaret came back inside, she announced her decision that they should give each piece an individual and personalized send-off. "It's too casual the other way," she said. "Too unceremonious." Margaret also produced—Wanda hadn't the slightest idea from where—two pairs of OSHA-approved eye goggles. "We should wear these," she said. "For safety's sake."

They brought several sturdy boxes up from the basement, filled them so that they weren't too heavy, and carried them outside.

The large patio behind Margaret's house was perfect for their purposes. It was enclosed on all three sides by a low wall constructed of gray, egg-shaped river rocks. There was a small wooden gate in one side of the wall; it was much weathered now, but Wanda could tell that it had been beautifully designed and expertly constructed.

She loved the pebbly, rustic look of the wall—although she supposed that certain people would regard it as an architectural affront; its lumpy surface was out of character with the rest of the house, with its flat, formal angles of brick and stucco. But there was something irresistibly whimsical about this wall; and although it took Wanda a little while to catch Margaret's enthusiasm—"This is FUN!" Margaret kept shouting—once she did, Wanda found that she enjoyed aiming her throws at specific places in its cobbled, friendly facade.

"WHEEEEE!" Margaret sang out gleefully. "BON VOYAGE!"

They began to experiment with various throwing techniques: over the head, under the leg, two-handed throws, backward throws, bowling throws, attempts at juggling. Margaret played horseshoes and shuffleboard with the dessert plates. Wanda shot hoops with the soup bowls. The pieces of china were beginning to accumulate, like exotic ice floes, forming random piles and patterns on the patio floor.

At one point, Margaret took off her goggles and massaged her forehead. "I think I'll take a break," she said, and then emitted a sharp, gooselike noise than could have passed equally well for a chuckle or a sob. She stretched out on a lounge chair.

As she watched Wanda dodge and weave skillfully from one end of the patio to the other, she began to whistle. Margaret hadn't whistled for nearly three decades, and at first her efforts produced more air than actual musical tone. But eventually she was able to manage a robustly out-of-tune rendition of "Sweet Georgia Brown," accompanied by hand-clapping and foot-stomping. Wanda made an impressive leap and executed a perfect mock layup. Margaret applauded and hooted wildly.

"However did you learn to do *that*?" Margaret exclaimed.

"Boys," Wanda said somewhat breathlessly. "I grew up around a lot of boys."

"Really?" Margaret was intrigued. This was the first personal information Wanda had offered since they'd met. "For some reason I thought you were an only child."

"I am," Wanda replied, "but I have a lot of cousins. James John Jacob Jesse Jordan Joshua Jeremiah."

"No other girls?" Margaret pressed.

"Jacqueline. We weren't especially close. I was more like their troop leader."

This admission, Margaret realized, was probably as much as she'd ever get from this girl on the subject of her childhood.

"Would you like some tea?" Wanda offered.

There was that distinct change in tone; Margaret recognized it now. Whenever their conversation became too intimate, Wanda reliably fell back into her default position—one of servitude.

"Not right now, dear," she answered. "Why don't you have a rest. You've been a wonderful help."

Wanda stretched out on the lounge chair next to Margaret. They gazed quietly at their work.

By this time, they had destroyed (*No,* Margaret thought. *Not destroyed—reconfigured*) all of the dinner, salad, and dessert plates, the soup bowls, and six teacups. The gold leaf reflected the sloping rays of afternoon light, giving the scattered pieces a look that spoke not of ruin, but of opulence and festivity, of things precious and celebratory and child-prized: ticker tape and pirate treasure, dress-up jewels and New Year's Eve confetti.

"Shall we?" Margaret said after a while.

They got up again, and—with a less athletic style, to be sure, for both women were feeling tired—they proceeded to finish off the rest of it.

"We're mad, aren't we?" Wanda said glumly. She seemed uncheered by the fact that she'd just given the gravy boat a unique launch involving the use of her nose.

"Quite possibly."

All of the boxes were finally empty, and Margaret held out a piece of porcelain which did not match the others. She regarded it briefly: It was an odd-sized, canister-like container with a domed lid. An Italian biscuit holder. In the thirty-some years it had spent in Margaret's china cabinet, it hadn't come within two miles of an Italian biscotti. Furthermore, if Margaret remembered correctly, it had been a wedding gift from a person completely unknown to either herself or Stephen by the name of . . . *What was it?* "My God," Margaret muttered, taking off the lid and producing a small rectangular card with white wedding bells and pink roses around the border. "The card is still inside! 'Fondly, with best wishes for your future, Mrs. Carmella Manzito.' I never did write her a thank-you note," Margaret said. "Oh, well."

Margaret pocketed the card, handed Wanda the lid, and grasped the biscuit holder firmly in her right hand. "Ready?" she said, settling herself into a wide stance.

Wanda mirrored Margaret's position. "Uh-huh."

"This is it, now. On three. Let's make it count!" In perfect synchronization, they revolved their arms in two fluid, generous circles as Margaret called "One! . . . Two!" . . . and then, on "Three!" simultaneously released their throws. The biscuit holder was smashed to smithereens.

"THANK YOU SO VERY MUCH, MRS. MANZITO!!!" Margaret yelled.

"WHOEVER THE HELL YOU ARE!" Wanda added.

They stood quietly for a moment. Their goggles were foggy. They looked like two explorers adrift on an exotic arctic sea.

"I would really appreciate an alcoholic beverage," Margaret said. "Wouldn't you? I have no idea what time it is, but I really do think that a drink is in order under the circumstances."

Wanda checked her watch. "It's twelve fifty-three. I don't have to leave for the theatre till five-thirty, so I say let's go for it."

"*Champagne, n'est-ce pas?*" Margaret asked. "*Un verre de champagne sera la chose parfaite!*" Margaret's use of French failed to animate her expression in the usual way. She frowned, and swiped her fingertips across her closed eyes several times. "The trouble is, I don't think there's anything in the house besides cooking sherry."

"I have some champagne," Wanda offered. "One of the designers gave me a bottle for opening night. Would you like some?"

"How generous of you, dear. That would be lovely."

"I'll bring out some blankets, too," Wanda said. "It's getting chilly."

"Don't forget the champagne glasses!" Margaret called. "All of them! *Tous!*"

Margaret reclined in her lounge chair, closed her eyes, and tried to imagine what it was like inside the house. Different, surely. Surely there was some form of discussion among her things as to what had just transpired. She imagined high-pitched, subtle resonances, muted versions of the sounds made by tracing a wet finger around the rim of a crystal goblet, or the thrumming vibrations of a tuning fork. Too faint for human perception, of course, but wasn't it true, hadn't scientists discovered, that inanimate objects gave off sounds? Who was to say that those sounds weren't utterances? Forms of intelligent communication?

She tried to accomplish a kind of cross-matter transference of energy, willing herself into one of her many fragile, valuable, and stolen things: the Royal Worcester jardinière, the one signed by W. Powell. Circa 1907, thirty-four centimeters tall, valued at $10,500. Perhaps it was feeling anxious and fearful. Perhaps it was quaking with a sudden, grave understanding of that old homily: "Whether the stone hits the pitcher, or the pitcher hits the stone, it's going to be hard for the pitcher."

Or perhaps, Margaret thought, her heart doing a sudden giddy-up dance, *it's delighted. Perhaps it's pleased that it's going to be touched again, after so long a time, in an intimate, familiar way. It's going to interact with something besides a feather duster. Perhaps all of them—the vases and figurines, the egg cups and inkstands and game pie tureens, the wall pockets and asparagus plates, the foot bath!—perhaps they're grateful that finally, finally, they don't have to wait anymore. They're going to come out of their dark niches and off their pristine shelves, into the sunlight, into human hands, to experience something riotous and passionate. Like the breaking of the glass at the end of a Jewish wedding!* Margaret thought, immensely pleased at how fitting it was. *Like that!*

Margaret pictured Wanda alone in her house, moving through the rooms with her brisk, light footsteps and her flickering, restless energy.

Yes, Margaret thought, closing her eyes again and settling deeper into the lounge chair. *They're happy. They're happy at last.*

"Shouldn't we save something for special occasions?" Wanda asked. They had each had three glasses of champagne. This meant several things:

1. There were shards of crystal glittering among the pieces of china,
2. They were drinking out of Dixie cups, and
3. They were both drunk.

"Maybe you're right," Margaret replied. "Like Easter!"

"Like Chanukah!"

"Like Bastille Day!" Margaret began to sing loudly, and badly, in her beautifully accented French. "*Allons enfants de la patrie, le jour de gloire est arrivé!*"

"Your birthday!"

"Oh, no!" Margaret said, refilling their Dixie cups. "Heavens, no. Much too far away. How about yours? When is it?"

"Don't celebrate birthdays."

"Why ever not?"

Wanda shrugged and took a swig of champagne.

There she goes again, Margaret thought. *Doing her disappearing act. Funny girl.* "My husband Stephen made this wall," she said.

"Really?" Wanda replied. "I wondered."

"It took months to finish."

"I believe it. This kind of thing is really hard to do."

Margaret had to admit, she'd never considered this. "I suppose it is."

Wanda got up. Stepping carefully, she made her way to the wall and let her hands explore its surface. "He did this all by himself?" Wanda asked. She liked wedging her fingers into the cool, smooth, shadowy recesses where the rocks touched.

"Yes. Stephen worked on this the whole time I was pregnant."

Wanda was surprised. She'd never heard Margaret mention children before. "That's nice."

"Day and night. I'd wake up at two or three o'clock in the morning—one gets so uncomfortable, you know; or else the baby wakes up and starts kicking up a storm—and Stephen would be gone. I'd find him out here, with one of the living room lamps plugged into an extension cord. I haven't thought about that for years. But then"—Margaret took off her glasses and massaged her closed eyelids with the tips of her fingers—"I don't come out here often."

Wanda sat down on the edge of the wall and took a deep breath. "Well, I like it."

"Daniel used to call this—the patio and the walls, I mean—his 'bubble house.'" Margaret paused and laughed. "It always came out 'Bubba!' 'My Bubba house!' he'd say, like a Southern sheriff, and Stephen would make jokes about boiled peanuts and moonshine."

"Daniel is—?"

Margaret didn't answer right away. "I'm sorry," she said. "Did you ask me something?"

"Daniel. He's . . . ?"

"My son. Stephen made this wall to keep him close to the house when he first started walking. To keep him safe."

"That is *such* a nice story," Wanda said, with the slurred emphasis of a person who's had too much to drink and feels just fine about it. She waited, assuming that Margaret was going to say more about her son. Instead, she fell silent and sipped on her champagne.

Wanda perceived nothing unusual about this—how could anything that happened between them be called unusual after today?—and so she cleared a place next to the wall with her foot, sat down on the patio floor, and began examining the china fragments surrounding her. She felt an odd tenderness toward them, and she sensed keenly that, whatever Margaret might intend, her relationship with these pieces was not finished, and would involve more than a broom and a dustpan and a trip to the city dump.

Margaret gazed westward over the large expanse of land that sloped down and away from the patio. Situated as it was at the top of a hill, the property looked out on an almost completely unobstructed view of the Olympics.

When is the last time I was out here? she wondered. *It feels as though it's been years. Surely not. Surely it can't have been that long.* She looked toward the carriage house, where a few crowded, anemic-looking daffodil and bluebell shoots had begun to emerge. She thought she could see Daniel, crouching under the empty window box, flinging a handful of bulbs into the air, and then laughing when they dropped onto his head. He was three. Margaret's eyes clouded. She rubbed them, looked up again, and saw an older Daniel—six or seven, maybe—waving to her from the upstairs window of the carriage house.

This is fascinating! Margaret's mother said, sauntering outside in a cranberry-colored peignoir. She was intent on reading a small book embossed with the words, "My Special Year." *I had no idea you spent so much time thinking about me, Margaret. And in verse, no less. It's really quite flattering.*

You don't mind that I had everything wrong?

Margaret's mother made a preemptive gesture. She began to recite in quavering melodramatic tones: *"As silent as one's conscience when temptation hovers near, she ne'er will sing a lullaby or hold her daughter near."* *That's quite good. . . . God in heaven, Margaret! What have you been doing out here?*

Lightening the load, Mother. Remaking the world in my own image.

What a blasphemous thing to say.

Mother, who was Carmella Manzito?

Who?

Carmella Manzito. She gave me a biscuit canister for a wedding present. She wanted me to have a happy life.

How should I know? I didn't go to your wedding, in case you've forgotten. I'd been dead for decades.

Sorry, Mother.

I mean really, Margaret!

Well, it's not as if you haven't been lingering. I thought you might hazard an educated guess.

What was the name again?

Manzito. Carmella.

Sounds Italian. Margaret's mother took hold of the edges of her peignoir robe and began twirling her wrists in small figure eights. She had a coy, self-aware look, as if she were trying to inspire a display from a male peacock. *Probably one of your father's chippies,* she said, lightly. *He had quite a few, you know. I'm sorry to dispel any illusions you may have about your father, Margaret, but the truth is, he acquired a lot more than fine antiques during all those trips to Europe.* She sighed and swooned gracefully into Wanda's lounge chair.

You know what, Mother? You're not invited to this party. Please leave.

What a rude thing to say. What's come over you, Margaret?

I already told you: I'm remaking the world.

You know what the world looks like, do you?

I know what my world looks like, Margaret replied, and turned her attention to Wanda. She was studying a large fragment of a dinner plate. It had cracked roughly in half, but much of its outer edge was still intact. *Hers, too, I imagine.*

From what I can tell, you know nothing about her.

Margaret emptied the last of the champagne into her cup. *Climb into this bottle, why don't you, Mother. I'll give you a ride.*

That's NOT funny! Margaret's mother replied. Then, with magnificent hauteur, she arose from her lounge chair and exited the scene.

"Heads up!" Margaret threw the champagne bottle against the wall farthest from Wanda.

"How much more of this sort of thing do you plan on doing?" Wanda was regarding the patio floor critically. She leaned over and adjusted the position of a tiny crystal fragment.

"Maybe all of it. Everything. I'm not sure yet."

Wanda put a finishing touch on her work, stood up, and stretched. The sun was low on the horizon, and it was chilly. Wanda gathered a blanket around her shoulders and snuggled into her lounge chair. "Champagne all gone?"

"Here," said Margaret. "Finish mine."

"Thanks. This was a really good idea."

"You know, I've never felt that the name 'Wanda' suited you. I've always wanted to call you something else."

"Really? What?"

Margaret paused, and then said, "Tink."

Wanda wasn't sure she'd heard correctly. "Tink, did you say?"

"Yes. That's right."

"Huh. Okay. Tink it is." She was almost asleep when Margaret spoke again.

"How would you feel about my taking in more boarders?"

"You mean, along with the overnight guests?"

Margaret laughed. "Yes."

"It's your house, Margaret. Do whatever you want."

"Yes, but, it's your home too now, Tink."

"Fine with me," Wanda murmured. "As long as they don't have cooties." She closed her eyes and instantly began to snore.

Margaret finished off the last of the champagne, and then got up and tucked another blanket around Wanda's sleeping form. She walked to the place where Wanda had been arranging the fragments of china and glass. In their new incarnation, the pieces formed a loose mosaic of a winged patchwork cow. Having escaped the pages of a dusty book of nursery rhymes, the old girl was finally off the shelf and out in the air, smiling broadly, vaulting breezily over a gold-encrusted, winking moon.

Fourteen

❧

Detective Lorenzini

Margaret woke her at five o'clock. Wanda shuffled zombielike into the kitchen, but was resuscitated by the spicy, muscular aroma of freshly brewed coffee. On the stove was her French press coffeemaker; Margaret was already pouring her a cup. A meal had been set out on the kitchen table: tuna salad sandwich on white bread, cut into four neat triangles; a cup of tomato soup freckled with oyster crackers; a glass of milk; a shiny green apple, and three Fig Newtons. Wanda was ravenous, and her head was pounding. "Aren't you having anything?" she asked.

"Not right now," Margaret replied. "Please, sit down and eat."

"Thanks, Margaret. This is really nice of you."

Margaret sat, pencil and paper in hand. "Help me write an advertisement, will you?"

"Did you decide to sell the rest?"

"The rest of what?"

"Your things."

"Oh, no. It's for the boarders. How do you think the ad should read?"

Wanda sipped her coffee. Perfect. The mere suggestion that caffeine was on its way instantly defogged her brain "'Two crazy women seek additional crazies to join our asylum. Must have good throwing arm. Cooking skills and caffeine addiction a plus.'"

Margaret laughed. "Really, though, are you sure this is all right? You'll be sharing your bathroom with another person."

"Sharing a bathroom?" Wanda said. "With one other person? Believe me, Margaret, it's no problem." As Margaret looked on, she dug in and ate everything, down to the last bite.

Inside the theatre, the house and work lights were turned off, and one of the Act One cues was set up. Troy was standing at the top of a large ladder in the middle of the stage. He had his arms over his head and was adjusting a lighting instrument. Normally, Wanda would have appreciated the early presence and initiative of an assistant; instead, she felt testy. She needed to confront him, and soon, about this tension between them, this unspoken *thing,* whatever it was.

She called to him from the back of the house. "Hey. What's up?"

He looked out across the darkened audience, shielding his eyes from the glare. "Hey," he said, as if he'd been expecting her. "It's this instrument. It's still not aimed right. You wanna stand where Nora is, for her special?"

"Sure." Wanda dumped her backpack and sprinted down the aisle. When she arrived at the lip of the stage, she planted her hands on the stage floor, pushed strongly, swung her legs to one side, and launched herself up over the edge. She stationed herself left of center stage, precisely where the actress playing Nora stood when she gave her speech. Food and coffee had left her feeling fortified. Her competence was restored, her confidence was back, it was business as usual. What a relief.

Troy began tilting the lighting instrument, working with a patient, minute precision that reminded Wanda of the way a musician tunes a violin. She closed her eyes. A fragmented cobalt-blue image, like an exploding comet, danced across the inside of her eyelids. As Troy continued to try and find the exact placement for the light, she felt a subtle warmth gliding across the planes of her face.

"There," he said finally. "That's good."

Wanda opened her eyes and watched him descend the ladder.

There was no denying that Wanda Schultz had long known and admired the musculature of men. She had observed with interest the physical changes that occurred in her male cousins' bodies over the years, as their marshmallowy limbs, torsos, and backsides transformed into something taut and sinewy, like saltwater taffy. Wanda knew men's bodies. She knew them well. And she was fully capable of appreciating bodies— especially those of her male coworkers—without engaging her libido.

Troy turned to face her. "Are you okay?" he asked.

Wanda frowned and swiped her palm across her forehead. Damn that cake. "Yeah, of course. Why do you ask?"

He started folding up the ladder.

She noted, reluctantly, certain attractive paradoxes contained in his hands: long-boned, graceful, callused, competent. "I never thanked you, by the way," she said, in the interest of politeness.

"For what?"

"For the flowers. Last night."

"You're welcome. I never thanked you for the card. And the candy bar." She shrugged. "Most boys like chocolate."

He surprised her by laughing—she had no idea why, but it was a nice laugh and she liked what it did to his face—and then he moved the ladder backstage.

Stepping carefully around the furniture, Wanda surveyed the set; it was a meticulously detailed, realistic representation of a dining room in a nineteenth-century tavern, and there were drinking glasses and bottles everywhere. "You remember Margaret? My housemate?" she called out, addressing the stage right wing space. "The woman who's not my mother?"

She could hear him backstage, putting the ladder away. "Mrs. Hughes."

"Yeah. She'd like to invite you over sometime. For dinner, maybe. Or dessert."

There was a long, eerily silent pause. Wanda stopped moving. She squinted offstage. Finally, Troy emerged from the darkness and stood in the stage right door frame. "Really," he said.

Wanda began tracing her fingers across the complex contours of a decanter. "Most people give roses on opening night."

He stayed where he was and regarded her from a distance. "I suppose that's true."

He looks like a casting agent's idea of a cop, she thought, *or a cowboy. That's it! He looks like a goddamn cowboy. Right off the Texas range.*

As he walked toward her (*Howdy, pardner. Yee-haw. Please don't come any closer*), she noticed the square set of his jaw and the faint tracings of lines in his lean face: a pair of parentheses around his mouth, the beginnings of crow's-feet at the corners of his heavy-lidded, sage-colored eyes. Lines that evidenced the laughter she'd just heard, wry humor, kindness. She suddenly had a clear vision of what he would look like when he was thirty, forty, even fifty. *A cowboy poet.* she thought, and then frowned. *He's too damn tall. He needs a hat. And a horse.*

He didn't stop walking until he was six inches too close. "You don't strike me as a roses kind of person," he said.

"No?"

"No."

"I strike you as a daffodil kind of person, I guess." Her voice sounded strangely immature and breathy, nothing like the way she intended. It was at this point that she realized they were standing on level ground, inside the theatre, talking in full sentences about matters which had nothing to do with theatrical collaboration.

"You strike me as someone who's hardy and surprising and beautiful," said Troy.

She studied his work boots. Size eleven. He'd need a half-size larger in a pointed toe.

"'Daffodils,'" he said, "'that come before the swallow dares, and take the winds of March with beauty.'"

His boots took a step toward her. She backed up and bumped into a table. The glass decanter wobbled. His hand reached out and grasped it.

"See you in the booth," Wanda said, exiting stage right.

Several hours later, she was calling the cue for Nora's special, the cue that he'd adjusted earlier in the evening. It wasn't until that moment that she realized where she'd heard his words before: years ago, while stage-managing a production of *The Winter's Tale.* The words were from Perdita's flower speech. In praise of her, the cowboy poet had quoted Shakespeare.

After the show, he walked her to the car as usual. They said nothing about the earlier events of the evening. On this night, they said nothing at all. These late night walks found her feeling more and more apprehensive. Within the past few days he'd ravished her hand, recited poetry—and that while they were still inside the theatre, where their respective roles should have kept her safe. Who the hell knew what he was going to try next, when they were outside under a campfire sky? The show had a three-week run, for chrissakes.

Her wariness was further heightened by a certain insidious smell in the night air. An early spring smell. A smell of things emerging which stirred a peculiar restlessness in her chest.

In an attempt to diffuse these tensions, she began to whistle "Old Chisum Trail" in a breathy, exuberant way that made her sound as if her mouth were full of saltines. After a few blocks, she suddenly noticed that Troy wasn't smoking. He was chewing cinnamon-flavored gum. This struck Wanda as extremely ominous.

They arrived at the car.

"Good work tonight," she said briskly, giving Troy a chummy punch to his upper arm. She turned and fumbled with the keys. "See ya!"

Before he could make any reply, Wanda slid onto the seat, pulled the door closed, and started up the car. She caught a glimpse of Troy's face in the rearview mirror as she sped off: he was staring after her with a somber, surprised longing—as if she were the Lone Ranger.

Wanda drove to a small, secluded park at the top of Queen Anne Hill. It overlooked the Space Needle and most of downtown Seattle. Peter was out there, somewhere. She popped a chocolate-covered espresso bean into her mouth and sighed expansively. *Finally,* she thought, *I can really look for him.*

She knew Peter. She knew his habits, his addictions. She had a precise, detailed, orderly plan which she intended to follow to the letter and which commenced tonight. Nothing could interfere with that, because the need to find Peter was not superfluous or trivial. It was an injunction, a genetic imperative. It felt like a medical condition.

It was opening night all over again—her opening night. She'd developed a character, physically modeled after the actress who played Charlie Parker's wife in the movie *Bird*—a movie she'd watched with Peter no fewer than six times. She'd given her character a name, an identity, authentic-looking props, a costume. She'd evolved a voice for her, a manner of speaking, physical traits, objectives, tactics. She'd plotted

the parameters that would contain her improvisations. This was guer-
rilla street theatre, and she was ready.

Her black dress, silk stockings, and high-heeled shoes were still in the
car. She changed into them while the radio played Rosemary Clooney
singing "May I Come In?" She tucked her hair into a glossy black,
pageboy-style wig. She put on a pair of black-rimmed, 1950s cat's-eye
glasses which she'd stolen from the Seattle Rep costume shop and taken
to one of those while-you-wait places, where she'd had the prescription
lenses replaced with clear glass. She fastened on Margaret's pearl earrings.
She put on some cassis-colored lipstick. After retrieving her red and black
book, she wrote for ten minutes nonstop, *I am going to find him.*

Then she pulled a Seattle map out of her backpack. As she studied
the city's confusing layout, she pondered the impact of landscape upon
personality. She wondered if Midwesterners owed at least some of their
steadiness and New Yorkers their ambition and drive to the fact that
they live on a flat terrain overlaid with predominantly perpendicular
streets. Wanda's study of native Northwesterners thus far hadn't done
much to either confirm or refute this theory. She wasn't sure she'd even
met any native Northwesterners. Everyone here seemed to be originally
from somewhere else. Except Margaret. She had a certain haziness of
disposition that might have come from growing up in a place where hills
and bodies of water forced streets to curve, intersect at odd angles, disappear completely.

Wanda considered the possibility that she'd been bewitched by these
insidious topographical forces. Maybe at least a small part of her current condition could be blamed on Seattle itself. A person could lose sight
of things in a town like this. A person could have her sense of direction
obliterated. Get behind the wrong hill, take the wrong turn, and—poof!
You could disappear. You could wind up wandering around in circles.
If you couldn't catch sight of the Space Needle, you'd be doomed.

Wanda shivered in her party dress. She pulled out the thermos of hot
coffee she'd brought along and poured a cup. It was just the fortifica-
tion she needed.

She regarded her map again with a renewed, right-angled confidence.
In red Magic Marker, she had circled the location of every store in the
greater Seattle vicinity which sold vintage jazz LPs. Each circle enclosed

a number, written in black marker, which was cross-referenced on a sheet of paper from Wanda's clipboard. The sheet contained the names, addresses, phone numbers, and operating hours of each of the stores; there were over thirty of them. Wanda had spent hours planning the exact sequence in which she would visit these stores, and they were numbered accordingly. Many of the stores, catering to their clients' nocturnal tendencies, were open late; those that weren't she'd visit during the day. She'd be most likely to find Peter at one of the night-owl places, though, between the hours of eleven and two. Some of the circles and numbers on Wanda's map were clustered together, forming complex intersections; other circles stood alone.

Wanda ceremoniously pointed to the circle enclosing the number 1. "YOU ARE HERE," she announced.

She started the car, feeling rejuvenated. She wouldn't let this town and its waffling curvaceousness deter her. She knew how to behave like she was in Chicago or Manhattan, where the streets were long and flat and set at perfect right angles, you weren't ambushed by the likes of callow cowboy poets, and your feet always took you exactly where you wanted to go.

She got to the first store in no time. Situated at the bottom of Queen Anne Hill, it was called Blissed on Bop. After perusing the bin of Charlie Parker LPs and stealing glances at the clientele, she sauntered to the checkout counter.

The clerk was a small man, probably in his early twenties. He wore wire-rim glasses. His hair was straight, strawlike, and parted unflatteringly in the middle; he looked like he was wearing a small thatched and gabled roof. He had on a dark blue, badgeless Boy Scout shirt. He was reading Kerouac.

She greeted the clerk in a quiet, husky voice. She asked his name. It was Dermot. She told Dermot it was nice to meet him. She asked if he was the owner. Dermot said no, he just worked here. She told Dermot that she hoped he'd be able to help her anyway; she could really use some help. Dermot looked at her legs. He said he'd be happy to help if he could.

She then introduced herself as Detective Tink Lorenzini, an undercover cop on assignment with the Seattle PD. She flashed a detective's badge and ID. She wondered if Dermot would be willing to answer a few questions. She was looking for a man in connection with a B&E charge.

"B&E?" Dermot asked. He was staring at her lips.

Detective Lorenzini pouted. "Breaking and entering," she said.

Sure!" replied Dermot. "Whatever I can do, Detective."

The detective held a finger to her lips, pressed her hips against the counter, and gestured Dermot closer. "Dermot, please," she half-whispered, using the kind of voice that sells lingerie and 1-900 phone calls. "We're going to be working closely on this. Why don't you call me Tink."

Dermot nodded. His mouth was open. Droplets of sweat popped up on his nose.

The detective asked Dermot if he'd seen a man in his early forties, six foot four, heavy build, long blond ponytail.

"No," said Dermot. "I don't think so."

She supplied more details: The man probably looked at the more obscure bebop recordings. No run-of-the-mill stuff. He may have even struck up a conversation. He would've been knowledgeable. A real expert.

"Everybody that comes in here is an expert." Dermot said with a sigh.

Detective Lorenzini started chewing her lipsticked lips.

"He has beefy hands. But artistic-looking, you know?"

No," said Dermot. "That doesn't ring a bell."

"He smells like virgin olive oil, rosemary, and Guinness?"

"That doesn't sound familiar, either."

"He looks like a pugilist monk."

"I'm really sorry," said Dermot, earnestly. "I guess I'm not being very helpful."

"That's okay," said Detective Lorenzini, her voice quavering. "Don't worry, Dermot. I'm going to find him." Dermot offered the detective a handkerchief; she used it to blot her lipstick.

She pulled a piece of paper out of her evening purse and smoothed it out on the counter.

"Wow!" Dermot said. "That's really good! Is that the guy you're looking for?"

"It's just a rough likeness," the detective explained, humbly. "Based on the suspect's description and so on. He's handsomer than that—probably—but you might find it helpful."

"I'm sure I will. A police artist did this?"

The detective then handed Dermot a business card with the Seattle Police Department logo. "Here's my card."

Dermot was still studying the suspect's portrait. "I see now what you mean about his nose. It's very distinctive."

"Listen closely now, Dermot," the detective said seriously. "The phone number on that card, it's *not* the regular police department number. It's the undercover unit. But the person who picks up the phone won't say 'Seattle undercover' or anything like that. They'll just say 'Hello.'"

"Just 'Hello.' Got it."

"And another thing: If you call that number, don't, under any circumstances, ask to talk to Detective Lorenzini. If you want to talk to me, you have to ask for 'Wanda.'"

"Wanda?"

"My code name. My alias. Are you clear on that?"

"Absolutely," Dermot said.

"The person on the line will put you through to me. If you have any information about my perpetrator. Got that, Dermot?"

He nodded obediently.

The detective returned Dermot's lipstick-tattooed handkerchief and sauntered toward the door. Several clients looked up from their album covers to watch her.

"Next time I'll buy something," Detective Lorenzini said, loudly enough so that the other customers could hear her. "And that's a promise." She winked at Dermot and disappeared into the night.

Fifteen

❧

Acting Lessons and Interviews

Margaret's next advertisement was not lengthy, but it was very specific. She requested that it appear in three different sections of the classifieds: "Wanted to Share," "Domestic Care & Services Wanted," and "Health Care."

After telephoning the newspapers, she fixed a cup of tea and sat down at the kitchen table. In front of her was a speech she had written. She was anxious about delivering it. She recalled a recent conversation in which Wanda had explained the concept of rehearsals and the thought process actors use when preparing a role:

"You don't just memorize your lines and do what you're told?" Margaret had asked.

"No. You have to think about what you want, your objective. You use the playwright's words in as many ways as you can to *get* your objective."

"Fascinating!"

"The different ways you try are called 'tactics.' A really good actor uses lots of tactics."

"I had no idea it was so involved. Actors must feel terribly misunderstood."

"Say, for example, that you want to find someone. That's your objective."

"I want to find someone," Margaret emphasized.

"Onstage, everything has to be really important. You can't just want something a *little* bit, you can't just *sort* of want to find someone; that would be a lousy objective. You have to want to find them more than anything, so much that you feel it in the very core of your being."

Wanda's speech was accelerating, her manner gaining intensity, as if she were a master storyteller about to arrive at the narrative climax, the moment at which the forces of good and evil met and did battle. Margaret was rapt. She half-expected Wanda to break into galloping verse. "Go on, please."

"You would try anything, everything, whatever you could, right?" Wanda said, urgently. "So you might not always be entirely moral about it. You might deceive people, charm them into giving you information, sneak around, spy."

"That's probably true."

"And it doesn't matter if the person you want to find wants to be found or not. You've still got to do it."

Margaret considered these concepts for a moment. "What if you had something important to tell someone, something you've been keeping a secret, say?"

"Oh, that's good. Very theatrical. Secrets are great because they involve obstacles."

"Obstacles?"

"You really want to tell somebody something—that's your objective. But there's something standing in the way. The reason it's a secret, the reason you're afraid to risk telling them—that's your obstacle."

Margaret jumped in. "You're afraid they won't care about you anymore! But if you don't tell them, you risk them finding out from someone else, and then being angry with you, maybe even hating you, because you were deceitful. On the other hand, you risk not knowing what kind of person they are. Do they really love you? Or not? If you don't tell them, you'll never know."

"Ah!" Wanda breathed admiringly. "Inner conflict! Subtext!"

"But do you *want* them to know?" Margaret mused. "Maybe not. Maybe ignorance is bliss."

Wanda had begun to applaud. "Mrs. Hughes," she'd said, "you were born for the stage!"

But Margaret remained unconvinced.

She looked down at her speech and began to read. " 'I have a proposition, Gus," she said stiffly. " 'But before that, there's something you should know. I'll understand completely if you don't want to see me anymore after you hear what I have to say.'" Margaret licked her lips. Her mouth felt as if it were crammed with steel wool.

She folded up the speech and tucked it into her apron pocket. It would be all right. Today was her day to clean the dining room, foyer, parlor, Aviary Suite, and library. She would have plenty of time to rehearse.

Margaret started receiving inquiries about the advertisement right away. At first, she was delighted—there were far more responses than she'd expected. However, it soon became clear that few people had read the ad carefully. Several candidates expressed surprise when she reiterated the precise qualifications for prospective boarders, and what they could expect if they chose to accept the arrangement.

One of the first applicants to call was named Nat. "You mean, you're actually going to die?!" Nat shouted. The voice on the other end of the line—which was low-pitched, staccato, and raspy as coarse-grade sandpaper—left Margaret mystified as to Nat's gender.

"Well, yes," Margaret replied. "But then, isn't everyone?"

"While I'm living there?"

"Probably. Yes."

"Christ almighty," Nat growled.

"There seems to be a misunderstanding," Margaret went on evenly. "Perhaps you weren't able to read the entire ad, or perhaps the job requisites weren't stated clearly enough. . . ."

"UN-FUCKING-BELIEVABLE!" Nat barked, and hung up.

"What kind of . . . tumor . . . is it, exactly?" another applicant had said. Her name was Stephanie. Margaret had to strain to hear her.

"It's a . . . Oh, wait a minute. . . . I want to make sure I get this right . . ." Margaret punctuated the air with her right index finger as she spoke, emphasizing the syllables of each important word carefully: "It's an as-tro-cy-*to*-ma of the left pa-*ri*-e-tal lobe. There! I did it!"

"Excuse me?"

"It's a Grade II."

"Oh." There was a long pause. Margaret could hear music from *Mister Rogers' Neighborhood* playing in the background. Stephanie made a few attempts to hum along. Finally she said, "Is that serious?"

Another applicant was named Buffy. "I don't exactly have all the qualifications you asked for," she said.

"That might not matter," Margaret said. There was a chirpy, musical quality to Buffy's voice that Margaret found appealing. "What qualifications *do* you have?"

"Well, I worked for six months in an animal hospital in Enumclaw," Buffy said proudly.

"I see."

"We specialized in large mammals. You know: cows, sheep, horses, hogs. . . ."

"I'm sorry," Margaret said, "but I'm afraid that's not really the kind of medical experience I'm looking for."

"Oh, no. Really?" Buffy sounded disappointed. "Are you sure? I mean, I know how to do intravenous injections, I can squat two hundred and fifty pounds, and I'm told I have an extremely soothing and empathetic manner."

"I'm sure you do, dear."

"I mean, really, I'm not exaggerating: These were very big mammals."

A handful of other applicants found the requirements and expectations acceptable, and with these women Margaret made appointments. She scheduled them for the early evenings, when Wanda would be at work.

Margaret decided to leave the patio as it was, as a final test. She would take the interviewees for a tour of the house interior, get a general sense of her personality, and then if it seemed as though the applicant was a strong possibility, she'd take her outside. Her response would be an important factor in settling the issue of compatibility.

Wanda maintained her own unique relationship with the patio; it was a canvas on which an intractable and resented impermanence held sway. Each day Margaret would find some new arrangement there, sometimes representative, sometimes abstract. In one sense, these patio mosaics were like the sand mandalas made by Tibetan monks, painstakingly assembled and then ritualistically destroyed. For Wanda, though—and in contrast to the monks, who cultivate a joyful acceptance of both creation and death—neither joy nor detachment was evident. The transience of life, the fragility of connection might be endured, but it was never to be celebrated.

Margaret witnessed this late one night when she got up to take some medication. Hearing a noise, she went to an upstairs window and looked down. Wanda was on the patio, wearing her fancy black dress, constructing a portrait. As Margaret watched, she began slapping at the pieces violently. Then she lay down on the concrete and wept.

"I've scheduled a first set of interviews next week in the evenings," Margaret said. "I know you'll be at work, but I thought I could weed out a few people so you wouldn't have to meet all of them." She was dabbing disinfectant on the nicks and cuts that crisscrossed Wanda's hands. "I'll schedule the most promising candidates to come back for a second interview."

Wanda gave a small laugh. "In the theatre, that's known as a callback."

Margaret lifted Wanda's fingers in turn and scrutinized them from every angle. "I wish you'd wear gloves."

Wanda shrugged. "I like being able to feel the texture. Gloves would ruin it."

Margaret harrumphed. "Stubborn." She screwed the cap back on the bottle of peroxide and opened a tin of bandages.

Wanda began shuffling through a file on the kitchen table into which Margaret had placed applicants' references and credentials. "This is weird," she said. "Have you noticed that all of these people have backgrounds as registered nurses?"

Margaret frowned; she was engrossed in peeling the back off a Band-Aid. "Uncanny, isn't it?" she muttered.

"I suppose it couldn't hurt to have a nurse around," Wanda mused.

"Especially if you insist on not wearing gloves." Margaret gently applied the center of the Band-Aid to the web of skin between Wanda's thumb and index finger, and then smoothed the adhesive ends into place. "There," she announced. "All done."

Wanda looked down. The worst of her cuts was being protected by Winnie-the-Pooh.

* * *

Five women came to the house for interviews. Margaret explained once again what they could expect if they chose to accept the position; she was also very clear in explaining her desire to keep certain aspects of the arrangement confidential, for a while anyway.

It was immediately obvious to Margaret that one candidate met her dual set of requirements—those she'd stated overtly and precisely in the language of her ad, and those she harbored in her heart. Still, she did not want to make the decision without consulting Wanda. She selected one other acceptable applicant and scheduled their visits on a Monday.

The first candidate called at the last minute to apologize, explaining that she'd found a more suitable arrangement. The second candidate arrived promptly, ringing the bell at seven o'clock. Margaret was fixing a pot of tea. "Would you mind getting that?" she asked.

Wanda opened the door and found a tall woman with the healthy face and workhorse frame of a farm wife. She had three children of indeterminate sex in tow; the older two were holding her hands, the third was snuggled into a backpack. Wanda had the impression that she was being confronted by a small indigenous tribe.

"You must be Wanda. How do you do? I'm Susan Meriweather." Her accent was British, but warm and unaffected. "I'd shake your hand, but mine are rather gooey at the moment."

"Hello, Susan!" Margaret called from the kitchen.

"Hello, Margaret!" Susan called back.

"SUE-SUE! SUE-SUE!" shouted the baby in the backpack, joyously. It sounded like "THOO-THOO! THOO-THOO!"

Susan guided her small herd into the center of foyer and went on. "As you can plainly see, I have company. This is Olivia, Ethan, and Zachary." She began to hoist the baby off her shoulders and onto the floor. "I've brought the chimps, Margaret!" she called out.

"The what?" Margaret called back.

"You mean, the *children*!" said the oldest child, seriously.

"Oh, yes. So sorry, Olivia. I MEANT, THE CHEETAHS!"

"No! No!" called the second child, frowning, "The CHILDREN!"

"Oh, yes, of course, Ethan. Silly me. NOT CHEETAHS AT ALL. THEY'RE CHIHUAHUAS!"

"NO! NO! NO!" called the two older children, cracking up. "THE CHILDREN! THE CHILDREN!"

"CHEE-DWEN!" yelled baby Zachary, outvoluming them all. "CHEE-DWEN!"

"Oh, God!" Susan called out, mock horrified. "I MEANT, THE CHILDREN, THE TOTS, THE WEE BAIRNS, THE ANKLE-BITERS, THE BONNY LADS AND LASSES!"

"THOO-THOO-THOO!!!" laughed the baby, clapping his hands. The other two children were somehow managing to giggle and hiccup in unison.

"Wonderful!" Margaret sang out. "I can hardly wait to meet them!"

Susan looked at Wanda and began unbuckling, unzipping, and untying various coats, belts, buckles, and bags. "Sorry. I hope this isn't a problem. Their parents called at the last minute to say they'd be working late."

"It's totally fine. I'm used to kids."

The baby gummed a hank of Susan's hair while she rummaged through the backpack and magically extracted enough plastic for a multifamily garage sale. It was something like witnessing the miracle of the fishes, but with yellow, orange, and blue sippy cups. "They'll stay occupied. We're used to schlepping, aren't we, darlings?"

After the tour of the house, Margaret and Wanda guided Susan and the children out to the patio. "Oh, darlings, look! Isn't this a big, glorious mess?"

"BIG METH! BIG METH!" shouted Zachary, showering Susan with gobs of saliva.

Olivia regarded Margaret and Wanda wryly, and then leaned close to Susan and whispered, "Maybe you should ask to see their rooms before you commit to anything."

"Now, Olivia, haven't you ever heard of creative clutter?"

"You always say that a messy room is a noisy room."

"HA!" blurted Margaret.

"Smarty-pants. But this isn't exactly a room, now is it? This is the great outdoors. And this may well be the most glorious great outdoor mess I've ever seen—and that's saying a lot, having lived with you lot all these years!"

"It reminds me of the beach in *Grandfather Twilight,*" Olivia said.

"I can see how it would!" Susan looked toward the middle child, who was standing near the French doors leading into the kitchen. "What does it remind *you* of, Ethan?"

Ethan grunted and turned to face the wall.

Susan handed the baby to Margaret and knelt down. "Ethan, can you look at me?"

"Don't want to."

"Are you feeling sad? Mad? Glad? Afraid?"

Wanda watched closely. She couldn't help but envy Ethan, standing—albeit reluctantly—in the spotlight of all this loving attention. She wondered what it would be like to move through childhood holding hands with someone who insisted that you not only face your feelings, but name them.

"NO!!!" Ethan screamed.

You might not like it now, Wanda thought, *but you'll thank her in about twenty years.*

"What then, love? Can you try and say?"

"STOP IT!" Ethan shouted. "STOP TALKING! WANT TO GO NOW!"

Susan drew Ethan into her arms. He flailed against her and then started to cry. "I don't want you to live here!" he said between gasps. "I want you to come with us! Come with us to New York New York!"

"I know, Ethe, I know." She began crooning something to him—not your typical British nanny fare, it sounded like a country-western tune. Dolly Parton maybe. Or Loretta Lynn.

"Now," she said once Ethan was becalmed, "let's see if we can make something of this. You'll help me, won't you?" She looked toward Margaret and Wanda. "Do you mind? If we play about a bit, I mean? I'll make sure we're very careful. Have you gloves we could borrow?"

"I rather thought they'd take me with them," Susan was saying to Wanda. They were alone upstairs and taking another look at Egg Cup, the room that would be Susan's. "I've been with these children ever since they were born. But their parents have already engaged another nanny through a service in Manhattan." Her eyes filled with tears. "There are, apparently, a lot of nannies in New York."

"You used to be a nurse?"

"Yes. Pediatrics." Susan stepped into the bedroom and looked toward the bath. "Your room adjoins this from the other side?"

"That's right."

"This will be nice," she said, feebly. "Sharing, I mean. Like university." Now that Susan wasn't tending her brood, she seemed uncomfortable, as if apologizing for her physical presence. Wanda could easily see her as the kind of girl who grew into those big-boned feet and hands too quickly and then slouched through adolescence, trying to disguise her stature and avoid ridicule. She probably never wore high heels or had a boyfriend in high school. Wanda wondered if Susan had *ever* had a boyfriend; she had a kind of asexuality that made her seem virginal. But then, she was British, and a nanny.

"By the way," Susan went on, "I'm not the sort that goes in for three-hour pedicures and cucumber masks."

Wanda laughed. "I'd be more used to that, actually. What will you do after your family moves to New York? Workwise, I mean."

Susan pulled a handkerchief from her pocket and fiddled with it. "Well, I'm taking a bit of a holiday after I move in here, and then eventually I'll be going back to nursing."

"Really. At a hospital?"

"No." Susan blew her nose. "Home hospice care. For the terminally ill." Her eyes zigzagged around the room once more; the look on her face could not easily be labeled as mad, sad, glad, or afraid. Wanda empathized, knowing very well herself that many emotions are not contained within the lexicon of Dr. Seuss.

"Shall we go downstairs then?" Susan sniffled. "Rescue Margaret from the wee ones?"

When they returned to the kitchen, Olivia and Ethan were already dressed in their coats and ready to go. Baby Zachary was fast asleep on a comforter laid out beneath the table.

"Susan!" Margaret said. "Before I forget: You should know that you're perfectly welcome to have overnight guests, anytime."

"A sleepover?!" Ethan was overjoyed. "Susan can have a sleepover?!"

"Exactly!" Margaret said. "Isn't that nice?" Then, sotto voce to Susan: "The children have been so good. May I give them each a cookie?"

"Please," Susan answered. "Give them several. I rely heavily upon the soporific effects of sugar at bedtime. Now, where did I leave my coat?"

Margaret began doling out cookies. Susan gathered her things, scooped up Zachary, and settled him, still sleeping, into the baby carrier.

Susan spoke softly to Wanda. "Overnight guests? I have the distinct impression she's giving me permission to get laid."

"She is."

"Unbelievable!"

"Can't say I've taken her up on it yet," Wanda confessed—Susan snorted sympathetically—"but she has a boyfriend. Wait till you meet him. He's a dear."

"Well," Susan said, sighing, "At least someone in the house will be dancing the mattress jig."

The house was eerily quiet after the departure of Susan and the chimps. Even Margaret's things seemed disappointed by the abrupt decline in sound waves. A shelf of Doulton vases looked positively glum, their round, empty mouths shaped as if voicing a single elegiac syllable uttered in the pear-shaped tones of the British Broadcasting Corporation: one long, sustained, and civilly mournful "Oh!"

"Heading to bed?" Margaret asked.

"Yep," Wanda replied. "How about you?"

Margaret nodded. They started up, side by side.

Margaret's mother appeared several steps above them, lounging against the wall, her terra-cotta-colored peignoir harmonizing perfectly with the mahogany paneling. She had a queerly benevolent look on her face.

"Susan's great," Wanda said. "When will she move in?"

"The day after tomorrow." Margaret awaited commentary from her mother. When none came, she felt a perverse desire to goad her. "I might be taking in more boarders, you know."

But it was Wanda who responded, blandly. "Yes?"

"I've been thinking of placing an ad for a handyman, a carpenter, someone like that." Margaret was baffled; her mother's silence was not only atypical, it seemed almost complicit. "The house could use some sprucing up, don't you agree?"

"Yeah," Wanda agreed sleepily. "I'm happy to help with the plumbing."

Margaret's mother swished into place beside them, alternately admiring her right hand, then her left.

"The house might become more noisy," Margaret cautioned. "Even chaotic. Are you sure that won't bother you?"

They arrived on the second floor.

Wanda yawned. "Nope. No problem," she said. "I'm good with chaos."

Margaret's mother drifted between them, brushed past them, and settled her back against the door frame leading to Margaret's bedroom. She stretched with annoying self-absorption.

"By the way, Mr. MacPherson is not my boyfriend. He's my companion. My friend."

"Well, whatever he is, I'm glad for you, Margaret. I really am. Good night."

"Good night."

Your companion? Margaret's mother said after Wanda had gone. *That's euphemistic.*

Is that all you have to say?

I'm sure you know what you're doing, Margaret. Is it so hard to believe that on certain subjects we might actually agree?

No. I suppose not.

All right then. Good night. She began to drift away. *Besides,* she said in fading dulcet tones, *I will so enjoy the presence of a handyman.*

Susan settled into Egg Cup and commenced weeping. She missed her young charges terribly, and she hadn't counted on the room's hundreds of diminutive yolkless vessels serving as a cruel reminder of her own steadily emptying ovarian sacs. Wanda derived small comfort from knowing there was another person in the house who cried at least as much as she did, especially since Susan's melancholia was powered by a biological imperative as well as an emotional one. In addition to their saltwater bond, they were well-matched adjuncts of the pink bathroom;

efficient and environmentally-conscious young women (Susan was a sponge bather, Wanda favored quick showers), neither spent more than fifteen minutes total within those rouged walls. Sometimes they brushed and flossed their teeth together. It was as much like sisterhood as either had ever experienced.

Only days after Susan joined the household, another boarder moved in. He was not the hypothetical handyman Margaret's mother had hoped for, but rather the intended witness to Margaret's acting debut. Even though she had meticulously penned and rehearsed her monologue, achieving a word-for-word memorization and a rainbow of subtly nuanced tactics, when the moment came, Margaret took one look at her audience and (as they say in the theatre world) "went up," forgetting everything. Her improvised speech was stunningly blunt. "I have a brain tumor," she announced. "I might live several years, I might not, but whatever time I have left I'd like to spend with you if you'll have me." Gus moved in the following morning, and the two of them began living in sin in the Cherub Room.

And as for Wanda, she found it a relief to come and go without enduring the keen scrutiny usually reserved for an only child. She went to the theatre in the evenings. She had occasional morning performances for school groups, and a couple of two o'clock matinees; but when she wasn't working she stayed away from home; she told her housemates that she was going out on job interviews. Her dress remained in the car; she carried her shoes, wig, glasses, hose, makeup, detective's badge, and phony ID in her backpack. She continued making her way to every used jazz record store in the city, moving gradually north. At each store, she spent a couple of hours, surveying the clientele and eventually making contact with one of the male employees. She inquired after Peter, left her phony business card and a Xerox of her sketch. In the car, she carefully recorded all her activities and contacts in her little red and black book—alongside her affirmation. She drank a lot of coffee. She ate little. She lost weight.

She discovered an assortment of cassette tapes in the glove compartment of Margaret's car: French language tapes, mostly, and books read in French by famous actors like Leslie Caron and Louis Jourdan. Sometimes Wanda put in one of the instructional tapes and tried to repeat the sounds without knowing their meaning.

"Love?" she said, reciting one of the speeches from *A Touch of the Poet*. "It's when you don't give a thought to all the ifs and want-to's in the world. It's when, if all the fires of hell were between you, you'd walk in them gladly to be with him, and sing with joy at your own burnin', if only his kiss was on your mouth." She practiced this speech over and over, pouting her lipsticked lips, trying to speak with a French accent.

Sixteen

❧

A Stage Manager on Easter, 1997

"Kosher Katz is coming today."

"Huh," Wanda grunted.

"Your friend?" Margaret prompted. "From opening night? He cooks, we eat?"

It's about time! said her mother. *Between you, you can barely open a can.*

"He'll be here at three for an interview."

"Ah. Well. Tell him hi."

On Easter Sunday, some people attend church services. Some get together with relatives, friends, or lovers, and go to brunch. They watch children dart around on spring grass lawns and fill baskets. Others, if they live far from family, might pick up a telephone. But in the Hughes kitchen, it was a Sunday morning like any other. No special rites of rebirth—religious or otherwise—were being observed. There were no chocolate bunnies or jelly beans. The atmosphere was not permeated with the odor of hard-boiled eggs and vinegar. No hymns were being sung. No one was dressed in their ecumenical best.

Wanda, monosyllabic and preoccupied, was slumped against the counter, staring out at the patio and sipping coffee before she headed off to work. Susan and Margaret were still in their bathrobes—flannel and silk respectively—sitting at the kitchen table. Susan was reading the comics with moist eyes; Margaret was trying to study an antiques guide. Mostly she was fighting off the presence of her mother, not quite formed, a blueberry shimmer hovering just over her right shoulder and leaning in to whisper the occasional aside.

She's nothing but skin and bones! she continued. *How could you let this happen, Margaret?*

Gus was practicing his sun salutes. He was several minutes into his routine and glowing with perspiration when he spoke.

"Wanda, dear, are you feeling all right?"

Wanda swirled the sludge at the bottom of the coffeemaker and then poured it into her cup. "Closings are a bit sad," she said, "especially when you don't have another job to go to."

"You'll get one," Margaret said.

"Of course you will," Gus echoed.

"You're part of this intense family for a while, and then everyone moves on. I've been at this long enough. Years. You'd think I'd be used to it by now."

"Maybe you're not supposed to get used to it," Susan said.

Wanda gulped her coffee. "Well. Anyway. Bye. See ya later."

"Ta," said Susan.

"OM," Gus intoned.

"Break a leg!" Margaret called.

In boca lupa! cheered Margaret's mother.

Wanda waved to them all, and then she was gone.

She called a sold-out matinee. Since it was closing weekend (actors are reliably indulgent as they near the end of a run, wanting to extend what may be their last gainful employment for months, even years) and since the play was by Eugene O'Neill, the pace was deadly, the running time predictably long.

In between shows, Wanda reminded the actors to please pick up their cues, clear their makeup tables, and take any personal possessions with them after the evening performance. It was a pleasure working with them. Maybe their paths would cross again.

On this particular Easter Sunday—one that coincided most unluck-ily with closing night—Wanda thought about good-byes. She found opportunities to stand too close to her assistant, realizing with anxiety that all her clothes smelled like cinnamon chewing gum, wet sagebrush, saddle leather.

When it was over, Troy walked her to the car as usual. He carried her things. She'd parked farther up the hill than ever. They were about a third of the way up before she spoke.

"Are you going to the party?"

"Are you?"

"No." They walked some more. The top of the hill came into sight. "I hate closing night parties," she offered.

"How come?"

"Why prolong the inevitable?"

When they got there, Troy held out Wanda's backpack. She took hold of it; neither of them let go. In this light, his eyes were glossy and dark, like Christmas holly. Wanda gave careful consideration to how she'd feel at the end of her life if she never saw him again. True, he was one of those thirty-three proverbial people in the theatre. There was a much more than even chance that they'd work together again, someday, on another show, somewhere. Those odds should have been a comfort. They weren't.

"Stay here," she commanded. "Don't look." She got into the car and changed into her black dress and rhinestone-studded shoes. Troy studied the night sky. She put on her wig and eyeglasses. Troy whistled; he was a very good whistler. She applied thick coats of lipstick and mascara. Troy rolled up his sleeves. She consulted her map to review the directions to tonight's destination: north, an easy five miles or so up Highway 99 to 85th Street, and then due west to Stan's Jazz Records in Greenwood.

When she was transformed into Detective Lorenzini, she slid out of the car and approached the suspect. "Hand over the gum," she said.

Troy complied. He hid it pretty well, but he was flustered.

Now we'll see, she thought. *We'll see what this boy is made of.*

"This is me," she began. "This is what I do when I'm not a stage manager. It's who I really am. I dress up like someone else and visit used jazz record stores all over the city and look for the man who dumped me. I'm still completely in love with him. He's the one who's got my heart, understand? He's the one. You wanna come along, great, you don't wanna come along that's fine too, but this is me. Do you think I'm crazy?"

Troy kissed her.

The kiss started out the way she wanted—aggressive, muscular, businesslike; but he turned it into something else—a beach vacation, a Mediterranean cruise—and made it last much longer than she'd intended.

She disembarked from his tongue, licked her lips, adjusted her wig. "Well?" she asked.

He still had his hands around her waist. His face was very close. "Yes," he said. "I think you're crazy. Yes"—he kissed her again, another slow boat to China—"I want to come along."

This was not the answer Wanda expected, which is not to say it wasn't the one she wanted to hear. "Have you ever heard of Rasaan Roland Kirk?"

"No."

"Get in," she said. And before he could wear away what little was left of her willpower and her lipstick, she left his arms and unlocked the car. "Let's see how you feel about bebop."

She waited two miles for him to say something. When he didn't, she turned on the radio. They listened to late night blues, that old bogeyman of the jazz family tree. Primal, raw, pained, unpretty, it was a good sound track for the scene playing out between them. At the same time, with its slamming rhythms and set forms, it matched the part of her that felt like a stupid bee, pollen-dopey, driven by pheromones from flower to flower just as the ragged-voiced singer dragged her blues-drunk self out of one chord and into the next.

This thing with Troy, whatever it was, was sloppy. An embarrassment. At least her pursuit of Peter kept on the course of a designed madness, one of her own creation.

Chemistry isn't love! she wanted to shout. *Pheromones don't last forever!*

Maybe he doesn't feel it, she thought suddenly. This was even more awful to contemplate. Maybe she was alone in this hot, insensible haze of attraction. Her eyes slid sideways. She glimpsed his left hand and forearm, daringly available in the space between their seats, producing so much heat that the terrain of his skin pulsed, as if he were a mirage. No. He felt it all right. She wasn't alone.

A dozen times she wanted to stop, pull over, slip out of her scripted craziness and into him. Here he was, after all, due east from her chest and a mere thighbone's distance from her belly. She didn't need a map to find him. She could triangulate his location and get them both out of costume in less than a minute. Getting laid on closing night had been a ritual event ever since she was fifteen. There was no need to break with that tradition now.

But she stayed in character and kept driving. A self-defined seeker, she was genetically and temperamentally predisposed to adopt desperate measures in pursuit of the unattainable.

He probably thought they'd kiss again. He was wrong. She'd put on the whole show for him, let him see how deep it went, how crazy she really was, and that would be the end of that.

They arrived. There was parking on the east side of the street, directly in front. It wasn't until she turned off the ignition that it occurred to her: Peter might actually be inside this very store, this very minute. That was the whole point: finding Peter. It was the hope that had brought her across the country and landed her here, deep in the heart of Greenwood, wearing fuck-me pumps and an evening dress. It wasn't for Troy that she was dressed like this, behaving like this. She hadn't found Peter yet, but that wasn't because he didn't exist. He wasn't some phantom—he was real; she wasn't insane—she was determined, and this might actually be the night. If there was ever a right time for the universe to reward her faith in affirmations, it was now. *I am going to find him. I am going to find him. I am going to find him.* The words were as true as anything she had ever told herself; her faith in their power was more potent than ever.

"Did you say something?" asked Troy. She reexamined his skin—he was all firm planes now, and clear boundaries. She sniffed the air—diffuse, and cool. His chemical hold on her was gone. The bonds had dissolved. The detective was back.

She smoothed her wig and reapplied her lipstick. "Listen carefully," she said in the throaty voice of her alter ego. "You can watch, you can listen, but you can't act like you know me once we're inside. Are you still sure you want to come along?"

"You promised me bebop."

She would not be charmed. "Get out. Let's go."

He stepped onto the curb, she got out street-side. The detective noted people strolling the streets—more than she would have expected in this neighborhood at this time of night. They looked happy, overdosed on Peeps and the promise of resurrection.

They went inside. She cased the place—no Peter, not yet—and introduced herself to the clerk. She was just beginning her spiel when Troy sidled over, gumshoe style. He stood next to her and pulled a notepad out of his pocket.

"Good evening," he said. "I'm Detective Bridges. I'll be taking notes on our conversation, just to make sure we have our facts straight, help my partner jog her memory later. I hope that's all right."

The clerk gave a knowing nod. "I know the drill," he said. "I live for *Law & Order.*"

Troy looked to Wanda, his pencil poised. "Detective Lorenzini, please continue. You were describing the suspect."

She stared at him. "You think this is a joke? You think this is funny?"

The clerk paled. "What? Did I say something wrong? Is everything all right?"

"We're investigating a *crime,*" Wanda emphasized to her partner.

"Really, detectives," the clerk rushed on, "I'm sure I haven't seen anyone that fits the description. I'd never lie to an officer of the law."

"Excuse us, please." Wanda yanked on Troy's arm and pulled him outside. "What the fuck do you think you're doing?"

His expression was teasing. "Are you aware that impersonating an officer is a criminal offense?"

"It's not funny, Troy." He really was a child; how could she not have seen it?

"Subject to fines, punishable by jail time?" He was moving in closer, laughing now. She felt maddened, endangered, because he was just about to capture her.

"I said, it's not funny!" The evening was ruined, her cover was blown. She flung out her arms, stormed around to the driver-side door, and started to open it.

"Wanda," he said placatingly, chasing around to her side of the car. "Wait. I'm sorry. I wasn't trying to —"

But she couldn't hear him. She was frozen in time, on the verge of ascent.

It was a smell that seized her first, a familiar smell that she couldn't name, not quite, other than to know that it was the perfume of comfort and love, and it led her eyes upwind and then she saw him: walking away, going north on Greenwood, a tall, lean pedestrian on the other side of the street, his hair long and ponytailed, his body the one around which her own had surely been molded.

It wasn't Detective Lorenzini's deductive powers that made her know the receding man was Peter, it was desire: ancient, sensual, and born of unshaped memory—the kind that is deeper and dearer than memory sculpted by words.

She called his name. She tried to run toward him, an awkward cartoon in her ridiculous shoes. Tendons, ligaments, ankle bones—forced into impossible anatomical relationships—strained for control, buckled crazily. She heard Troy call her name as she stumbled into the street after the man, that man, the man that got away, but it was cut in two ("WAN!") by the sound of screeching tires. And then she was airborne.

Stupid, she thought mid-flight, the pain already excruciating and knowing that something even worse was on its way. *What a stupid, girly thing to do.*

Spinning through space, she thought of Margaret's porcelain plates. Maybe they'd wondered too if they could maneuver their bodies, take hold of some lucky thing at the last minute, ride an unseen current of migrating molecules to a safe, soft landing. And there he was: her luck, her partner, Detective Bridges backing her up, his beautiful face horribly transformed, running toward her, arms outstretched, desperate to catch her as she had been to catch—and save!—the pure porcelain offerings to a marriage that didn't hold, and maybe for her it wasn't too late, she could still be won where found and sail gracefully effortlessly straight into his arms without falling into the fires of hell but no, no, no, oh . . .

Trying to escape her body, landed now and imprinting the macadam of the street in a way that no human body was ever meant to, she briefly imagined herself from above, and then sank to the street again and into the reality of searing pain. She struggled with her cat's eyes—where were her glasses?—dimly aware that one of them wouldn't open and the other had something dripping into it. Suddenly there were perplexing, ominous swirls of black and white closing in on her. *It's the nuns, the nuns!* she thought, terrified. *Oh God, oh please please save me from the nuns!* But then she recognized a small gaudy puff of color moving among the evil nuns and their black and white habits, protecting her, dispersing them, and she was quieted. *Thank you,* she wanted to say, *thank you thank you,* and closed her eyes.

Easter colors, she thought dully as she began to go, remembering the poor doomed chicks and bunnies of her childhood, dyed in unnaturally vibrant shades of bubble gum pink and lime green and put on display in pet store windows. How sad it was, how heartbreakingly sad.

"Dyed, then they died," she tried to whisper; but to the paramedic, leaning close to this ruined girl who might be uttering her last words, it sounded like "Da. Da."

Seventeen

❧

Margaret's Dream, Part Two

This time, it is Margaret and Wanda, riding in a train, sitting inside a private coach. *But it's not a real coach, is it?* Margaret realizes gradually. *Not a real train. It's more like a theatre set for a children's play. That's it! We're in a play! Why, it's* The Little Engine That Could!

There are theatre flats arranged like walls on three sides of them, painted in the clear yellows, reds, and blues of the 1931 illustrations by Watty Piper. When Margaret looks toward where the door of their coach and a fourth wall should be, there is nothing there; it is completely black. *Maybe that's where the audience sits,* Margaret reassures herself.

Margaret and Wanda sit opposite one another on large, comfortable armchairs upholstered in floral-patterned chintz. Between them is a child's wooden school desk; it is laid out with a Ludwigsburg tête-à-tête and an unopened box of animal crackers.

Wanda is busy writing in her little red and black book. She is wearing her high heels and lovely black dress, which shows up especially nicely against the colors on the wall behind her. *Oh my!* Margaret thinks when she looks down, pleasantly surprised to see that she, too, is fashionably dressed in black. *Mother will be so pleased.*

"I can't figure this out," Wanda mutters intensely. "The laws of probability do not apply. There is evidence of a midline shift. There is mass effect upon the cerebellopontine angle. How on earth did a star get in my head?"

The engine whistle toots happily. Margaret hears the clackety-clack of wheels on track. She reaches up to touch the painted curtains on the wall to her left. Instantly, they are three-dimensional, coming apart to reveal a real train window with a real scene outside.

It's the French countryside! Margaret thinks, happily. The fields are a vivid green. The sun is shining. There are quaint cottages along the way. Farmers and their wives and children stand along the railroad track. They wear old-fashioned peasant costumes. They wave gaily, as if to royalty.

"Bonjour!" Margaret calls as they pass by. *"Bonjour, mes amies! Ça va? Est-ce que vous savez ou nous allons? Regardez, Wanda! C'est si parfait!"*

Margaret turns to look at Wanda. She is now a little girl of eight or nine. She is drinking coffee, looking at Margaret over the rim of the tête-à-tête cup with her enormous, dark eyes. Her black dress is much too big for her—it looks like a shroud—and Margaret sees that she has kicked off her high-heeled shoes.

There is the sound of a heavy knock. It reverberates unnaturally, as if electronically amplified. It seems to come from nowhere, and at the same time, everywhere. A loud booming voice says, "Conductor."

"Come in," Wanda answers in her adult voice.

Margaret looks toward the invisible fourth wall. Stephen emerges from the blackness, dressed in a dark blue uniform. He is young. *Goodness me,* Margaret thinks. *He does look fetching.*

"Tickets please."

Wanda hands Stephen the box of animal crackers.

"Where are we going, Stephen?" Margaret asks.

"We're going to the factory, Mom," Wanda answers. "Don't you remember? The cookie factory."

Margaret is puzzled. "But if you're here," she says to Stephen, "who's driving?"

"Next stop, Hungary," Stephen says, then leaves.

Margaret looks out the window. The peasants are gone. The French countryside is gone. It is getting dark outside, and they are moving through a flat, eerily featureless landscape.

"I'm hungry," Wanda says. "Is Dad going to stop soon?"

"What?" Margaret asks. "Who's Dad? Whose dad? Where's Dad?"

"Dad!" Wanda gets up, pulling her black dress up to her ears so as not to trip over it. She pads toward the fourth wall. "Dad!" Margaret hears her call as she disappears into the darkness. "Where are you taking us? I thought we were going to the cookie factory. . . ."

"Wait, honey!" Margaret calls. "Don't go that way!" She jumps out of her seat, toppling the desk and sending the tête-à-tête crashing to the floor.

As she stumbles toward the edge of the darkness, a bright light is suddenly switched on. Margaret finds herself in front of a large audience of schoolchildren. Daniel and Wanda are sitting next to one another in the front row, smiling.

The children wear school uniforms. Pinned to their shirts are little yellow construction paper name tags. Margaret isn't sure—her eyes can't seem to adjust to the bright light—but it looks as though all of their names begin with the letter D. "This is different," Margaret says, puzzled. The children laugh and clap riotously, as if this were the funniest thing in the world.

Margaret looks around. The setting now is much more realistic. The coach is elegant, with polished brass fixtures, wood that's been buffed to a high gloss, velvet curtains, plush leather seats, and maroon-colored carpets. The tête-à-tête still lies in pieces on the floor. Margaret turns back to the children. Their faces are happy. Trusting. Expectant.

"Break a leg!" she says.

The children laugh.

"I think I can. I think I can. I think I can."

The children laugh harder. Tears start streaming down their faces.

Margaret sings, in a loud, tuneful, Wagnerian voice, "I'm a little teapot, short and stout. Here is my handle, here is my spout. . . ."

The children open their mouths wide, laughing harder than ever, but suddenly Margaret can no longer hear them. She realizes that she is looking at the children from a distance. The fourth wall of her coach has materialized. She is in a real train now, completely enclosed, and she is looking at the children through a long rectangular window. The children are in another train which is parked on an adjacent siding.

Margaret sees Stephen. He is holding on to the outside of the coach door with one hand, smoking a cigarette with the other. *That's much too reckless,* Margaret thinks. *He's setting a bad example for the children.* Stephen still wears his uniform, but there is something different about it now. Before Margaret can figure out what it is, the train starts to move, very slowly.

The children's expressions change from delight to mild surprise, from surprise to alarm, from alarm to terror. They press against the glass, beating on it, calling to Margaret, trying to get out. The train starts picking up speed.

"I'm coming, honey!" Margaret yells. She turns around to look for a way out, but finds that her coach has filled up with crates and boxes. She can barely move. She makes her way around the coach. There is no door. She goes back to the window, pounding on it frantically, trying to break the glass. "What is it?" she screams. "What is it, honey?"

"We're going to the factory!" Wanda screams.

"We're going to the factory!" Daniel echoes.

The train hurtles out of sight. There is the sound of an explosion. Margaret collapses, sobbing, on one of the leather coach seats, and then screams. It is made of human skin.

"Margaret. Margaret, dear."

Margaret woke up to see Gus standing over her. He was wearing his bathrobe.

"What is it?" she said, rubbing tears out of her eyes.

"There was a phone call just now. From a police officer."

"What—?"

He took her hands and spoke calmly.

"We need to get dressed and go to the hospital. Something's happened to Wanda."

PART

TWO

Eighteen

❧

Bowling Alone

A few months before Margaret sits down in Desserts, Etc. and composes the ad that brings Wanda Schultz to her doorstep, you get out of a dusty Greyhound bus in the middle of downtown.

Everything about your appearance is designed. You dress plainly, in black, a costume suggesting membership in an order of secular ascetics. You keep your long graying hair pulled into a neat ponytail. Your body is lean and rangy, as if you've forsworn sustenance that hasn't been hunted and gathered with your own hands and out of the wild. There's a thrifty animalism about the way you move, too, and your eyes take in everything. Your worldly possessions, the things you need to survive, have been culled to a minimum and crammed into a large bulky knapsack; its superior end towers several inches above your head and gives you the appearance of a giant, dour, bipedal mollusk.

This is how you look. Except nobody's looking.

That's fine. That's your intention.

People have good instincts when it comes to certain things. In their hearts they're afraid that loneliness, like tuberculosis, can be contracted, and you look contagious. You look like what you are, what you deserve to be—somebody who's lived a long time without a tribe, without tenderness—so strangers avoid you like the plague. You scare the hell out of them. They worry they might be looking at future versions of themselves.

Let 'em worry, you think, noticing how their eyes run away from you. Maybe they'll go home and kiss their wives like they mean it, hold their kids like there's no tomorrow, write a letter to someone they haven't seen in a hundred years. That's fine too.

You get busy, following the same procedural steps you take every time you arrive in a city: First, you find the nearest public telephone and start examining the directory. You look in the personal pages under L. No luck there. You look in the Yellow Pages under B. You write lists. You buy a city map. You make a plan. You don't expect your plan to succeed—you've been doing this for years without success and you're not an optimistic sort of person to begin with, but it's a force of habit.

This time, though, you do something you haven't done for a long time: At the bus station newsstand, you buy a postcard. You address the postcard to an address in Chicago, stamp it, and shove it into a mailbox before you can change your mind. You don't know why. You played an impulse. It was stupid. You regret it already.

You need some privacy for what comes next, so you go to the men's room and lock yourself inside one of the stalls. You open up your knapsack and start digging. Your hands close around a bubble-wrapped framed photo; the glass is still intact. You'll unwrap it later, after you get settled. You pull out a book—your book of faith, the only book you carry: a 1962 copy of the collected works of William Butler Yeats, edited by the esteemed Professor M. L. Rosenthal. Laying the book against your chest, you close your eyes, ask your heart a question, open the book at random, and point. This is where your finger lands:

But one man loved the pilgrim soul in you, and loved the sorrows of your changing face.

The words are scripture. They guide you, uphold you, help you persevere. Wherever you've gone, whatever variables you've encountered, the book's wisdom—and your interpretation of it—has always led you to the same course of action. Today is no different. You wish to hell you hadn't mailed that postcard. Why the fuck did you do it?

The book goes back in your knapsack. You take care of business, splash cold water on your face, washing away the dirt of the last thousand miles and the memories of whatever city you just came from. You're here now. There is no past. No immediate past, anyway.

You check your wallet. You'll get something to eat, find a place to stay—maybe you can get a room at the downtown YMCA until you find work—and then you'll set about the business of looking for your wife.

Have you been to Seattle before? Maybe. You can't be sure. You should keep better records, probably.

Nineteen

❧

Bowling Together, 1959–1969

Michael Francis Joseph O'Casey was crazy about bowling alleys. He loved them for many, varied reasons.

There was the easy mixture of society and rowdy athleticism; the smell of cigarettes, hamburgers, and paste wax; the ice-cold bottles of beer; the sharpened pencils.

There were the neat rows of oiled and spray-disinfected two-toned shoes. They reminded Michael of his car: a 1957 candy-cane red and white Ford Fairlane in which he'd spent many blessed hours making out with an assortment of willing sinners. Michael O'Casey didn't credit the church with much, but he had to admit that his sex life owed a great deal to the Vatican for its part in shaping the psychology of those pure, darling, infinitely repressed and inexhaustibly libidinous Catholic girls.

Michael loved the sounds of bowling alleys. Bowling alley noise was like a big huzzah of the world not going gentle into that good night. He loved the resonant thud of the balls, the staccato brattle of colliding pins. The sounds of a bowling alley made you know that—beyond any doubt, and in this little corner of the universe at least—earthly objects were making real, true, happy, honest, and uninhibited contact with one another. There were the sporadic, papery sounds of applause. Bursts of laughter. He loved the seeming randomness of it, when in fact the whole thing was underlaid with an inexorable, ordered ebb and flow. Over the course of several hours, the sounds of a bowling alley induced meditative calm that nothing, with the exception of reading William Butler Yeats—or engaging in prolonged, athletic sex—could duplicate.

Then, of course, there was the game itself, about which he could wax poetic for hours.

He was a good player. He had a lot of bravado, a rough-edged style, and amazing power for someone so lean. Nobody knew more about drilling a ball than Michael O'Casey. His nickname was "The Oilman."

Last but not least, bowling alleys were a grand place to meet members of the opposite sex. There was nothing like eyeing female fannies as they sashayed down the throw line.

"I hate to see you go, darlin's, but I love to watch you leave!" Michael called to a departing group of sorority coeds. They giggled and cantered toward the door. Michael and Jerry O'Connell—his roommate, bowling compatriot, fellow student, and countryman—gazed wistfully after them.

"Jesus, but I love capri pants," Michael said.

"Poodle skirts are nice too," added Jerry.

"Yeah, but you can't see their lovely asses nearly so well."

"God, Michael, you're such a pig."

Michael lit a cigarette. "You're thinking the same thing, don't tell me you're not. You're up."

They were two frames away from the end of the game. Jerry bowled a split.

"You're still hookin' the ball, man. Stay straight." Michael scanned the room. Things were winding down. "Damn. I was hopin' for a bit of fun this weekend."

"You've got studying," Jerry said. "We both do."

"Idiot."

"Fine. I for one don't want to lose my scholarship and get sent back to bloody Eire."

"You're like an old woman sometimes, Jerry."

Three lanes away, Michael noticed a little girl, practicing. "It's a bit late for that one. I wonder where her parents are," he said, half to himself.

"Who?"

"That little girl down there. Lane sixteen. She's not half bad."

Jerry sat down and marked his score. "Look out, Mike, you're eyesight's goin'. That's no little girl."

"What are you talkin' about?"

"Are you blind, man? It's a woman. Your turn."

Michael walked to the throw line, hoisted his ball, and then casually glanced over his shoulder at the girl's profile. Jerry was right. When he studied her face—the angular set of her jaw, her riveted stillness—he saw that she could be anything from eighteen to thirty. But God, she was a wisp of a thing.

"Come on, man," Jerry prodded. "Move it. Let's finish this frame at least before they give us the boot."

The woman turned and caught Michael staring at her. Her face was pale, waifish, her hair short and black. Her eyes, undershadowed with faint bluish half-circles, were enormous; against her skin they were dark as roasted coffee beans. "What are you looking at?" she called defensively.

"Uh-oh," said Jerry.

"I'm not lookin' at anything, darlin'," Michael volleyed. "I'm just getting ready to send these pins to kingdom come. Maybe you'd like to come down here and have a look."

"I don't think so." She turned her back and picked up her ball. Michael bowled a spare. She bowled two strikes.

Michael stared. "On the other hand, maybe I'd better go down there instead. Jerry?"

"I'm headin' home."

"You want a ride?"

"Nah. I'll take the El. You might be needin' the backseat of your car tonight after all."

"Not so sure about that," Michael said, still staring.

"Good luck, man. I'll see you when I see you."

Michael moved his gear to lane sixteen. She paid no attention; she was back at the throw line, so still and focused that the atmosphere around her seemed ionized. He sat down in the scorekeeper's chair. He lit another cigarette.

She was wearing blue jeans and a white sleeveless blouse. From a distance, she had merely seemed skinny and small-boned—fragile—but up close you could see an undulating landscape of muscle just beneath her skin. A fierce, tensile strength. She had a tiny ass. She had a chest like a boy. She threw the ball like she was God's avenging angel. She bowled four more consecutive strikes.

When she was done, she walked over to him. She was breathing hard. She licked the sweat from her upper lip. She pulled a flask from a brown paper bag and took a swig. She offered it to him.

"No thanks."

"What's your name?"

"Michael. O'Casey."

"My name's Gina."

"You've got a lead pipe for an arm, Gina."

"I paint," she said, as if that explained everything.

"Do you paint as well as you bowl?"

She took a drag off his cigarette. "What do you do?"

"I'm a student at Northwestern."

"Not one of those fraternity boys, are you?"

"God, no."

"What do you study?"

"I'm writing a thesis on Yeats."

"That's a very good answer, Michael O'Casey."

"I'm glad to hear it."

"Buy me a beer. Recite something for me."

He could have chosen another—he knew dozens by heart—but the words that ignited his breath and passed across his lips were these:

"'When you are old and grey and full of sleep, and nodding by the fire take down this book, and slowly read, and dream of the soft look your eyes had once, and of their shadows deep. . . .'"

Thus began the courtship of Michael O'Casey and Gina Lorenzini. It was a courtship conceived in a bowling alley, against a sound track of collisions; probably that in itself should have told Michael O'Casey something. So, too, should the way Gina could drink anything—beer, wine, bourbon, whiskey—without ever seeming to get drunk. And then there was her moodiness, which in Michael's love-blindness he labeled as mysterious. Mercurial. Italian. He should have seen the signs.

But it was no use: From the moment he met his future wife, Michael O'Casey was lost.

*   *   *

They said good-bye in the bar and Gina disappeared into the night.

Next Friday, there she was again. And so it went on, week after week. Michael would come in with Jerry; they would find Gina already there, by herself, bowling.

"Are you sure she's worth it, boyo?" Jerry had asked. "This one is taking 'playing hard to get' to new heights."

"That's not it," Michael said. "She's not like that."

After the bowling alley closed, they would go to a bar. Sometimes Jerry joined them. He and Jerry would talk about school, she'd tell stories about the restaurant where she waitressed. They'd mostly just shoot the shit and have a good laugh. She didn't talk about herself.

One night when Jerry left early to go to the library, she said, "Take me home, Michael."

They did not have sex that night, in Michael's room. Strangely, he didn't feel like it. They didn't even make out. They drank beer, Michael read poetry, and Gina fell asleep in his arms. Eventually, he fell asleep too.

When he woke up, she was gone. She left behind a drawing of him, sleeping, under which she had scrawled, "Dear sweet Michael O'Casey, You are one of the good souls and i think you deserve a good girl but i do love the way you read poetry and hold me safe in Innisfree. Thank you and Mr. Yeats for dropping slow peace and an evening full of linnet's wings. i can almost hear them singing. You look like an angel when you are sleeping. g."

The next week, she wasn't at the bowling alley. Michael couldn't bowl a strike for the life of him. Jerry stopped hooking his throw and bowled a 190.

When they left, just after midnight, there she was: standing in the parking lot, bareheaded, bare-legged, wearing a sleeveless blouse and skirt, shivering. She gestured to him, pulled him close, and whispered urgently, with what sounded to Michael like passion, "Come home with me, Michael. Please. Be home with me. We can walk. It's not far from here."

Michael tossed his car keys to Jerry.

"You sure, Mike?"

"Yeah, Jerry. Live it up."

They didn't speak. She walked with a grim urgency, hugging herself, not letting him touch her. After a few blocks, they arrived in front of an

Italian restaurant. She stopped. "That's where I earn my bread and but-ter," she said. Then she pointed to the upper floor. "And that's where we're going to fuck." She laughed then and started pulling him up the stairs.

Inside her apartment, it smelled like oregano and turpentine. They'd barely made it across the threshold before she unzipped his trousers, pulled him onto the floor, hiked up her skirt, and took him inside her. Viscous wet dense heat baptized his cock and—*Christ, Jesus, holy Christ*—they both came at once.

They lay in the dark, blood pulsing in sync. Beneath them in the res-taurant kitchen, pots clanged, dishes were scraped, somebody sang a song in Italian.

"Usually it's us boyos who like a quick bang like that," he said, once his heart recovered its own rhythm. "I hope to God you're wearin' protection."

"It's my time," she answered. "I'm bleeding."

Ah, he thought sadly, *Catholic girls.*

"Does that bother you, Michael?" Her eyes, *Jesus,* were unmined coal.

"I don't mind at all. But next time, give a man a chance to put on a raincoat, willya? We won't tell the Pope." He turned to kiss her. She rolled away and got up.

"I'll get some wine."

She went into the kitchen. He lit a cigarette, turned on a lamp, and inhaled sharply: An inquisition of faces glowered at him.

It was Gina, over and over, frozen in oil and varnish, staring from canvases that were propped against the walls and ringed the apartment on all sides. Self-portraits they were, done in a kind of Italian Renais-sance style, and masterful, too, no question. The backgrounds were out-door scenes painted in pastel blues, pinks, greens—the luminous colors of a Tuscan landscape in spring—and dotted with winged innocents: plump cherubs, butterflies, birds. But the light that gave a honeyed glow to the angels did not lend warmth, color, or succulence to her skin, which was taut and blanched and strangely without the varnished sheen that covered the rest of the painting. He imagined her scouring her painted skin with a scrub brush to achieve this effect.

She'd costumed herself in one of two ways—either as a member of the church or as some kind of sinner. But this was the only element that varied. Priests, prostitutes, acolytes, KKK wizards, and saints—

all wore the same bloodless complexion, the same sourness of expression, a mask that was both damned and damning. Her dark figure was advanced to the forefront of the paintings—she was life-sized—and took up most of the canvas. But compelling as she was (she'd gotten the bottomless quality of her eyes right, that was sure) his attention was drawn to the airy landscape in the distance, toward the vineyards and rolling hills.

Was she bewitched? Was she daring him to reach into the window of the painting and take her forcibly by the shoulders? Because that was what he wanted to do: force her to stop staring at whatever it was that gave her the look of someone whose heart was being charbroiled on a spit for all eternity. She'd designed a special form of punishment by painting herself this way, dooming herself to stare out toward a hell beyond the canvas when heaven was so close, just a romp down the hill behind her. All she had to do was turn around.

Had she painted all these while sitting in front of a mirror? Yeats's "The Two Trees" came to mind: *Gaze no more in the bitter glass the demons, with their subtle guile, lift up before us when they pass. Or only gaze a little while.*

He stood before a painting of her dressed as a nun, the funereal folds of cloth so realistic he could almost smell the sour sweat and suffocating steam of a magdalen laundry.

"You're a believer, I see," he said, an idiotic understatement if there ever was one, but he'd been quiet for who knew how long and she had to know he was looking at all this.

Her voice came from the kitchen. "Aren't you?"

He laughed—not at her, but because he bloody well needed to. "No."

She was walking toward him then, holding out a bottle of wine in one hand and two glasses in another. "Maybe I'll have to convert you."

He uncorked the bottle and filled their glasses. "You'll need to spend a long time tryin', darlin'." There was a red stain on the front of her skirt, a sign overhanging the shrine where his hands and mouth and cock most wanted to go. He was hard again already. *Wine comes in at the mouth,* he thought, *and love comes in at the eye.*

She stared at him, downed her drink, and then walked to her easel. She pulled away a cloth, revealing the canvas underneath. It was a half-finished portrait of him, wearing wings.

"I'm flattered," he said.

She poured more wine. "Will you model for me sometime, Michael?"

He put down his glass and started taking off her clothes. "Only if you'll model for me."

He didn't offer his thoughts about her paintings. They were brilliant, sure, and if she'd asked to hear his opinion he would have obliged her—though perhaps not in an entirely honest way.

Thankfully, though, she didn't crave his artistic opinion. All she wanted was simultaneous sexual satisfaction, as frequently and in as many ways as possible. He could give her that, by God, and something more. He'd make her laugh. He'd bathe her in light the color of whiskey. He would see to it by Christ that she'd gaze no more into that bitter glass.

After a few weeks, he took Gina to meet Maureen and her family. At that time the Schultz brood was entirely male and numbered only three.

"Isn't she a wonder, Mo?" he'd said. They were in the kitchen. Michael was doing the dishes. Maureen was trying to feed Jacob, who was eight months old; they were both festooned with chartreuse globs of Gerber puree. Gina was outside, smoking a cigarette, standing apart and watching the two older boys roughhouse with Artie.

"Have you asked her about her family at all?" Maureen said.

"I get the feeling she hasn't any, or else she's on her own."

"That's a pity. She's very . . . serious, isn't she? Does she ever laugh?"

"She's a wonder. She's a genius."

"Not to mention a great roll in the hay, I'm thinking."

Michael spun around. "Maureen O'Casey, I'm shocked!" he exclaimed in falsetto. "Shocked, I tell ya! This from the mither of three! With Bun Number Four bakin' the oven! Be Jaysus!" he said to the baby. "What's the world comin' to at all at all, I ask you, boyo!" Michael scooped the baby out of his high chair and whirled him around, flinging droplets of strained green beans in a perfect arc around the kitchen. Maureen shrieked and laughed. Michael hugged the baby close and stage-whispered, "'A great roll in the hay,' your mither says. That's a bit like the pot givin' names to the kettle, wouldn't you say, Jakey?" Jacob smiled broadly and promptly threw up.

"HA!" Michael snorted.

"Oh, for God's sake." Maureen grabbed a wet dish towel. "Look at the two of yous. Give me the baby, and wipe yourself off with this." She started peeling off Jacob's clothes. "I just worry, you know. I'm still your older sister."

"I'm fine, Mo. Really. We're fine." Michael banged on the window to get Gina's attention. When she turned around, she began laughing so hysterically that her knees buckled.

"Ah," Maureen said. "So she *does* have a smile now and then."

Gina was kneeling on the ground, shaking with laughter, tears streaming down her cheeks. Michael started kissing the window, leaving a profusion of green-tinged lip prints. Artie, James, John, and the now-naked Jacob stared as if they were in the presence of alien life-forms.

"All right then," Maureen went on. "Get that shirt in the laundry and put on one of Artie's. Then you can start in cleanin' the walls and that window!"

Michael blew more kisses as he exited. Gina mimed grabbing them out of the air and stuffing them into her shirt.

Maureen didn't ask any more questions about Gina. She was a good girl like that, not the prying sort at all.

Michael and Gina were together constantly, sometimes at her place, sometimes at his. Michael's grades suffered; he lost his scholarship and had to drop out of school.

"Marry me, Gina."

She stared at him, unblinking. "I'm older than you."

"Marry me."

"I'm an artist. I smell. My hands are never clean."

"I'm an atheist. I'm in desperate need of savin'."

"Don't joke like that. I don't like it."

"Forgive me. Marry me."

She backed away. "I should have broken it off. I shouldn't have let it go this far."

"Oh, no, darlin'!" Michael said, affecting his exaggerated brogue. "You've got the wrong idea entirely." He pulled her toward him and started to unbutton her blouse. "You were thinkin' I was proposin' because I was mad for you, is that it? No, darlin', I can't stand the sight of you." He parted the folds of her blouse and drew slow feathery circles around her areolas. "It's only that I'll lose my visa unless I can get some homely, unwitting American spinster to say 'I do.'"

Michael teased her nipples with his tongue until they stood erect, like two tart raspberries. Nothing mattered but the taste of her.

"No babies."

He looked up, startled.

She seemed to be staring at something far away. "I wouldn't be a good mother."

He didn't know what to say. They hadn't talked about children. He hadn't really thought about it.

"And I can't have an abortion, either, Michael." She looked at him. "God would punish me."

"Gina—"

"I don't care if *you* believe or not, Michael. I know I'd be damned. So you have to promise me that we'll be very, very careful. No babies."

God, but she was beautiful. His enigma. His secret-keeper. *Maybe she'll change her mind,* Michael thought. *Or maybe she's right; maybe we don't need kids. It's a sure thing that Maureen has already done her bit, procreating on behalf of the O'Caseys.* He decided he didn't care. "Whatever you want, Gina. Just say yes."

"All right, Michael," she answered. "I will join my flesh with yours." She giggled then, pressing frantic hands against his hard-on, starting to unzip his trousers.

Within two months, they were married. At Michael's insistence, and despite Gina's protests, they had a civil service at the county courthouse; Jerry and Maureen were their witnesses. They lived at Gina's place.

For a while, everything was right as rain. Michael got a job managing the front desk of the bowling alley. He took one university class each semester, working on his degree, studying at night. Gina waitressed part-time and painted. She was moody, yes, but he didn't care. He could always fix it. With sex. With a joke. He'd read poetry to her. They'd go bowling.

Then one day she showed up at work, sobbing so hard he could barely understand her.

"It's happened it's happened oh Christ Michael Christ what am I going to do?"

"It'll be all right, darlin'." But he was shaken. Her desperation was terrible to see.

She tried hard during her pregnancy, probably for his sake. She drank less. She read Dr. Spock, obsessively. She cut curtains for the baby's room. She shopped with Maureen. She let Michael pamper her. She let the waitresses at the restaurant give her a baby shower.

Gradually, she stopped painting—the smell of turpentine made her nauseous—and just before Wanda was born, Michael came home one day to find that she'd destroyed all her canvases; they'd been torn off their frames and slashed into strips. They lay in a twisted, serpentine mess in one corner of the room.

Gina was on her hands and knees, naked, her belly swollen and ripe, trying to scrub the remnants of oil paint from the living room floor. "You were right, Michael!" she said. Her face was unnaturally luminous, her voice singsong. "Everything's wonderful! Everything will be for the baby now! The baby will make me good!"

After Wanda was born things got worse. Gina seemed to have no feelings for her. She couldn't stand to hold or feed her. When Wanda cried, it was Michael who went to her, picked her up, gave her a bottle, sang to her. He didn't know any lullabies, so he crooned jazz and blues ballads. Wanda's favorite song, the one that never failed to soothe her, was "Blues in the Night."

Gina didn't eat. She drank heavily. Michael had been taking night classes, but when he started coming home to find Gina passed out, Wanda awake, wailing, needing a diaper change, he gave up going to school. He was afraid to leave them alone any longer than necessary.

"Why don't you ever come to see us, Michael?" Maureen asked.

"It's hard to get Gina out of the house." He was ashamed to ask for help. "She's still having trouble, you know, getting used to the baby."

"She can call me, Michael, anytime. I hope she knows that. I remember how lonely it can be, especially that first time. I'm sure it would help her to talk to someone."

"Thanks, Mo. I'll tell her."

Wanda became accident-prone. "She fell off the couch," Gina would say, her voice frowsy and confused. "She banged her head on the door." "She tripped on the stairs." "Her arm got caught on the fire escape railing. She was trying to fly and her wings aren't ready!"

When Michael gave Wanda her bath, he found scratches, bruises. "How did you get this, darlin'?"

"Sing the song, Da," she'd say as she decorated his face with bubbles. "About the blue night and the man in knee pants."

Then she broke her arm. She was four.

"It's very rare that we see this, Mr. O'Casey," the pediatrician had said. They were looking at an X ray. "Children's bones are still unformed and malleable, so it's unusual for them to actually break. Usually we see something called a 'greenstick fracture,' in which the bone bends." The doctor fell silent. He looked Michael in the eye. "Just make sure Wanda is getting proper supervision," he said, finally. "I wouldn't want to treat her for another injury this severe."

That was when Michael started taking Wanda to work with him. They had a nursery at the bowling alley. It wasn't busy during the day, so Wanda got lots of attention and he could look in on her frequently. At least he knew she'd be safe.

Gina had good days sometimes, days when she seemed almost normal. Sometimes in the afternoon she would come over, play a bit with Wanda, bowl a few games. "Come watch Mommy make the pins go 'crash!'" She was still a helluva bowler. Now and then she would even compete.

The photograph of Gina was taken in 1970, at tournament time. Michael stood facing her, in the adjacent lane; he caught her just after she released the ball. Her throwing arm was cocked in front of her, framing her startling, haunted face. Her other arm floated out to the side with a peculiarly light and graceful extension of the fingers. She was standing on one leg, with her other leg cocked behind her. She looked like an exotic crane poised for flight. Wanda was in the photograph too, barely visible behind the scorekeeper's desk in the background. Her eyes—dark, enormous eyes just like her mother's—peeped over a Styrofoam cup. Michael loved the photograph so much that he ordered two prints. Soon after, Gina vanished.

She left a note: "Dear street sweet brawler Michael love, i'm sorry i'm sorry i'm sorry i'm sorry. Cracked. Can't fix it. Satan has made his bed in me. It's hell, the hell of this. i'm never going to change i hurt. Her. You. Split. God can't forgive. Mary can't forgive a rotten evil mother who cannot keep our human child safe from the weeping world. A hole in the soul that must be it. Can't fix it. Stop trying. Say one rosary for me and then Hail Mary Hell Mary. Going away. Going far away to the sinning place the mouth of Hades the land without birds and Michael don't please don't come looking. Wish me your beloved dead. Take care of our sweet faerie, our magic wand protect her plant your nine bean-rows and a laurel tree so those with the will of wild birds can have shelter. I will always love you always always love you angel your virginia."

"She can't have just disappeared, Maureen. People don't just disappear."

"They do, Michael. Sometimes they do."

"I'm going to find her. Can you take care of Wanda for a while? I know it's a lot to ask."

"Don't worry about that. Of course she can stay with us, but—"

"She mentioned family in Kansas City once. She was estranged from them, but they might know something. I'm going down there to see what I can find out. Can I bring Wanda over on Saturday?"

Michael gave away most of his possessions. He sold his car to Jerry. He kept one of the photos of Gina for himself; the other he tucked into Wanda's small suitcase just before he delivered her to the Schultz doorstep. He would travel with little else but cloth and poetry; his book of Yeats was a talisman now, a reminder of how they met, an emblem of his love. To have the book always with him was to stay connected to her. He would look to it for guidance.

In the beginning, he called Maureen every weekend. There was always a lot of noise in the background. Kids yelling.

"When are you coming home, Michael?"

"Not yet. I showed her picture around here, and somebody thinks they may have seen her. Have the police there turned up anything?"

"Sometimes people don't want to be found, Michael. That's what they told me."

"That's not a proper answer! That's just a way for them to excuse their own bloody incompetence! Are the bastards even tryin' to find her? Am I the only one who cares?"

"Come home and be with your daughter, Michael. She misses you. Do you want to talk to her? She's in the backyard."

"No!" he shouted. "Christ, Maureen. No."

His calls were fewer and fewer after that. Eventually he stopped calling altogether.

He moved frequently. Whenever he arrived in a new place, he picked up a postcard and mailed it to Chicago, just so Maureen would know where he was and that he was still alive.

After a while, though, he started to wonder if that was a good idea. Maybe it would be better if they forgot about him. Yes, he decided, it would be best if they all thought he was dead. After all, he was a different person now. So, surely, was Gina—if she was still alive, which was doubtful.

So, he stopped sending the postcards. He began dressing entirely, exclusively, in black. He changed his name. He disappeared from view. It was, to tell the God's truth, a blessed relief to be untethered to his old life, a life which included people who loved him when they should hate him for the wreck he'd made of all their hearts. The one punishment he could impose on himself was that he keep looking for Gina, bowling alley by bowling alley, from one end of the country to the other, back and forth, round and round, for the rest of his ignoble life. It was a fine castigation, the right way to simulate hell's damnation: He knew he'd never find her.

But deep down, some part of the man who'd once been Michael Francis Joseph O'Casey still hoped to see his wife walk in to whatever bowling alley he found himself in, shimmy her darling, unrepentantly plumlike ass up to the throw line, and let one go in that way that was only Gina's, unique in all the world.

Twenty

Nothing Like South Pacific

Several miles from Margaret's house is an area of Seattle which, like many such places in American cities, has no name; it is a connecting area, an urban corridor. Its main artery—Greenwood Avenue—is born out of and then disappears into other streets, arising and vanishing with no demarcations to mark its origin or its termination.

For a brief time, at 85th Street, Greenwood Avenue achieves a distinctly cheery and extroverted personality, when it serves as the heart of the Greenwood Neighborhood: a tidy collection of businesses housed in mostly old but well-maintained, squat brick buildings. Like maiden aunts, they have a kitschy, apple-bosomed feel to them. Appropriately, many of the businesses in this neighborhood are stores containing all manner of knickknacks: Depression glass, milk glass, Fiestaware, Hummel figurines. There are also more practical-minded establishments: a grocery, a bank, Buddy's Homesick Café, the retail center for the Progressive Animal Welfare Society, the Greenwood Academy of Hair. Newer, trendier stores are starting to spring up as well: a sushi restaurant, a store selling items related to Tibetan Buddhism, a used jazz record store.

Festive banners are perennially hung across 85th Street to announce community events: neighborhood meetings, parades, street fairs, etc.

The citizens of the Greenwood Neighborhood, one senses, are involved. They take an interest. They are most likely social, outgoing people with nothing to hide. They suffer no major complaints, physical or otherwise. They are rarely gripped by guilt or shame. And Greenwood Avenue, for a brief time, shares the plucky and unsinkable disposition of the residents here.

But by the time Greenwood Avenue crosses 90th Street, even though it adamantly maintains its northern course, it begins to seem depressed, becoming wide and flat and undistinguished—a lackluster ribbon of gray that is flanked by an unrelated collection of businesses and rental properties which, although probably reputable, share a certain seedy and impermanent look, as if they've been hastily installed and might just as hastily vanish. They seem always to be casting a backward, guilty glance, like fathers who've been ducking out on their child support payments.

Cars speed past, sometimes using this section of Greenwood Avenue as an alternate route when the major north-south routes of Highway 99 and Interstate 5 are congested.

There are no sidewalks in this part of Seattle. Tourists do not flock to it. It is does not serve as the backdrop for family photographs. It is not called a "neighborhood" because it seems to lack identity. On the other hand, maybe it doesn't want an identity. Maybe it's incognito. Maybe it's in disguise.

In this unnamed northern part of the city—near the complicated confluence of Greenwood Avenue, 100th Northeast, and Holman Road, south of Broadview and east of Crown Hill; not that hard to *find,* but a little hard to *see,* unless you happen to be looking for it—is a bowling alley. Its sign is easy to miss, crowded as it is by other signage that has grown up around it since 1962: Mailboxes, Etc.; The Dollar Store; Jiffy Lube; Texas-Style Barbeque; Windemere Real Estate. But here it is: one of the last independently owned bowling alleys in Seattle, the Aloha Lanes.

Soon after he arrived in Seattle, M. J. Striker began searching for work that would draw on his extensive experience and afford him a living wage. He also required a form of employment that would allow him to stay true to his twenty-seven-year quest, his peculiar form of self-punishment, and his marital vows. It didn't matter that those vows had been uttered in a secular setting; in his loyalist heart, M. J. Striker was as married as if the Pope himself had tied the knot. In short, he looked for work at a bowling alley.

A place in North Seattle had an opening, and M.J. scheduled an interview with the general manager, a man named Rudy Hahn. He boarded a bus at the downtown Y. It was a long ride that took him through a lot of landscape and ended up on a street that had seen better days. He was mightily glad when he finally got where he was going.

From the outside, the Aloha Lanes looked like every bowling alley that had been built in the early 1960s and then outlived its popularity: big and unsightly, in a state of scruffy disrepair. Its windows were streaky; its paint job was old. The only external greenery was a palm tree that had been pruned so aggressively over the years that it was little more than a hairy stump. M.J. viewed places like the Aloha as Ozymandian ruins of the day, built by people who'd believed that America's favorite participation sport (and the way of life that went with it) would rule forever.

M.J. went in. From the sound of things, only a couple of lanes were in use.

There was a large circular stone bench in the lobby. It surrounded a concrete fountain which M.J. assumed was supposed to look like an exotic island, complete with lava flows, dusty plastic palm trees, and fake orchids. The fountain was neither full of water nor functioning. Its basin floor was inlaid with turquoise tiles—chipped, cracked, groutless—and littered with cigarette butts. Children probably used to make wishes here. Couples probably used to sit on the bench and neck. A fetid smell— part mildew, part stale cigarette smoke—emanated from pink and maroon, palm-frond-patterned carpet that had surely been laid in the 1970s. Tiki statues lined the facade of the front desk. They must have once resembled jolly Polynesian sprites; now they looked more like a small army of pissed-off dwarves who'd been pressed into riot-control duty. This was not James Michener's Hawaii. M.J. felt right at home.

A kid with pimply skin and a mouthful of hamburger slouched behind the desk.

"I'm here to see Mr. Hahn," M.J. said. The kid turned his glassy eyes in M.J.'s general direction—he was obviously stoned—and pushed a fistful of French fries into his mouth. His fingers had the same pallid, limp greasiness as the fries, and for a moment it looked to M.J. as though the kid was about to devour his own hand. Oddly enough, M.J. envied him; the kid—in spite of his apparent hygenic and intellectual short-comings—was, after all, a kid.

"Rudy Hahn," M.J. repeated, slowly. "I'm here for an appointment at ten o'clock."

The kid squinted obliquely at a place above M.J.'s head, as if he were receiving instructions from an invisible celestial source.

There was a burst of laughter from a group of elderly women. The kid blinked and tried to focus his eyes on M.J.'s top coat button. He muttered incomprehensibly and sank behind the desk. M.J. awaited further nonverbal communication. He watched the old ladies.

They all looked nice, the way old ladies do when they go bowling. They were wearing slacks, dangly earrings, lipstick, and sweatshirts decorated with shiny doodads or pictures of things like orca whales, sea lions, and turtles; it was, after all, Seattle. They'd all had their hair done. Furthermore, they all looked young; even old ladies look young from behind when they're bowling. M.J. knew that if he got close, the ladies would smell of fabric softener, dry talcum, floral perfume. None of them would smell like turpentine, sweet onions, oregano, and sweat. None of them would be Gina.

He looked toward the video arcade. A couple of truant teenagers with pierced body parts and sunken edgy eyes were shooting at something. Girls or boys? Who could tell.

The kid resurfaced with some papers. He slid them across the desk to M.J. and then shuffled over to the diner. M.J. pulled a pen out of a cracked ceramic bowl sitting next to the cash register—it was made to look like a halved coconut—and began filling in the blanks, for the thousandth time recounting his recent employment history, his expec-tations, his qualifications, and printing "N/A" in response to questions related to emergency contacts and next of kin.

When he was done, he walked over to the diner counter, where the kid was hunched over a plate of nachos. M.J. held out his paperwork. The kid couldn't be bothered—he was enraptured by a glob of Velveeta—but to M.J.'s complete surprise, he blurted a surly multisyllabic utter-ance ("Dohntgivituhmee. Hahnzinthere. Gowahnin. Fuckinay.") and gave M.J. a disgusted sideways glance.

It took M.J. a moment to decipher this message, fraught as it was with complexity and nuance. Finally, though, he smiled broadly, and in his best parody of the Lucky Charms leprechaun said, "Tanksulaht, eejuht!"

The kid jerked his head up to squint at M.J., momentarily lucid, completely dumbfounded. M.J. grinned and headed for the office.

Rudy was sitting behind his desk, listening to somebody on the phone. When he saw M.J., he smiled and gestured for him to come in. He wrapped a hand around the mouthpiece and whispered, "I'll be done in a minute."

Rudy had on a short-sleeved bowling jersey which was unbuttoned to mid-chest—a function not of fashion nor of vanity, M.J. realized, but of necessity: Rudy Hahn was built like a brick shithouse. It was hard to imagine a collar anywhere in America that could comfortably accommodate Rudy Hahn's neck. He wore a white undershirt and a large silver crucifix. He had thick black hair that, from what M.J. could tell, was abundant everywhere but on his head.

"Yeah, I know," Rudy said, nodding patiently. "Listen, I've gotta go. I've got a prospective employee here. . . . Okay. Bye."

Rudy hung up, sighed, and stood. He reached across the desk to give M.J. a handshake. "Sorry about that. One of my gloom-and-doom colleagues complaining about the sorry state of the PBA."

"That's okay."

"Glad you could come in, Mr. Striker. Have a seat."

"Thanks." M.J. handed over his employment application and resumé. Rudy studied M.J.'s credentials. "Perfect name for a bowler, by the way." He looked up and squinted through his thick black eyelashes. "I see here that you've traveled around a lot."

"I like seeing the country."

Rudy clasped his hands behind his head and leaned back in his chair. "I ask because, to be honest with you, it's getting hard to hold decent people in these front desk jobs. I started working here when I was seventeen—can you believe that?—and I took it serious. Still do. I've got people who've been bowling here for three generations. They're as good as family to me." Rudy ran his fingers over the top of his head—a gestural remnant, M.J. guessed, from the days when Rudy had something up there to run his fingers through. "But I get a lot of flakes now. You know what I mean. Kids who think they can get paid by the hour to eat burgers and play video games." Rudy glanced out at the vacant front desk and grimaced. "They're not here for long. I get a lot of turnover."

"Sure."

Rudy looked down at M.J.'s paperwork. "You've got age, experience. I'm sure you're more than qualified to do the job. My question is—and I hope you'll be honest with me here, no hard feelings either way—will you be able to stay?"

M.J. shifted in his chair. "What kind of commitment are you looking for?"

"At this point—" Rudy winced and rubbed his stomach. "Damn. My doc tells me I'm working on an ulcer . . . Hell, I'd settle for six months."

M.J. looked down at his shoes. He liked the look and feel of this place, and Rudy seemed like a straight-up sort of fella.

"Okay, yeah. I can do that."

"Can you start tomorrow morning? Not that I'm eager or anything."

"Sure."

"Great." Rudy stood up and shook M.J.'s hand. "On your way out, ask for Jean, our bookkeeper. She can get you set up with your paperwork."

"Thanks." M.J. started to leave.

"You bowl?"

"No. I just like to watch."

"That's too bad. I was hoping to lure you into a league." Rudy got up and walked M.J. to the office door. "Do you follow the pros? Do you have a favorite kind of bowler?"

M.J. paused. He looked at the old ladies—who weren't all that much older than he was, come to think of it. "My favorite bowler is the one who's shown up at three-thirty every Friday for twenty-seven years. Do you have anybody like that?"

"Oh, yeah." Rudy laughed. "We do. You'll meet 'em all."

Twenty-one

❧

The Origins of the Hawaiian Shirt Collection

M.J. had been working at the Aloha Lanes for a few weeks when Irma Kosminsky, one of the Aloha's regular patrons, came back from her annual vacation to Hawaii.

M.J. had seen her often enough. She was hard to miss, with her dyed orange hair and her floral print outfits. Mrs. Kosminsky bowled twice a week: on Tuesday morning with the ladies of the Hadassah League, and on Thursday afternoon in one of the senior leagues—The Hits and Missus—with a quiet, frail-looking gentleman that M.J. assumed was her husband. But he couldn't remember ever speaking with her; so he was surprised when, after distributing leis to practically everyone in the bowling alley, she marched over to him carrying a large straw tote bag, embroidered with bright yellow pineapples and bearing the words "Maui Is for Lovers."

"Here," Irma said, thrusting the straw bag at M.J.'s chest. She leaned close and squinted up at him. "You're a handsome man. I bet you're not even seventy yet."

"Excuse me?"

"Stop looking like such a cloud!"

"What is this?" M.J. asked, eyeballing a sheaf of tissue paper in the bottom of the bag.

"I've been watching you," Irma went on, standing on her tiptoes and lassoing a lei over M.J.'s head. "I'm not asking you should be happy or anything, God forbid, just that you should wear something with a little spirit, a little pizzazz, a little flash."

"What is this?" M.J. repeated. He reached into the tissue paper and extracted a neon-pink and lime-green rayon shirt. Someone with a grossly inaccurate understanding of mammalian anatomy had designed the fabric; its pattern featured grass-skirted, topless women with bowling-ball-shaped breasts and men with engorged biceps. The men were riding on the backs of creatures M.J. guessed were supposed to be dolphins—although they looked more like quadruple-amputee dachshund puppies.

"It's a shirt, for God's sake!" Irma bellowed. "A Hawaiian shirt!"

"I don't understand."

"Wake up, Junior. You work at the Aloha Lanes. The lounge serves cocktails in ceramic coconuts. Half the songs on the jukebox are Don Ho singing 'Blue Hawaii,' the other half are Don Ho singing 'Bali Ha'i.' YOU figure it out!"

M.J. accepted the shirt but didn't wear it.

A week went by. Irma started pestering him.

"What's wrong with you?" she said. "You don't appreciate my gifts?" M.J. was deeply unsettled by her use of the plural; he was afraid it foretold of future planned assaults on his wardrobe.

"It's a lovely shirt, Mrs. K. It's just not my style."

"Come for dinner tomorrow night."

"That's nice of you, Mrs. K., but—"

"I'll serve something black. Bean soup, licorice, coffee. It'll be very grim, I promise. We'll cover the mirrors. We'll listen to Piaf. We'll read passages from Dostoyevsky."

"Why are you doing this, Irma?"

"It's a mitzvah, doll. You should come by a quarter of six, and leave by seven-thirty. My sweet husband Sammy needs his beauty sleep." Irma helped herself to a front desk brochure about kids' birthday parties and scribbled her address on the back. "If you don't come, I'll never forgive you."

* * *

The Kosminskys lived about a mile and a half northeast of the bowling alley. M.J. expected a retirement community, or even a nursing home—there were plenty of them in the area—but the address Irma had written down led him to a regular apartment building called La Belle Mer (a confusing name, since from what M.J. could tell there was nothing whatsoever aquatic about the place). He climbed the stairs and found Apartment 204. Irma opened the door. She was wearing a voluminous, floor-length Hawaiian print muumuu and cradling an obese, black, three-legged cat.

"So who died?" she asked.

"Hello, Mrs. K." The cat hissed at him. "Thanks for inviting me."

"Sammy!" Irma called over her shoulder. "Did somebody in the building kick the bucket? This poor man got lost on his way to a funeral." Mr. Kosminsky was half-dozing in a recliner in front of the television and did not respond. "Never mind," Irma continued. "You're here now. You might as well come in." She lugged the cat onto her hip and pulled M.J. inside, elbowing the door closed behind him. She lowered the cat to the floor. His tripod stance and bulk made him look like a furry milk stool. "This is Maurice," she said matter-of-factly. "He has diabetes. He's deaf as a post. He won't bother you if you don't bother him." She turned to Mr. Kosminsky. "Sammy! Sweetheart! Say hello! Our guest is here!"

Sam Kosminsky looked up at M.J. and smiled. "Welcome," he said.

"Thank you."

"Let's eat!" Irma proclaimed. She disappeared into the kitchen.

M.J. helped Mr. Kosminsky out of his chair and into the dining area. The table had already been set. Mr. K. took his place and indicated M.J.'s chair. He withdrew a yarmulke from his cardigan pocket and placed it over his head.

Irma emerged from the kitchen wearing large pink oven mitts. She laid out three steaming Salisbury steak TV dinners. From the fridge, she retrieved three dishes of fruit cocktail sprinkled with miniature marshmallows and flaked coconut. She took off her oven mitts and stood at the table across from M.J.

Mr. Kosminsky lit two candles, closed his eyes, and sang: "*Baruch atah Adonai, Elohaynu melech ha'olam . . .*"

M.J. had rarely heard Mr. Kosminsky speak, much less sing. He would have been surprised at any lengthy utterance from Mr. K., musical or not.

But the fact that Sam Kosminsky's singing voice was beautiful, liquid, sonorous—the voice of a Welshman, M.J. would have thought, had he not known different—made M.J. feel something akin to reverence.

"... *hamotzi lechem min ha'aretz. Amen.*"

After dinner, they played a game of Scrabble. Irma won. At seven, Mr. Kosminsky excused himself, shook M.J.'s hand, kissed his wife, and went to bed. M.J. helped Irma clean up.

"That was nice, Mrs. K.," M.J. said. "Thank you."

"He's not well, you know, my Sammy."

"He looks fine to me."

"At least he dresses like a live person. You want coffee?"

"Sure."

"I know, I know: You take it black. Go sit out there. I'll finish up."

M.J. went into the living room. He had expected Irma and Sam's apartment to be more colorful, more cluttered. He'd imagined knickknacks, souvenirs, pictures of grandchildren, things like that. M.J. assumed that most old married folks would have acquired a lot of stuff. A lifetime of it. But for a place occupied by a couple in their eighties, the apartment contained very little that was not strictly functional. There were a few books, some framed prints. On top of the TV, Irma and Sam looked out of one of those stiff studio photographs. It was a few years old; Mr. K. had aged considerably since it was taken, while Irma looked about the same. Maybe even younger.

In one corner of the room was a small glass-fronted cabinet; Maurice had spent the evening sleeping next to it, but when M.J. approached, he half-opened his chartreuse eyes. He hunkered down and slithered his tail. He growled.

"Piss off, you old fur sack," M.J. growled back. "I want nothing to do with you." Maurice dropped his feral act. He looked crestfallen.

M.J. drew closer to the cabinet. Inside was a menorah, a set of silver goblets, a chalice. On one shelf was a single, saucerless teacup.

"That belonged to my daughter," Irma said. She set down a tray containing two mugs of black coffee and a plate of Oreos. "Before that, it was mine when I was little. It was the only thing that made it out with me."

"Out?"

"Of Europe."

Irma walked across the room and stood next to M.J. She opened the cabinet door and spoke in a matter-of-fact tone. "I was thirty in '42. Lucie was five. We were playing dress-up, having a tea party. They dragged us out and put us on a truck. I never saw Albert—my first husband—again. Lucie died in a transit camp."

Irma reached into the cabinet and lifted out the teacup. It was bright green mostly, rimmed with a fancy gold leaf design; on one side, a white oval enclosed a painting of an orange bird sitting on a branch. "Isn't that something? A person can almost hear it singing." She grasped a fold of cloth at the front of her muumuu and used it to wipe the inside of the cup.

"Sam came with the Allies," she went on. "I was as good as dead. He was so kind to me. A gift. He saved my life, in more ways than one." She tilted the inside of the cup toward M.J. "See that? The little bouquet there at the bottom?"

M.J. nodded.

"Poppies, penstemon, larkspur, rosemary. You know about perennials?"

"No."

"They're hardy plants," Irma said, "easy to grow. They come back, year after year. But they won't grow inside. They have to have fresh air. Sunshine." She looked up at M.J. as if she were going to say something more. Instead, she replaced the cup in the cabinet and crossed the room to the television. She kept the volume on mute. "My Sammy is a light sleeper," Irma explained seriously—even though it was clear that Mr. Kosminsky was quite the opposite; M.J. could hear regular, reverberant snoring from behind the closed bedroom door.

They drank coffee, ate cookies, and watched *Jeopardy!* It was a rerun; Irma knew all the questions. After a few minutes, Maurice limped over. He looked up at M.J. with big, watery eyes, and then, with more grace than anyone would expect from a fat three-legged cat, he leapt into M.J.'s lap and began purring and farting in equal measure.

"Well, what do you know about that?" Irma said. "He likes you."

At seven-thirty on the dot, Irma walked M.J. to the door.

"Want some free advice?"

"Sure."

"You feel BLUE? Get up and DO!"

"I'll try and remember that," M.J. said.

He leaned down and kissed Irma on her rouged, papery cheek. Her eyes were green—the same green, M.J. realized, as Lucie's cup. She must have had her hair done recently; the skin at her forehead and around her eyebrows was tinged with orange.

"I want to see you in that shirt before I die!" she yelled, pushing him out the door. "And that could be any day now!"

Irma continued to pester him about the shirt. M.J. continued to dress in black.

Sam Kosminsky passed away a few weeks later. Among the funeral mourners were Rudy, many Aloha Lanes staff members and patrons, and M.J.—who chose this occasion to wear Mrs. Kosminsky's gift for the first time.

When Irma saw him—a one-man riot of pink and green in a sea of somber black—she laughed so hard she fell off her chair.

After that, M.J. wore the shirt on Tuesdays and Thursdays, Irma's bowling days—hoping that it would continue to have a cheering effect. For a while it seemed to work.

About a month after Sam died, however, Irma dropped out of The Hits and Missus. No one asked her to, of course, and there were numerous protestations, but Irma was resolute.

"A couples league is a couples league," she said. "I'd be a fifth wheel."

Her participation in the Tuesday morning Hadassah League declined as well. She'd show up, but oftentimes she either played halfheartedly and left early or didn't play at all; she'd sit, slumped, at the scorekeeper's desk, letting her cup of coffee get cold while the other ladies bowled. She stopped wearing lipstick.

One Tuesday, M.J. knocked on Rudy's door.

"Yeah. Come in." Rudy was in a bad mood; he was working on the books.

"I'm sorry to bother you but . . . Irma's not here."

Rudy looked up. "What?"

"Mrs. K. She's not here."

Rudy checked his watch. He frowned. He spun around in his desk chair and looked at the wall calendar behind him. He started massaging the top of his bald head in a circular pattern. He massaged with such vigor and rapidity that M.J. began to worry he might give himself a blister. He stopped. He swiveled back to face M.J.

"But it's Tuesday," Rudy said. He looked like a medieval monk who'd just heard a rumor that the world wasn't flat.

"I know, Rudy," M.J. answered.

Rudy yanked open his top desk drawer and threw his car keys at M.J. "Go."

"Are you sure?"

"Yes!" Rudy was out from behind his desk and striding toward the door. "I'll watch the front. Now go!"

M.J. was at Irma's door in less than five minutes. He rang. He knocked. He waited. He was just about to kick in the door when it opened. There was Irma. Alarmingly—for it was well after ten o'clock in the morning—she was still dressed in her bathrobe. She was not wearing makeup. Her hair was uncombed. Worst of all, her roots were showing.

"What are you doing here?" she mumbled.

"What are *you* doing here?" M.J. answered.

"I live here."

"It's Tuesday morning, Irma. You've got someplace to go."

"I don't feel well."

"I don't believe you."

"Go away. I'm tired."

"Let me fix you something to eat."

"I'm not hungry."

"Coffee, then. I'll make it black."

The joke fell flat. Irma shrugged, turned around, and shuffled into her bedroom.

Maurice limped into M.J.'s view. He stared up at him and uttered a single plaintive meow.

"What do you want, fur ball?" M.J. barked. He started for the kitchen, but Maurice meowed again, louder and even more pathetically. "What?"

Maurice scampered down the hall, his belly swinging freely from side to side. He stopped just short of Irma's bedroom door and turned around. M.J. sighed and followed. Maurice went into the bathroom. He planted himself underneath the sink and looked up at the medicine chest.

"You want me to open that?" M.J. said, and then muttered, "Fuck all. I'm talkin' to a deaf cat." But he walked across the room anyway and opened the medicine chest. Along with the prescription pain pills, toothpaste, denture adhesive, mouthwash, Ben-Gay, and milk of magnesia, there was a box of Garnier Nutrisse Conditioning Color Masque Number 68: "Luscious Mango."

M.J. opened the box and removed various bottles and tubes: "Conditioning Color Masque Developer," he read aloud. "After-Color Conditioner with fruit extracts. Colorant. Fruit Oil Concentrate." He opened the instructions, to which a pair of clear latex gloves had been adhered. "Well, would you look at that! Isn't that clever?"

M.J. sat down on the toilet seat lid and began to read; he emphasized the most vital bits of information to himself by reading aloud: "'Never leave tip closed after mixing; the container might burst.' Jesus! 'Do not point either end of tube toward the face while opening or using.' 'If any mixture gets on your skin, dip a towel in shampoo and gently remove stain before continuing. . . .'" After a while, Maurice settled himself on the floor near M.J.'s feet and fell asleep.

When M.J. was sure he understood the procedure, he got up, gathered some bath towels, and began filling the sink with warm water.

"Irma," he called, snapping on the latex gloves, "get in here! We're going to by God infuse your lovely hair with lasting color and fragrant fruit oil!"

M.J. did not quit his job at the Aloha Lanes. Nor did he leave Seattle. Six months came and went without comment, and over time M.J.'s paychecks began to reflect a steady, substantial raise. Without being asked, he took on more responsibilities—including employee scheduling, firing, and hiring. He was good at it, which surprised him at first. Eventually he figured out that it was because—unlike Rudy, bless his heart, who saw only the best in everybody—he had an unerring eye for wankers. Furthermore, he didn't give a rat's ass if people liked him or not.

Rudy's incipient ulcer went into remission. And since he no longer had to function as a one-man Human Resources Department, he was able to focus his creative and managerial efforts on the resurrection of the Aloha Lanes. He secured a bank loan. He replaced the carpet. He got the fountain working. He installed a light show, fog machines, a new sound system. In order to attract a new generation of bowlers, he implemented "Rock 'n' Roll Bowl" on Friday nights—with a professional DJ and shows at ten and midnight.

"How can we get more families in here?" Rudy asked M.J.. "You know, people with young children."

"Make a playroom for their kids. It wouldn't take much. I could buy some toys and stuff at the Thriftko."

"We could put it in the newsletter, too; I bet we'd get lots of donations." So the two of them cleared out a large storage room and transformed it into a child care center. M.J. found a social services agency that helped place teenagers in decent jobs, and he hired a couple of good girls to run it.

Rudy instituted a no-smoke policy on weekends. He added things like Gardenburgers, Tofu Dogs, and Caesar salads to the menu. He bought an espresso machine. Business picked up.

Irma eventually returned to her lipsticked, coiffed, and colorful self. M.J. did her hair on a regular basis. He accompanied her on trips to the grocery store, pharmacy, and veterinarian. They shared dinner at Irma's place four nights a week. She showed up at the Aloha, either to bowl or socialize, nearly every day; when she didn't, M.J. or Rudy called to make sure she was all right.

M.J.'s Hawaiian shirt collection grew until it acquired legendary status. Nearly everyone in the Aloha community contributed at one time or another. Sometimes the shirts arrived, gift-wrapped, on major holidays; Irma, of course, remained the major benefactress, presenting M.J. with shirts on Rosh Hashanah, Yom Kippur, Chanukah, Passover, Veterans Day, St. Patrick's Day, and the Fourth of July, and other members of the Aloha Lanes brought gifts in observance of occasions like Christmas, Valentine's Day, and Halloween. Most of the time, though, M.J. would arrive at work on a nondesignated holiday to find yet another shirt on the front desk, sometimes with a note, sometimes without.

"And what have we got here?" he'd yell to the clientele at large. "Are we celebratin' Be Kind to Lapsed Catholics Day?"

Before long, M.J.'s black wardrobe was crammed into the back of his closet. He had so many Hawaiian shirts that he could wear a different one every day for weeks in a row. His favorite shirt, however, remained the first one Irma bought him.

"When will you bowl with me?" Irma demanded. Having transformed M.J.'s wardrobe, she had made it her new mission to appropriate his leisure time. More to the point, Irma had rejoined The Hits and Missus and was actively recruiting a regular partner.

"It'll never happen, Irma," M.J. replied. "I'm strictly a spectator."

"Never say never!" she said.

They had similar conversations about religion.

"Come with me to shul. What could it hurt?"

"Irma—"

"Be quiet. If somebody like ME can believe in God, what's YOUR excuse?"

M.J. had no answer for that. But the question continued to intrigue him.

Without meaning to, M.J. Striker had become a resident of somewhere. He'd acquired a family and a colorful wardrobe. He was no longer invisible.

Twenty-two

❧

An Atheist on Easter, 1997

Fɪʀsᴛ, know this: A disbelief in God does not mandate a rejection of ritual. Atheists have traditions too. Like many people on this day, you have observances to make, spiritual concepts to ponder, prayers to recite.

Services are conveniently held in the privacy of your own basement apartment and while you're still in your Skivvies, for your church has a congregation of one. Commencing with the solemn uncapping of a good ale purchased specially for this occasion, you fill a tumbler and drink it down. Since Easter is the only day on which you partake of your native brew (or of *any* alcoholic beverage, for that matter, and here's another stereotype blasted to dust: Not all atheists are godless anarchists and not all Irishmen are drunks), in a manner of minutes you're thoroughly squiffed.

The invocation of the ale is followed with a ritual poetry reading, taken from the book you've chosen as your scripture, your book of common prayer. The poem's title is "Easter 1916," and among many, many other things it commemorates a famous uprising in your homeland. It is the greatest poem of the twentieth century.

You refill your glass, clear your throat, and begin to recite for no one in the clearest, most sonorous voice you can manage: "'I have met them at close of day, coming with vivid faces . . .'"

The reading reminds you of sacrifices bigger and more lofty than the ones you've made: "'I have passed with a nod of the head, or polite meaningless words, or have lingered awhile and said polite meaningless words . . .'"

The poem is about transfiguration—what better subject to contemplate on this day?—and how the deaths of plain folk made martyrs of them and caused others to cast off their motley wear and change: "'Transformed utterly,'" as the poet says, "A terrible beauty is born.'"

The poem is about misjudgment, too. Regret and redemption: "'He had done most bitter wrong to some who are near my heart, yet I number him in the song; he, too, has resigned his part in the casual comedy . . .'"

You are nothing like these martyrs, nor like those who came after, transformed, and took up their cause. This poem does not memorialize your uprising, your self-annihilation. Your courage is a pale watery thing, your love petty—the narrow love of one man for a spirit-ravaged, sorrowful woman—and your sacrifice is laid on the altar of romantic obsession. But you read because it's Easter—by Christ, that's the title— and because the greatest poem of the twentieth century was set down in English by a man bred in Dublin city and the sea cliffs of Sligo, and isn't that one of the best jokes Himself ever played? (This is another thing people don't appreciate about the atheistic sensibility: You don't have to believe in God to talk about him, for God's sake.)

"'Too long a sacrifice can make a stone of the heart. O when may it suffice? . . .'" You're near the end. This is the section that is hardest to bear, harder still to read aloud with composure. "'That is heaven's part, our part to murmur name upon name, As a mother names her child when sleep at last has come On limbs that had run wild . . .'" Your eyes are almost blind with tears begot of these names and the memory of others: "'I write it out in a verse—MacDonagh and MacBride and Connolly and Pearse . . .'" *and Virginia and Maureen, and our sweet faerie wand. . . .*

Besotted with weeping, as well as brew, you close the good book and go back to bed.

And thus the service endeth.

Hours later, you reawaken, take a shower, make coffee. The main event is over; you ponder how to proceed. There are things you won't

do on this day, that's sure; avoiding certain activities constitutes a less
formal but still integral element of your holiday tradition. For example,
you won't turn on your 10-inch black-and-white television for fear of
being assaulted by a young, sweet-faced Judy Garland, wearing a hat
as big as a tent and singing the theme from *Easter Parade*. You won't
venture within earshot of an alleluia. You won't gather with friends at
a restaurant for brunch. You'll avoid eye contact with little girls wearing hair ribbons, floral dresses, white tights, and shiny black patent
leather shoes.

You might consider calling your only sister in Chicago, saying hello,
and talking about something safe, like the weather; Midwesterners love
to talk about the weather. You could inquire after your sister's health,
her husband's health, the health and whereabouts of her eight biological children—and her only niece.

This plan sounds too redemptive. You light a Lucky Strike and put
it out of your mind.

Then you remember your commitments to your boss. You remind
yourself of your duties as an amateur hairstylist. You recall the admo-
nition of a certain Jewish matron and friend, a person you consider a
martyr in her own way: "You feel BLUE? Get up and DO!"

In the end, you're not very original. You dress in the most god-awful
Hawaiian shirt in your collection—a gift from the martyr, it's your
hands-down favorite—leave your apartment, and start walking with
purpose. You behave like every other idiot who's desperate to believe
that the lost will be found, the sinners will be redeemed, and the dead
beloved—arisen and full in earthly flesh—will find their way back to
your arms. In short, you end up at the church of your choice, because
no prayer in the world comforts your soul like the sound of someone
bowling a strike.

It was one of those cool, early spring nights. The quiet that followed
closing time would make it hard to sleep, especially tonight, so M.J.
threw on a coat, belted it loosely over Irma's shirt, and headed south for
a walk. Other people were out walking—spring fever was his guess—
so 85th and Greenwood was busier than usual for this time of night, and
a Sunday, too.

Across the street in front of the record store, a young couple was quarreling. Even though M.J. couldn't see the lovers' faces or understand what they were saying, it was a sure thing that the girl was roundly pissed off about something, and her sweetheart was trying to jolly her out of it. There was wildness and strength in her lithe body. She kept fluttering against his trunk and limbs, pushing away from him one moment, inclining toward him the next. M.J. saw in an instant what a pair they made. *Linnet's wings and laurel tree,* he thought, hoping against hope that they knew what they had and would do whatever needed doing to keep it close.

At 85th he turned around and started back uptown. He didn't look at the couple again; they'd loosed a feeling in his gut, spiraling now and gaining momentum, and even though he could easily dredge up a poem to shape that feeling into artful expression, he'd had enough of Mr. Yeats for one day, enough poetry, enough bloody feeling—*Can't you for one blessed minute give it a rest, man?*—so he sank his head between his shoulders, looked down, and skulked north on Greenwood like an asshole trying to leave without paying.

He'd gone half a block when he heard shouting: a name, he thought, but the name was not his.

Suddenly a car gave voice to some unlucky horror: There was a prolonged, desperate shriek of braking tires. Any fool within earshot knew how that sound would end. M.J. ratcheted his eyes shut and waited—for the crush of steel, the shattering of glass. But there was no crash—only a terrible arrhythmia in the city's heartbeat, paralyzed breath, a battlefield silence.

Then people started screaming. M.J. turned around. He was sorry when he did.

She was lying in the middle of the street. Probably dead. Had to be, or dying. She wore the remnants of a fancy black dress.

The street was stilled and numb with aftershock until a young man bolted toward her, running like a soldier to a fallen comrade in the field, skidding on his knees to where she lay, draping his coat over her—and when M.J. saw them, spotlit in the pink-smeared headlights of the SUV that looked obscenely big, big as a tank, he realized who they were. *Oh Christ,* he thought, *it's that girl and her boyo and they'll never be able to patch things up now. Poor bloody bastard. Poor son of a bitch.*

He stepped off the curb and started toward them, but then a middle-aged woman stumbled out of the SUV, pale, shaking, barely able to walk. She shuffled toward the girl, muttering, her eyes glazed, and M.J. veered away from the lovers and took her by the shoulders, fixing her at a safe distance and blocking her view, taking off his coat and wrapping it around her, making her sit on the curb because she was going into shock. He said words to her, stupid, meaningless words, but the only ones that came to mind: "You're all right, missus. It will be all right."

There was the sound of more doors opening then and he looked up to a sight like a clown car at a Shriners parade: They tumbled out from all sides, an entire soccer team, boys they were, a dozen of them maybe and young, too young to be in the middle of this, looking for all the world like Dublin lads after a proud hard-won game of hurley, dirtied faces and scraped knees and still wearing their black and white jerseys. They walked silently, slowly toward the dying girl—as if some ill-intentioned hypnotist were reeling them in—and formed a circle around her, some of them dumbstruck, others choking back sobs, all transfixed.

Suddenly, unbelievably, the girl started flailing her crushed hands and trying to make sounds. *Holy Christ,* M.J. thought, his guts churning in sympathy, *she's not dead, she's not even unconscious, those boys can't be there,* and he rushed over then, knowing all about boys, the roughened bluff outsides that mask the tenderest of underbellies, how they march into places where they shouldn't go and then are too ashamed to lead themselves out. He knew what they needed now: to be told what to do, to have rules and a straw boss. He moved among them and steered them away, not roughly, but with the firmness of a father, he hoped, because that's who he had to be now, that was what was being asked of him and he would take it up, the cause of fatherhood, just this once, and stand in for all the absent fathers of all these hapless boys. Their das would not want them to see, to know—and neither did he—how easy it is for these bodies of ours to be utterly ruined.

"Boyos!" He forced each one to look into his eyes. "Come here now, boys, come away, over here. I need yous all to listen. That lady over there, is she somebody's mum?"

A shaky voice spoke up, "She's my mom, sir," and a boy with thick, smudged glasses stepped to the front. "She didn't mean to . . . That girl, she ran right in front of us and my mom—"

"I know that, son. Listen now. Your mom really needs you. Go sit with her, can you do that? Get her talking, about anything. Make sure she stays warm. A couple more of yous," he said, pointing, "go with him. Is there a cell phone in the van? You, son, go get it and call the police."

And so he went on, talking to them, mobilizing them, keeping them occupied until the paramedics and officers arrived. When they did, he stepped out of the street and took his place in the shadows. He hadn't seen what happened. There was nothing more for him to do. Still, he couldn't make himself leave. He stood there forever, even after the ambulance pulled away and the scene started to clear. No one noticed him. No one questioned his loitering presence.

His coat lay in the street where it had dropped unnoticed from the woman's shoulders when she got up and spoke with the officers. The night was well on—it was chilly damp now—and he stepped off the curb to retrieve it.

There was something else in the street too, and just then another figure moved like the dead out of the shadows from the other side and bent down to pick it up: It was the girl's shoe, a foolish high-heeled thing, the kind of shoe a woman wears when she has no faith in her own beauty. M.J. wondered again about the girl, what her reasons were for wearing that kind of fancy getup, in this neighborhood, on this night.

Her sweetheart cradled the shoe carefully in his two hands, as if it were a relic made of finest glass. And then he started to weep.

He was the only one here who knew her name, thought M.J. *Poor boyo. Poor dear lad.*

He could have easily taken up the cause at that moment too—he could have stood in for this young man's da, put an arm around him, led him to the nearest pub and bought him a beer and listened to his sad, sad story. He wanted to, in fact, and that surprised him.

But a police officer walked over to him—an older, heavier man who surely had more experience at this kind of thing—and laid a surrogate hand on the young man's shoulder, so M.J. turned away and headed north.

Easter.

Bloody hell.

He should never have come out in the first place.

PART

THREE

Twenty-three

Post-ORIF

The language of medicine is varied and precise when it comes to skeletal fractures and orthopedic repair. As an example, let's say that a small-boned person with impaired judgment and stiletto heels ran into a busy intersection and was struck by an SUV being driven at 30 mph by a woman chauffeuring her son and his victorious soccer team to Pagliacci's Pizza. This unfortunate person would almost certainly incur bilateral Colles' fractures of the wrists upon impact. Other injuries might be comminuted, compressed, avulsed, compacted, blown out, and so on.

The professionals treating our patient would schedule her for "reduction"; this involves restoring a bone to its normal anatomical position and alignment. The manner in which a fracture is reduced depends upon its severity: In less serious cases, repair is accomplished without surgical intervention; when a fractured bone projects through the skin, however, it is fixed by an "open reduction with internal fixation," or "ORIF." Since our patient's injuries are especially severe, her body will be literally retrofitted—in much the same way structural engineers fortify buildings, bridges, and homes in earthquake-prone cities—through the insertion of steel rods, compression screws, wires, nails, pins, plates, and adhesives.

The hospital staff who treated Wanda when she was brought into the ER as a "pedestrian versus SUV" were presented with a smorgasbord of orthopedic challenges. There were many X-rays taken of Patient Schultz over the course of her hospital stay—X-rays obtained to confirm appropriate positioning of the orthopedic hardware and to assess for evidence of healing. On one occasion, a radiologist reading a standard three-view exam of her right forearm noticed a subtle detail, one that his colleagues had either overlooked or considered unremarkable.

He dictated, "Incidentally noted is very slight palmar angulation at the distal radial epiphysis, suggesting evidence of a remote trauma with malalignment and/or nonunion. One wonders, did the patient break her arm as a child?"

It is often said, in consolatory tones, that "time heals all wounds." But radiologists, who study and interpret physical proofs of the body's ability to store memory, know that this is a crock of shit.

In the first weeks following the accident, Wanda slept; and while her physical body was tended by medical professionals, everything else—those aspects of her which could not be X-rayed, measured, laboratory-tested, or clinically assessed—was overseen and controlled by other entities, chiefly her dreaming self: a self which had been so long silenced, neglected, and relegated to the brain's cramped, under-the-table places that, once freed, it poured forth its messages nonstop.

Wanda's dream-self knew her helplessness and had no compunction about turning this to an advantage. It was relentless. It showed no mercy. Wanda—unconscious, immobile, unable to resist—could do nothing but watch as images were played out on the screen behind her closed eyes. The stories told by her dream-self were not structured in the long, smooth, leisurely, wide-screen Cinerama way of a movie epic. Uninterested in truth, beauty, accuracy, chronology, or narrative flow, Wanda's dream-self was a historical revisionist with a handheld camera and an unlimited budget. Wanda was forced to watch and participate in a nightmare, a horror film with endless variations on one theme:

But I'm not meant to be an actor! she wanted to yell, as an unseen director cast her in production after production: as Eliza in *My Fair Lady,* Wendy in *Peter Pan,* Perdita in *The Winter's Tale.* The productions were underrehearsed, the dressing spaces were inadequate, she had no stage makeup, her costumes were the wrong size. She was clumsy, ill-prepared, the set pieces were flimsy, the doorjambs too low—the sets were built for children, it seemed, or for midgets—and she kept bumping her head, tripping, stumbling around like a colorless, unfunny clown. There was no privacy, her humiliation was public, the actors and actresses—some of them famous, all of them more beautiful and competent than she— were crowded together in the dressing rooms. The audience saw all the flaws. The wiring was faulty. There were no lights at the makeup tables. Where was her Cleopatra wig? How was she supposed to get out of a corset without help? How could she manage such quick costume changes? Why were there crayons and paint tubes and glue sticks and cracked coffee cups rolling all over her dressing table? Where was her lipstick? Where was she supposed to hang up her dress?

I'm calling the union! she longed to shout. *I'm going to report this! You're in violation of Equity rules!*

But she was the only one who cared. Everyone else regarded her as a pain in the ass, a diva without a diva's talent. Backstage, it was dark, so dark. It was dangerous. The set was hazardous, unorganized, a free-for-all. Where were the Equity lights? Who was the stage manager? And they hadn't rehearsed the "Rain in Spain" number! A pivotal turning point in the character's development! The showstopper! The audience was already out there, waiting, waiting for her. Could she even do the dance steps? The high kicks? And the singing! She had no musical background. Her voice was untrained, weak, it couldn't possibly carry to the back row. No one would hear her. Everyone would know that she'd been miscast. Someone else should be doing the lead. Maybe they'd throw things at her. Tomatoes and plates. Where was she supposed to stand? Where did she enter from? Where was she supposed to go? What was her blocking? Why did everyone else know their place onstage? And flying? She'd have to fly? No, surely not, her harness was ill-fitting, too loose; but suddenly she was up there, way up by the lighting instruments that were cold, turned off, up in a black starless sky, and she was looking down into the open jaws of hundreds, thousands of empty seats, and then she was falling, falling, with no net, no one to catch her. Where were the techies? The Flying Foys? They were supposed to be the best, but they'd abandoned her! Where was the father? The paterfamilias? Peter Foy? Troy? Where were the well-trained airographers? And then she was hoisted up again, and dropped, and hoisted, and dropped.

Who's manning this operation? she wanted to know. *Aren't you supposed to die if you fall in your dreams? Am I dead already?*

And the venues, they were so large, the largest she'd ever seen, like Greek amphitheaters, Shakespeare's Globe, like the outdoor theatres she'd heard about in the South, where whole communities gathered to see the crucifixion of Christ, the resurrection. Where hundreds of towns-folk acted out the story of the Passion Play.

Finally, she realized the truth: *She* was the stage manager. It was all her fault. She'd put on a costume, forgotten to do her job, and now she was suffering the consequences. No one had walked the set. No one had scheduled rehearsals. She deserved whatever she got.

I'm not meant to be an actor! Wanda tried to scream, over and over. But her mouth would not open. It was a cage, and she was trapped inside.

The outward effects of this dreaming were evident—Wanda often cried as she slept, tried to move or make sounds. These physiologic activities were comforting to the doctors and nurses. They were proof of brain activity, a near-sure promise that consciousness would one day return to this young woman in whom they had invested so much of their time and skill.

Her colleagues and housemates too were heartened by these signs of life—Margaret and Troy more than anyone. But the two of them recognized these signs as symptomatic of an untreatable sadness and isolation, and their relief was tempered by a terrible impotence. Wanda was in another country, one without access, one from which she could not be rescued. She would have to find her own way out. She would have to come to them.

When she finally opened her eyes, for reasons both physical and pharmaceutical, she still could not move or speak. Her legs, arms, and pelvis had undergone numerous open reduction/internal fixation procedures and were immobilized by casting material; fractures to her mandible and facial bones made it necessary for her jaw to be wired shut. Her needs for food and water were met intravenously. Percocet minimized her pain; it also kept her in a continuous, sedated haze. She was unable to write her affirmation.

Over time, she slept less. She started taking in more of the waking world:

Sounds came first—the drone of hospital noises, electrical beeps and burps; a Muzak of voices. Doctors and nurses. Chatty visitors. She preferred to tune out content. Being unable to speak had given her a new relationship with words. She had a disdain for those who required them—a disdain which included her former self and all the cajoling commanding handling vocabulary she had used her whole life, all the ways she had labored with language to get the misbehavers to behave, the intractable to give a little, the fighters to make peace, the deserters to stay, the sons-of-bitches to do the right thing—and she had a new appreciation for those who could do quite nicely without. It was a relief, really, to be free of words. A relief to be silent.

Then came blurs of color, reflected light. Just as Wanda preferred to block out the content of sounds, so she refrained from focusing her sight in a way that delineated form. She liked the way matter blurred together so that whatever or whoever was in the room had no identity, no hard edges. Just an opus of color.

Nevertheless, sometimes content came through. Sometimes words and images took on more distinct shapes.

Taking care of that. Margaret speaking. *Medical bills come to me.*

Internal damage. One of the doctors. *Possible infertility.*

Everyone at the theatre. Blah-blah. Actors. Directors. *Miss you! Job waiting! Can't wait!*

Bruce has joined us. Margaret again. *Marvelous cook! Everything ready when you get home.*

Frequently, at night, she heard hollow spasms of breath: a man, sobbing. At other times she woke to see a still, shadowy figure in the bedside chair or standing guard at the window. Once she awoke to feel his face close to hers on the pillow, her skin warmed by his breath.

Come back, babe, the figure whispered. *Don't run away.*

Eventually, with medical attention, physical therapy, and time, Wanda regained full consciousness. She recovered some mobility and strength. She learned to maneuver a wheelchair. When she felt up to it, she could peregrinate slowly with the help of a walker. Her hands and arms once out of casts were free to flutter. Her bodily pain, although never completely absent, subsided. She was occasionally able to abandon prescription drugs—and their numbing effects—for over-the-counter ibuprofen. Her jaw could once again open and close—in a limited and painful way—and she could eat solid foods, if she chose. She had the ability to talk.

But for reasons not attributable to medical science or understood by her professional caregivers, Wanda chose to remain mute. She communicated through the use of facial expressions, or a simple nod or shake of her head. On the infrequent occasions when words were required, she scrawled her responses on a yellow legal pad. And in order to clarify her choice to those with whom she was unacquainted, she hung a sign around her neck.

"Not deaf," the sign said. "Mute by choice."

"Do you like it?" Margaret asked.

The current residents of the Hughes mansion were standing in the hall outside the first-floor guest quarters, otherwise known as the Aviary Suite—or rather, Margaret, Gus, Susan, Bruce, and Margaret's mother were standing; Wanda was sitting in her wheelchair. Everyone waited.

Wanda nodded wanly, but affably. She wheeled in. No one quite knew what to do next.

"Maybe you'd like to be alone for a while?" Margaret suggested.

Wanda's back was to them. She seemed to be looking out of the large bay window. It was a rainy July evening, still light outside.

"All right then!" Margaret plowed ahead. Turning to the rest of them, she half-whispered, "Why don't you all go ahead. I'll join you in a minute." She extended her arms and made expansive sweeping movements, as if she were a Canadian mother goose herding the goslings to another part of the picnic grounds.

Then, having shooed the living away from Wanda's door, Margaret gripped the edge of the door frame, took a deep breath, and prepared to deal with her mother—who had not only slipped into Wanda's room, but was now nestled among the pillows on the window seat. She looked disturbingly comfortable, as if she were planning to either take a lengthy nap or read the collected works of Leo Tolstoy.

She's in a bad way, your wounded bird, Margaret's mother remarked, airily.

Margaret ignored her and spoke to Wanda's unmoving silhouette.

"Is there anything I can get you, Tink?"

A length of rope? Margaret's mother prodded. *Some sleeping pills?*

Margaret forged on. "I hope you don't mind us moving your things downstairs. It just seemed as though this room would be more convenient."

Margaret's mother gazed out the window. *Too bad it's on the first floor,* she remarked.

"I'd be happy to fix you a plate and bring it in," Margaret continued through gritted teeth. "Bruce cooked the most marvelous meal."

Did he season it with strychnine?

"We're a completely vegetarian household now, did I tell you?"

Oh, really, Margaret! The girl needs psychiatric help, not lentil loaf.

Margaret advanced brusquely into the room and installed herself between her mother and Wanda. "The room is all right, isn't it? Will you feel comfortable here?"

Wanda looked up, her face a blank.

Be realistic, Margaret. The girl can't possibly stay. You must know that. Look at her. She's a basket case! Looney Tunes! She belongs in a bughouse!

Margaret spun around and began fluffing the window seat pillows aggressively. Her mother, unbudging, regarded Margaret with saintly tolerance. She reached out and traced her delicate fingers along the contours of a porcelain figurine which sat on a nearby table.

Your father was particularly enamored with this piece. He bragged about it, the way he bragged about everything. "What finds!" your father would say. "What treasures! Don't you understand? They'd go to waste if it weren't for me."

The figurine was a white porcelain parrot from the Meissen factory, c. 1739, one of the works of a gifted artist named Johann Kandler. He was famous for his attention to naturalistic detail. The bird was life-sized, about twelve inches tall, and so true-to-life that whenever Margaret tended it— on alternate Fridays—she always expected it to speak. But it never did.

Your father felt that Germans had no innate sense of delicacy or poetry, no ability to appreciate anything fine. "That's one thing I'll give the kikes," he'd say. *"At least some of them have decent taste. But the krauts! They're all Sturm und Drang, sig heil, and sausages. It makes me sick to think of the goods they must have smashed on Kristallnacht! What a waste."*

The figurine was in perfect condition and, if Margaret recalled correctly—she was cursed with a near-photographic memory when it came to the inventory and assessment of these things—it was most recently valued at nine thousand dollars.

Your father did enjoy German women, however, Margaret's mother continued. *He liked to remind me that the typical German hausfrau could make him come in thirty seconds flat. He even fucked the occasional German Jew. I don't believe those encounters were consensual, but I'm sure your father enjoyed them just as much, if not more.*

Margaret snatched the figurine and smashed it on the floor.

Well! Margaret's mother said, sitting up. *If you're going to start that again, I'm leaving.* She swiveled off the window seat and swooped toward the door. *Be sure to check the room for razor blades before you leave!*

Margaret leaned against the table. She was out of breath, her forehead was clammy, her balance unsteady. When she was able to speak again, she muttered, "*Quelle dommage.*"

Wanda looked up. Her eyes focused, brightened. The fixed bones of her skull appeared to shift subtly. The overlying skin softened and pinked. The muscles of Wanda's face, Margaret gradually realized, were trying to remember how to smile. She reached down and took one of Wanda's hands. Her skeleton felt dense and weighty now, no longer the hollow, crisp infrastructure of a creature designed for flight.

"I'll get the glue, shall I? In case you feel like doing some fixing."

Wanda sat in her wheelchair, unmoving, absorbing a sense of being present with something completely exotic, almost naughty—*what was it?*—something to which she had not had access for what felt like an eternity. Was it a quality of sound? Something about this room?

She was alone, that was it. It was that simple. And she could stay alone as long as she wished. Forever, if she wanted. That long.

She had to pee. The bathroom seemed impossibly far away. She tugged her backpack onto her lap and started wheeling across the room, bumping into the furniture (*Ha!* she thought. *Like a bad actor!*) and slowing to a crawl each time the chair dragged over one of the oriental rugs.

The door leading to the bathroom had been widened. Inside, there were more changes. The claw-foot tub had been removed and there was an enlarged shower stall at floor level with a built-in seat and handheld shower unit. The sink and medicine cabinet had been lowered. Metal bars had been affixed to newly tiled walls. *It's handicapped-accessible,* Wanda marveled. Her astonishment was bipartite: half for the realization that she was the handicapped person for whom the bathroom had been remodeled, half for the fact that Margaret must have hired someone to make these alterations—*And for a tenant, for chrissake. A boarder.*

The enormity of Margaret's kindness engulfed her, not as a comfort, but as a shroud. She dumped her backpack on the floor and hoisted herself onto the toilet. She peed. She pushed herself off the toilet and back into the chair. She wheeled to the sink and washed her hands. She stared at her face in the medicine cabinet glass.

The bruises and swelling were gone. There were no overt traces of the damage that had occurred under her skin. No sutures. No disfiguring scars. Most people would have considered that lucky. But her face now had a brittle fixedness and asymmetry—as if she were wearing a malformed, degenerating rubber mask. She reached into her backpack and pulled out one of her black markers. Slowly, she drew a heavy black circle around her reflection and spoke to the face in the mirror:

"You. Are. Here."

She opened the medicine chest. Someone—Margaret again, probably—had thoughtfully stocked it with all her medications, including the last of her Percocet. Wanda pulled out the bottle. She gave it a rattle. She regarded it with detachment.

It wouldn't take much, she thought. *It wouldn't take many.*

Margaret stopped in the entrance to the dining room. Classical music was playing softly. Laid out on the table were five, gleaming, mismatched place settings; Bruce and Susan had spent days scouring thrift stores in search of antique china and glassware especially for the occasion of Wanda's homecoming. Gus had instructed them all in the art of napkin folding, and each setting was graced with a white linen swan.

From the kitchen came the workaday sounds of final premeal preparations: busy feet, cupboards opening and closing, serving utensils being set against platters, questions, answers—the bustle of a well-organized informal workforce. A family. Margaret stood quietly, marveling at the miracle of these sounds in this house.

"Hello?" she called finally. "Where is everyone?"

Instantly, the swinging door inched open and Bruce peeked out, cheeks florid, chef's hat askew. "Well?" he said, edgily. When mealtime was imminent, he often exuded the nervous energy of a milling multitude. The door opened farther and Margaret saw Gus and Susan, attendant with platters, flush-faced and eager, putting her in mind of Santa's elves.

"I think we should go ahead without her. I'm sorry, dear. I know you worked especially hard on this meal."

Bruce sagged, a limp meringue, but when his assistants burst through the door and plunked their serving dishes on the table—Susan lisping jauntily, in a spot-on impersonation of a Southern belle, "Well, all I can say is, that child is goin' to regret it!" and Gus proclaiming, "Absolutely splendid!"—he puffed up like reconstituted potato flakes.

There were a few more minutes of back-and-forth between kitchen and dining room as more plates were delivered to the table, followed by a great clumping of heavy oak chairs as they settled at table—making them sound like a diminutive but dogged herd of migrating bison.

Then they turned to Bruce—who had taken up a formal stance behind his chair—and gave him the kind of hushed attention that might have preceded the Sermon on the Mount. He donned his reading glasses and snapped a piece of paper out of his pocket.

"As prologue," he began, "we have Brie and Hazelnut Bakes. . . ."

Meals—especially dinner—had become quite an event. There were naturally nights when Margaret's appetite failed—she took medications for edema, seizures, blood clots, etc., and their side effects occasionally left her feeling no desire for food—but she never failed to show up at the table, even if only long enough to savor Bruce's menu recitations.

". . . Our soup is Iced Melon with Violets, very mild, very cleansing. . . ."

Although Bruce still retained his round contours, Margaret was sure that he'd grown lighter in the months since the day of his interview.

He'd chosen Bon Bon, a small room on the third floor. When asked why he preferred this to one of the larger rooms on the second floor, he said, "Ma'am, I'm a fat, single, gay, depressed, Jewish boy from Alpharetta, Georgia. When I'm not cooking, I need to be as far away from a refrigerator as possible. If I do happen to get an uncontrollable urge in the wee small hours of the night to confuse food with love, at least I'll have to carry myself down and up three flights of stairs to do it."

That was Easter Sunday. It seemed a lifetime ago.

After the accident, Margaret suggested that he reconsider. "The mood around here is going to be awfully dreary." She could barely speak. No one at that time believed that Wanda would live. "Not the best for someone who's . . ."

". . . fat, gay, depressed, and Jewish?" he prompted, taking her hand. "No ma'am. I'm still movin' in. Y'all are gonna need good food now more than ever."

Maybe because he'd come to them during such dire times and nourished them at a cellular level, she had a special fondness for him.

He concluded his reading—"Ginger Cake with Lemon Icing and a Mandarin Orange Curaçao Sorbet"—and Susan began clapping her hands with genteel enthusiasm.

"All hail the gustatory Jew!" she huzzahed. Gus and Margaret joined in.

Bruce blushed. "Oh, y'all stop now." He tucked away the paper, and—as Susan stood to light the candles—began to sing the blessing.

Wanda opened her bottle of pills and poured them into her hand. They were scored through the middle. She broke one. She broke another. All. Now there were twice as many. They filled both hands. She reached out and sprinkled them among the white porcelain pieces on the carpet. Outside and inside, the gray light darkened. Wanda did not turn on a lamp. She lowered herself to the floor. She scooped up handfuls of pills and porcelain.

No glue, she thought. *So many choices.*

In the other room, she paused to listen to the low, indecipherable tones of conversational speech. Laughter. The startling sound of a male voice lifted in song.

"It's bound to take some getting used to, being back here," Gus was saying. He dabbed delicately at a bit of béchamel sauce on his mustache. "So many changes."

"Do you think she'll stay?" Susan asked.

"I'm not sure that she has anywhere else to go," Margaret replied. "And anyway, at this point she doesn't really have a choice."

"Poor wee thing," Gus added.

They stared at their plates. The doorbell rang.

Susan spoke up. "I'll bet half a crown it's someone selling the *Encyclopaedia Britannica*."

"Girl Scout Cookies!" said Bruce.

"The King James Bible," Gus offered.

"Cemetery plots!" Margaret hollered, laughing.

"NOT FUNNY!" they all hollered back.

"Party poopers." She bit into a ginger-glazed carrot stick for emphasis. "I'll get it."

On the way, she paused to listen at Wanda's door; all was quiet within.

Troy stood on the porch, a wide-brimmed hat in one hand and a yellow bouquet in the other. His oilskin coat glistened with water droplets, and his face and hair were damp. "Troy, dear!" Margaret said, more loudly than necessary. "Please, come in. I'm so glad to see you."

She ushered him into the dining room. "Look who I found! Out on a night like this!"

Troy's arrival produced an unusual effect: Anyone who didn't know better would have thought they hadn't seen him in years, and they showered him with a prodigal's welcome of hugs and back-claps. "Please don't let me interrupt dinner," he protested, but they were already flying into action: Susan scurried to the laundry for towels, Bruce vanished to the kitchen, and Margaret set tasks for Gus—would he please fetch epoxy from the pantry and retrieve the boxed-up remains of her wedding china?

"I just stopped by after work," Troy said. "Really, ma'am, I wasn't intending to stay."

"Don't be silly." Margaret pulled an ironstone Mason pitcher off a shelf and began filling it with water. "I'm sure she wants to see you." Her mother had returned; she was lurking in the corner of the dining room and assessing Troy's physique in an entirely inappropriate manner. It was downright beady. Margaret shot her a twitchy, sour look. "Let's get those lovely flowers into this pitcher," she said pointedly. "I'm sure Wanda will love them."

The others came back to the dining room and recommenced their fussing over Troy. Before they could abduct him to the table, however,

Margaret broke in. "Would you please take these things in to Wanda?" she asked, gesturing toward the box and epoxy.

"Sure." When Troy took up the box, it rattled with the unmistakable sound of broken contents, and his face reflected mild alarm.

"Don't worry, dear," Margaret said. "Wanda will know what to do with that."

"See if you can get her to come out," said Bruce. "I made enough food for the Army Corps of Engineers."

"But please," Margaret whispered, "don't hurry." She took Troy by the shoulders, turned him around, and gave him a small push in the direction of the Aviary Suite.

Cream was drizzled into cups with chipped handles. Sugar cubes were plunked and stirred. Fork tines chimed mildly against mismatched plates. Dessert spoons dawdled over melting spheres of sorbet. They nibbled. They sipped. They steered clear of certain subjects. They watched the clock.

Finally, Gus spoke. "They're probably playing Monopoly."

Margaret gave a violent, imploded snigger, sending a mouthful of ginger tea up her nose and setting off laughter all around. Even Gus let loose with a series of staid yuks.

After they all helped clean up, they started for their respective rooms— Susan and Bruce outpacing Margaret and Gus on the stairs.

"Good night!" they called out to one another. "Good night!" "Good night!"

Margaret loved the way their conjoined voices reverberated against the angled planes of wood, marble, plaster, and porcelain. *I should have had concerts here,* she thought, suddenly regretful. *Boys' and girls' choirs. Madrigal singers. I could have done that much, at least.*

Gus drew Margaret's hand through his arm. He placed one of his warm, puff-pastry hands over hers as they strolled toward their room.

"Your barbershop quartet," she said. "I'm sorry, dear heart, I've forgotten the name."

"The Crooning Clansmen."

"Yes! I want them to sing at the wake. Here in the house. Would they, do you think? Would you ask?"

Gus stopped. "When are you planning on telling her, Margaret?"

"I can't see how it would do any good, not now anyway. She's still so fragile."

"But everyone else knows, my dear. It hardly seems fair."

Margaret stroked his cheek. "Don't worry, Gus. I'll let her know when the time is right."

Wanda woke suddenly. Had she heard someone talking? She was in bed, still dressed, but her shoes were off and she was covered by a blanket. How did she get here? She looked around the room, so huge and unfamiliar. It was almost completely dark, and it took time to realize that she was no longer in the hospital. The only light came from a street lamp outside the bay window. No moon. No stars. It was still raining, harder now, and there was a wind blowing.

She'd been on the floor, she remembered, doing—what? Margaret had been here, and smashed something—a bird, yes. And left the pieces behind, Wanda remembered; she'd been turning the pieces over in her hands. She was out of the hospital, in this new room, this room full of birds, on the main floor, so that she wouldn't have to manage the stairs. They'd been so thoughtful, so kind. She could hardly bear their kindness.

Someone besides Margaret had been here, she realized—and not only because she'd been moved to the bed, but because of the smell: dewy sage, laundered flannel. It was Troy.

Wanda's eyes refocused in the dark and she saw him, slouched in the window seat—awake or asleep, she couldn't tell. She had seen him like this often in the last months, keeping watch near her bed, like a soldier. She had heard him crying. He was the only one, of all of them, who had not pressed her to speak, had not tried to cheer her with petty conversation. Silent, the way horses are silent. The way cowboys are silent.

With effort, she sat up and moved her legs over the side of the bed. Troy stirred.

"Wanda?" He got up and walked across the room.

She'd forgotten how tall he was. In silhouette, it was clear to her in a way it hadn't been before: He wasn't a boy at all. His hair was longer and his face leaner, as if he'd lost weight. Even in the dim light, she could see that he'd aged. She started to pull him toward her on the bed. She felt his hesitation, his wariness, and beneath that, their old unfinished business, and an offer she knew he would never make on his own.

"Don't worry," she whispered, pulling harder, until they were face-to-face and she could taste the warm cinnamon breeze of his breath. "I won't break."

It should have been a sweet pleasure to come at last to the feast of his body—plum wine, the oil of grapes, honeyed butter, peasant bread—to reward his long months of fasting and withholding, his bedside vigil, and what might even have been a guilty love. She tried the old enticements and teasings, tried to draw lines with him, for him: sinewy curves, thick swirls of color. She tried to braid her body with his, conjoin flesh and fluid—but all she could offer was gracelessness and pain. The only lines she could draw were sharp and splintered, gouged from dead wood. He tried too. He didn't want her pain. He slowed her, gentled her, quelling for a time her desperation with touch. He tried sweet applications of wet here and there, as if to soften and then glue her back together. He made promises she knew he couldn't keep, assurances he didn't mean. How could he? Because he was breaking too against the rock that she'd become. He had to be thinking—as she was—of what their bodies could have been together before the accident. She mourned the loss of what she might have given—not love, maybe, but something of worth: oblivion, nourishment, an improvised tango, a good fuck. Now and forever she could only be an obscene assemblage of cast-off parts that did not cohere and could not adhere to this or any other man's beauty. *Cripple,* she thought, seeing the angularity of the word in space, tasting its imploded bitterness.

Outside, the rain fell harder. She tried to become rain, create some place within where a pool could form and he could come and drink and be blessed. But she could make nothing. She was baked earth, mouthfuls of sand, an empty table. Even as they held each other and cried, her body could not squeeze out a single tear for him to drink.

Sometime later in the night he got up and dressed. For a long while he sat on the bed, resting his hand on the back door of her heart. She tried to smooth out her breath, make it sound like the breath of a dreamer. She hoped he was fooled. She could not bear the thought of wounding him further. Finally, he leaned down, whispered her name, and left.

Wanda wrapped herself loosely in her bathrobe and got into her wheelchair. She retrieved her backpack. She pulled out her red and black book and leafed through its pages. *I am going to find him.* she'd written, the dates recorded on page after page, as if they were journal entries, with the last entry made the day of the accident. She'd been meticulous in her madness. She wondered without caring what had become of her black dress, her rhinestone shoes, her black wig and cat's-eye glasses.

She wheeled to the fireplace, put a match to the book, and threw it in. She watched it burn. "I will never find him," she said, as the pages blackened and shriveled. "I will never find him." She added kindling, logs, and the fire grew hotter. She was good at this. She watched the effortless transfiguration of her words, their release into a form that was weightless, airborne, capable of flying everywhere, seeing anyone. She watched the firelight ricochet over her bare skin and its new covering of scars; they were like hieroglyphs carved in granite. She wondered why the heat of bodies opening to one another didn't always lead to the reduction of a broken heart, and from there to union, alignment, love. She understood suddenly that her heart had healed, but wrongly, in the way of bones: It had sclerosed.

She noticed a tube of epoxy and a cardboard box on the dresser; inside the box were a pair of safety glasses, heavy work gloves, pieces of the gold leaf china that she and Margaret had demolished months ago, and a note: "Dearest Tink, Do with this as you'd like, but for God's sake, please use the gloves. Love, M."

Putting the box on the seat of her wheelchair, Wanda made her way back across the room, where—alone in the firelight, and because for the time being she had nothing better to do—she went to work.

Twenty-four

≈

A Brief History of the
Hughes Collection

When Wanda awoke the next morning, the fire was out and the rain had stopped falling. The light coming through the windows had a flat pallor, the color of steel—a December palette, she thought, not at all the way light should be in midsummer.

The room was cool. The smell of Troy was still here, mixed now with the incense of dying wood smoke and rainwater, embedded in the fibers of bedsheets, pillowcases, and the dermis of her skin. On the bedside table was a porcelain vase; it held a bunch of flowers so saturated with yellow pigment that they hurt Wanda's eyes. She recalled a line by one of those suicidal poets she'd studied in college. *The daffodils are too excitable,* she paraphrased. *It is winter here.*

She'd worked until first light and then gone back to bed. She must have fallen asleep. She had no idea what time it was—her wristwatch was long gone, and for months now time had been doled out in milligrams by doctors and nurses—but she could hear vague, sporadic thumps and bumpings throughout the house, so other people must be awake.

She pushed herself up and gazed at her work, laid out on the marble floor in front of the fireplace: nothing figurative, just a piecing together of the fragments from Margaret's parrot and her gold leaf china. An abstraction. A jigsaw puzzle without narrative. It gave her no satisfaction to look at it, but at the time, the act of handling the pieces—trying to find in their jagged shapes surfaces that suggested intersection, connection—had quieted, soothed, and distracted her. And here she was. She had made it to morning. She was still alive.

Where were those handy dandy prescription narcotics? Where had she dropped them?

She lowered herself into her wheelchair. She was about to conduct a search when someone knocked on the door.

Ha! she thought. *Deus ex machina! This really is a bad play.*

"Hello?" It was Margaret. "May I come in?"

Wanda wheeled to the door and opened it.

Margaret entered with a tray containing an antique porcelain coffee service. "Good morning!" She moved briskly to the window and set the tray on the table where the porcelain parrot had spent its last intact moments. "Did you sleep well?"

Wanda nodded.

Margaret poured. "Everyone's just left. Gus went to work, and Susan and Bruce have gone to do the weekly marketing."

She was immensely irritated by Margaret's voice. Had she always sounded like this? Like an excessively chipper talk show hostess from the Christian Television Network?

"They'll be back later this morning," Margaret concluded, giving her a sparkling smile and handing her a cup and saucer.

Then Wanda realized that it wasn't Margaret's voice that had changed; Margaret was the same as always. Everyone's voice—including, Wanda supposed, her own—sounded false and trivial. And whatever shabby, stupid content their words contained had little to do anymore with what she could bring herself to regard as meaningful communication. At the same time, Wanda recognized the arrogance and self-pity implicit in this brave-new-world view, and hated herself for it. The Percocet was still on the floor, somewhere. Wasn't it?

She inhaled the steam from her cup. *Jesus.* She'd tasted nothing but soapy, weak hospital coffee for so long, this was as good as an aphrodisiac.

Margaret walked over to the fireplace hearth. She studied the arrangement of pieces on the floor. "I didn't get to say good-bye to Troy," she said nonchalantly. "I suppose he left after the rest of us went to bed."

Wanda felt her cheeks go hot.

"He's been very helpful in the past few months."

Wanda grunted. She was starting to feel dizzy.

"He was the one who did all the remodeling in the bathroom, did he tell you?"

Margaret strolled toward the bathroom door as she spoke. "I mentioned something at the hospital to him—about wanting to make this room more serviceable and so forth—and the very next day, before I had time to call a contractor, Troy brought sketches and a supply list and volunteered to do the job! I still don't know how he managed, all by himself."

Wanda's heart was pumping in triple time. *It must be the caffeine,* she thought. *Or—saints be praised!—maybe it's a massive myocardial infarction.* She set her coffee cup aside and tried to think how to begin. Finally, she picked up her legal pad and wrote, "Can't stay here."

"Why not?" Margaret answered sharply. She was no longer smiling. "Why not?" she repeated, her voice angry, accusatory.

Wanda hadn't expected this kind of reaction. It caught her off-guard. She felt like a shamed, ungrateful child. Inside her body, something was happening. A kind of unnatural loosening had commenced. A breakdown of engineering and design, a failure of inner centrifugal force, with Ferris wheel parts hurtling into space and the atmosphere of her skin unable to contain them. Orthopedic hardware could do only so much. Steel screws and rods and plates and pins couldn't hold her together, and even her shameful attempt at therapeutic fucking had failed. There was too much collateral damage, so that finally and now she was truly coming unstuck and how funny, really, when you thought about it, when she'd held herself together for years and years and quite successfully, too, but with what? How had she done it? Where did it go?

She needed Margaret to leave. She needed to find her Percocet. She scanned the place on the floor where the pills should have been, but they were gone, gone, gone.

Shit! she cried inwardly. *Troy. He must have picked them up.*

She gripped her pencil. When she was sure she could write legibly, she printed, "No one is this kind to someone who isn't kin."

Margaret drew close. "I see. You think I'm some kind of saint? You think I don't expect anything in return?" She spoke gently. "You've got me all wrong. My motives are nothing but selfish. Here."

Margaret handed her an envelope and then sat down on the bed. She reached toward the nearest bedside table and picked up the vase, with its decorative family of swans. Margaret began polishing them with a corner of her cardigan sweater.

"Read that," Margaret said. "It will help you understand what I'm going to ask you to do. And why."

The envelope was made of expensive paper, a blend of linen and pulp. It was old, and looked as though it had been handled frequently. Wanda pulled out the letter within, a single sheet of yellowed paper. Again, she was struck by its exquisite texture. It had the feel of a finely laundered handkerchief.

"'*Dear Oscar,*'" the letter began. The words had been written with a fountain pen in a flamboyant script. The letterhead was in a foreign language; Wanda guessed it to be Dutch. "'*It will be a damn bloody shame if this lot doesn't arrive in brilliant condition. You will find several nice tableware pieces of Worcester, a Sevres jardinière, a couple of Delft plates, a Meissen coffeepot, a pair of apothecaries from Capodimonte (I had to give my left nut for these, you bastard!), some Minton novelties, and several of those appallingly tasteless figurines the Popov factory is so fond of putting out: Pie Seller, Hunter with Rabbit, Balalaika Player, etc. Ah, these kikes and their tchotchkes! The whole lot came from the Paris apartment of a French professor named Lazar, and the details, as always, you will find on the attached inventory. Business is good, my friend. Very good. Sincerely yours, Edvard Krabbe.*'" The letter was dated 5 May 1942.

Wanda looked up. Margaret's eyes were full of tears.

"That letter was written to my father."

Wanda remembered the day of her arrival. The odd, expressionless manner in which Margaret had catalogued her possessions during the house tour: Capodimonte. Meissen. Popov. Sevres. She thought about Margaret's fluent French, about the section of books in the library on World War II. She suddenly saw the whole of Margaret's life, tending these things, not going anywhere, living a life apart.

Margaret wiped at her eyes. She took the letter from Wanda and replaced it in the envelope. "My father was well-connected and wealthy, even before the war. When the Nazis began their work, he saw a great opportunity. He was skilled that way, really gifted—a kind of diviner when it came to money. So he began a new business: as a broker of fine antique European china and porcelain."

Margaret massaged her forehead. She stood up, walked over to the window, and looked out toward the carriage house. "I took over after he died in '46. I was twenty-four years old. And still so stupid. One day, I was showing a piece of soft-paste Capodimonte to a client—I'll never forget it, it was a Recumbent Slave. I was explaining how Capodimonte is prized for its translucence, its warm, milky-white color—some idiotic art dealer nonsense like that—when a man burst in. His face was awful. Haunted-looking. Skeletal. He was wearing a black wool coat and a yarmulke. He started yelling at me. His English was very broken. 'You are standing on the dead!' he shouted. 'On the bodies of the six million you make your fortune! I curse you! I curse your family!'"

Margaret stopped speaking for a few moments. She was shaking.

"I thought he was crazy. Then I started going through my father's account books, his correspondence, his personal papers. I asked questions. I looked where I hadn't wanted to look before, and I found the unthinkable."

Margaret began pacing erratically around the perimeter of the room, pausing now and then to lean against a wall or a piece of furniture, absentmindedly picking up and replacing figurines of birds as she went. She spoke quickly. "I closed the shop after that, packed up everything and moved it all here, into the house. I thought that would be enough, you see. I thought that would make it right. To not sell any of it, to not profit by it. I thought that was payment enough and that I could have a life."

"You married," Wanda whispered.

Margaret nodded. "We had a child—Daniel—and then when my husband found out—as he was bound to, of course, I can't imagine how stupid I was, how wrong, to think I could hide it—he . . ." Margaret stopped. She slowed her pace and her speech. "Stephen was—is—a good person, and it was too awful for him to have been deceived, and about something so horrible."

She'd completed her circle of the room. She stared at another pair of adult swans adorning a bud vase, surrounded by reeds and water lilies, nuzzling their cygnet, frozen in time.

"Our son died," she announced blandly. "After that, there was really nothing to bind us to one another."

Wanda forced herself to speak. "I'm so sorry, Margaret."

"It was all a very long time ago." Margaret picked up the vase. "The point is, there's never been atonement. People I love have been punished. I won't have it anymore." She sat on the bed and stared at the swan family in her cupped hands. "The right action, of course, would be to return these things to their owners, or their surviving kin. I've placed ads in art and antique journals, that sort of thing, but these objects, they're not like paintings or bank accounts. Rare as they are, they are hard to trace. Much of the documentation was lost. Or destroyed." Margaret placed the swan vase in Wanda's hand. "You've heard of Kristallnacht?"

Wanda nodded.

"Then you know what it means: 'The night of broken glass.'"

Wanda nodded again. Where was Margaret going with this?

"That poor man," said Margaret, and her eyes no longer focused on anything in the room. "I never knew his story, never knew his name. I've wondered ever since, what could I do? How could I repay it? These things have outlived their time, it seems to me. If all they do is sit on a shelf, no one will ever know their worth. I think it's time for them to die."

Wanda shook her head. She didn't understand.

Margaret turned sharply, her eyes like lamps. "They should all be broken. I want you to do it."

Wanda was trying to take in what Margaret was saying; at the same time she was imagining the next few minutes after Margaret's imminent departure. She was playing out a couple of possible scenarios in her head, working things through.

And then Margaret did something surprising: She leaned in close, smoothed a slow hand across Wanda's hair, brow, and temples, and kissed her warmly on the cheek. It wasn't a series of gestures a person would expect from a landlady. "There's more, you know," she said, in a light, conspiring voice. "Pieces that aren't on display, that are still in storage. There are boxes of it. Boxes and boxes. There's so much here that needs doing. You're going to be very busy."

After Margaret left, Wanda pondered her options. They were fairly straightforward, really: She could either kill herself in one of several ways or she could break things. She could do both, actually, but that would be messy and Margaret had done enough; she didn't want to stick her with the expense of carpet cleaning on top of everything else. Maybe she could do this for a while, especially if Margaret wanted it so much. There would always be time to off herself. It wasn't as if she was going anywhere.

She looked at the swan vase Margaret had placed in her hands. She didn't especially like its style—it was too excessively pretty—but she could appreciate its artistry and the fact that it had survived intact for centuries. That would have been the extent of her knowledge before today; but now she knew that its perfect appearance was propaganda, the worst kind of lie, a campaign of misinformation and denial. Margaret was right: This flawless thing could never tell its most important story, not the way it looked now, not without help. Who had this vase belonged to? A child? A young bride? A maiden aunt?

Wanda became aware of the other residents of this room: hundreds of exquisite porcelain birds. She stared at them. They stared back.

Twenty-five

❧

What Is Woven

The members of the household all but gave up on Wanda's ever emerging from her self-imposed exile. It was as if she weren't there. She became the madwoman in the shuttered room, the resident invalid of whom no one dared speak. She admitted access to only two people: her physical therapist (an avuncular former wrestler named Nestor; he came to the house four days a week), and Margaret, who delivered her meals in hotel room-service manner— wheeling a serving cart into Wanda's room, taking her leave, and retrieving the cart from the foyer later.

During their few minutes of face-to-face contact, Wanda did not speak, a state of affairs which didn't bother Margaret in the least. Since the girl hadn't been a chatty confiding sort of person before the accident—except when powder rooms were involved—Margaret wasn't about to press her for confessional heart-to-hearts now. Margaret knew she was considering her proposal. She was such a complicated soul, so independent in her way, and now the only privacy she had, the only place she could be alone really, was within her own silence.

The others were concerned, of course, and curious, but Margaret— ever the best of secret-keepers—invoked landlady-patient privilege. She wouldn't allow Wanda to be treated as the object of gossip or speculation, and any mealtime conversation which inclined in that direction was abruptly—and firmly—squelched. It was not for anyone to talk about Wanda when she wasn't ready to talk about herself. And it was not Margaret's place to discuss what she was up to.

Not that she knew, not exactly. She only suspected. Her suspicions derived from Wanda's eating habits.

Bruce put special care into all of Wanda's meals; every plate was a work of art. At first the dishes came out looking much as they did when they went in—as if Wanda were not only disinclined to eat, but loath to disturb Bruce's masterfully composed presentations of color and texture. Eventually, though, Margaret detected subtle changes: One of the plates was lighter; teeth marks indented a piece of linguini; linen napkins were rumpled and striped with sauce. And then came a morning when cream cheese and mandarin clownfish romped in shoals of blueberry syrup. An afternoon when baby peas, pimentos, and pearled onions formed a pointillist face. On the evening Wanda's mashed potatoes, homemade herbed croutons, and white chocolate mousse came back as a miniature replica of the Taj Mahal, Margaret knew she was getting better.

Two weeks after Wanda's return, they had just sat down to eggs Florentine, crumpets, and glazed fruit when she appeared in the dining room entrance, leaning on her walker. Her chest was conspicuously free of signage.

"I'd like another tour of the house," she announced.

Margaret restrained her glee and spoke levelly. "The whole house," she inquired, "or just the first floor?"

"All of it, of course. I've been practicing with this. I can manage the stairs."

"Don't be ridiculous!" Margaret shot back. "I'll make some phone calls and see about putting in an escalator." She pushed away from the table and shook a finger at Wanda. "And don't you dare pull a face!"

As she darted into the kitchen, Gus stood up, pulled out a chair, and waited; he seemed confident in his impression that Wanda did not desire assistance. Around the table, an eggy-eyed, dumbstruck silence prevailed.

A full minute passed as she made her way from the dining room door to her place at the table. Gus held her chair as she awkwardly hinged her body into it and set her walker aside, then he moved to the sideboard and began fixing a plate of food.

From the kitchen, Margaret's voice broke the silence. "I wonder if Troy has experience building escalators. Does anyone know his telephone number off the top of their head?"

Gus delivered Wanda's plate to the table. "Thank you," she said. Then she jerked her napkin into her lap, barked out seven digits, scowled at her bed of spinach and eggs, and began to eat.

Wanda wanted to know more this time. She questioned Margaret about the minutest details: "Where did this piece come from? Who designed it? How was it made? What is it called?" She listened intently. She was assiduous in her documentation. Her clipboard came out of storage and her legal pad was reappropriated for a more traditional use: She made notes and sketches on sheet after sheet of yellow paper as Margaret spoke.

In most cases, Margaret could give scant information about her things, other than what was provided on the insurance schedule and what she'd been able to glean from reference books and her father's correspondence. There was nothing personal. Nothing about the people who'd owned them and from whom they'd been stolen—besides the fact that they'd lived in France at some point between 1933 and 1945, and they were Jewish.

Wanda pressed her. "These things need to have stories, even if the stories aren't true. What we don't know, we'll make up."

"We will?" Margaret was dubious.

"Actors do it all the time. They call it 'personalizing the prop.'"

"They do?"

"You've lived with these things a long time, Margaret. You must think about who owned them, invent stories for them, don't you?"

Wanda opened a cabinet—they were in the smaller downstairs parlor—and picked up a figurine. "Start with this."

Margaret replied automatically: "Staffordshire bulldog, twelve inches tall, circa 1860, valued at three thousand five hundred dollars."

"Those are the facts," Wanda said. "I want the *story*."

Haltingly, Margaret began. "A schoolteacher in Chartres—his name was Ernest—spent a good part of his savings to buy this for his younger sister in Paris after her beloved dog died. She . . . Simone . . . always thought it the ugliest thing, but she couldn't bear to part with it."

Wanda nodded thoughtfully. She carried the homely bulldog to the hearth. After studying it for several seconds, she took a breath and let it fall. Pieces skittered along the floor, originating from the point of impact and shooting out in all directions. Wanda squatted—her pain so evident that Margaret winced—and stared, picking up certain fragments and inspecting them. With effort, she stood again. She stepped awkwardly on some of the larger pieces, breaking them further, until she seemed satisfied with the result.

"I like that story," she said, so quietly that Margaret thought she might be talking to herself. "Write it down for me, please. Write it all, whatever you can think of."

The dogs in the cabinet started wagging their tails. Margaret smiled.

"Very well, Tink. I'll write it down."

It was clear that Troy was fully qualified—and eager—to take on the planning and supervision of their construction projects. There was the escalator, of course, which Margaret realized she'd be needing herself at some point. There would also be necessary modifications to the main floor of the carriage house, since—to Margaret's surprise and delight—Wanda had asked if she could use it as a studio.

"How would you feel about Troy moving in?" Their current field of operations was the library; Wanda was sorting fragments of several smashed Meissen harlequins and two completely decimated commedia dell'arte troupes, Margaret was working on the fictionalized version of her insurance schedule. "Since he'll be working here for the better part of every day," she continued, "taking meals with us and so forth, I thought it might be more practical if—"

"Your house," Wanda cut in, "your decision."

Margaret enjoyed Wanda's new way of speaking—now that she was speaking. It was a kind of verbal shorthand, efficient and unadorned without being rude. Familial. Yes, that was what Margaret liked; it was language one would hear spoken among "family" in the broadest sense of that word—not only blood relatives, but consorts of all kinds. A language shared by people secure in the knowledge that words are not the real adhesive of love.

"Good," Margaret said. "He's in then. Let's break. Tea?"

Later that afternoon, Troy arrived and began unloading boxes into the foyer. Just before Margaret began taking him on a tour of the house, Wanda emerged to lean in her doorway. "When did you get the Chevy?" she asked.

He turned to face her and mopped his face with a bandanna. "Fifty-three days ago."

Wanda was stone-faced. "You should have bought a Ford." She went into her room and slammed the door—conclusively squelching Margaret's hope that they'd share the Aviary Suite.

Margaret took Troy upstairs so that he could see the rooms on the second and third stories. He lingered at the door of a remote corner room on the second floor: the Soldier's Room. It was the last one Margaret showed him and, of all the rooms in the house, the one she found most difficult to visit. It was also the most spare and eclectic, containing a hodgepodge of nineteenth-century furnishings—all of which, Margaret noted with embarrassment, were slightly dusty: a four-tier rosewood whatnot, a knee-hole writing table with barley twist legs, a painted pine marriage chest from Hungary, an overstuffed Victorian reading chair and ottoman. The room's prior furnishings had been moved to the upper floor of the carriage house almost thirty years ago, along with the rest of Daniel's things.

Some of the porcelain soldiers displayed here commemorated real people: Louis Napoleon, the Duke of Cambridge, Wellington. Others were commissioned representations of high-ranking officers in military finery, astride their horses, posed next to cannons or flags. These Margaret had placed behind glass doors on the shelves of the whatnot. Most of the figures, though, were of the callow, the low-ranking, the nameless. Teenagers in oversized uniforms from the Spanish Civil War, privates wearing rumpled Union blues or Confederate grays. Margaret's heart was raw for these boys; she imagined them more than any of the other pieces in her house as carrying the spirits of their owners. They stood in a place of prominence above the Italian tile fireplace, a ragtag infantry stretching the entire length of the mantel.

"This'll do," Troy said.

"But Troy, dear," Margaret protested, "there's not even a bed."

He walked in. The resonance of his footfalls seemed to startle the room and awaken its inhabitants. Margaret could feel the soldiers coming to attention. She could hear distant echoes of marbles rolling across the floor, books being thumped open, blocks being toppled. The laughter of rough-housing boys. She caught a glimpse of Daniel at seven, brandishing a wooden sword that Stephen had made for him. He was slaying dragons.

There were built-in cherry wood bookcases flanking the fireplace, and above these, quarter-moon, stained glass windows in shades of amber, garnet, amethyst, and jade.

"This faces east, doesn't it?"

"It does."

"This room must be pretty in the morning."

Troy picked up a young Irish soldier and cradled him in his hands.

Who could have believed it, Margaret thought wonderingly. *A young man, in this room again, after so long.*

"Don't worry, ma'am," Troy said, his eyes still downcast. "I've got a sleeping bag."

Wanda was surprised by how easy it was. Most of the time it took no effort at all. She remembered the theatrical manner in which she and Margaret had hurled pieces against the pebble wall and watched them shatter all those months ago. It had been unnecessary. All it really took was the simple act of dropping them.

The way the pieces broke depended on several factors: the type of clay from which they'd been made, whether they'd been thrown or hand-built, the temperature at which they'd been fired, the type of glaze, the manner of decoration, their shape, size, weight, porosity, and thickness, whether they were dropped singly or in groups, and the surface on which they were dropped. Wooden floors yielded one kind of break—even the kind of wood affected the result, Wanda discovered—and, of course, using any of the fireplace hearths guaranteed the most dramatic and thorough breakings.

The pieces all had their own music, too, brief but distinct. A porcelain soup tureen could thud hollowly, darkly, like the striding bass notes in Monk's "'Round Midnight." Shattering aperitif crystal might remind her of the crisp jubilance of a bebop trumpet. The cacophony of dessert plates dropped en masse could imitate Bird's raggedy sax.

She began to vocalize as she worked, emitting a kind of half-sung accompaniment for the pieces as they fell, and then improvising vocal codas—short requiems after they lay still, silent, and in pieces.

She loved the random shapes. She knew early on that she wouldn't want to manipulate them much further, unless it would be to drop them more than once and/or walk on them. No nippers, certainly. She pondered the ethics of employing hammers, deciding finally that she might use them—but only occasionally, and only as a last resort if she couldn't get pieces sized for her purpose in any other way. She didn't know yet what that purpose would *be,* but Margaret trusted her, so she tried to have faith.

Some days were breaking days. Some days were sorting days. She sorted logically—by color, shade, size, shape—but she used other means too, means which she couldn't explain even to herself. She had a special place for pieces which attracted her, spoke to her in some way, setting them aside until she had a clearer idea how she could use them.

Sometimes she broke several pieces before sweeping and sorting the fragments; at other times she would break only one item at a time.

Often she'd wake in the night, unable to sleep. She'd hear quiet, acoustic music: solo guitar, hammered dulcimer, cello and violin, Guatemalan flute. These were the kinds of things Troy listened to when he couldn't sleep. She pictured him in the nearby dining room at the massive antique desk which now served as his drafting table, working on Margaret's construction plans in his calm, meticulous way, standing in a circle of light on the other side of her bedroom wall. She'd get up then. Drop a couple of birds. Sort pieces.

Eventually she realized there could be only one source. And—accepting her natural inclination toward narrative—she also knew that her mosaics would illustrate only one subject.

She began poring over Margaret's collection of books on Judaism and World War II. She examined hundreds of photos. She took notes, made sketches. There was so much to learn, so many stories to tell.

She walked the rooms of the house with Margaret—who had imagined owners for every single piece, from the largest Chinese garden
seats to the smallest snuffbox, from the most valuable and rare items
in the collection to those which were more common, less dear. Sometimes Margaret's imaginings were scant: "Moshe. Widower. Wore garters. Fed pigeons. Shot in the head, in the night, in a forest." In most
cases, though, her stories were full of details: "Adele, nine years old,
sitting at a school desk, proud and straight, wearing a plaid blouse,
white anklets, her hair in braids. She was going to be a journalist. She
loved horses. She won the school essay competition and her grandmother gave her this as a prize. When she starved to death, she was
holding a pencil."

Soon these fictions began to blend with points of fact, and Wanda
could no longer separate them. Was the father with the bloodied head
who waved to his children from the yellow taxi real or imagined? Did
the little boy who was pulled from the pickle barrel really exist? Her
head swirled with ghosts, her dreams were full of the persecuted, the
condemned, the dead—all telling their stories. She did not mind listening. It did not cost her in the way it cost Margaret. She knew she was
taking dictation, but for what kind of document? She wasn't sure. How
would she use these words, these stories? She didn't know, not yet. She
could only keep prospecting.

"What do you call someone who derives pleasure from the bread of
affliction?" Bruce asked. He was making challah while Wanda studied a kosher cookbook.

She looked up and waited for the punch line.

"A 'matzochist'!" He paused and frowned at her. "That's a good one.
You're supposed to laugh."

Wanda smiled and laid her book aside. She watched Bruce's hands—
so practiced, so full of ease and grace.

"How did you learn to do that?" she asked.

"My *bubeleh*. Grandma Katz. She was my first and finest culinary
arts professor." Bruce punched his fist into the center of a large mass
of dough; it sighed audibly as it deflated around his hand. He divided
the dough in half, divided one of the halves into thirds, and then began

rolling each third into a long strand. "'Slow down, boychick!' she was always saying. 'Cooking is not to rush. It's a prayer. A gift of love. It's family. It's standing in the company of your ancestors and feeling their hands, helping you.'" Bruce started weaving the strands into braids. "When you're Jewish, everything that matters happens in the kitchen."

Wanda closed her book and stood up. "Teach me," she said. "Show me with your hands. Tell me what it means."

One day she found a book leaning against the door of the Aviary Suite. A note said, "I found this at St. Vinnie's sandwiched between *I'm Mad at You, Ernie!* and *The Wonderful Feast.* The other two will go to Ethan and Bruce, respectively. You get this. Love, Sus." The book was a collection of artwork and writings made by children interred in a Jewish ghetto called Terezín from 1942 to 1944. The children were secretly schooled there. They wrote poems. They drew pictures. They made collages out of torn office forms, trash, wrapping paper—whatever they could find. Somehow they had access to paints, too, and there were bright images of numbered bunk beds, flowers, fairy tale towns. Some of the paintings were abstractions of color and pattern. One child drew a long row of stick figures holding hands and riding the boxcars—not jammed inside but standing on the roofs, as if they were daring circus performers or stunt artists. Terezín was built in the shape of a star, Wanda learned. Its prisoners were marked for extermination from the moment they arrived. Of fifteen thousand children who passed through, a hundred survived. They were stars of light, imprisoned within a star of darkness.

Wanda smoothed her hands over the pages of the book. Studying was not enough. She'd never understand anything if words and pictures stayed only in her mind; she needed them in her body. She began copying the children's poems and line drawings onto brown paper grocery bags and flattened cardboard boxes. She did the same with the other stories—those that Margaret had made up, and those that had really happened. She rummaged through the household garbage and made collages from what she found there: bills, receipts, labels from canned goods, newspapers.

By now, she'd smashed the contents of many rooms. She'd accumulated several boxes of fragments and a huge palette of colors and shapes. In her mind, she was seeing pictures. Imagined amorphous forms were becoming defined. There still were techniques to learn, problems to solve, but the studio was nearly habitable. She was almost ready to start.

"You could use more sets of protective eyeglasses," Margaret said as she wrote. "Respiratory masks and gloves too." Over the dessert course one night—chocolate ginger cake with pear glaze—she and Wanda were making a list. "And books on mosaic-making, don't you think? I might have something in the library, but they'd be more in the nature of art history books. Nothing on technique."

"I know a bit," Wanda said. "I helped my uncle tile a bathroom when I was eleven."

There was instant silence. It was the first time Wanda had ever shared anything like a family story.

"It was a pink bathroom," Wanda continued, ominously. She was staring at a bit of pear glaze as it ribboned off her fork.

They waited. Nothing. End of story.

Margaret sighed and resumed. "All right then. What else?"

"Adhesives," Wanda blurted. "Grout, too. I'm not sure what kind."

"For what you'll be doing, you'll want sanded." It was Troy, in his corner, drafting plans. "Unless you'll be using tight, uniform joins."

"What?" Wanda said.

"And you'll want to try mixing a couple of ways. It should feel like cake frosting when you're done."

"What?" Wanda repeated, looking suddenly feverish. Margaret fought off an impulse to feel her forehead.

Troy's brow was still furrowed over his plans. "The consistency of the grout. It should be like frosting."

When Wanda didn't respond, Margaret asked, "How is it you know all this, dear?"

"My sister back home has a flooring business." And he did look up then, but not at Margaret. He stared at Wanda as if she were the only person in the room. "Mosaic techniques aren't exactly the same, but I can show you a thing or two. If you want."

Margaret looked at Gus. Susan looked at Bruce. Troy looked at Wanda. Wanda broke her dessert dish.

* * *

Once the plumbing and wiring were roughed in and the bathroom was usable, everyone helped move in supplies and furnishings. Afterward, they ceremoniously donned safety glasses and gathered around a large worktable.

Gus brought out a chilled bottle of sparkling apple cider and popped the cork. He then filled nine eighteenth-century tankards, all painted in the Chinese style, which Margaret had retrieved from storage. "To Wanda's new studio!" he proclaimed. "You've done a brilliant job in here, lad," he said. "Cheers!"

They downed their cider.

"Shall we?" Margaret offered, indicating her tankard.

Bruce held up his hand. "Listen, y'all. I have to say this. I don't mind what everybody else does with these things, really I don't, but I have to say that it doesn't exactly sit right with me. I mean, my sweet grandmother almost kicked the bucket when I came out. She'll flat out DIE if she finds out I'm impersonating a Nazi thug breaking dishes on Kristallnacht."

"That's not what we're doing," Wanda spoke up suddenly, her voice serious and emphatic. "We're breaking things as ceremony. We're breaking them in remembrance."

There was a pause after that, not only in response to the content of Wanda's speech, but because it was the most anyone had heard her say since she'd come home from the hospital.

Bruce spoke. "I think that would be good enough for Bubie Katz." He hurled his tankard to the floor. "L'chayim!" he shouted. They all followed suit.

The carriage house was thus officially reappropriated as Wanda's studio.

From then on Wanda spent her days and nights breaking, sorting, and making more preliminary sketches, paintings, and models. It was strange to be engaged in such an amorphous creative process. There was no structure to it, no deadline. No calendar of events that led in a linear way from preproduction meetings to actor auditions to casting sessions to rehearsals to techs to opening night. And the end was nowhere in sight: With no final performance, no closing night parties, no striking of the set, how would she know when her work was finished?

Troy was often near, also working. One night when they were both up late—he was putting up drywall, she was planning the colors for a wall mosaic—he came over and stood next to her.

"I have an idea." He'd started to grow a beard; this had the unfortunate effect of making him look both older and more handsome.

Wanda's heart started pounding. "For what?"

He leaned on the table. She stared at his arms, dismayed that she still found them immensely compelling.

"Your three-dimensional pieces," he said. "I think I've solved the problem." He brought his hands together and mimed the action of molding something pliable. "You start by sculpting a model in clay."

Wanda dropped her pencil.

"You cover it with fiberglass resin." His hands described the action of painting.

Wanda tilted leeward, enough to feel the heat of his body.

"You let the resin harden and then saw the sculpture in half—it's rigid now, understand—and then you scoop out the clay." Troy's hands made slow scooping movements.

Wanda leaned her cheek against her hand; she felt woozy.

"Then," Troy concluded, slowly bringing his hands palm to palm, "you resin the halves back together again. See?"

Her gaze was level with his jaw, and she forced herself to look there instead of into his eyes. His beard was a tangle of chestnut and auburn, flecked with gold.

"It'll be structurally strong," he said, "hollow, and lightweight. You'll be able to glue your pieces onto the fiberglass form."

"What if it doesn't work?" Wanda murmured.

"It will," he whispered. "I already tried it." He put something on the table in front of her. "Good night."

Wanda stared. Troy had mosaicked a life-sized sculpture of one of her high-heeled shoes. Not with black pieces, though. As she gazed at the shoe's pieced-together surfaces, Wanda felt like a high-flying bird winging over fields that were every imaginable shade of yellow.

*   *   *

Her first work would be two-dimensional, a wall mosaic; of all the ideas she'd planned so far, it was the most simple technically. She didn't want to start with anything too complicated, too structurally risky. Certainly not the sculptural pieces—even though Troy's suggestions for their execution seemed like sound ones. There was just too much at stake.

She cut two large sections of cement board that would serve as substrate. She framed and hinged them—this mosaic would be a riff on Renaissance diptychs. She transferred her drawings. She laid out her palette of tesserae—opaque fragments of porcelain and china; pieces of paper on which she'd scrawled the stories, poems, drawings; clear and colored glass.

She spent days moving things around. It was like doing a jigsaw puzzle—but a jigsaw puzzle with endless possibilities. Or like painting, without the headaches of paint. She liked the way you could lay in a color and change it if it wasn't absolutely right.

In the beginning, it was easy for her to become obsessed, hard to stop, especially when she couldn't find the right piece.

"Give it a rest," Troy would say. "Take a break."

But she'd keep on anyway, angry, miserable about being thwarted in this way. She'd make something fit if she had to.

Once in a while, though, the right piece seemed to simply find her hand. That was the way it felt. She struggled to understand how this happened, and why. The more she struggled, the less she understood, and the harder the work became.

But then it would happen again: The right pieces would find her. It was a mystery.

After several days, when she was finally satisfied with the layout, she moved on to the next step: application—buttering the thousands of pieces one by one with adhesive and applying them, gluing the torn paper to the substrate and over this adhering bits of glass so that the words and pictures were visible.

Halfway through this process, she stopped.

"This looks like shit."

"Wait until you're done," Troy said. "Keep going. You need to grout it."

"But it looks like shit."

"Grout it," he repeated. "You'll see. It's all in the grout."

She finished adhering the tesserae. Then, she waited: one day, two days, three days. She had to be absolutely sure that the pieces were set, that they wouldn't move—not even one single millimeter—once she started to grout.

"Ready?" Troy asked.

"I suppose."

As Troy looked on, she added water, bit by bit, to the grout. "That's it. Take your time."

Wanda mixed slowly. The next step would involve covering the mosaic completely, working dollops of hardening cement into every gap, and then waiting—for thirty minutes—before sponging off the excess. She had been dreading this. Grouting meant losing sight of the familiar. There was risk here, terrible risk. The risk of separating herself from those in the picture—people she'd imagined, tended, and come to love. The risk of stepping aside as the subtleties of color and shade and placement were bulldozed behind a wall of gray. The risk of losing Margaret's faith and trust if all of this went to shit. The risk of failing, again.

When the grout was the right consistency, Troy said, "That looks good. We've got to work fast now. Remember, it's not drying, it's setting."

The two of them started slathering grout over the mosaic, pushing it into the crevices, obscuring everything. When they were done, Wanda sat down on the floor.

"I hate this part," she groused.

"I figured," he answered. "I'll make coffee."

Half an hour later, they wiped the surface clean.

Troy was right. The space between the pieces, the *negative* space, was hugely important—maybe even more important than the pieces themselves.

The grouted space was what literally held the fragments together, gave them their definition; it also made the colors—especially the yellow stars on the children's coats—even more vivid. But more than that, it was there, in the space, where order was created, rhythms of line, movement. The space made a pathway for the eye, a route which the viewer could take to get from one part of the picture to another.

Space unified all. Space made everything possible.

"See?" Troy said.

"Yes," Wanda replied. "I see."

"Do you have a name for it?"

"*Étoiles,*" she answered. "'*1942–1943.*'"

Troy nodded. "Perfect."

Wanda was still looking at the mosaic—it had turned out better than she'd hoped, and for the children's sake and Margaret's she was glad— but her real preoccupation was with the shape, color, and quality of space between her body, and Troy's.

The more she worked, the more she became familiar with a kind of magic which only happened when she let go. For years her mind had looked like a legal pad, lined and occupied with carefully written numbers, to-do lists, counts, cues, imperatives: "Fade #2, bring up moon and star gobos on a slow 3 count," "Make this week's plan for Operation Musical Beds," "Check rigging and harnesses," "Finish homework, take Jackie to the mall," "Cue Hell: moans, smoke, chains," "Buy grocs, pay bills, pick up cleaning, call AA for Peter," "Delay door slam to 4 ½ counts after his exit," "I am going to find him, I am going to find him, I am going to find him."

This was the kind of inner noise she struggled to eliminate; it was this chatter which kept the pieces from finding her hands—and kept her hands from giving life to the dead. Only when she was quiet inside, when her mind was a large empty room instead of many cluttered ones, only then did the magic happen.

She became more familiar with this state of being. She began to rec-ognize when she was in its presence and when she was not, and she got better and better at getting there: The Land of No Words, she came to call it. She had heard artists sometimes describe themselves as "vessels"; now she understood what they meant. An abandonment of ego was required, an evacuation of the self, and—this was hardest—a letting go of the need to be constantly in control.

She began to trust when the elements fit, when the crisscrossing roads between bits of clay, paper, and glass made sense in a way that couldn't be sensibly described and weren't necessarily what she'd had in mind.

She brought Monk, Bird, Miles, and Trane into the studio with her. They helped transport her to the Land of No Words. They set up a col-laboration—her hands, the Holocaust, smashed clay, and bebop. An improvisation that was underpinned with structure and technique, but played out with a pure heart open to the possibility of surprise. It was crazy, but it was right. The pieces started finding her hands more frequently. She took to filling her pockets. She sounded like a walking crash box.

Her thoughts still sometimes turned to Peter, to losses in her life, and to what she regarded as her failings, faults, sins. The nearness of Troy, the pain and the pleasure of that nearness, reminded her of futures that were no longer possible. This could have been hazardous; she was, after all, surrounded by sharp objects.

But she was held together more and more by the practice of traveling to and residing in the Land of No Words, and by the physical rituals of her work—breaking, sorting, planning, adhering, grouting.

There were things owed, promises to be kept. And as time went on, she accepted the fact that, in taking on this work, what she owed and promised was not only to Margaret and the living; she was just as much in debt to the dead.

Twenty-six

❧

Artist Glues the World!

"God," Bruce griped good-naturedly. "When you're built like Audrey Hepburn you look stunning in anything!"

"'Gamine' is the word," Susan added. "I always longed to be gamine."

"You're statuesque!" Bruce said.

"I have size-twelve feet."

Bruce and Susan had set up chairs in the foyer near Wanda's door. They were watching her model the dozen evening dresses they'd taken out on approval from clothiers around the city.

"Which reminds me," Susan continued, "what's your shoe size?"

"Five," Wanda answered sheepishly. "Sometimes five and a half."

Susan sighed. "I would really hate you if I didn't love you," she said.

Wanda modeled dress after dress. Bruce and Susan praised the way she looked in all of them, but Wanda was harder to please. Nothing seemed right.

"I've wondered for years what the inside of a 'Petites Department' looks like," said Susan, wistfully.

"I have to admit," Bruce added. "I'm living out several fantasies."

A year had passed since Wanda's accident. She still had no idea what strings Margaret had pulled, what connections she'd reeled in, what deals she'd struck, but somehow she'd arranged for Wanda's mosaics to be part of a small group show at a downtown gallery. The opening of the exhibit was tonight.

"You have to like something," Bruce admonished. "There's no way we're going to let you wear jeans."

Finally, she appeared in a two-piece black ensemble: a floor-length full skirt made of silk and flocked with swirls of velveteen, and a short, tight-fitting jacket with a peplum, stand-up collar, jet buttons, and leg-of-mutton sleeves. Bruce and Susan literally gasped.

"It's gorgeous!" Susan exclaimed.

Wanda wasn't sure. It was so different from anything she'd ever worn before. She did like the fact that it covered up all but her face. She also liked the tightness of the bodice; it made her feel contained, boundaried, separate, safe—although from what, she wasn't quite sure.

"It's rather nineteenth-century, isn't it?" Susan went on, admiringly.

"Yes, ma'am. If I were sheriff, I'd sure as shootin' tip my hat at THAT!"

"That's the one! That is definitely the one!"

The front door opened. Troy was back from a trip to the hardware store; he carried bags that jangled with drywall screws, nuts, bolts, and nails.

"Bruce. Susan," he said. "What—?"

And then, seeing Wanda, he stopped dead in his tracks and stared. Troy brought his fingers to the brim of his hat, nodded slightly, and continued on his way.

Wanda knew then what she needed to be safe from. Why her heart craved a corset.

"I'll take this one," she said. "It's just right."

Irma's head was wrapped turban style in a bath towel and she was wearing a bulky chenille robe which came down to the middle of her shins. Her feet were snuggled into gold-lamé, open-toed, beaded-and-sequined sandals. Her toenails were painted ruby red. She was scowling up at M.J. as he foraged around in her bedroom closet. With her arms crossed and her thin legs planted wide, she looked like a very tiny, mightily displeased member of a monarchy whose custom it was to hold court wearing terry cloth.

They'd already had dinner, washed the dishes, and applied a new shade called "Sassy Cinnamon" to Irma's hair. The timer was set for thirty-five minutes. M.J. was standing on a small stepladder, looking squinch-eyed into the dark recesses of an upper shelf.

"See them?" Irma asked.

"What is it I'm looking for, Irma?"

"I told you already. Shoe boxes!"

"No. I don't see any shoe boxes."

"Well, look! They're up there! Behind the lightbulbs."

"I don't see any lightbulbs, either."

Irma frowned. "I thought that's where Sam kept the lightbulbs."

"Jesus, Irma, can't we just watch TV or play Scrabble or cards like we usually do?"

"For such a young man," Irma said, in a tone suggesting she'd just discovered something wondrous about M.J.'s character, "you're a terrible stick-in-the-mud." Then she frowned again. "Keep looking," she snapped. "And don't come down till you find them. I'm going to get the glue. Meet me at the kitchen table."

Wanda and Susan sat side by side on a padded bench in the middle of the largest room. Gallery-goers swirled around them. The buzz of lively conversation, the drinks, the food, the bumper-car movements of people navigating through a crowded space—all of it was familiar, reminding Wanda of an opening night party at the theatre. But this was different. It was nerve-wracking, watching these strangers interact with a world which up until now had been completely private. On top of that, these clothes. She should have stood up to Bruce and Susan, sweet and well-intentioned as they were. There were plenty of people here dressed in jeans.

Not for the first time, she wished she hadn't come.

"Cheer up!" Susan bumped against her playfully. "The show is fabulous. They're all enthralled."

Wanda had been scanning faces in the crowd, seeking out certain body types. She felt anxious and let-down. Susan had no way of knowing that the lion's share of this anxiousness and disappointment had nothing whatsoever to do with the show. She turned to her and whispered, "Nobody's touching anything."

Susan leaned close and whispered back. "They're not supposed to, darling. It's Art."

They were missing the point, being so polite. "They should be touching," Wanda murmured, turning her attention back to the crowd.

She had been imagining this night ever since Margaret told her of the exhibition. But her fantasies did not revolve around praise for her work, paparazzi, or being launched into stratospheres of fame and fortune; they centered on the dramatic appearance of Peter.

Surely he was still sculpting. Maybe he'd become less isolated, more connected to other artists and the Seattle art scene. Of course he'd be miserable. That was certain. Completely bereft, still drinking, deeply tortured by his decision to leave her. In spite of this, though, it was possible, completely possible, that he'd be aware of local gallery openings, attend the ones that interested him. This one would interest him—not necessarily because of the mosaics, but because one of the other exhibiting artists worked in wood. Yes, he might show up. There was nothing in the least far-fetched about it.

He would appear in the gallery entrance, attractively dissolute and tousled, his long mane of hair unbound, his shirt unbuttoned, his massive chest powdered with sawdust. He would have come from his studio, which would of course be nearby. She would see him long before he saw her, but she would hold her ground. She would not approach. He would walk the exhibit, lingering over her work, letting his hands travel the landscape where her hands had been. Finally, he would notice her from across the crowded room—a stunning figure, dressed entirely in black. Inviting, seductive, and yet remote. Familiar somehow. Could it be? Was it possible? He would come toward her, slowly. The crowd would part. All eyes would be on them.

Would he kneel?

No. Too melodramatic. Too corny.

Or, maybe not.

Fuck it. He'd kneel.

"Life has been meaningless since I left you," he would say, with tears streaming down his beautiful beat-to-hell face. "I haven't been able to work. The angels have deserted me. The Muse is gone. I can't function. Please come back. I need you. I promise I'll never leave you again. Can you forgive me?"

She'd smile in a way that would be half I-forgive and half come-hither. He'd rise, cup her face tenderly, and pull her into a world-class, end-of-the-movie lip lock. Then he'd whisk her up into his arms and off to his studio, where he'd tear off these ridiculous clothes and they'd spend the next decade in bed.

But the party was over two hours old now. Inside her unripped bodice, Wanda's heart beat time with the words *I told you so, I told you so.* She should stop looking for Peter in this crowd. He wasn't here. He wouldn't be coming.

When M.J. finally emerged from Irma's bedroom, carrying three shoe boxes so crammed with contents that their lids were held in place—just barely—by thick rubber bands, he found Irma perched at the kitchen table wearing a pair of latex gloves. The tabletop was almost completely obscured by scrapbooks, glue sticks, scissors, sheets of stickers, colored markers, and the substantial body habitus of Maurice, who had situated himself in the center and was snoring.

"You're coming with me to Hawaii this year," Irma said.

"What?"

"It's all arranged. I'll be the envy of the AARP."

"You can't be—"

"Unless you're younger than fifty. ARE you younger than fifty?"

"I'm fifty-nine."

"Ha! At last. A fact."

"Irma—"

"Don't argue. This might be your only chance to see palm trees and dance the hula with an octogenarian. Now, put on some gloves. We're going to create an archival record of my Hawaiian vacations with Sam."

"Excuse me?"

"See this?" Irma pulled out a sheet of colorful stickers and pointed. "Acid-free. That's very important. So are the gloves. Body oils, dirt, chemicals. Over time, they degrade the photographic image, so that in the end you've got"—Irma clapped her hands dramatically—"nothing but gray! Pictures that look like a laundry mishap! Completely washed out!"

"What in the name of God are you talkin' about?"

"I heard about it on *Oprah*. Lucky for us we only have three boxes; there were women in the audience who had hundreds! Can you believe that?"

M.J. rifled through the supplies on the table. "Where did you get all this stuff?"

"From Ruth Epstein's daughter-in-law, Traci. I went to a party at her house yesterday. It was fun! And you should see what that girl has done with her family pictures. It's art, I tell you! It's an inspiration! Here's her business card."

M.J. squinted. "'Traci Anderson-Epstein, Creative Memories Consultant?'"

"She gives senior discounts."

M.J. responded, dully. "So, we're spending the evening gluing pictures into a scrapbook?"

"No," Irma said, "we're going to create an archive!"

M.J. raised an eyebrow.

"All right, it's a scrapbook, but you don't have to be such a snob about it. You have something better to do?"

"Yes," M.J. replied. "In exactly twelve minutes I have to rinse your hair."

"Well, for the next twelve minutes it won't kill you to be a family archivist. Stop complaining and put on those gloves." Irma reached for a box and opened it. "Oy!" she exclaimed, pulling out the first of what were surely hundreds of pictures in that box alone. "Look at that."

M.J. leaned closer. Irma held a remarkably ill-composed black-and-white photo, probably intended to feature a couple wearing 1940s-style bathing suits and leis and posed in front of a huge palm. But the photo's dominant subject was the tree; it seemed to sprout from the man's head, and its fronds loomed large and dark, curving downward in a menacing, slightly arachnid way. "Invasion of the Killer Coconuts" was the caption that came to M.J.'s mind.

"That's me and my Sam, on our honeymoon," Irma said, her voice so full of reverence that she might have been regarding a work by

Leonardo da Vinci. "Let's start with this one," she went on. "I think it should have a whole page all to itself, don't you?"

"Sounds fine, Mrs. K."

"Hand me a glue stick, will you? Let's get started."

"Hello?" Susan said, startling Wanda back to the present moment.

"What? Sorry."

"It's all right." Susan gave her arm a squeeze. "He's outside."

"Who?"

"Troy. That's who you're looking for, isn't it?"

Wanda focused on her plate and started picking at a quiche crust with her fork. "I wish Margaret could have come," she said. "Why didn't she? Do you know? It's not really because Gus is working tonight, is it?"

"I think she's still afraid of being seen in this context. You know, in association with these things. I think she's still ashamed." Susan looked toward the catering table, where Bruce was presiding over a table of hors d'oeuvres. "Look at Bruce. He's in heaven."

Wanda sighed and poked at her quiche.

"He's gone out for a smoke, in case you're wondering," said Susan.

"Who?"

Susan emitted a short, bemused exhalation through her nose. "Troy, darling. Troy."

"I thought he quit."

"He's started up again."

Wanda frowned and pushed crumbs around her plate.

Susan gave her a peck on the cheek. "I'm going to check in with our Mr. Katz. Back in a minute."

Wanda kept her head lowered and began to eavesdrop.

"My God," one woman remarked with incredulity. She was studying the show brochure. "I just read here what she uses for tesserae!"

"Tess who?" her male companion grunted, affable but perplexed. Wanda grinned. He reminded her of Uncle Artie.

"Tess-sir-ray," the woman emphasized impatiently. "The pieces she uses. It says here that she smashes antique porcelain that was stolen from . . ." They moved on.

"You're Tink Schultz!"

Wanda startled. A woman sporting an orange pantsuit and a complicated haircut hailed her from several feet away and started zeroing in.
Wanda was mortified; up until now, no one knew who she was—now
half the room was staring in her direction. "Are you Tink Schultz?" the
woman said, her voice obnoxiously familiar, in the way of politicians and
talk show hosts. She had protruding, eggish eyes and a nervous demeanor.

Wanda immediately felt a kind of energetic repulsion, as if the
woman were wrongly magnetized. She nodded.

The woman pulled Wanda's hand into hers and began shaking it
brusquely. "I'm Kat Brandt with *The Seattle Times*. I have to say, your
work is simply extraordinary—even without its obvious sociopolitical
resonances." She hefted a large leather satchel into view and pulled out
an electronic date book. "I'm wondering, could we schedule an interview sometime this week?"

Wanda spotted Troy across the room. He seemed to be the only person in a sea of faces who wasn't staring at her. She reached up and sema-
phored a distress with her linen napkin. Something tore, a side seam
on her bodice maybe, and she quickly tucked her arm back into her side.
Troy had seen her, though, and he was already pushing through the
crowd toward her: Sporting a string tie, vest, and boot-cut jeans, he was
Louis L'Amour cover art come to life.

"I'll have to okay it with my editor, of course," Ms. Brandt was saying, "but I'm pretty sure he'll jump on it after I tell him about you."

Troy arrived. "Jump on what?"

Ms. Brandt smiled blandly in Troy's general direction and then refocused her hyperthyroid attention on Wanda. "I want to do a feature
on you. Your background, your training, your personal and artistic in-
fluences, your philosophy . . ." Ms. Brandt leaned closer. "You may not
realize this," she said, in a conspiring voice, "but you are about to turn
the art world on its ass."

Wanda felt wilted. She looked to Troy. "Are you really smoking
again?"

"Now and then," he replied. "Here, I brought you some water."

"Thanks." Wanda gulped gratefully, keeping him in her sights.

"Who—?" Ms. Brandt seemed flustered. She hunched forward
slightly, trying to make her presence known. When that didn't work,
she started waving. "I'm sorry. This is—? You are?"

Wanda downed the rest of her water. Fortified, she set her glass aside and stood. "This is Troy Bridges," she announced, using the authoritative, projecting voice that had served her well in the management of actors and children. Heads that weren't already turned in their direction did so now. "Mr. Bridges is my . . ." She yanked on the reins of her speech momentarily, mentally checklisting various titles for Troy until she landed on one with the ring of professionalism. ". . . technical director. None of this would have been possible without him."

Wanda was wearing the pair of flat-heeled shoes that Susan had picked out to go with her dress, so Troy was a good foot taller than when she'd stood next to him as Detective Lorenzini. Nevertheless, Wanda felt that they were symbolically, if not literally, hip to hip, so in the interest of presenting a chummy, professional, unified front, it seemed perfectly natural at that moment to put her arm through his, draw him closer, and look into his eyes. She immediately regretted it.

"Gotta go," she said, blushing. "Pheromones." She grabbed two glasses of champagne from the nearest tray and bolted for the bathroom.

"Five pages! That's enough for one night, don't you think?" Irma said, admiring their work. "And so nice they look too. Are you too worn out for a game before you go?"

"No," M.J. lied. He felt weary. "But I could use some coffee."

"Help yourself. I'll clean this up." They busied themselves. "Do you have any photos you'd like to organize?" Irma said offhandedly. "Now that you see what's possible, I mean. How artistic you can get. Not to mention the fun. Don't you think these stickers are cute?"

"No."

"No, what?"

"I don't have any photos."

"None?" Irma asked, incredulous.

M.J. measured the coffee. "All right, Irma. I have one photo."

"One."

"That's right."

"What's it a photo of?"

"You are a nosy broad, Mrs. Kosminsky, anybody ever tell you that?"

"'Curious' is the word I prefer. I'm a curious broad. And let me tell you, mister, along with honey and apple cider, a curious nature is the secret to my longevity."

M.J. pulled two coffee mugs out of the cupboard. "Scrabble or gin rummy?"

"Scrabble." Irma scooped up her coffee mug and marched into the living room. "Don't think I'm going to let this go!"

Her voice was loud enough to rouse Maurice, who awoke with a start, rolled onto his side, and fell off the table with a thud.

Wanda peeked her head out of the bathroom. "Is she gone?"

"Yes."

Under the fizzy influence of six gulped ounces of champagne, Troy looked more delectable than ever. It was his blurriness she liked most, his indistinctness.

"Thank God."

"I told her she could have an interview—"

"Fine. As long as you do it with me." He had the look of a memory.

"—but I think she's still looking for you."

A memory of woods and their colors: ebony, the auburn of burnished oak, the white of paper birch, the swirl of burled mahogany. "Can we sneak out the back way?"

"The party's not over."

"It is for me." Annexation—that was what she wanted. A dissolution of borders. He wanted it too, didn't he? She came out of the bathroom and scatted a snatch from Monk's tune "Ask Me Now." She held out her hand.

Troy hesitated. "I'll tell Susan and Bruce. They'll be wondering where we are."

"No they won't. Come on. Let's go home."

Even through her champagne-and-adrenaline-induced haze, Wanda knew there was a reason she was supposed to keep her distance from this angel, but she couldn't remember what that reason was, and besides, it surely couldn't have been a good one. She leaned against him, letting her cheek sink into his chest and her lungs fill with his scent. "Aren't you tired of this?" she asked. "Aren't you exhausted?"

She presented her face. He kissed it. She presented her mouth; he kissed that, too. She roamed around inside him, savoring the flavors of spice and tobacco smoke on her tongue. The tobacco was new. It was nice. Peter used to smoke.

Troy withdrew from her arms and backed away. "No."

"What's wrong?" she asked.

"I won't do this again."

"Do what?" Wanda tugged at the collar of her dress; it suddenly felt too tight.

He looked at her. "You'll have to find another way to get fixed."

Wanda felt as though she were choking. "What do you mean?"

The muscles around Troy's eyes contracted. His face reflected a mixture of feelings that Wanda couldn't read. "I won't play doctor. I won't be part of your physical therapy program."

"What are you talking about?" Wanda asked defensively, pretending not to understand.

His voice was even, his expression neutral. "I won't fuck you to help you feel better."

"Why not?"

"You know why. I want more than fucking. Don't come to me until you do too."

Reflexively, Wanda grabbed at her collar and pulled hard. Two buttons popped off and rolled toward the back door. She hobbled after them and snatched them up. Then she pushed open the door and stood outside, breathing in the night air greedily, trying to sober up. What the hell just happened?

Her breathing slowed. She checked in with her heart. She could picture it in there, in its calcified condition, encased in the bodice of her dress. Maybe it hung suspended, caught in something that had once been liquid—like a woolly mammoth in ice, or a dragonfly in amber. Or maybe it bore fossilized impressions. If someone were to autopsy her heart, they'd find traces of life, evidence of eons gone by. Times when she'd been able to feel and the feelings left imprints. Maybe her heart was wearing a cast. Maybe it wasn't sclerosed at all but atrophied, shrunken, and the cast enclosing it was scribbled over with stories written in a dead language. Wanda checked further. Was there any softness left in there? Any spot that was still unfired, unformed, unglazed?

Was there access? Entry? A place still open to impression? No. Her heart was finished. It bore, perhaps, records of life, but it wasn't alive. Too late for decoration. Too late for effects. Further handling could only result in cracks and fractures. People could cut themselves on the edges of her heart, she was sure of it. Troy was right to stay clear. His good sense was commendable.

She sensed him behind her, too close. She took a step, widening the space between them.

"You still want a ride?" he asked.

"Yes. Please."

She wouldn't touch him again, so help her God. She would keep her distance. She would remember—*Ah, this was the reason!*—that she was a hazard to the living. Her intimacies would be with objects, memories, and dreams. She'd hold in her heart only the missing and the dead.

M.J. and Irma were pulling their Scrabble tiles. "Don't you ever want to go back there?"

"Back where?"

"To Europe."

"Why would I want to do that?"

"I don't know. To get something back, maybe."

"What? Nah. That part of my past, it's like a street that only goes one way."

"If I'd lost someone—"

"Oh, stop. We've been friends for a year. The mystery man routine is wearing thin. Stop being coy and tell me about your photograph."

M.J. squinted at his tiles. "My wife left me, years ago. She's one of the people in the photograph."

"Who's the other one?"

Damn, M.J. thought, *the old dame doesn't miss a trick.* "It's nothing like what you've lost, Irma. It's not worth talking about."

"Loss is loss. Heartbreak is heartbreak. You think I'm sitting here gloating. Telling myself that my suffering beats yours? Hurt is hurt. You don't measure these things."

"It just seems plain ridiculous to talk to someone like you about suffering."

"'Someone like me'?" Irma looked genuinely angry. "A survivor, you mean? Listen. If I thought that way—like we've got the market on suffering and the rest of the world doesn't know the meaning of the word—then I'd be a pretty poor excuse for a human being, wouldn't I?"

"Sorry."

"Your wife. When did you see her last? When did she go missing?"

M.J. pretended to study the Scrabble board. "Almost thirty years ago."

"Oy. Is she dead?"

"I don't know."

"Do you think you'll ever find out?"

"Damn, Irma."

"Well, what does your heart tell you?"

M.J. started arranging and rearranging his tiles, looking for a word. "My heart tells me, No, I'll never find her."

"So this is what you do? Close the door to love and spend your life looking for a person you're not going to find?"

"It's what I deserve."

"Oh," Irma said knowingly. "Now I get the picture. What did you do to deserve to be so guilty?"

"I abandoned my daughter."

"Aha!" Irma cried. "On the street, you left her?"

"No."

"With people who beat her and starved her?"

"No, of course not. I left her with my sister."

"So she's a bad person, this sister of yours. A real witch."

"No!" M.J. felt his face go hot. "Our Maureen's the best there is."

Irma was staring at him, her face calm and neutral. She'd made him give up a name, the trickster, ridden him until he'd said it out loud. He hadn't spoken any of their names in years. There was a reason for that. Saying their names was like throwing open a door in his chest to a world full of nothing but storms. He was pissed at her, soundly pissed. He shut up.

She pressed on, her words slow and deliberate. "You know where your sister is, don't you? You could find your daughter if you wanted to. If you ever gave her a second thought."

"I'm not risin' to the bait. I'm not talkin' about this anymore."

"It's an insult to God, you know—to choose to suffer."

"Irma, it's not that simple. She has every right to hate me, and probably does. They probably all do. What good would it do any of them to see me again?"

"Ah, boychick," Irma said, clucking. "It's not about them. It's about you." She looked down and began moving her Scrabble tiles around. The tiles made little clicking sounds that M.J. liked. "Maybe if I'd never met Sam," she continued, "I would have put walls around my heart, dressed in black, and gone through the rest of my life shaking a finger at the world. But I did meet Sam, thank God, and he helped me choose to live, to love. Not to forget the dead, no, never that—we said the kaddish for Lucie and Albert every year of our married life. But to live; like the Torah says: 'Choose life.' Make friends. Play cards. Bowl. Go to Hawaii." Irma paused then and looked up. "'Tikkun Olam'—you know that phrase?"

"No."

"Repair the world. Fix what you can."

"You'll just have to believe me, Irma. In this case, it's too late to fix things."

"Maybe. You could be right. My point is, it's never to late to try. And that's all God really wants from us. That we try. I'm no smartypants, doll, and really I don't mean to meddle. I just want you to think about it."

"Okay, Irma," M.J. said. He wondered what Irma's God would have to say about lapsed Catholics who lie to little old Jewish ladies. "I'll think about it."

Irma took a slow sip of coffee. "You asked before, is there anything I would have wanted." She gazed at Lucie's teacup. "I wish I could've had their bodies. No matter how they ended up. When you say is there anything I'd like to get back, that's it. Not having that . . . it's always been the worst part for me. A lot of people have tried to get . . . What do they call it?"

"Restitution?"

"Restitution, that's it. Money, paintings, stocks, bonds, insurance policies. It's in the newspapers all the time. I don't blame them. It's the principle of the thing, I know that, and they've got the right. It's just not something I ever felt like doing."

Irma returned her gaze to the Scrabble board and started laying out a word. "What I lost was my husband and my child. You don't look for teacups in a cemetery."

M.J. studied Irma's face. She didn't usually look her age, but tonight she did, even wearing "Sassy Cinnamon," and he felt a pang of tenderness and fear.

He looked down at the word Irma had laid out on the board. "A–Z–Y–G–O–U–S," he said. "What's that?"

"Azygous," Irma replied matter-of-factly, as if it were the most common word in the world. "It means 'not one of a pair'; 'having no mate.' 'Odd.'"

M.J. smiled and shook his head.

"What, you don't believe me? Look it up. It's the last word under A. 'Azygous.'"

"No, Mrs. K., I believe you."

"That's sixty points—plus fifty more for using all my letters. Not a bad start." Irma pulled out a pencil and notepad. "Are you keeping score?"

M.J. picked up his I and his N and lined them up under Irma's S. He spelled a three-letter, three-point word meaning the breaking of religious law or moral principle.

"Why bother, Mrs. K.?" he said. "We both know you're going to win."

Troy turned off the truck motor. They sat for a while, silent, sad, not facing one another.

It was midnight. The sky was dark, the moonlight tangled in a congested swirl of mists. The porch lights were on. Everyone in the house was surely asleep.

He spoke first. "That was nice what you said, about my being your technical director."

"I meant it." Wanda turned to him. "I really do count on you for . . . so many things." His profile was a dark, unreadable silhouette. "I'm sorry, Troy. I wish I could—"

"God I love your body." Sound waves came to a standstill in the space around them, defying physics. It was an enclosed space, Wanda realized, containing commingling molecules of their breath, too, and minuscule flakes of genetic code. "Good night."

She sat still, alone, unable to move. Her heartbeat grew oddly amplified. Her blood tides pounded with a pressure so fierce that all sounds had the ebb and flow of a storm at sea. For the second time that night, she felt as though she were suffocating. She began breathing in short, quick gasps that, had she been physically self-aware, she would have recognized as sobs.

God I love your body.

Wanda was trying to remember a time in her life—any time—when anyone had said words to her that meant as much as the words Troy had just spoken.

Twenty-seven

Reviews

Ever since her initial diagnosis, Margaret had undergone a CT scan every three months; this was in the interest of what neurologists call "following the tumor," a phrase which had always struck Margaret as amusing. Where were they following the tumor to? Did they expect it to lead them somewhere? She sat in Dr. Leising's office, reviewing the most recently reconstructed images of her intracranial space. Gus was with her, as was Susan. It was a routine visit.

"As you can see," Robert said, "compared with the January CT, the tumor demonstrates no appreciable change. There it is," he continued, "and there, and there. . . ." He pointed to several images with the tip of a ballpoint pen. "In this slice especially, you can see that the margins of the tumor are still well-defined and there has been no growth." He used his pen to trace the edges of the star. Margaret fancied that she felt an accompanying tickle, deep in the recesses of her brain. "Frankly, Margaret, I'm dumbfounded. All I can say is, you are one very lucky woman."

I know, Margaret thought, but dared not say it. She smiled and squeezed Gus's hand.

Subsequent meetings went much the same way: They'd gaze at thin-section CT images of her astrocytoma (Margaret preferred to call it "The Star") while her doctor, docentlike, pen in hand, would enumerate The Star's stable characteristics. Margaret always made an effort to feign polite surprise when the words "no change" were uttered; she did not want to give the impression that she was gloating. She often sensed a tinge of disappointment in Robert's voice. Perhaps he felt embarrassed by the fact that his dire predictions for her future had not come to pass. Or maybe he hoped The Star would be more of a challenge to follow, less constant. "Just keep doing whatever you're doing," he'd repeat, glumly, shaking each of their hands in turn.

"Don't worry," Margaret would chirp. "We will!"

Reviews of the group show first appeared in local and regional publications:

"A mosaicist named Tink Schultz—along with two other local artists—is exhibiting a collection of small-scale sculptures and wall mosaics. In style, they are reminiscent of the *pique assiette* tradition made famous by Raymond Isidore, the 'crazy plate stealer' who spent thirty years applying ceramic and colored glass mosaics to every interior and exterior surface of his home in Chartres. Historically, this type of mosaic construction is nothing new; even Seattle has its counterpart, in Milton Walker's West Seattle rock garden. And the *objets trouvé* nature of Schultz's work is commonly employed by contemporary artists. But Schultz is no crazy plate stealer. Nor do her materials come from thrift stores or Dumpsters. Schultz's tesserae are generated by breaking antique porcelain from the massive collection of a woman named Margaret Hughes, and they are the by-products of Jewish persecution."

Another:

"In a large wall mosaic entitled, *Étoiles, 1942,* a line of smiling, round-faced schoolchildren proudly wear the yellow star on their winter coats as they stand before a school playground. The other half of this grim diptych, *Étoiles, 1943,* shows the same children, still wearing their stars, but in this image they are emaciated, haunted-looking, and imprisoned behind the real barbed wire with which Schultz has wrapped this group portrait. Having seen these pieces, it is virtually impossible to imagine a more apt medium for the subject matter."

And another:

"Schultz's sculptural mosaics are stunning reinterpretations of objects related to Judaism: In *Winter Miracle,* she gives us a fully lit menorah with swordlike shards of gilded porcelain standing in for the flames. In *What Is Woven,* a dozen loaves of braided challah are laid side by side, cradled in cloths, like nursery newborns. And nowhere is the union of artistry and materials more profoundly expressed than in *Seder Plate*— in which thousands of pieces join to form a large Passover platter. Its five sections, for the components of the Seder meal (lamb bone, egg, bitter herbs, honeyed apples, and parsley), are delineated with distinctive figurative designs and Hebrew characters. Although the symbolism here is obvious, it is staggering to behold."

At first Wanda pooh-poohed the significance of reviews; but then she tracked them down with assiduity, shut herself in her room, and scrutinized every syllable. She soon learned, though, that giving weight to other people's opinions was creative nihilism; it was like being banished from the Land of No Words and exiled to the Land of All Bullshit. The arts section of *The Seattle Times* was routinely used for fire-starting.

She was contacted by a gallery owner who wanted to give her a solo show, so she spent the next months obsessively applying herself to the design and execution of three new works: *Shoes of the Dead, The Choo-Choo Circus,* and *Holy Book.*

On opening night, Margaret once again stayed home. Wanda didn't mind; she put in only the briefest appearance herself before heading back to the studio. She wore jeans, drank apple cider, and stayed well away from Troy.

After this, Wanda's work—and Margaret's collection—received even more publicity. Travel magazines and domestic and international flight publications printed feature articles:

"The Seattle summer art scene has much to offer. In her solo show, mosaicist Tink Schultz continues to excite controversy with her choice of materials (see page 38, 'The Hughes Collection Scandal: Desecration or Deification?') even as she presents us with stunning works related to the Jewish faith. In this exhibition, the large scale of her newest sculptures makes it evident that Schultz is grappling with even grander themes.

"As an example, a piece entitled *Shoes of the Dead* references the horrific display of victims' shoes in the Washington, D.C. Holocaust Museum. But in this case, a mosaicked pyramid of jumbled, unmatched footwear of all sizes and styles—ingeniously and gorgeously crafted from vividly colored tesserae—is not a grim monument to despair and death, but a joyous affirmation of life. Another of Schultz's more transcendent works is simply called *Holy Book*. From a distance, it resembles a large, ivory column. Drawing closer, one sees that the column is an unadorned cylinder upon which lies a massive scroll. It might be the Torah. It might be the Bible. It might be the Koran, the Bhagavad Gita, the Upanishad, or any of countless other religious texts. We cannot know: The book's pages are blank, pieced together from millions of minute fragments of unadorned translucent white and gilded china. This piece by Schultz—who describes herself as a 'spiritual atheist'—reminds us that the words of faith are not only divisive, but insignificant; it is the book's flaws which give it a distinct authority and holiness."

There was a feature article in *Vanity Fair:*

"The story behind Schultz's tesserae is almost unbelievable: Her work is fashioned from antique European porcelain which was stolen from Jews in the 1930s and 1940s. The thief? One Oscar Hauptmann (1880–1946), a noted antiques broker and shipping magnate. Permission to break these rare and in some cases priceless antiques—which remain unclaimed by their original owners or surviving kin—comes from Hauptmann's daughter, Mrs. Margaret Hughes, with whom Schultz resides. Mrs. Hughes has made many attempts over the years to track down the owners of these pieces, but her efforts have been wholly unsuccessful.

"Is it possible to separate our knowledge of these facts from the art itself? No, it is not. Even if Schultz's work were shabbily crafted (which it is not), it would still be elevated to a different status. One cannot view this oeuvre without entering into a discussion of the significance of materials coupled with artistry. There have already been strong outcries from many groups and individuals about the nature of Schultz's work and the legitimacy of claims made by Mrs. Hughes; some have expressed vehement support, others equally vehement condemnation. What is Schultz's responsibility to these priceless objects she destroys? What is Mrs. Hughes's responsibility? What is their joint responsibility to the Jewish community at large? And to the community of art historians, curators, and collectors who consider Schultz's process and Hughes's patronage nothing less than desecration? And finally, how much are these controversies and concerns fueled by the fact that the artist herself is not Jewish? These questions will certainly be taken up and debated endlessly in both secular and religious settings, but they are not within the scope of this review.

"It is fair to say, however, that at the center of this controversy is the concept of worth: what we as humans value—and why. In Schultz's work, context is everything."

The telephone began ringing almost nonstop. There were calls from journalists, museum curators, civic and religious leaders, agents, and others. Not all of the calls were complimentary; not all of the callers were fans.

From those who did appreciate her work, Wanda began getting offers for commissions. These ranged from commercial projects— solicitations from interior decorators begging her to design kitchen backsplashes, shower stalls, and fireplace facades—to larger, community-related projects and public art for places like libraries, schools, theatres, hospitals, government buildings, and community centers. She found it hard to turn these projects down and ended up saying yes to many of them. They were worthy. They needed doing. The people who approached her were earnest and good-hearted. She would just have to manage her time and energy better.

"Did you have any idea the sea of treacle you'd be stepping into, becoming famous?" Susan asked one night at dinner.

"Sea of grout would be more like it," Bruce joked. "You look tired, girl."

"I'm fine," Wanda insisted, but without much conviction. She felt haggard, drained. She'd spent most of the day taking calls, having meetings, trekking back and forth between the house and the studio. Her bones hurt. Her mind was a rattletrap. Her hands were lonely.

"Clearly," Margaret said, "you need some help. At the very least we need to put in a second phone line—would that be possible, Troy?— and hire a secretary. Someone to answer the phone, screen calls, field requests, that sort of thing."

"I believe they're called 'administrative assistants' now, dear heart," Gus interjected.

"Well, of course they are. I'll place an ad in the paper tomorrow." Margaret stood to get a notepad. "You shouldn't be tiring yourself with business concerns, Tink."

"I'm telling you," Wanda said testily, to the table at large, "I'm fine!"

Margaret looked hurt. She sat down. Everyone else ducked their heads and tucked into their suppers—except Troy. He was sitting at the other end of the table, staring at Wanda in a way that made her pissed at him and ashamed of herself. She dragged her fork through her mashed potatoes and waited for someone to send her to her room.

Instead, Troy made an announcement: "I think we should start offering classes." Around the table, necks lengthened and faces began to reemerge, slowly, warily—as if summer had suddenly arrived at a turtle pond in Antarctica. "In mosaic technique," he went on, "laying tile, design. We have the resources and the space."

"Tell us more, lad," Gus said.

And so he did, outlining ideas for weekend workshops, community classes, collaborations with vocational programs and high schools. Wanda was stunned. He must have been thinking about this for weeks, maybe longer.

"But those are just rough ideas," he concluded, shoving his dishes aside and taking up pencil and paper. "What do you think? Can we raise this barn?"

Wanda watched as Troy drew everyone into the discussion. They continued to brainstorm well into the night. With Troy as leader and facilitator, they planned classes, delegated responsibilities, designed marketing strategies, and composed a simple statement that clarified their goals: the establishment of a nonprofit teaching facility dedicated to the art and craft of making mosaics, with the broader mission of fostering community through artistic collaboration. It would be called the Crazy Plate Academy.

As if Troy's vision coincided with some deep, unmet collective need, the academy was instantly, eerily successful. Students streamed in. Word spread. Classes filled quickly. Anyone who had difficulty paying benefited from another of Troy's ideas: Free instruction was offered to any student who could volunteer his or her time sorting pieces and assisting in the assembly of Wanda's larger works.

In effect, by starting the Crazy Plate Academy, Troy had not only birthed a teaching facility; he'd seen to it that Wanda had all the help she would ever need—without the humiliation of having had to ask for it.

* * *

"Hello, Robert."

"Hello, Margaret. Alone today?"

"Yes," Margaret said, settling her pocketbook on her knees. "I thought I'd give Susan and Gus a reprieve for once."

"Ah," Robert said. "Beautiful fall we're having, isn't it?"

"Yes. Beautiful."

He nodded. "Well," he said with a sigh. "Here we are." He flipped on the lights. "No change." He pointed to a few images, made some perfunctory comments. His lectures had become shorter and shorter, which was somewhat disappointing to Margaret, since she never tired of hearing about The Star or being reminded of its presence.

But, of course, her relationship with it was quite different from anyone else's. To Margaret, The Star was a perfect physiologic manifestation of her life's preoccupations. The Star caused her pain, as it should, but the pain was manageable. The Star necessitated procedures and medications, but that, too, was bearable. A whole society had sprung up because of The Star's presence. A community. Maybe it would stay this way forever, never changing, never growing. Just a reminder, a cautionary tale—like the raised, white, scallop-shaped scar on her right knee from that time when she was seven: Running too fast through Volunteer Park, she'd slipped on wet autumn leaves and fallen on a nail.

"Until next time, then," Robert concluded.

"See you in the new year!" Margaret replied.

Twenty-eight

❧

The Unveiling

On October 1, 1998—not coinciden-
tally, they all learned later, the day after Yom Kippur—a woman showed
up unannounced at the Hughes household. She did not present herself at
the front door in the manner of a regular visitor; instead, she walked
around the north side of the mansion toward the carriage house. Bruce
saw her from the kitchen, where he was slicing vegetables for Pumpkin
Tortellini Soup. He was sufficiently alarmed by the woman's unexpected
presence, her demeanor, her surreptitious approach, and her dress ("How
was I supposed to know? She could have had a surface-to-air missile under
that cape!") that he impulsively dialed 911—a fact that would embarrass
him deeply for years to come, since the visitor was none other than Barbara Cohen, soft-drink heiress, arts advocate and patroness, human rights
activist, philanthropist, and the woman known to many sectors of the Seattle community and the world at large as "Babs C."

It was a clear, crisp autumn day. Troy was outside, giving a work-
shop to a group of vocational students. Wanda was adhering tesserae
and tiles made by community volunteers to a memorial obelisk which
would stand in the entrance of an AIDS hospice.

The caped woman strode over to her—her coarse salt-and-pepper
hair cropped short, her maroon cape billowing like a set of wings—and

clasped Wanda's gloved hands, not appearing to notice, much less mind, that they were gooey with polyvinyl acetate adhesive.

"You're Tink Schultz?" she asked. "I'm Mrs. Cohen. Please call me Babs."

"Hello," Wanda said. "Your gloves are ruined." Before she could get another word in or extricate her hands from the woman's firm grasp, Mrs. Cohen continued.

"I'm wondering, is there a place we can talk?"

Wanda got her hands free. They stripped off their gloves in unison; Mrs. Cohen tossed hers into the trash. "We could go into the studio," Wanda offered. She glanced at Troy and nodded, hoping to communicate her gut feeling that this woman, in spite of her strange behavior, was probably not a Ku Klux Klanswoman or professional assassin. He relaxed and turned his attention back to his students.

"You've done a good thing," Mrs. Cohen began earnestly once they were inside. "A mitzvah. And that's mostly what I came here to say to you. All these community projects, this teaching . . ." Pivoting with perfect leading lady grace, she executed a maneuver that stage directors like to call the big turn. It caused her cape to ripple magnificently. "It's wonderful," she said. "Just wonderful . . ." She stilled, and her grave, gray eyes settled on Wanda. "And your other work," she said solemnly. "Your work about the Shoah. Thank you."

Of all the words that had been spoken in reference to Wanda's work, these had never been among them. For the first time since she'd set foot in Margaret's house, Wanda once again broke one of her own commandments and, in the presence of a total stranger, began to cry.

"May I?" Mrs. Cohen went on, gently. "Snoop around, I mean?"

Wanda nodded.

Some artists keep their source ideas out of sight and neatly organized—in file cabinets or closets perhaps, or in carefully labeled boxes. These artists are serial monogamists. They take on one project at a time and see it through to its completion. They focus with exclusivity, putting up firewalls that cannot be breached by the incursion of other ideas. If other inspirations whisper to them, they might take notes, but they shelve them. This kind of artist makes her ideas stand in a queue. She asks them to kindly wait their turn. She promises she will get to them, she keeps her appointments, but she insists upon seeing them one at a time. It is one perfectly viable way of working. It was not, however, Wanda's way.

Besides the works-in-progress that were arrayed around the studio, and the models, boxes of grout, adhesives, mixing tubs, piles of porcelain, and so forth that were the tools of Wanda's trade, there were enormous bulletin boards affixed to all the walls—the kind one sees at community centers or in other public places. Over the years, the bulletin boards had become covered with a thick strata of postcards, magazine pictures, Xeroxes, scribbled words, newspaper articles, phrases, sketches, paintings, lists—any item of interest, no matter how small or seemingly insignificant, was tacked up on the studio walls. Wanda kept every token of inspiration readily accessible, if not directly in view. She believed that these neonate ideas and inspirations worked on her, with her, in a peripheral, indirect, and powerful way. They hovered, tangibly. They seeped into her consciousness.

Be true to what attracts you had become her motto. *Keep it near. Its voice may be far away and faint, unformed and obfuscated, but that's no reason to shutter it in darkness.*

To most visitors, Wanda's studio looked like a colossal monument to detritus and disorganization. But she could pinpoint the location of every scrap. She remembered what lay at the bottom of every box. She could document the identity of every layer. All of it had meaning.

Mrs. Cohen stopped suddenly at a place near a dim corner. "Huh," she grunted. She started peeling apart the sketches that were thumbtacked there, squinting at each one in turn.

Wanda's breath quickened; Babs was excavating the whisperings of ideas that were farthest from view and closest to her heart.

"Do you mind?" Mrs. Cohen murmured vaguely, but she didn't wait for an answer. Carefully, she took the sheaf of sketches down, separated them, and then tacked them back up on the wall, side by side. She hinged forward on her fashionably booted feet so that her nose practically rested on one of the sketches, and the toe-to-crown line of her body made a perfect scalene triangle with the floor and the wall. She emitted a quiet symphony of nonverbal responses which seemed to reflect a mixture of surprise, amusement, relish, pathos, and discovery. Finally she turned and regarded Wanda with the unblinking expression of a benevolent raptor. "Why are you hiding this?"

"I'm not hiding it, Mrs.Cohen—" Babs seemed about to say something; but then she changed her mind. "It's just a completely different kind of work."

"Personal, you mean?" Mrs. Cohen looked strangely troubled.

"Yes. Personal."

"I see." Wanda's visitor was obviously wrestling with something. "I'm Jewish, you know," she said with a slow emphasis—as if this information was neither self-evident nor a non sequitur. She considered Wanda for a moment or two longer. "We must talk more," she concluded. "Now, where's Mrs. Hughes? I must see her as well."

There was a Seattle police car in the driveway, its cherry-top flashing. Two grim-faced officers stood side by side on the carriage house path in a stance suggesting a kind of athletic readiness. Behind them on the patio, Margaret, Susan, Bruce, Troy, and the vocational students were gathered in a tight clump, their expressions reflecting everything from mild concern to feverish trepidation. Bruce looked as though he might faint.

In little time the police officers were convinced that Mrs. Cohen did not pose a criminal threat. Bruce was mortified, especially since he was the one person who knew Babs by reputation ("If Jews had saints," he'd say later, "she'd be one!"). But Mrs. Cohen took it all in stride. "I've been mistaken for a lot of things," she quipped, "but never a soldier in the army against artistic expression. Senator Helms will be thrilled."

"Now," she said, once the officers were gone. "Will someone please introduce me to Mrs. Hughes?"

Margaret emerged from the crowd. "Here I am."

"It's an honor to meet you." Mrs. Cohen pronounced. Then she confounded them all by pulling Margaret into a lengthy, impassioned hug, as if they'd known each other forever. "I'm so sorry for not coming to see you sooner. Please forgive me. What you've done is a goodness beyond belief."

Wanda's first full-scale installation—commissioned by Mrs. Barbara Cohen—was a project which would take over a year to complete; the planning phase alone would take weeks. Wanda and Troy labored extensively on the technical demands of creating and—equally important—transporting the finished work; it would be traveling to museums across the country. Keeping construction on schedule would also require the help of hundreds of Academy student and community volunteers.

Wanda began training everyone in her methods for transferring designs. She and Troy schooled them in the application of sealants to the various substrates she'd be using for the two-dimensional components. There were lessons in mixing adhesives and grout.

They kept Mrs. Cohen apprised of their progress; she listened and nodded and wrote checks. A filmmaker from New York was given permission to document the construction process, so that even before its completion, the project referred to in shorthand as "M.K." had the art world buzzing.

Margaret had another unremarkable CT in early January. She commemorated the occasion by presenting Robert with a bottle of French champagne.

"What's this for?" he asked.

"Our two-year anniversary."

"Thank you, Margaret. I don't know what to say."

"You don't have to say anything, Bob. I'm just glad to still be here."

"It's not as if you've just been waiting around, is it? There's been quite a tizzy about you and that boarder of yours who breaks things, what's her name?"

"Tink. Yes. She's an artist."

"Tink?" Dr. Leising was at a loss.

"Short for 'Tinker Bell,'" Margaret explained. "Believe me, Bob, it suits her perfectly."

"Well then, I'll see you in three months," he said, standing to shake Margaret's hand. "Unless, of course," he added with a slight surge of energy, "you experience any change in your symptoms before then."

Babs planned a huge gala for the opening exhibit. Those invited included journalists, friends, members of the art community, and political, civic, and religious leaders. Also in attendance would be several Holocaust survivors who wanted to show their support for the project—including Babs's great-aunt Tessa.

Clearly, in Babs's mind the event was part art opening, part diplomatic détente. "I want to get all the people who are talking about desecration-this and responsibility-that in the same room, face-to-face, in dressy clothes. I want them to hear from Tessa and the other survivors—who are the only real authorities on anything. Most of these protesting, indignant types haven't even seen Tink's work, much less made anything but the most reactionary response."

Furthermore, she was adamant that Margaret attend. "You have to be there," she stated. "Your not coming to the other openings, I have to tell you, has made people think you're ashamed."

"But I am ashamed," Margaret said.

"Of what? You're not some Nazi sympathizer."

"My father was."

"Yes. And here you are, not hiding that fact, doing so much more than just being sorry."

Margaret massaged her temples. "But it took me so long, Babs," she said. "Too long."

"There's no statute of limitations on good deeds," Babs concluded. She squeezed Margaret's hand and then went back to perusing a last-minute checklist. "By the way," she said, "did I tell you that you're getting a special award from the Mercer Island Chapter of B'nai B'rith? I'll be introducing you."

"You mean I have to stand up in front of people and say something?"

"They'll clap, you'll smile. Nothing to it. You'll be perfect."

Margaret heard Gus return from the bathroom. He pressed a warm, lavender-and-rosemary-scented cloth onto her forehead. "Grim, is it, lassie?"

"A bit," Margaret muttered. She tried to concentrate on Gus's gentle touch, on the pleasantly resinous smell of the herbs, on the agitated slashes, loops, and pinpricks of light—like a foreign alphabet—written on the inside of her eyelids. What did the words say? In what language were they written? She tried to send healing, even breaths deep into her core, as Gus had taught her, tried to smother the molten pain in her head with a cooling blanket of blue.

"Shall I go get Susan? Should we tell them we can't come?"

". no, Gus, I can't disappoint them. I'll just rest a bit longer."

Margaret's mother was on her left, filing her nails; Daniel was on her right, nearer the foot of the bed. He was crashing metal Hot Wheels cars back and forth over the knobby terrain of Margaret's knees, shins, and ankles, and providing the requisite nerve-twanging vrooms.

They'd appeared around five, just as she started to get ready. Hovering on either side of the vanity table mirror as she fixed her hair and applied her makeup, they primped too. Darting amongst clothes, shoes, hatboxes, and garment bags in the walk-in closet, they acquired their fancy clothes when she did. Now they were sitting close as she lay on the bed. Margaret couldn't remember exactly when Daniel had evolved from a barely visualized aura to a distinct and multiwardrobed figure; lately, however, he'd found not only defined form but enthusiastic speech.

You look great, Mom! he cried. *Look at this! Screeeeeech! It's the Grand Prix!*

Thank you, sweetheart; you look nice too. But you know, this is a grown-up affair. . . .

She heard Gus's voice as if from afar. "Are you sure, Margaret? Should I call the doctor?"

They were never with her at this time of day. In the morning, yes, she expected them, and true, sometimes they shadowed her until well into the afternoon, when finally and almost always they'd drift away, make themselves scarce, do whatever it is that dead mothers and children do when they're not socializing with the dying. But they shouldn't be here now, in the early evening. And not tonight, of all nights.

She had to get up. It was almost time to go.

You're just afraid someone will call you names or throw rotten produce, Margaret's mother said.

I'm afraid of more than that, Mother.

It was bound to happen sooner or later. You didn't expect to stay in the shadows forever, did you?

I expected, Margaret emphasized, *to be a worm sandwich.*

Daniel laughed. It felt as though the inside of her skull were being excavated with a pickax.

Oh, Margaret, really! You must enjoy this hoopla while you can. Believe me when I tell you that it's no fun being part of a scandal after you're dead.

Come on, Mom! It's time to go!

She rose then, slowly. Gus helped her to her feet. She looked into his eyes and found in their blue depths a brief, cooling offshore breeze. She smiled at him and straightened his tie. "Ach, laddie," she said, in her best attempt at a Scottish accent. "Don't you look fine in your fancy clothes!"

He laughed, took her arm, and they started downstairs.

The pain in her head, slicing and dense, had the force of millions of exploding stars.

The installation, entitled, *The Magdalen Kitchen, 1972,* had three walls which enclosed a completely realistic kitchen. Aunt Maureen's kitchen, to be exact. Every surface, including the floor, was covered in tesserae. There was a sinkful of dishes, a stove, a fridge, cupboards. Every minute detail had been attended to, down to the grease spots on the dishcloths and the dead fly on the windowsill. From a mosaicked radio on the kitchen counter came period music. A crazy-quilt tesserae clock kept time. Placed within this setting was a long table covered by a mosaicked cloth. Crowded on the upstage edge of the table was a family of seven boys eating breakfast. And pouring juice for the boys was Aunt Maureen, dressed not as a 1970s housewife and mother, but as a fifteenth-century servant.

This was not what anyone had expected. The room vibrated with the sound of voices engaged in discussion, praise, celebration, and debate. Babs couldn't have been more pleased.

After an hour, she moved to a microphone and got everyone's attention. She welcomed and thanked the guests. She directed a speech of special thanks and recognition to the survivors. Then she began her introduction. She reiterated what everyone already knew about Margaret's collection. She described Margaret as "a woman who has cherished, maintained, and protected a precious part of Jewish history and culture—in the same way that many brave individuals during the Holocaust tried to protect the persecuted Jews from whom these things were stolen." Babs paused and made eye contact with a few select members of the audience. "Although no person asked her, no secular laws required her, and no religious laws commanded her, Margaret Hughes chose to be generous enough—and courageous enough—to come forward and share the gift of her collection with all of us now, in this way. It is a gift that will resonate for generations to come. Please join me in recognizing Margaret Hughes."

The room exploded in applause. Babs kissed Margaret on the cheek and presented her with her award.

Margaret stepped up to the microphone. She gripped it with one hand and smiled. She noticed her mother and Daniel beaming at her from the back of the room. "Thank you!" she said. She tried to smile again and stepped aside.

Wanda then made a speech thanking Margaret, Mrs. Cohen, Troy, and all the volunteers. "Had it not been for the help of all these remarkable people, *Magdalen Kitchen* would have taken years to finish. You'd be looking at a ninety-year-old."

There was laughter, more applause, and then Babs leaned into the microphone. "So go! Eat! Drink! Discuss!"

The crowd dispersed and the babble of voices resumed.

"Are you all right?" Gus said, taking Margaret lightly by the elbow.

"Some water. Please, dear heart. Could you?" Margaret said.

It was the last thing she would remember.

She regained consciousness in the Radiology Department, in the arms of a CT technologist. "Well hello, Mrs. Hughes!" It was Gerald, one of her favorites. He positioned her carefully in the CT coil. "That's quite a getup you were wearing when they brought you in. You didn't need to dress up on my account. Clothes don't make the gal, you know. How about some Bach transcriptions for cello?"

Margaret smiled weakly. She had come to know all the hospital personnel by name—the admitting staff, the technologists, the radiologists. Goodness, it had been more than two years that she'd been coming here! The technologists she knew especially well; they treated her so kindly, called her by name, played music during the procedures.

Gus had taught her breathing techniques that kept her relaxed while she lay confined in the CT coil and the machine acquired helical pictures of her brain. She used these techniques every time she was in the coil, but they were a special comfort on this occasion; it was the first time Margaret had felt genuinely frightened—not only because she dreaded the results of the scan, but because there was no escaping it now: She would finally have to tell Wanda about The Star.

"You can see, right here"—Dr. Leising pointed to one of the images—"how there's been growth compared to the previous study."

There were a few moments of silence.

"Have you had a worsening of your symptoms, Margaret?" Dr. Leising wanted to know.

Gus and Susan stared at her. She felt exactly as if she'd been summoned to the principal's office for cheating on a test or filching extra desserts from the lunch line.

"Margaret," Gus said, taking her hand. "The doctor is asking you a question."

She glanced toward the door. Wanda and Troy were on the other side, in the lobby.

"Will you excuse me for a moment?" she asked.

She got up and went through the door to the reception area.

"Where's Wanda?"

"In the bathroom," Troy answered. "Down the hall. I'll take you."

She could hear crying even before she pushed the door open. "She knows?"

Troy looked pained. "Couldn't really keep it a secret after this. I'm sorry, Margaret."

She reached up and squeezed his shoulders. "It's all right, dear. You did the right thing. I'm just sorry that you had to be the one to tell her. I should have done it long ago." She faced the door. "Will you wait?"

"Of course."

Margaret went into the bathroom. Wanda's crying instantly stopped.

Margaret located the bottom of a black silk skirt in one of the stalls. She opened the door next to it, put down the lid, and sat.

"Well," she began, "here we are again."

Reviews of *The Magdalen Kitchen* were mixed:

"The source of Schultz's tesserae is well-known, and many Jewish community members regard the new direction and subject matter of her work as a betrayal."

Another: "Smoke and mirrors. A clear case of the Emperor's New Clothes. Were it not for the incendiary nature and scope of Schultz's achievement—it's BIG, all right, no one can argue with that—her work would rank among that of the average mosaicist."

Another: "When will we see the end of this trend? No matter what the subject matter or the materials used, 'art' of this nature is best left to Girl Scouts and Martha Stewart devotees."

And: "What distinguishes Ms. Schultz's work is the scandal surrounding it. Other than that, she takes us to no new ground in terms of artistic significance. Ever since Judy Chicago, we've had feminists reinterpreting 'women's work'—i.e., the family kitchen, hearth and home, etc. etc. ad nauseam. My prediction is that this flash-in-the-pan body of work, once the legal and ethical issues it has raised recede into the distant past, will be quickly forgotten."

These reviews were in the minority, however, and most art critics agreed that *The Magdalen Kitchen* secured Tink Schultz a significant place in the world of contemporary art.

But setting aside these critical analyses, good and bad, consider the artist's point of view. When she creates, she does not imagine the world entire, but one—just one—of us, as her audience. It is that person's tokens she carries, that one she labors for, longs to please, and holds in her heart.

She wouldn't want us to be intimidated by fancy French phrases or the ubiquitous Art with a capital A; we all harbor something of the crazy plate stealer. We may not have the intimate and (let's face it) just-this-side-of-pathological relationship with objects that Margaret does, nor are we likely to be inclined toward Wanda's laissez-faire attitude regarding the destruction of material goods. But we've all been involved in willful damage and reconstruction. Every last one of us.

"Everyone else knew, Margaret. Why not me?"

"I'm sorry, Tink. I just never found the right time."

Most of us can't keep our eyes off mosaics, especially if they're like Wanda's, built up from the damaged, the cast off, the orphaned. They are infinitely seductive. We marvel at the time involved, the patience, the technical mastery, the detail. We do this with other kinds of art too, but why does a mosaic invite our bodies—as well as our eyes and intellects—in a way that the *Mona Lisa* does not? Why are we content to keep our distance from the Sistine Chapel? Would we really want to touch it, even if we could? Whereas, if someone tried to keep us from laying our hands on a mosaic, especially a *pique assiette* mosaic, we'd feel deprived, wronged, pissed as hell. These are good questions to ponder.

"You lied, Margaret. From the very beginning. From the first day we met."

"You were fragile."

"Bullshit."

"You cried in the powder room."

"That's not the reason."

The surface of any mosaic, even the most artfully executed, is always slightly irregular, and a patchwork of textures. We can be sure that touching the marble of Michelangelo's *Pietà* would be a different experience than touching Simon Rodia's Watts Towers, or the patio of Raymond Isidore's house in Chartres, or Isaiah Zagar's outdoor murals in the South Street neighborhood of Philadelphia.

"You were busy with your play, your technical rehearsal, your performances."

"I was not busy with my play every waking moment, Margaret."

Of course, no one can fault the *Pietà*. She's exquisite. A masterpiece. But with her smooth sinews of bloodless marble, who can deny that she is also intimidating?

"Then there was the accident. You were recuperating. You were weak."

"I was strong enough to hear about your Nazi father. You showed me *that* closet of skeletons."

Imagine the *pique assiette pietàs* that Wanda will make someday: A rabbi cradling the corpse of an Auschwitz prisoner. A father holding a young victim of a gang war. A mother clasping the body of a son who has died of AIDS.

"There was no change in the tumor for so long. I hoped, maybe . . ."

". . . it would get better? That's no excuse, Margaret. You still should have told me."

Mosaics also appeal to the side of us that has been reprimanded, punished, shamed. They are our rescued mistakes. Vindication. *Pique assiette* is revenge against those who inhaled sharply when we fumbled something, lifted a hand to us in anger, called us names—Idiot! Clumsy! Failure! Fool!—and said, Now look what you've done, what a mess you've made!

"If you'd known I was ill, would you have stayed?"

"Of course not. No. Absolutely not."

"Well, then. There's your reason."

When confronted with a dropped plate, what is your proclivity? Keep it? Repair it? Relegate it to the dump? Sometimes a single *I'm sorry* is all it takes; sometimes a person can say *I'm sorry* a thousand times and that glue will never dry.

"I'm a selfish old woman. For years I looked forward to dying in that house with nothing but those things and their ghosts. It was the only picture of my life that gave it value. I don't know why I changed. I just got an idea that I'd been wrong all along about what penance looks like. I never cared what it would cost you. I wanted someone to know me before I went. I'm sorry that person had to be you."

This metaphor culminates, obviously, in relationship, which is, after all, a marvel of construction, built up over time and out of fragments of shared experience.

"Margaret. Please, don't cry. Come out of there now."

Maybe we feel such a strong kinship with *pique assiette* because it is the visual metaphor that best describes us; after all, we spend much of our lives hurling bits of the figurative and literal past into the world's landfill—and then regret it. We build our identities from that detritus of regret. Every relationship worth keeping sustains, at the very least, splintered glazes, hairline fractures, cracks. And aren't these flaws the prerequisites of intimacy?

"It's all right, Margaret. Please come out. Of course I'm not leaving. How could I leave?"

The next time you break something, consider the action that might not immediately come to mind: Say a prayer of thanks over what has been broken.

Then, give it a place of honor.

Build it a shrine.

Twenty-nine

꒦

Like God in Paris

"You thought I was serious about this being one of those AARP trips, didn't you?"

M.J. gave a monosyllabic response, but didn't look up.

"Sight-seeing by bus," Irma went on. "Lunch stops at McDonald's. Mai tais by the hotel pool."

He was planting plumeria seedlings along a park trail. The flowers were white, delicate, waxy—unlike anything M.J. had ever seen. Their centers were illumed with blurred stars the color of softened butter. There were clusters of people grouped along the trail—their traveling companions—all doing the same thing.

"Admit it, mister. You were expecting a lot of blue hair and bingo."

They spent their days on Kauai like this, engaged in habitat restoration one day, trail maintenance another. Last week they'd helped a local farmer put in a taro field.

"You're right, Mrs. K. A service trip with the Sierra Club was not what I envisioned."

This work was new to him, and he enjoyed it. He tamped down the soil around a plant, making sure it was snuggled into its new bed. He brushed rich, dark crumbs of earth from his hands and took up another seedling.

They were a diverse group, ranging in age from ten to eighty-five. One of them had caught M.J.'s attention: a middle-aged woman with long hair and freckles. He'd noticed her right away, from the moment they boarded the plane in Seattle a week ago. He kept finding her in his field of view; there she was now, working intently by herself on the other side of the trail.

Irma punched him on the arm. "See? What have I been telling you? Life is full of surprises!"

Their hotel was in the Marais district in the eastern part of Paris, convenient to the airport buses, the Metro, and a major hospital. It was a quiet, working-class section of the city, within walking distance of tree-lined bridges, canals, locks, and barges that put Margaret in mind of the locks back home. Paris had the same compactness born of geographic necessity as Seattle.

As for the Parisians, they were nothing like the arch, contemptuous snobs of most Americans' imaginings; on the contrary, Margaret found them to be friendly and helpful. But then, Gus and Susan—who thus far had done all the talking—spoke impeccable French. Every tourist knows, or should know, that speaking good French to a Frenchman guarantees you a saint's welcome; speaking bad French lands you in the same moral sludge as that of a murderer.

Margaret's plan was to stay in Paris for the first four weeks and then relocate to Chartres, from whence they would make day trips to rural sites. A two-month vacation in all. Not surprisingly, Dr. Leising had objected strongly.

"They have physicians in France, don't they?" Margaret had cooed, borrowing a lilting cadence from her mother's voice. "I'll be accompanied by a registered nurse; we'll be near a hospital. It's not as though waiting around is going to make the tumor get better, is it?"

Robert regarded her coolly. His jaw clenched. "No, Margaret. It will not get better."

"I die in Seattle, I die in France. . . . I ask you, Bob: What's the difference?"

To that, he had no response but a sigh.

Gus was more sympathetic to Margaret's wishes, but Susan—whose demeanor had changed a good deal now that she was functioning in full-blown Licensed Registered Nurse mode—had made no secret of her opinion that the plan was unreasonably ambitious, even foolish, and her efforts to deter Margaret had been tireless to the point of stridency. No one had had the heart to tell her that her protestations were futile—clearly, short of physical restraint, Margaret was going to board that plane and travel to France—and no one had yet found words forceful enough to shut her up.

"Couldn't we at least stay in North America?" she'd implored one night as she, Wanda, and Margaret were setting the dinner table. "How about a trip to French-speaking Quebec?"

Bruce's voice called from the kitchen: "I can cook all the soufflés you want right here!"

Susan turned to Wanda. "I mean really, don't you think she's being irresponsible?"

Wanda plopped a dinner plate heavily on the table and turned to face her. "I think," she said, in the voice of a head ward nurse in a Catholic hospital, "that the job of a hospice caregiver is to give the dying the dignity of their final choices. Now let it go, Miss Meriweather."

Susan's eyes widened, her lips wobbled, she burst into tears and ran into the kitchen.

"Sorry," Wanda said sheepishly. "Somebody had to do it."

"Thank you, Tink," Margaret said, then hollered, "Dinner, boys! Time to wash up!"

A week later, Gus, Susan, and Margaret arrived in Paris.

In the beginning, they made the usual tourist expeditions: to Notre Dame, the Louvre, the Jeu de Paume, the Tuileries. Susan and Gus were very strict, allowing Margaret only one major outing per day. If they went sight-seeing in the morning, she was required to rest for the remainder of the afternoon and evening. If they were planning dinner out, followed by a night at the opera, cinema, or theatre, she was practically kept under lock and key from sunup to sundown. The slightest sign of fatigue on her part was met with extreme consternation.

She had experienced only one seizure—a far less serious seizure, Margaret was quick to remind them, than the one after the gallery opening. She had not even lost consciousness, for goodness' sake; it was just a mild episode of hemiparesis. The hospital was less than five minutes away, the medical staff spoke even better English than Susan and Gus spoke French, and she'd received excellent care. It had been nothing, really. But after that, she practically had to beg them to stay.

Their vigilance was such a burden, not at all what she had wished for. Even though she understood that they were motivated by concern, and that all this constant supervision was probably necessary, she chafed under it. This was her first trip—her only trip—to the place she'd dreamed of since she was a girl. Everything, even the astonishing sight of Winged Victory, was tainted by the awareness that Gus and Susan were unable to relax, even for a moment, because they were the self-appropriated caretakers of a woman who, in their minds anyway, could drop dead at any second.

One morning, she woke up early. They had been to the theatre the night before, and Gus was still asleep. She got up carefully and listened at the adjoining door. There was no sound coming from Susan's room either. She felt especially well, the morning air was laden with the earthy smells of spring, and so she decided to go for a walk.

After taking her medications and tiptoeing into her clothes, she wrote a note: "Please don't worry. I've gone for a stroll. Meet me as planned at the Musée Picasso at ten. I have to see how my French holds up without you two! Love, M."

She went downstairs to the dining room and asked the maitre d' if she might take her breakfast with her. "I'm going for a walk this morning," she explained. *"Une promenade."*

The maitre d' smiled. It was a genuine smile, Margaret felt. Maybe her accent wasn't too terrible. "Really? Where are you going, madame?"

"La Musée de Picasso," she enunciated, with special attention to the u in "Musée."

"Ah! Very good!" the maitre d' said. "One moment, *s'il vous plaît."*

Margaret adjusted the brim of her straw hat. She swayed slightly in her new floral skirt. She liked the feathery way it swirled against her legs.

The maitre d' returned and presented her with a small lunch basket crammed with fresh rolls, butter, jam, fruit, a carton of yogurt, a thermos of coffee, and a yellow rosebud. *"Voilà!"*

"Oh! It's beautiful! *Merci, monsieur!"*

"De rien, madame. Bon appétit!"

Margaret set off, city map and basket in hand. "*Bonjour!*" she said to each passing stranger, feeling braver and braver. How wrong could her pronunciation of such a small word be? "*Bonjour!*"

It was the first time she had been alone in Paris, and the sense of freedom and relief was intoxicating. The morning, at last, was hers. If she tired, or if it grew time to meet up with Gus and Susan, she could always hail a taxi.

"April in Paris," she sang under her breath. "Chestnuts in blossom. Holiday tables under the trees . . ." She headed east on one of the major boulevards. After a few blocks she consulted her map and saw that on this side of the Place des Vosges was a northbound street that would take her almost directly to the Musée Picasso. She had plenty of time. She'd find a park and have her breakfast of bread and yogurt—and French coffee, of all things! Wanda would never believe it. Then she'd look for a street on her left called Rue de Turenne.

"God makes it so easy for us," Irma said offhandedly—as if it were a perfectly natural conversational segue, and she'd just been talking about religion instead of extolling the virtues of Dr. Scholl's shoe inserts.

"What?" It was midday and the group was taking a break, eating lunch at the picnic benches on either side of the trail they'd been working on.

"To do mitzvoth."

"Good deeds," M.J. said distractedly. "Is that what you're talkin' about?" There was that woman again, the tall one; she was sitting with a couple of twenty-somethings at a table on the other side of the trail. "Yes!"

He'd noticed her taking meals alone in the dining room, or in the lobby at the end of the day, reading. She wore eyeglasses attached to one of those necklace-type things; it was strung with polished stones and beads, almost like a rosary.

"You, for example," Irma went on. "It wasn't as if I had to go looking. God practically dropped you in my lap. All I did was pay attention."

"You've done a helluva lot more than that, Irma."

"And you've done a few things for me too, boychick, don't forget."

M.J.'s attention was tugged to the other side of the trail again. The woman was laughing, but there was something muted and reserved about the sound of it, as if she was out of practice.

"You should go over there and introduce yourself," Irma said. "We're only going to be here for another few days."

"What are you talking about?"

"That woman. The tall one with the bracelet. You've been staring at her."

"No I haven't," M.J. lied.

"Fine, then. You haven't! Such an A.K. you can be sometimes."

"I don't even want to know what that means."

"*Alter kocker!*" Irma barked. "You're right! You don't!"

They ate their lunch in silence for a while. Irma made a show of shifting around and sighing loudly, as if she were vastly uncomfortable. Finally she spoke up again.

"Just say this: 'Hello. My name's M.J. That's an interesting bracelet. What's your story?' How hard can it be?"

M.J. laughed.

"You want me to introduce you? Her name's Joyce Gallagher."

M.J. squinted. "You've met her already."

"Not everybody on this trip hides in their room at the end of the day. Some people actually came here to make friends."

"I have a friend: you."

Irma bulldozed past him. "We had a little chat in the ladies' room after dinner the other night. She's fifty-two years old, she's a professor of English, she teaches at the University of Idaho at Moscow—that's just over the border, you know, a stone's throw from Spokane—and she's divorced with two grown kids, Annie and Theodore. Annie's here too, but Joyce hasn't seen much of her because Annie brought her boyfriend. That's them over there with her." Irma waved and shouted. "Helloooo!"

"You learned all this in the ladies' room?"

"What, you think we just go in there to take care of business?"

Joyce smiled and waved back.

M.J. hunkered down and studied his pineapple juice.

"The thing is," Irma said, "God put you in front of me. I just used my eyes. Then I had a thought—that you were lonely, maybe, that you needed a friend. Then I had an idea, an idea that I could do something about it, and after that there was no turning back, see?"

"No. I don't."

"Once a person has an idea—to do a mitzvah, I mean—then it becomes a promise to God. And believe me, He hates to see us let a good thought slip through our fingers."

"How do you know my thoughts about her are good?"

"Very funny. You're not the big bad sinner you think you are. My point is, nothing makes God madder than when He goes to the trouble of putting someone in front of us and we don't follow through."

M.J. sighed. He knew that trying to explain for the umpteenth time that God didn't occupy a place on his moral compass would have no impact on Mrs. K. whatsoever; nor would it keep this conversation from continuing until dinnertime. "You're not going to leave this alone, are you?"

Irma smiled and took a bite of her fruit salad.

M.J. sighed. "Fine, Irma, fine. I'll go say hello to the woman."

"Good boy!" Irma shooed him off with a wave of her napkin. "You won't regret it."

He got up and started stomping across the trail, toward Joyce's table. "Idiot," he mumbled. His heart was pounding as if he were fourteen years old. "I'm an idiot."

"Will I see you guys at dinner?" he heard Joyce ask as he got closer. The daughter and the boyfriend had already packed up their gear and were heading off.

"Maybe," the daughter said. "Bye, Mom. Have fun."

They hiked away, leaving Joyce behind to clean up the picnic mess. She watched them go, wearing a face that M.J. wished he hadn't seen— a brave, worn face that would take up at least three chapters in a book with a sad ending.

She didn't notice him until he was a couple of feet from the picnic table.

"Hello," he said. "I'm a friend of Mrs. Kosminsky's"—he gestured— "over there."

Irma waved. They waved back.

"My name's M.J."

"Hello," she said. "I'm Joyce." Her hair was a white-and-auburn mass that went down to the middle of her back. It must have been neatly braided earlier in the day, but now there were fuzzy wisps—like dandelion seed tufts—arching over her forehead. Not a large person, she nevertheless gave an impression of solidity. M.J. thought of lighthouses and docks—structures one could steer toward, tether to. "It's a pleasure to finally meet you."

She held out her hand; it was a temperate hand, in spite of the Hawaii heat, and when M.J. took it he breathed in the smell of something like mulled cider. But there was another scent, too; it had an arid, ashy quality, and he was startled by its familiarity. *Does loneliness have a smell?* he wondered. *The loneliness of resignation?* It did. He knew it to be so. He smelled it on Joyce, and surely his own skin was scented with it as well.

He noticed the wide silver bracelet Irma had mentioned, patterned with a labyrinthian design. "Is that Celtic?"

"Yes. I understand from Mrs. Kosminsky that you're originally from Dublin."

"That's right." She was wearing a sleeveless purple shirt—it was a good color on her; the shirt was open at the throat and revealed more freckles on her chest. M.J.'s mouth felt suddenly parched.

Joyce went on. "Did she tell you that I have a great love for Irish poetry? In fact, I'm working—ever so slowly—on a biography of your great kinsman, Mr. Yeats."

That old broad. What a trickster. "No," M.J. said, smiling. "Irma didn't mention that."

Soon after she turned onto the Rue de Turenne, Margaret began to feel weak and unwell. She hailed a taxi. She directed the driver to take her to the Musée Picasso and then slumped against the car door in the backseat—next to Daniel, who was playing with a toy sailboat, and her mother, who was studying a pocket-sized Berlitz volume of *French for Travellers.*

Maybe taking this trip was selfish, Margaret thought. *Maybe everyone else was right.*

"*Où est la théâtre?*" Margaret's mother intoned with confidence. Her accent was terrible.

It's "le," Mother. "Le théâtre."

"*Où est la—le cinéma?*" Margaret's mother looked up from her phrase book and inhaled deeply. *Foolhardy, perhaps. I wouldn't call it*

selfish. Everyone should have at least one day in Paris, in the spring. Je
adorez le France!

Margaret winced.

Her mother returned to her phrasebook. *"Où est les archives?"*

It's "ee," Mother, not "I." And "sh." "Les-ar-sheev." "Où sont les archives?"

You can be very snobbish sometimes, Margaret. Are you aware of that?

Look, Mom! Daniel cried. *It's a man selling balloons!*

The taxi had stopped at a traffic light. Margaret glanced up and, sure
enough, there was an old man wearing a beret and a dark woolen coat.
He was holding two enormous bouquets of yellow balloons. Daniel
waved. The man opened his hands to wave back. Instantly, the balloons
floated skyward and revealed a modern-looking building at 37, Rue de
Turenne.

"Let me out here, please," Margaret said sharply.

"Pardon, Madame?"

Margaret fumbled for the right words. *"Arrêtez-vous!"*

Your French is good, Margaret's mother said grudgingly. *I'll give you
that.*

The cabdriver looked confused. "This is not the Musée Picasso,
madame."

"Yes, I see," Margaret answered, swiveling around in the seat. "What
is that building? *Qu'est-ce que c'est là?"*

"C'est le C-D-J-C." He gave the letters their French pronunciation,
so to Margaret it sounded as though he said, "Say day gee say."

"Pardon? Plus lentement, s'il vous plaît."

"Le Centre de Documentation Juive Contemporaine."

"I'll get out here, thank you," she said.

"But, madame, it's too early. *C'est fermé.* Closed."

"That's all right. I'll wait. *Merci."*

Margaret got out, paid the cabdriver, and found a nearby phone.
"Gus? No, dear heart, nothing's wrong. I'm fine. I'm sorry if you and
Susan were worried. It's just . . . there's been a change in plan. Can the
two of you meet me somewhere else?"

After hanging up, Margaret glanced at her watch; it was only just
nine o'clock, and the museum didn't open until eleven. Still, she had
no desire to be anywhere else, so she settled down on the front steps of
the CDJC and opened up her basket.

A woman walked by, holding a curly-headed toddler by the hand. *"Vous choisissez un jour parfait pour votre pique-nique, madame!"* she said.

"C'est vrai!" Margaret replied, without hesitation. *"Aujourd'hui c'est un jour parfait!"*

The next morning at breakfast, Irma was writing postcards. She pushed a pile across the table to M.J. "Here," she said. "I bought extras, in case you want to send some."

"Irma," M.J. said. "Who am I going to write a postcard to? You're the only friend I've got, and you're sitting across from me."

"You're so wrong I'm not laughing," she said. "Rudy Hahn? Rudy's not a friend? The staff at the bowling alley?"

"All right, all right."

"The customers? Those nice girls, Carrie and Joanna, who take care of the kids? No friends, he says. What a bunch of baloney."

"But you're already sending them cards. Just say I said hello."

"That's a lazy attitude! Besides, a person can't get too many postcards from Hawaii. Here!" Irma jabbed a pen in his direction. "Get to it!"

M.J. sipped his coffee and then took the pen. He twirled it, thumped it, tapped it, made it do flips.

Irma gave an exasperated groan. "Why are you schlepping now?"

"I don't know what to say."

"What's so difficult? You're living like God in Paris, tell them."

"What's that supposed to mean?"

"It means," Irma said, "you're doing well. You're happy. You had an actual conversation with a lady professor from Moscow, Idaho. You took a walk with her. You sat with her at dinner. That's plenty of news, coming from you." She returned to her postcard.

After a few more seconds, M.J. began to write. It didn't take him long.

"There," he said, stamping the postcard with a flourish and dropping it onto Irma's completed pile. "You happy now?"

Irma picked it up. "But there's no message on here. Just an address in Chicago."

"That's okay," M.J. said tightly. "They'll know who it's from."

* * *

"They must have records," Margaret explained excitedly. "Documentation. Inventories." Susan and Gus exchanged a look. "I know how many people died," she continued, reading the subtext in their expressions. "I know it's probably impossible. But here it is and here we are. I can't just walk away. Couldn't we at least wait until they open and talk to someone?"

Gus replied, "Of course, lassie."

Susan added, "I just don't think you should get your hopes up."

"Where have you been?" Irma said, pretending to read her paperback. "The seat belt sign has been on for ten minutes."

"The head," M.J. replied. He buckled up and then pulled the flight magazine out of its seat pocket. "Also, I figured it'd be a good time to say good-bye to Joyce. It'll be pretty chaotic once we get to baggage claim."

"I see."

He feigned interest in an article about a Seattle artist who liked to break things. "We exchanged addresses."

"Good," Irma said. "You'll have somebody else to send a postcard to."

The serious, bespectacled young woman who answered their initial questions about the CDJC was named Sylvie. She had been courteous enough at first—but then Margaret stated her request: that she be allowed to access inventories of possessions confiscated from Parisian Jews. Sylvie was adamant about CDJC rules, which required anyone who wanted access to the archives to submit a "legitimate request" in writing, and well in advance of visiting the Centre.

Gus placed a hand on Margaret's arm. "May I try and explain, dear?"

"Please," Margaret replied. She felt as though she were going to cry; her French was clearly inadequate to communicate the urgency of their situation.

Although Margaret did not completely understand the content of Gus's speech—and it was quite a long one—she recognized a gradual softening of Sylvie's expression and demeanor.

"*Je vois,*" Sylvie kept repeating. She glanced frequently at Margaret—who found she didn't mind being on the receiving end of a pitying look if it meant she could get what she wanted.

When Gus came to the end of his monologue, Sylvie muttered a few quick phrases and gestured, indicating that they should sit and wait. "*Excusez-moi,*" she said, making a brisk exit.

"Where's she going?" Margaret asked.

"She's getting her supervisor," Susan answered, grinning at Gus. "Mr. MacPherson, you could have had a career in the diplomatic corps."

"Ach, but I have, my dear! I've been a hotel valet for fifty years."

Sylvie returned with a trim, impeccably suited man in his late forties. He extended his hand to Margaret. "Hello, Mrs. Hughes. I am Claude Berger, the director." His resonant voice had only the barest trace of an accent. "I have read of your remarkable collection in the art and antique journals." Margaret glanced beyond him to Sylvie, whose cheeks were noticeably pink. "You are of course welcome to use the Centre and all its resources during your stay in Paris. We have just the smallest bit of paperwork to fill out—Sylvie, could you see to that, please?—merely a formality. And then of course you are free to access the archives in any way you see fit." Director Berger leaned down and kissed Margaret's hand. "It is an honor to meet you."

The next morning, Gus and Margaret told Susan that they would be spending their days in the CDJC archives, doing research. They insisted that she spend this time on her own. Gus assured her that he'd make certain Margaret didn't overextend herself.

"But I'll feel so guilty!" Susan protested. "What if something happens?"

Margaret presented her with a beeper. "Now go!" she ordered, à la Babs. "Enjoy! Be a tourist!"

The Germans and their French assistants were very good about keeping records, Sylvie told them. She suggested that Margaret and Gus begin by examining the inventories dating from July of 1942. "That was when the big *rafles* started in Paris," she explained as she led them through the archives. "It is as good a place as any to commence to look."

"*Rafles?*" Gus asked.

Margaret eyed the towering shelves of books, the file cabinets, the drawers. The rooms and their contents seemed to go on forever.

"'Roundups,' I think you'd say," Sylvie continued. Her English was good, but she spoke quickly and in a rote manner, like an overworked tour guide. In addition, her accent was quite strong, so Margaret had to struggle to understand what she was saying.

"Jews were dragged out of their homes and taken to the Vélodrome d'Hiver—a large sports arena—for registration. As soon as their apartments were empty—if the German police or the French police or the neighbors didn't get there first and start stealing things—the ERR would appear."

Thankfully, Gus jumped in again to get clarification. "The ERR?"

"The Einsatzstab Reichsleiter Rosenberg," Sylvie rattled off. "It was a special operations unit of the Nazi party. A man named Alfred Rosenberg had special permission from Hitler to steal whatever he thought would further the Nazi cause. The ERR took everything: furniture, books, toys, dishes, kitchen utensils, photos, paintings, curtains . . . even socks and underwear, if you can believe it. And every bit of it was inventoried. This way."

Sylvie turned a corner and kept walking. Gus had no trouble keeping up, but Margaret felt like a tardy child being tugged along by a punctual parent.

"After they were processed and registered at the Vel' d'Hiv, they were sent to one of the holding camps in France—Pithiviers, Beaune-la-Rolande, Drancy. Anything they had of value on them at that time was inventoried and confiscated. These were small things, though—wedding rings, cash, jewelry, things like that—so what you're looking for wouldn't be found in those records." Sylvie paused and glanced back. "Is this helpful?"

"Oh, yes," Margaret said breathlessly. She was already exhausted.

Sylvie resumed walking and talking in her glib manner. She might have been telling them how to make paper clips. "After they left the holding camps, they were put on the convoys—the cattle cars, you know, to the concentration camps. Drancy was the worst. It was basically a dispatch station for Auschwitz. Here we are."

Sylvie stopped abruptly. Gus and Margaret almost ran into her.

"Please, sit," Sylvie said, indicating a large table.

Margaret plopped down and tried to catch her breath. Her face felt sweaty.

"So," Sylvie said. "The inventories I'm going to bring first for your studies were made by the ERR."

"Thank you," Gus replied.

"Is Madame all right?"

Gus answered, "It's all just a bit overwhelming."

Sylvie smiled. It was a pinched, cynical smile—oddly out of place on the face of such a pretty young woman—and Margaret puzzled over it. Then she realized that Sylvie probably saw a lot of people come and go through here, people who began with energy and good intentions that wearied fast. People for whom this kind of work was just too hard. That was it, Margaret thought: Sylvie was like an old soldier indoctrinating a pair of new recruits who weren't going to make it.

"I'll be right back," Sylvie said.

"Do you think this is a mistake?" Margaret said.

Gus put a hand on her shoulder. "Why would you ask that?"

Because it is, she wanted to say. *Because I can't do this. It's too much.* Instead, she said, "It isn't a very romantic way to spend our time together, is it?"

Gus sat down. He took out a handkerchief and began gently pressing it to Margaret's forehead, temples, and cheeks. "Do you know what it reminds me of?"

Margaret shook her head.

"The day after we met. You remember? I called every 'Hughes' listing in the Seattle phone book, playing detective, looking for you. I felt like a teenager." Gus took her hands. "That turned out just grand, didn't it? So will this."

Gus leaned close, so that their foreheads were touching. A few of Margaret's tears fell onto their hands.

"Besides," he stated, "it's what you have to do, isn't it, lassie. Before you go? I'm going to help you. You're not going to have to do this alone."

When they separated, Sylvie was there, giving them a look that was equal parts disapproval and surprise. She placed a large drawer on the table in front of them.

"So." All business. "Perhaps you will find something in here, yes?"

"I hope so," Margaret said, still holding tight to Gus.

"If you need me for anything, do not hesitate to ask. I'll be just over there."

"*Très bien, mademoiselle,*" Gus said. "*Merci.*"

"*Merci,*" Margaret echoed.

"All right, then. *Bonne chance.*"

The inventories, penned in hundreds of small notebooks and receipt-voucher ledgers, were meticulously detailed.

"One silver spoon, bent," one of the entries read.

Another: "*The Story of Babar* with flyleaf inscription: 'To Georgy, 1941. Happy 4th Birthday. Love, Auntie Gitu.'"

Another: "Porcelain girl doll with four ensembles: ballerina, equestrienne, ball gown, nurse. Missing ribbon from one ballet shoe."

As the days went on and their research continued, it became clear that—whether out of choice or directorial mandate—Sylvie had been assigned to Gus and Margaret for their exclusive use as a research assistant. She checked in with them frequently, answering questions and bringing them whatever they needed. She even reserved their table; when they arrived at the start of each day they always found a pitcher of water, glasses, pads of paper, and sharpened pencils.

One morning their table was graced with a large bouquet of lilacs, and fresh flowers greeted them every day after that.

"I guess we've passed the test," Margaret joked. "She likes us."

Near the end of their second week, Gus said, "Didn't we move a box of children's ware into the studio?"

"At least one."

Gus placed his index finger on a line from the ledger he was examining. "Do you have a green and gold chocolate service that's missing a piece?"

Margaret's heart thumped. "The tête-à-tête. Yes."

"What's the factory name?"

"Sevres."

"You should look at this."

Margaret leaned close and read the page heading: "Sendler Residence, July 16, 1942." Her eyes traveled down the page to where Gus's finger indicated one of the inventoried items. Margaret inhaled sharply.

"We need to cancel our trip to Chartres," she declared. "And we need to call home. Right away. Tell Tink not to break anything for a while."

The next step was to find out what happened to the Sendlers after they were evacuated.

"If they were taken to Drancy or one of the other substations on the way to the camps," Sylvie explained, "there might be a record of their arrival there." She took off her eyeglasses and looked at Margaret. "Why don't you two leave early today. Go to le *cinéma,* perhaps, or *faîtes vous une promenade.*"

Let's go to the park, Mom! Daniel cried.

Oh! Margaret's mother whined. *I'd much rather go to the cinema, wouldn't you?*

The dead, Margaret thought. *They can be so loud.*

Sylvie's voice seemed muted and indistinct by comparison. "Let me see what I can find out about the Sendlers," she said. She placed a hand on Margaret's arm. "There will be time enough tomorrow, and Madame looks tired."

The next day, Sylvie met them at the entrance. She held a small notebook. "They went to Drancy," she said, handing the notebook over. "Look."

"*#293: July 17, 1942,*" Margaret read to herself. "*Madame Irma Mariska Sendler; born 4 April 1912 (Rovno, Poland); current resident Marais district, Paris; Twenty-two thousand francs (22,000); 40 pounds sterling; 1 platinum and diamond ring; 1 gold wedding ring; 1 gold watch.*" Margaret handed the notebook back to Sylvie. She felt nauseous.

"She must have been evacuated with her daughter," Sylvie said. "Listen. The next entry reads: '*#294; July 17, 1942; Lucille Sendler; born*

10 December 1937. Marais district, Paris. Costume jewelry only. Nothing of value."

"What do we do now?" Gus asked.

"She was four," Margaret muttered. *Only four.*

"Convoy lists. I think we should look at those next. If we find them on one of the convoys, then we can know which camp they went to. That will help narrow the search."

Susan insisted on joining them. "Please let me help. I've seen enough sights. And," she added in the voice she always used when she was in her professional mode, her *Cherry Ames, War Nurse* voice, "I don't like the way you're pushing yourself, Margaret."

They spent their remaining days in Paris examining lists of names.

They were beautiful names, Margaret thought, all of them: *Azaria, Berman, Vogel, Stein . . .* She could not bring herself to scan the names with the speed and efficacy that Sylvie and the others mastered; she felt compelled instead to read the names slowly, trying to picture the people to whom the names belonged. *Abovitz, Weisman, Friedman, Morgensztern . . .* She moved the muscles of her tongue and mouth in a conscious and attentive way, as if the names were poems. Meditations. As if she had known them all. Made them all. As if she were God, numbering the hairs on their heads.

Picková, Cohen . . .

Her mother and Daniel drifted in and settled on either side of her, silent at first. Watching.

Dreyfuss, Blumenthal, Törsch, Mikova.

After a while Margaret began to whisper the names, and then half-speak them, so that over time the process began to feel as it should: at first like an act of prayer, and then finally like an act of contrition. Daniel and her mother began speaking the names with her.

Rabinek, Gettelman, Singer, Schwartz, Bronicki, Eszenyi, Fischl, Fabry . . . The names went in and out of focus; she read more and more slowly.

Synková. She could feel the names permeating her skin, sinking deep into her cells. *Mif.* Each one added its light to The Star, enhancing its density, its brightness.

The rare, fragile things the Nazis had stolen—things that had survived well into this century, intact—had been packed more carefully than the people who belonged to these names. *Koleba. Klein.* Seventy-five to a hundred people per railroad car, Sylvie told them, and two buckets: foul water in one, urine and feces and blood in the other. No sleep for how many days? Nauseous with hunger and thirst; pain and then numbness.

Salomonovitz, Laznowski, Lazar, Paltiel . . .

Bodies had been shattered and things had not.

Katz, Levi, Persitz, Frank.

At one time in her life, she had pronounced names like Sevres, Meissen, and Capodimonte with more reverence than the names on these pages. Obscene. Unholy. What kind of God was she anyway?

She felt ashamed. She felt ill. The sound of the trains. The smells inside. All of it was constant now. Just as it should be.

They found nothing of the Sendler child.

"She very well might have died at Drancy," Sylvie said. "The conditions there were terrible, and thousands died on French soil, you know, not in Germany or Poland. Many of the survivors who lost loved ones there instead of in the camps say that, later, they were relieved."

"How can you do this?" Margaret asked. "How can you work here, day after day?"

Sylvie paused. She shrugged slightly. "I grew up with this," she said. "My family lost people in the war, and these stories . . . I have heard them my whole life. One does have to . . . detach, a bit, in order to be useful."

Finally the name "Sendler" showed up on a convoy list.

"I found her," Margaret said, flatly. "She went to Auschwitz." She fell silent and massaged her temples. The cattle cars were rumbling through her head. *Clickety-clack, clickety-clack . . .*

"What now?" Gus asked.

"The next step is more difficult, I'm afraid," Sylvie began. "There is of course a good chance she died in the camp. Or she may have been put on a work detail, or evacuated in one of the forced death marches, or even sent to another camp. What I mean to say is, there may or may not be any further record of her." *Clickety-Picková, clickety-Klein . . .* "If she did survive, then we might be able to find something on the other side of the war—hospital discharge papers, emigration papers, something like that." Sylvie stopped speaking; Margaret was dimly aware that the young woman was staring at her. "The good news is, you have a name, and it is not a terribly common one. Only twenty-five hundred French returned, so there are not so many names to look at."

Picková, Cohen, Koleba, Klein . . . "So many lists," Margaret mumbled. She tried to move her arm, her hand, to rub the sides of her head, but . . . Where was her head? Had she misplaced it? Had it floated away?

"Are you all right, madame?"

"Margaret?"

"Margaret?"

Margaret?

Mom?

The whistle blew. The train arrived at the station. The door slid open. She was blinded by the light, overcome by the stench of burning flesh.

She woke up in the camp infirmary. *Oh, no!* she thought, terrified. She tried to sit up. *But I can work!* she wanted to cry. *I can still work!*

She heard a familiar voice—Cherry Ames, War Nurse, was it?—speaking nearby. "The day after tomorrow, if we can," Margaret heard her say. "It's very bad."

There was something wrong with her vision. She saw everything as blurry and undulating, as if it were being reflected in a fun house mirror. Her mother was there, as lithe and stringy as saltwater taffy. She was wearing a ballet tutu, riding boots, and a nurse's cap. She was practicing tricks with a bullwhip. Daniel was nearby too, wearing Babar's becoming green suit and derby hat. He was examining Margaret with a toy stethoscope.

Hi, Mom, he said. *You're sick.*

But I can work, Doctor! I can still be useful!

Hello, Margaret, her mother said. She sidearmed her whip and came closer.

Are you going to gas me? Am I going to the crematorium?

No, Margaret. We're going to take you home. She placed a cool, gentle hand—a mother's hand, Margaret realized—on Margaret's forehead. It felt very nice.

Sylvie came to say good-bye. "I am so sorry, madame," she said, "that you could not leave with the answers you came for."

"Thank you." There was something different about Sylvie's face. At first Margaret couldn't make out what it was. Then she realized that Sylvie was not wearing her eyeglasses. Her eyes were huge and round and hazelnut brown. Most surprising of all, she was weeping.

When Margaret got back from Paris, the CT showed an increase in the size of the mass. Dr. Leising babbled on about herniation, brain stem compromise, neurologic dysfunction. He recommended radiation therapy.

"It could shrink the tumor," he said. "Lessen your symptoms, at least temporarily. Prolong your life."

"For what?" Margaret said.

"Dammit, Margaret!" Dr. Leising snapped. "You're signing your own death warrant."

But she would not be dissuaded. The disappointment she felt—after coming so close—left her with nothing to stand on but shame and failure. She had tried, she had failed, she could do no more.

She put her affairs in order, made adjustments to her will. She named Gus as proxy and gave him durable power of attorney. She dictated commands related to her medical care and end-stage treatment, including a "Do not resuscitate" order.

Members of the household took turns in an effort to rally her. Bruce tried enticing her with her favorite foods; she wasn't hungry. Troy brought in blueprints and outlined a planned offensive on the kitchen; she deferred to his judgment. Gus and the Crooning Clansmen gave a bedside concert. They even wore their kilts. This she liked a good deal, but she refused to let on.

Wanda's tactics were the most unvarnished. "I'm going to be so pissed at you if you die."

"Break a plate," Margaret suggested. "You'll feel better."

One day, Susan came in and roused her.

"Margaret. Wake up." Her Cherry Ames voice had lost any hint of sweetness. *Whatever happened to bedside manners?* Margaret wondered, sluggishly. *Whatever happened to letting people die when they want to?* "It's Sylvie on the phone. She has news." Susan propped Margaret into a sitting position and handed her the receiver.

"*Allo?* Madame Hughes?"

"*Allo,* Sylvie."

"Listen: It's about Madame Sendler. I found her, through the armed services records." Sylvie was making an effort to speak very slowly. This, in combination with her beautiful French accent and cadence, made Margaret feel as though she were being read a bedtime story. "After the war, she married an American GI."

Margaret tried to put a face to Sylvie's voice, but all she could picture was a pair of thick-framed eyeglasses, moving stealthily through the night sky like some strangely designed surveillance craft.

"I was also able to locate her emigration papers. She came to the United States in 1947. I have put all the particulars in a letter which is on its way to you now."

"I see." On board the eyeglass spacecraft now, Margaret balanced expertly on one of the earpieces. She was wearing a white lab coat and holding a clipboard, writing long, precise columns of numbers in a coded language that only she could decipher—a scientist, drifting through space, recording the fluctuating energies of stars.

"I have sent out letters to several Holocaust research centers in America. It may well be that one of them may know of Mrs. Sendler's whereabouts."

"All right then," Margaret said distractedly. "Good-bye."

"But Madame Hughes," Sylvie said, and there was an urgency in her tone that made Margaret shake off her drowsiness. "You don't seem to understand. It is so very important. Are you still there?"

"Yes. I'm listening."

"This means that she is a survivor. Her life did not end in the concentration camp. She had another life. A third life. Madame Hughes, there is a very good chance that she—or her family—are living still."

In Margaret's mind, a clear image of Sylvie's face finally materialized behind the eyeglasses. Such a pretty thing, but so serious. Did she never smile?

"That's wonderful news."

Sylvie continued. "You know what they say, that every survivor's story is a history of miracles? *Petits et grands.*"

"*Oui?*"

"Mrs. Sendler's name. The name of her second husband. It is *un petit miracle,* I think, that it should be such an uncommon name."

"What is it?" Margaret asked.

Sylvie started to laugh. "Kosminsky!" she said. It sounded as though she were singing. "Can you imagine? Irma Mariska Kosminsky. *C'est incroyable, n'est-ce pas?*"

"*Oui,*" Margaret agreed. "*C'est incroyable! Merci,* Sylvie. *Merci bien.*"

"Well?" Susan said after Margaret hung up. "What is it? What did she have to say?

Margaret wiped her eyes and started fumbling with the buttons of her pajama top.

"Help me get dressed please, and then call Robert. I'm ready to talk about radiation therapy."

Thirty

❧

Mrs. K.'s Last Frame

M.J. was speaking with a chubby girl wearing torn jeans and cloddish shoes. He'd seen her before; she was hard to forget. She had gone out of her way—the way young girls seemed to nowadays—to make herself look as ugly as possible: ratty clothes, bleached hair, pale makeup, blue lips. A small gold hoop extruded from her left eyebrow. Behind her, arrayed in attitudes of studied nonchalance around the fountain, were six or seven other kids of indeterminate sex, looking and smelling like they'd rolled a bum for his wardrobe.

"I don't think so," M.J. was saying.

"Whaddya mean?"

"I mean, I'm not gonna put up the bumpers for you."

"Why the hell not?"

"How old are you, anyway, darlin'? Eleven? Twelve?" M.J. knew she was probably more like fourteen, but he wanted to piss her off.

"What the fuck does that matter?" the girl said. On her cheeks, two pale spots of pink struggled up through her pale makeup. "I'm not trying to buy a beer, for chrissake. I just wanna fuckin' bowl."

"You're too old to be asking for a bumper lane. And too young to be usin' that kind of language."

"Who the hell are you, anyway? God?" One of Eyebrow's admirers gave a snicker. "Just give us the lane that's got the goddamn bumpers."

M.J. turned on his most charming accent. "Let me explain somethin' to ya, darlin', so that you'll have the whole picture clear in your darlin' head. For one thing, I got a birthday party comin' at one and the bumper lane is reserved for one Alexander Anderson-Epstein, age five, and the darlin' boys and girls in his party who actually need to use it. For another thing, I've seen you here before. You're name's Roxie, isn't that so?"

"How do you know that?"

"You'd be amazed what a person with a curious disposition can learn eavesdropping on an eleven-year-old's phone conversations, especially if they have as many as you do. I've seen you here, without this lot"—he jerked his thumb toward the crowd behind her—"and I've seen you watchin' the sport. Like a hawk." M.J. leaned closer. "You have," he enunciated, "an interest. An interest in somethin' besides pissing off your mum and dad and flunking out of school."

Eyebrow was fuming. M.J. took a long drag on his cigarette and gave her a steely stare. "Let's cut the bullshit, shall we, Roxie? Listen closely: You're never gonna get any good if you rely on the bumpers; you wanna be some slop-ass bowler your whole life? Take lane nine. It's open. If I get a minute, I'll come around and give you some pointers."

"Thanks a lot. Asshole."

"Yeah, well, I may be an asshole, but I'm a helluva good bowler. Come back with a clean mouth and a willingness to learn the greatest game ever invented by humankind!"

M.J. had to shout the last part of his speech, since Roxie and her friends had turned en masse and exited in a group huff toward the video arcade.

"Hoodlums," he muttered.

"Old fuck!" countered Roxie, spinning around with a flourish and giving him the finger.

"You're right about that, darlin'!" M.J. replied. He took another drag on his cigarette and went back to writing next week's schedule.

"That poor girl," Irma clucked later that night. They were eating macaroni-and-cheese TV dinners.

"What poor girl?"

"That girl today. The one you were talking to at lunchtime."

"Poor girl, my ass. She's a hoodlum."

Irma raised an eyebrow. "So, you think she's getting a lot of love at home, do you? A lot of attention?"

"How would I know, Irma?'

"Summer's over."

"So?"

"Things may have changed a lot, but as far as I know kids are still supposed to be in school during the day."

"What is it you're suggesting, Irma?"

"Nothing! I'm not suggesting anything! Just that maybe a girl that age, she still needs someone. A grown-up. You could do a little something. Like you said. Give her some pointers."

"Right, Irma. Like she'd listen."

They ate dessert: cherry Jell-O with celery, walnuts, and cream cheese balls.

"You don't have to bowl, God forbid, and you shouldn't have any fun, but you could show a little interest. Pick up a ball. Give her a lesson."

"Give it a rest, Irma. A kid like that does not want somebody like me butting into their life."

They did the dishes. They brought their coffee into the living room.

"What do you want to do tonight?" M.J. asked as he settled on the sofa. "Cards? Scrabble? TV?" He snatched up the *TV Guide* and started reading it. When Irma didn't answer, he looked up.

She walked over to the cabinet, where Maurice was in his cat bed, standing guard as usual. She hoisted him into her arms and stood there, stroking him. "I almost didn't marry Sam, you know. I almost had a different life." She fell silent. Maurice purred and nuzzled her neck.

"Irma?" M.J. was struck by how small and frail she looked.

"I knew he loved me. I just didn't think I had anything to give. After we'd been together for a while—this was in '47 and his tour was almost over—he asked did I want to go back to Paris one last time. Visit the old neighborhood. Maybe take a look at my apartment."

"I thought you said you didn't want to go back."

"I didn't, but . . ." Irma shrugged. "Sam was trying to be kind. Maybe he thought I'd regret it later if I didn't go, and I halfway thought he might be right. I knew that, whatever happened, I could never live in Paris again. So, we went. Our neighborhood was in the Marais district. It was so strange being there after the war, all the familiar faces gone.

We got as far as across the street from our apartment, and then I started shaking and crying. It was terrible, like it was happening all over again. I couldn't go any farther. I couldn't have walked in the front entrance or up the stairs even if I'd wanted to. Sam said—and I'll never forget this, it was so like him—'I'll do it for you, sweetheart. You wait here. I'll go up first.'"

Irma paused. She settled Maurice back in his cat bed and mewed at him. He looked up at her adoringly and uttered a high-pitched squeak. Then she went on.

"Sam came out with this old woman on his arm and they started to cross the street. She could barely walk, and she looked older than God. At first I didn't recognize her. And then I remembered. She was our next-door neighbor. Our shriveled-up, snoopy, pain-in-the-ass neighbor. You know the kind: living alone, nowhere to go, always home, always squinting through the crack in their door, with their noses in everybody else's business. Old. Old in the worst possible way a person can be old. Albert—my first husband—and I, we couldn't stand her. I remembered thinking that she was probably a sympathizer. And maybe she was—who could tell in those days? Lucie liked her, though. She called her 'Madame Polar Bear.' I never knew why." Irma opened the cupboard. "'*Madame L'Ours Polaire.*' Anyway, I was terrified, seeing her again; I don't know why. It was all too close, and people . . . you just didn't know what they were going to do if you were a Jew in those days. Liberation or no liberation. Sam must have seen it in my face, because he came over and put his arms around me and said, 'Do you remember your neighbor, Miss Levendel? She has something for you.' She didn't smile, she didn't say anything, she just took my hand and put this in it."

Irma reached inside the cupboard. When she turned around, she was holding Lucie's teacup.

"It had rolled onto the carpet, under the table, and after we left she picked it up. It was the only thing in our apartment that the Nazis didn't steal once we were gone. And she saved it, can you imagine? All those years, thinking maybe somebody would come back? It was like that all through the war, things like that, little things that people did. Somebody in the camp, forcing you to put up your arm, holding it up when they asked for volunteers to work, even if you didn't know the first thing about sewing or making bullets or building a road. Even if you wanted to be dead.

Somebody like Sam, feeding me in the hospital, the tiniest mouthfuls, like a baby, so that I wouldn't eat too much. Those little things, those kindnesses." Irma looked down. "She picked up a cup. Such a small thing. How could she know how much it would mean? To have something of my daughter to take away, to keep, when I thought I had nothing."

Irma paused again. Her voice had been steady, but M.J. saw now that she was crying. "It was the first time since it all happened that I thought, Maybe there's some hope in the world. Maybe I can love again. Maybe I can live."

Irma pressed the cup into M.J.'s hand. "Keep this."

"Irma. No. I couldn't."

"Don't argue. I want you to. It's got a little crack there, see?" Irma blew her nose and opened the drawer in the coffee table. "Okay," she said, bringing out a deck of cards and starting to shuffle. "Five-card stud. Penny a point. I feel lucky."

The next day Roxie came in again. It was the middle of the day, and she was by herself. M.J. watched her wander over to the video arcade.

Irma marched to the front desk, waving an envelope. "Guess what? I got a letter from Joyce in the mail."

"Who?"

"Joyce. You know. That nice woman we met in Hawaii?"

"That's nice."

"She says she'll be in Seattle next month for Thanksgiving. For a whole week she'll be here. Isn't that terrific?"

"Uh-huh."

"You don't seem very surprised."

M.J. squinted at her. *Crafty old carrot-top.* "I got a letter from Joyce today too."

"Oh, really? Well now. Isn't that swell?" Irma tucked her envelope into her shirt pocket. Then she leaned closer and stage-whispered, "She's here, did you notice?"

"Who?"

"Don't be funny. You know who. She's all by herself, too, so this might be a good day to, you know . . ."

"Give her some pointers?" M.J. suggested.

"Sure. Why not?"

"Pick up a ball?"

Irma shrugged. "What harm could it do?"

M.J. reached for her hand and kissed it. "All right, Mrs. K. Go finish your lunch. I'll see if somebody else can cover the front desk for a few minutes."

It didn't take more than M.J.'s lacing up a pair of bowling shoes for the Aloha Lanes clientele and staff to take notice. The regular customers started elbowing each other and whispering. Carrie and Joanna stopped hanging Halloween decorations in the kids' room and came down from their ladders. The gal who sold Lotto tickets stopped buffing her nails. The cooks went pop-eyed in the kitchen. Irma and her girlfriends, who'd been in the diner having the Wednesday Special (hot turkey sandwiches with mashed potatoes and gravy), declined dessert, dabbed at their mouths with their napkins, reapplied their lipstick, and poured their coffee into Styrofoam cups. The waitress went on break.

As soon as Jean, the bookkeeper, came to watch the front desk, M.J. pulled a pair of women's shoes off the shelves and headed to the video arcade.

"Come with me," he said to Roxie, taking her by the arm.

"Why?" Roxie tried to summon up her usual smart-ass demeanor and vocal delivery but failed. Without her crowd, she was a different person. She seemed younger. More vulnerable. More like a kid. Also, thank God, for whatever reason she'd left the eyebrow hardware at home.

Rudy cut short his phone call and came out of the office. He was surprised to see Irma standing at the forefront of a small phalanx of customers and employees who were behaving like bad house detectives, affecting nonchalance while conversing furtively and stealing glances at the video arcade. "What's going on?" he mouthed. Irma smiled and pointed.

"Rule Number One," M.J. said, starting to escort Roxie to one of the empty lanes. "You have to let yourself be led by the ball, not the other way around. You have to honor the weight of the ball, give yourself over to it."

"I don't know what the hell you're talking about."

"You will. Sit down and try on those shoes."

Roxie obeyed. "They fit okay."

"You sure? You don't want 'em loose. You don't want 'em tight, either."

"They're just right."

"Good." M.J. picked up a ball. "Here. Try this one. How's it feel?"

"Fine, I guess. How's it supposed to feel?"

"Heavy. But not so heavy that you can't travel with it. Now come over here and stand on the throw line. Hold your ball, like this. Look at the pins. Are you looking?"

"Yeah."

"Okay. Rule Number Two—you can't think, not once you start moving. Do all the thinking you want while you're standing on the throw line, but before you move an inch you have to make your mind empty. You have to be all instinct. All heart. Now let me see you throw."

Roxie looked unsure. "Are you gonna show me how? I mean, are you gonna play too?"

M.J. felt Irma's eyes on him. He turned and looked up at her. She was due for a dye job, he noticed. At the same time, she'd never looked prettier.

"Yeah," he said, nodding. "I'm gonna play."

And so it was that, after a twenty-seven-year hiatus from the sport he loved best in the world, M.J. Striker bowled. He gave Roxie a two-hour lesson. The girl had potential, she really did. After that, he bowled with some of the regular customers. He bowled with Rudy. He even bowled two games with Irma. Both times, she won.

When M.J. arrived at work the next morning, there were five new Hawaiian shirts waiting on the front desk and a slew of notes from customers and staff. A person would've thought he'd finally graduated college or something.

Early in the afternoon, The Hits and Missus started drifting in. M.J. checked his watch. He called Irma's apartment. He waved to Rudy.

"Mrs. K.'s a little late," he said. "She's probably already left, but . . ."

"Go ahead," Rudy said. "I can watch the front."

M.J. walked; it was a nice day—clear blue skies, warm for October. He figured he'd run into Irma on the way and they could walk back to the bowling alley together; they'd done it before. Maybe he'd finally give in and be her partner in The Hits and Missus. That would get her out of the house on time.

He arrived at Irma's door and knocked. No answer. He knocked again. He waited. "Irma?" he called, his chest tightening. He pressed his ear against the door; he heard Maurice on the other side, scratching at it, meowing. "Irma? Are you in there?"

Irma's neighbor opened her apartment door a crack and glowered at him. "I haven't heard a peep all morning," she said. "Just that damned cat. You want me to call the building manager?"

"No," M.J. said, taking a few steps back, getting ready to kick in the door. "Call 911."

A few days after the funeral, Rudy and M.J. were cleaning out Irma's apartment.

"You'll be leaving, won't you," Rudy said.

M.J. was folding some of Irma's clothes. They still smelled like that perfume she wore. Like Hawaii. She'd left instructions about where she wanted everything to be donated: a shelter for battered women, Northwest Center for the Retarded, the Goodwill. She was still doing mitzvahs.

"We agreed to six months," M.J. reminded him. "It's been a lot longer than that, you'll have to admit."

"I was just hoping. Any idea how soon you'll be taking off?"

"I don't want to leave you in the lurch. How about another couple of weeks?"

Rudy groaned. "You think I can find somebody to replace you that fast? And then train them? You underestimate yourself. How about another month, at least?"

"Sure."

Maurice squeaked.

"Did she make plans for him?"

"Yeah. The lawyer said she wanted me to take him, but . . . Would it be okay if he lived at the alley? Jean said she'd make sure he got fed. She likes cats."

"Won't he get scared, with all the noise?"

"Nah. He's deaf as a post." Maurice looked up at M.J. and squeaked again. M.J. reached down and petted him.

Rudy finished labeling the last of Irma's things for pickup. "I'll start taking the boxes down to the curb. Then we can get the furniture. The truck should be here pretty soon."

"Sounds good."

M.J. went into the bathroom. Maurice followed him, playing up his limp. He'd been doing that a lot lately. M.J. opened up the medicine chest and started dropping things into the wastebasket. Maurice jumped up onto the toilet seat and started crying.

"I'm sorry, okay? They don't allow pets at my apartment. And besides, you heard me: I'm not staying. You wouldn't be happy traveling around the country in the luggage compartment of a Greyhound bus."

In the back of the cabinet, M.J. found an unopened box of hair color: Tropical Red Ginger Glimmer. "Fuck all," he said. He sank onto the edge of the toilet seat lid. Maurice climbed into his lap. Sitting there together—transcending vast differences in species and temperament, and with an empathy that, if studied, could have earned some zoologist the Nobel Peace Prize—they keened and wept as if the world were coming to an end.

He called Joyce to let her know, because Irma would have wanted him to.

"I'm so sorry, Michael," she said. "She was a remarkable person."

Nobody had called him Michael in almost thirty years, and he didn't like the fact that his heart slid sideways in his chest when he heard her say it. "Will I be able to see you when I get to Seattle? I'll be there in a month, for Thanksgiving break. We could get together. Have coffee."

"No," he told her. "I'll be gone by then."

Thirty-one

❦

Mannerly Devotion

The effects of radiation hit Margaret hard. She was tired always, frequently nauseous. There were more medications to take, injections to receive. There were trips to the doctor's office and the hospital. It took a great deal of work, she discovered, to arrest the expansion of The Star, now that it had acquired a will and power of its own.

On days she felt well enough, she made use of Troy's escalator and came downstairs. So many things had changed. The Hughes mansion had entered another era.

The living room and parlor had been appropriated as sorting and construction sites, and were filled from morning until evening with volunteers. Margaret loved meeting them, shaking their hands, hearing about their lives and their reasons for being here. They were young and old and everything in between. They were art enthusiasts and history teachers; women who called themselves "stay-at-home moms" and men who called themselves "house husbands"; nuns, pastors, rabbis, swamis, young people on summer vacation, retired Boeing workers, yoga students, Veterans of Foreign Wars. Occasionally, she joined them in their labors. It was so restful. Sorting was like beachcombing on a shore where every pebble is precious and time is boundless. And the familiar way everyone chatted—so many hands in constant, purpose-

ful, attentive motion—gave Margaret the feeling of being at a quilting
bee, a barn raising, or a wake.

There had been changes in the live-in community too. Bruce—who
had his hands full with cooking for such a large and diverse population—took on the help of a sous-chef, who moved into the Satsuma
Geisha Room. (Margaret had been unable to remember his actual name.
He was one of those people whose appellations do not in any way match
their appearance, so she called him "Gaylord." He didn't seem to mind.)
And once Wanda was strong enough to manage the stairs without the
escalator, she reclaimed the privacy of her old upstairs bedroom, while
Nestor, her physical therapist, took the Aviary Suite. He massaged the
aching hands, forearms, and wrists of the volunteers, and performed
administrative duties related to the Academy and Wanda's career.

One day when Susan brought Margaret downstairs—she'd started
to use a walker by then—Stephen and Marita were standing in the foyer.
Margaret hadn't seen either of them in years. Stephen, more jowly in
face but trim in body, still wore his hair on the longish side; Margaret
had to remind herself that he was a sixty-something architect, not the
twenty-eight-year-old art student she'd fallen in love with and still pictured whenever she thought of him. Marita still favored a dramatic and
colorful style of dress; however, she was clearly no longer a size 6.

"I wasn't sure we should come," Stephen began, "but your nurse said
she didn't think you'd mind."

"Of course I don't mind. This is a wonderful surprise."

"I thought you might be angry—our showing up, well . . ."

". . . When I'm so close to kicking the bucket?" Margaret joked. "I
know that you're not after my money, Stephen, if that's what you're
worried about." He smiled, and Margaret stilled an impulse to reach
up and touch his face. "You'll enjoy seeing what's become of all the . . .
What did you used to call it?"

Stephen cringed. "The loot. That was wrong of me, Margaret."

"No it wasn't."

Marita—unsuccessfully stanching her tears—tottered toward her,
wearing too-small pink and black shoes with impractical heels. She
hugged Margaret with such force that had Susan not stepped in to act
as a human buttress, the two of them would surely have toppled over in
a heap. "I'm so sorry, Margaret. I'm so very sorry. . . ."

"There, there, Marita." Margaret patted her fleshy back. "Susan, would you please get some gloves and goggles? Let's find these two something to break."

Other changes were behind-the-scenes in nature; Margaret had put her hand to a number of legal documents in the past months, making sure that all of this—the work, the Academy, the use of the house— would stay in place after she was gone. That much, anyway, was a relief. But they had heard nothing from Sylvie since her phone call in June.

On bad days, Margaret remained upstairs. Gus bought a VCR and a new television for their room so that she could watch movies in bed if she wished. It was wonderful, seeing films she hadn't seen in years. Everything, apparently, was available on videotape. Susan and Bruce, the dears, were quite the film buffs, and they enjoyed the challenge of finding whatever movies she requested, no matter how rare or outdated, even if she could only provide the scantest details about plot or character. They always came home with exactly what she wanted.

Sometimes she had trouble opening her eyes to actually watch the films, but it was still a decadent pleasure to lie in bed and listen to the voices of the old stars—Greta Garbo, Leslie Howard, Myrna Loy, Fredric March, Paul Henreid, Ingrid Bergman—and the lush sound tracks that never left any doubt where the sad parts were; when there was peril, betrayal, frivolity, or tenderness; when a tragic loss or a joyful reunion was taking place.

Then, too, she learned a great deal by eavesdropping on Susan and Bruce's conversations when they thought she was asleep:

"We should start trying," Bruce half-whispered. Margaret could hear the voices of Charles Boyer and Irene Dunne in the background. "I have a whole stash of muscle mags waiting to get some use. We could have a Leo! Leos love to eat. Especially if they've been conceived by turkey baster."

Susan laughed feebly. "Not yet," she said. "Not until Margaret is . . ." She started to cry.

"You're taking wonderful care of her."

"So are you," Susan sniffled. Her voice put on a brave face. "You know, her not eating, it's not because your food isn't marvelous. It is. It's just . . . she can't. Their bodies—when they're this close, you know, this far along, they seem to understand instinctively that food . . ."

"I know, Suzy-Q. It's okay."

Susan started weeping again. "I don't think she's suffering too much, do you? Oh, bloody hell. This is why I gave up nursing in the first place."

"I think," Bruce said, in the exaggerated Southern accent that always signaled a joke, "it would tickle her no end to hear you've got a biscuit in the oven."

Susan laughed—from the sound of it, expelling a great deal of mucus in the process. "You don't think she'd consider me morally unfit? Unwed mother and all that . . ."

"An immaculate conception? Hell, no. Here. Blow."

Margaret's mother and Daniel were often at her side, munching on popcorn, gummy bears, Junior Mints, and nonpareils. Their appetites were just fine. Thankfully, they didn't talk much. They seemed to enjoy the films as much as she did—although Daniel sometimes griped at what he called "the mushy parts."

Yuk! Gross! They're KISSING! I'm glad I *never had to do that.*

You're so right, sweetie, Margaret's mother said. *In my opinion, all that nonsense is wildly overrated. You didn't miss a thing.*

You two, Margaret scoffed. *No sense of romance.*

Every day, Wanda wheeled in the serving cart and fed her small mouthfuls of soup, if she could tolerate it, pureed fruit, sips of herbal tea. She also used this time to share sketches, paintings, and models of whatever projects she was involved in—the room was full of these—and often she surprised Margaret with some delightful whimsy: a mosaic portrait of Daniel, modeled on his last school picture and assembled out of buttons, beach glass, beads, and marbles in all the colors of a candy store; a tesseraed clock set to Paris time, its face framed, raylike, with dozens of tiny souvenir shop Eiffel Towers; a functional teapot decorated with little-boy treasures, things of Daniel's that Wanda had unboxed after Margaret gave her the key to the upstairs floor of the carriage house: race cars, action figures, LEGOs, coins, dominoes, dice. A tin kazoo.

Wanda had several small-scale commissions going, and recently she'd received grant money to begin another large work, her biggest yet. On the day she arrived to unveil the plans, she seemed oddly reticent.

"Before I show you all this," she began, "I should tell you that this next installation is more . . . personal, I guess you'd say, than anything I've done before."

"Yes?" Margaret queried. "You say that as if you're worried."

"It's just that we've never talked about how I've . . . changed gears, and the fact that I'm still using tesserae from your things to do it. I've never asked how you feel about that."

"How I feel?" Margaret was baffled. "Why would I—?" In a moment of realization and contrition, she understood. She'd drawn this hapless girl into her cursed world, and now Wanda needed to be released. "I feel fine, just fine, about it. Now show me. Please."

Timidly, shyly, Wanda showed her: dozens of sketches, color drawings, paintings, a detailed model. The work was astounding. Its main subjects were three full-scale figures—man, woman, and child—who defined the points of a huge equilateral triangle. The man and the woman faced one another; the child looked on, unnoticed. The work would be called *Family Recreation*.

"I've seen this woman," Margaret said. "Where? How?"

"It's based on a photograph," Wanda said softly, "the only picture I have of my mother."

"You keep that photo in your backpack, don't you?"

"I used to. It hangs in the studio now."

"And this man behind the camera. Who—?"

"Da. My father."

"I see. So this little girl with the suitcase must be . . . ?"

Wanda looked down. A sheaf of longish bangs fell across her forehead.

And there she went: behind that wall she ran to whenever she wanted to disappear. But for once, Margaret decided to chase her. And there it was: She saw the door.

"I'll have some of that broth, dear," she said, though she was not at all hungry.

Wanda gathered up her things and set them aside. She placed the bed tray across Margaret's lap, smoothed a linen napkin across her chest, ladled broth into a bowl, and began to bring warm, gingered soup to Margaret's lips, blowing gently on each spoonful first. "That's delicious,"

Margaret said. After swallowing a few more mouthfuls, she asked, "Will you please tell me about that photograph?"

Wanda's eyes grew large with surprise, and then—holding fast to the physical comforts of servitude—she told the story of how Wanda O'Casey became Wanda Shultz. She told it with a great deal of humor, without self-pity, and with a shy, flattered, heart-eased look that made Margaret feel certain she'd been waiting her whole life for someone to ask her that question.

At the Aloha Lanes, Rudy finally hired somebody, a kid in his late twenties who had a love for the sport and didn't seem to have his thumb up his ass. He'd work out fine.

M.J. gave his landlord notice—he'd be leaving on November 25— and started canceling utilities and packing up his apartment. He was surprised by how much stuff he'd accumulated over the past couple of years. But then, he'd been in Seattle longer than he'd been anywhere since 1969. He took most of what he didn't want to the Thriftko. Some of it—his TV, his books, his bike, and all but a dozen or so of his Hawaiian shirts—he gave to folks at the Aloha. The rest of it he set out on the curb with a handwritten sign: "FREE."

Irma hadn't left him any money—she probably had the good sense to know he wouldn't accept that—but she had left him things, things he couldn't possibly sell or give away: her menorah, the scrapbook they'd put together, her Scrabble game, a framed picture of her and Sam. And of course, Lucie's cup. He realized that, even after paring down to the bare essentials, his life wouldn't fit in his backpack anymore. He'd have to travel with a box, go through baggage claim.

He wouldn't go to Idaho; Joyce lived there. Oregon would be too much like Seattle. He wanted to get away from water. Maybe he'd go southeast, to one of those desert states.

By October, Margaret's sight had started to fail, and she grew even more sedentary. She was still dimly aware of the life of the household, comings and goings above and below and around her—breakings, assemblings, meals, music, voices—but more and more, she felt drawn to the calm, shadowy company of the dead. There was something she had to do (*what?*) before they would take her in, but The Star was growing quickly now. She wasn't sure how much longer she could hang on.

"Family?" Margaret breathed. "How going?"

"All right," Wanda said.

"Really well," Troy added.

"When finished?"

"Ten years at the earliest."

"Maybe fifteen."

"Liars, both of you," she whispered, then laughed and closed her eyes, imprinting the watercolor image of their twining faces on the canvas of her eyelids.

The next thing she knew, Gus was there.

"Margaret?" he was saying gently. "Lassie? Are you awake?" He was holding the telephone. "Do you want to talk? I think it's long distance."

"You," she exhaled with a rasping effort. "Please."

His replies were short, but his face reflected a mild degree of shock. He thanked the caller and hung up. "That was Sylvie." He was reaching for the nightstand drawer, pulling out the phone book. "She sent out letters a few months ago. To Holocaust research centers." He was thumbing through the pages. "They ask survivors to tell their stories— 'oral histories,' they call them—and put them on video. One of the centers answered Sylvie's letter and told her that Mrs. Kosminsky did this for them, some time ago." He found the page he was looking for. He helped Margaret sit up; then he sat down on the bed and put an arm around her. With his other arm, he drew the opened phone book into her lap.

"All right, lassie," he said, slowly and clearly, "we've got one more search before us now. Have you got it in you? We're going to start looking under 'K.'"

"'K'?"

He put his cheek against hers. It was wet. "'K' for Mrs. Kosminsky, dear heart," he said. "Her last known address is in Seattle."

The day before he was supposed to leave, M.J. was saying his good-byes. Parting company with the customers and staff was hard enough, but then around three-thirty Roxie showed up. When he told her he was leaving, she was pissed as hell.

"Rudy'll be happy to give you lessons."

"Yeah, right."

"He'll be a much better teacher than I am, believe me. He's got kids of his own."

"Whatever."

"Just remember to—"

"I know, I know. 'Let myself be led by the ball.' Whatever the fuck that means."

"Roxie—"

"Have a good life. Write if you get work." She turned around and walked out without looking back.

Jean called him to the front desk, where she was holding the phone with one hand and petting Maurice with the other. He was stretched out next to the cash register, looking listless and ungroomed. "For you."

"Thanks." Jean's eyes were red and watery. M.J. hoped she wasn't allergic to Maurice.

It was Irma's lawyer. "I'm so glad I've been able to reach you," he said. "Your home phone number has been disconnected."

"Yeah. So. What's up?"

"Someone looking for Mrs. Kosminsky has been in touch with me. Apparently they have in their possession one of her belongings. As the sole person named in her will, it comes to you."

"What is it?"

"I haven't the faintest idea."

"But I'm leaving town tomorrow afternoon."

"That's fine, Mr. Striker. I'm sure they won't mind if you come in the morning."

"I have to go there?" M.J. protested. "But it's Thanksgiving Day. They'll be . . . basting, or carving, or something, won't they?"

"The party indicated that it's crucial you get in touch as soon as possible. Do you have a pencil and paper? Here's their name and number." M.J. looked at Maurice. Maurice squeaked, feebly.

Shit, M.J. thought. "Yeah. Go ahead."

* * *

The day before Thanksgiving, Margaret was in bed—on this occasion not watching a movie, but a videotaped interview on loan from the Washington State Holocaust Education and Resource Center.

A woman's face was projected onto the screen. Her hair was a riotous, bottled shade of red. She was dressed in tropical colors and wearing large dangly earrings. In a deep voice that was almost comically bullfroggish, she was telling the story of her evacuation from Paris, her internment in Drancy, the death of her daughter, her subsequent transport to Auschwitz, her experiences there, in other camps, and after the Liberation. She cried, but she also smiled. She laughed. It was hard to believe she was dead.

They had just missed her, as it turned out. Her name was there, in the Seattle phone book, plain as day, along with her husband's: Samuel and Irma Kosminsky. But their number had been disconnected. So Gus called the Holocaust Center which in turn made some inquiries and discovered that Mrs. Kosminsky had died a month ago.

But was there kin? A surviving heir? Someone to whom they could return something that belonged to the Kosminsky family? It was an emergency, Gus explained, using the full force of his diplomatic powers.

Une histoire de miracles, Sylvie had said. *Petits et grands.*

Yes, they were told, Mrs. Kosminsky had named someone in her will.

Margaret closed her eyes and listened. Her mother held her hand. Daniel snuggled up next to her and drove his race car, quietly.

Gus came in. He picked up the remote control and pressed the "pause" button.

"Hang on, lassie," he said, stroking Margaret's forehead. "I just got off the phone with Mr. Striker. He'll be here tomorrow."

Margaret smiled up at Gus; his face was a moon-shaped, glistening blur.

Then she looked past him, to the television screen, where the stilled image of a redheaded woman looked back at her and laughed.

Thirty-two

※

We Gather Together

If you're coming to the Hughes house for the first time—whether you're an unsuspecting solicitor, substitute mail carrier, FedEx driver, or fledgling volunteer, and whether your visit represents a perfunctory business matter or the proverbial end of the line—here's the way it goes:

You'll arrive—on foot, by car, van, taxi, train, plane, bus, or a combination of methods—and you'll stare. It's all right; everyone does. It will take a while for the size and grandeur of the house to register. *This is it?* you'll think as you walk up, incredulous. This can't be the place. It's unreal. It's a big house. An un-fucking-believably big house. Whoever thought that somebody like you would get to see the inside of a house like this one?

As you come closer, you'll notice what at first looks like small drifts of snow. Closer still, and you'll see that it's piles of shattered china, mostly white but sprinkled here and there with touches of color, shimmers of silver and gold. The pieces are everywhere, scattered through the flower beds and around the trees like an exotic garden mulch. Fragments line the sidewalk leading up to the front porch and the paths winding through the grounds; in other places the pieces have collected into dense mounds, little multicolored islands of varying sizes and configurations. Their presence in the landscape has the appearance of being both randomly chaotic and exquisitely designed. Pay attention. Let your mind embrace metaphors. It's your first clue about what goes on here.

Reaching the porch, you'll ring the doorbell. You'll be greeted by someone—a young woman, you think—wearing work clothes and protective eyewear. She holds an old teacup, saucer, dessert plate, something like that. It doesn't look especially valuable.

"Welcome," she'll say, and offer up to you the small thing in her hands. Maybe you'll take it, maybe you won't.

"Hello. I'm M.J. Striker. I'm here to see Mrs. Hughes."

Instead of getting a normal response, without so much as a how-do-you-do or we're-not-buying, the small fragile thing will be pressed into your hands. "That belonged to a woman named Alta Fogle," you might be told. "She was the child of Norwegian immigrants who owned a farm in northern Minnesota. Harsh country. Cold country. The Iron Range, they call it. Alta's mother died in childbirth—the cup you're holding was part of her dowry—and Alta was raised by her father. Sometimes they went ice fishing. They'd sit in the bob house and drink hot cocoa. Out of that cup. The one you're holding in your hand. Alta never married. She never left Minnesota. She kept the farm after her father died. When she was ninety-two, in the middle of February, she took a thermos of hot milk and brandy out to the bob house, put in a line, and died. She left behind a farmhouse full of things: abandoned, alone, with no heirs to claim them."

"Jesus Christ," you mutter.

Maybe this is true. Maybe not. You can never be sure: All objects in the Hughes house have to have meaning, and if their past is not known, stories are invented. Even the lowliest, most solitary unmatched object— the lone surviving salad plate acquired at Goodwill Industries—has significance, weight, relevance. The tale you just heard might be a big fish story, but right now you believe every word. You feel like you're about to fuckin' cry.

"Are you ready?" your hostess will say, indicating the cup.

You're confused. What are you supposed to do? You just came here to settle a legal matter, meet someone named Mrs. Hughes about something and then be on your way. You're only here because of Irma, because of something she wanted you to take care of. But dammit, you didn't expect this. It's bad enough you had to hear this story about Alta Fogle and her lonely life. It bad enough that it's Thanksgiving. This Mrs. Hughes couldn't wait one more day to do this, whatever it is? There's probably a bunch of people inside: noisy kids, women in aprons, men talking about football. Families. On top of all that, now there's this weirdness.

"Excuse me? Ready for what?"

"You have to break that before you can come in."

"Why?"

"Do you want a short answer or a long one? I could tell you a nice story about the Buddha and the teacup."

By now you're thinking, *I shouldn't have come. I should've just left. Irma's dead. She's dead. She's not gonna know. Except, knowing Irma, she probably would.*

"The short answer will do."

"It's a custom, like"—here your hostess pauses, giving you an assessing look—"taking off your shoes."

"Do I have to do that, too?"

Your hostess laughs. "Oh, no. Definitely no. That would be hazardous around here." She stamps her hiking boots for emphasis. "Hard soles only."

"Okay. Where—?"

"Anywhere is fine. Most people just use the wall of the porch. Here, wear these."

She hands you a pair of protective eyeglasses. You put them on. You take a few steps back. You feel like an idiot, but the face of the person standing in the massive doorway registers nothing but a disconcerting neutrality. You look down at the thing you're holding. You wish to Christ she hadn't told you about who it belonged to. But you go ahead anyway. You throw Alta's cup against the wall. You don't throw it hard, you don't put any juice into it, but it still shatters into a million pieces. You stare. You blow your nose. You think you'll leave the glasses on for a while.

You're ushered inside.

"I'll tell Susan you're here," your hostess says, as if nothing out of the ordinary has just happened. "Feel free to look around."

Your hostess disappears up the stairs. You're left alone in the foyer. There's some kind of contraption that runs down one side of the banister; it must be an escalator.

The house is huge. Unbelievable. But familiar, somehow. Maybe because it's as grand as something you'd see in the movies—the setting for some heroic climax. You imagine Gregory Peck carrying Ingrid Bergman down the stairs.

You become aware of people in the room to your left, probably fifteen or twenty of them in there. They're all doing something, working on something. A couple of them glance at you and smile, but mostly they keep at whatever it is that they're doing. They all wear gloves. The room is full of tables, with boxes. There is the sound of plates being shuffled around. It's like music. Some of the people are standing, some are sitting, all are concentrating hard. There's a gaming mood overlying the whole thing; you half-expect someone to call out "B-53" followed by "BINGO!" Drawings and paintings cover the walls.

"Hi! Are you a new volunteer?" It's a round-faced man in a chef's getup.

"No." *Volunteer for what?* you wonder.

"Oh. Well, please stay anyway. I made enough food for the Mass Assembly of the United Nations. Have you met Tink? She's out in the carriage house."

"No, I'm here to see Mrs. Hughes."

The cook looks like he's witnessed the Ascension. "Oh my God! You're the one!" His face lights up. His eyes go teary. He grabs your hand and starts pumping it like you're old friends. "This is incredible. Susan!" he calls up the stairs.

"Yes, darling." A tall, horsy-looking woman appears on the first-floor landing.

"Mr. Striker's here!"

"Hello, Mr. Striker. Please come up." She's a Brit, but her accent isn't high-tone.

"Have you checked your basal body temp?" the cook hollers.

"Not yet, but I'll do it soon, I promise."

"Okay! I'll get my magazines!" The cook turns back to you. "We're having a baby." He grabs you and gives you a full body hug. "This is such a great day." He rushes down the hall and out of sight.

Your hostess skittles down the stairs; as she passes you she says, "Go on up. Margaret can see you now."

You ascend and meet the horsy gal on the first-floor landing. "I'm
Susan," she says. "Margaret's nurse."

"Is Mrs. Hughes sick?"

"Please, come this way." You walk down a long hallway. "Dublin,
is it?"

"That's right. Good guess."

"I'm half-Irish myself. Grew up in Birmingham."

What are the odds of that? you wonder.

"We're in luck," she goes on. "Mrs. Hughes is feeling well. She thinks
she might even come down for dinner."

"I didn't know she was ill. I can come back another day."

She turns to face you. "Mrs. Hughes has been waiting a long time to
meet you, Mr. Striker. There won't be another day."

She taps gently on the door and inches it open.

"Margaret?" she calls, softly. "Margaret, are you awake?" You hear a
small rustling from inside, like wings. Susan opens the door wide. "This
is Mr. Striker," she announces. "The beneficiary of Mrs. Kosminsky's
estate."

Her room, strangely, didn't smell like death. Not that M.J. had had any
experience with the dying; it just wasn't the smell he expected. There
was a dense sweetness to it, almost but not quite overpowering—like
the way certain flowers smell after a heavy rain.

She was sitting up. He was aware of her eyes—bright, blue, shiny—
and how they seemed to be the containers for whatever life was left in
her.

"Mr. Striker, this is Mrs. Hughes." She held out her hand. If it were
not for her eyes, M.J. might have been afraid to touch her, she was so
thin.

"Nice to meet you," he said.

"Have a seat, please, Mr. Striker." Susan indicated a chair next to the
head of Mrs. Hughes's bed. "I'm sure you're confused about why you're
here. I'll go get the box, Margaret. I'll be right back."

She left the room. M.J. smiled awkwardly at Mrs. Hughes and then
sat rigidly on the chair. He didn't know why, but he felt like he was

back at Catholic school, a kid in trouble, and one of the priests was about to give him the strap.

There wasn't any fancy medical equipment, just a collection of prescription medicines on her nightstand. Maybe she really wasn't that sick after all. He noticed paintings and drawings on the walls up here, too, and all around the room were colorful, odd-looking knickknacks—vases and plant pots, pictures, a crazy-looking teapot, a small table fountain, candleholders. They'd been made out of pieces of plates that had been glued together. Even the fireplace was decorated with smashed crockery. *Irma would have loved this,* he thought.

Margaret motioned M.J. close. There was a hiss of air.

"I'm sorry?" M.J. said. "What was that?"

"Nice shirt."

"Thank you."

Susan returned, holding a medium-sized cardboard box. "By the way," she said, "I forgot to say that you're more than welcome to stay for Thanksgiving dinner."

"Yeah. The fella downstairs—the cook, I guess—he already asked."

"Do you have plans?"

"No, but I couldn't—"

"You don't have to decide right this minute." Susan held out the box. "This is for you."

M.J. took it and pulled open the flaps. Inside were crumpled sheets of yellowed newspaper.

"Go ahead," Susan urged.

He started to pull the paper away. He found a lid first, a saucer, a small pitcher. Then it dawned on him what he was looking at: Lucie's tea set. Minus the single cup Irma had left him, which was wrapped in three layers of bubble plastic and nestled in his backpack. He looked up at Mrs. Hughes, and then at Susan.

"How did you—?"

"It's a long story," Susan said, "and an interesting one. Mrs. Hughes has provided all the details for you in this letter." She handed him an envelope. "Briefly, though, Mrs. Hughes inherited a great many possessions that were stolen from Jewish evacuees during the war. This tête-a-tête of Mrs. Kosminsky's is unique because of the painting of the herbs and flowers inside the bottom of the cups. Only a few sets were made like this, and the others are accounted for. It is the only thing Mrs. Hughes has ever been able to trace and return. So you see, it means so much to have found a member of Mrs. Kosminsky's family."

M.J. looked down. He tucked the envelope into the box and started rewrapping the pieces. "What should I do with it?"

"That's up to you, Mr. Striker. What do you think Mrs. Kosminsky would have wanted?"

"I have no idea."

"Well, it's yours now, to do with as you wish."

"What will you do with the other things?"

"You mean, the things that were stolen from the other families? We're breaking them. Or rather, Tink and the others are breaking them."

"I'm sorry—?"

Susan laughed. "We must seem like an awfully strange lot."

"We are," Margaret whispered.

Susan crossed the room and took her pulse. "Do you still feel well enough to come downstairs?"

Margaret nodded and smiled. Her eyes were amazing. *She would not have us sad because she is lying there,* he thought. *And when she meets our gaze her eyes are laughter-lit.*

"Let's get you ready then. Excuse me, Mr. Striker."

He got up and moved aside as Susan brought the wheelchair closer. She folded back the covers and bent down.

One of Mrs. Hughes's hands floated up and hovered in space, her fingers undulating mildly, like the tendrils of an undersea plant. "Go now, Susan," she said, with more volume and tone than he'd heard in her voice. "Let him take me."

"Are you sure, Margaret? Mr. Striker, do you mind?"

"Not a bit."

"All right then. If you two will excuse me, I need to take my temperature, and then I have an appointment with a turkey baster. I'll meet up with you later and show you around, all right?"

Margaret gave Susan the thumbs-up sign. Susan leaned down and kissed her. "I'll see you both downstairs," she said, and then left.

Mrs. Hughes looked at him. Within her calm, canny look, there was mischief, too, as if she was amused by his discomfort. *Give her a little grace*—Yeats's words could have been written for her—*What if a laughing eye have looked into your face? It is about to die.*

As he'd imagined, she was nearly weightless; it was as if the solid structures of her body had begun to disintegrate. He could tell now what an effort it had been for her to speak with him. When she was settled in her chair, she held out her hands and he placed the box in her lap.

He wheeled her through the hall. The second-floor rooms were all empty, but M.J. couldn't shake the feeling that they were being watched. They arrived at the top of the stairs, and he maneuvered her chair onto the escalator platform. As they descended, M.J. heard a rapid, energetic thumping of footsteps—the kind of sound kids make inside a house. He turned and looked up, fully expecting to see a child standing at the top of the stairs watching them. But there was no one. He looked down at Margaret. She was smiling.

A table had been set up on the back patio—it was unusually warm and fine for the end of November—and people were coming and going from the kitchen, the way people do before a big holiday meal. M.J. noticed that all of the dishes had cracks or chips, and that none of them matched.

Margaret gestured toward a lounge chair and M.J. lowered her into it.

"Thank you." Her eyelids drooped, and for a moment M.J. thought she'd fallen asleep. But then she opened her eyes wide and looked at him. She started trying to lift the box, but she was too weak. M.J. set it on a table next to the chair. She settled her hands in her lap.

"Is there something I can do to help?" M.J. asked. There was a new energy and clarity in her eyes, he thought, and with it, a kind of ease.

She inclined her head toward the carriage house. "Visit Tink. She won't mind."

M.J. squatted in front of her. "It's been a pleasure meeting you, Mrs. Hughes."

"Please stay," she said, smiling. Then she closed her eyes again.

He got up and started making his way. He looked back, just once. A shaft of sunlight fell across Margaret's hands—palms up, fingers separated and lightly curled—giving them the appearance of luminous, cracked, empty bowls.

* * *

The carriage house stood about fifty yards from the main house; they were connected by a blue flagstone path, and—just as in the front yard—there were fragments scattered through the landscape, trodden into the cracks between the stones. As the sounds of the people behind him faded, he had a sense of moving into a different world. The path led to the back of the carriage house—where new windows showed that somebody had done some remodeling, and made a good job of it, too—and then curved around and led to the street side.

There was the massive original carriage house door, with a smaller entrance just next to it. Without quite knowing what to do, he knocked. There was no answer, so he went in.

What he saw took his breath away.

It was Gina's ass, attached to Gina herself—or rather, a sculpture of Gina, made of what had to be millions of pieces of smashed dishes and having the same mesmerizing, cobbled-together look as the objects he'd seen in Mrs. Hughes's bedroom. She was posed, he realized incredulously, exactly as she was in his photograph of her, balanced precariously on one leg, one arm stretched to the side, the other reaching strongly forward, palm up. Without the context of setting, he saw the gesture for what it was: a supplication, a plea. She was naked. Attached to her sinewy, narrow shoulders—so like a child's—were two impossibly enormous wings.

"Hello," he heard someone say. He became aware that he was not alone in time and space with this figment of Gina; looking around, he saw and felt the presence of other physical entities. Beneath his feet, a floor. He was standing on it. There were walls, too. A ceiling. Shelves, tables, sheets of plywood, boxes, buckets. It was really quite a cluttered place, he realized. "Over here."

His eyes tracked through the room, trying to find the source of the voice. On the way, he saw the unadorned form of a little girl, holding a cup. He saw a child's valise, a bowling ball, a shoe. He saw a man aiming a camera at Gina.

Eventually he found a young woman with dark, tousled hair. She was sitting on a stool next to a large worktable. In front of her was a bowling pin, half-covered with more fragments.

"Are you one of the new volunteers?" she asked.

M.J. came closer. Shards of crockery crunched under his feet.

"I'm Wanda Schultz," she said, taking off her eyewear, "but everybody here calls me Tink."

Her eyes filled out the shape he had seen a million times in his dreams: looking up from a plate of pancakes, peeking over a Styrofoam cup. *Sing the song, Da. What's wrong with Mother? Why aren't you staying with Aunt Maureen too?* No fortress of will could keep him from remembering, no vow of deprivation could turn off what he felt. When had he stopped searching for Gina? When had he started looking for her?

He said his name. It was all he could risk.

"Oh! You made it! I'm so glad."

She slid awkwardly off her stool and limped toward him. Her boots against the floor made a gritty noise, but there was another sound too, like something shattering: the sound of a town in the middle of a tornado, of car wrecks and buildings being shelled. Eventually he realized that the sound came from whatever she was carrying in her pockets.

"We should get back to the main house," she said. "Bruce will have a hissy fit if we're late. You are going to stay for Thanksgiving, aren't you?"

Thirty-three

≫

Margaret's Dream, Part Three

*W*hy, *it's Babar's gorgeous yellow balloon!* Margaret thinks. *How delightful!*

All of them are already on board, in the backyard, waiting. Although
the balloon does not appear to be tethered in any way, it is still earthbound.

"Why aren't we moving?" Margaret hears people murmuring. "Why
are we still here?

The passenger compartment is huge—so huge that it accommodates
not only all of the household boarders and Thanksgiving guests, but
hundreds of boxes of all sizes and shapes. *Oh, no,* Margaret thinks. *Not
this again.*

"All right, everyone!" she shouts with authority. "We need to lighten
the load! Throw out the boxes!"

"But Margaret," Marita says, "they're all marked 'Fragile.'"

"Don't fret, Marita," Stephen answers.

Everyone starts heaving boxes overboard. The boxes land with a dramatic series of crashes. Sure enough, the balloon starts to rise, slowly but
steadily.

"It's working!" Margaret shouts. "We're going up! Up to the stars!"
She turns around. Everyone on board is shouting, cheering, applauding.

They rise straight up to the level of the roofline, and then the balloon
stops, suspended over the patio.

The passengers begin to mutter with concern. "Is there something wrong?" "Why have we stopped?"

Margaret hears her mother shout, "Still not light enough! You need less weight!"

"Mother?" Margaret shouts back. "Where are you?"

"I'll go," someone says. Margaret turns and sees a child wearing a school uniform and a backpack. *Why, it's that little boy with the jelly doughnuts,* she thinks.

"Jack?" she asks. "Is that you?"

"We're BRITISH!" Jack replies, and promptly throws himself over the side.

Margaret screams, horrified. But he pulls at something on his backpack and—*Oh look!* Margaret thinks, immensely relieved. *He's wearing a parachute!*

Jack's parachute explodes with a loud ruffling sound. It billows wildly until it forms a large circle. *It's decorated!* Margaret realizes, enchanted. *Like a plate! The majolica plate, Florence, 1640, but who cares about that. It's orange and yellow and blue and green and I have always loved the colors of Italian majolica.*

"Your father considered it gaudy," Margaret hears her mother say.

"I know, Mother. So you've told me, and I don't care. It's beautiful and brave. Just the thing for little boys to eat jelly doughnuts off of."

Margaret watches Jack's parachute settle safely on the ground. He peeks his head out and waves. "See, Mum?" he yells up to her. "I'm fine! No crashing!"

More people start jumping off—strangers at first, and then people Margaret gradually comes to recognize: School friends from when she was a girl. People she and Stephen knew, couples. The mothers of the children Daniel went to school with. Gay Paxton!

"Hello, Gay!" Margaret calls. "I'm sorry I broke your teapot!"

"It's all right, Margaret!" Gay calls back.

The girl with the nose ring who served my desserts. She's put on weight. I'm so glad. And Dr. Leising, too, and all the kind nurses and technologists. Even Marita. Everyone has a plate-parachute. All different, all beautiful.

Then come the volunteers who help with Wanda's mosaics. The adults. The schoolchildren. Babs. Sylvie. Then Bruce and Sue and—

Oh! Margaret gasps, thrilled. *They've had their baby! It's a boy!*

Gus goes next, followed by the Crooning Clansman in their kilts; they sing a barbershop arrangement of "I'm a Little Teapot" on their way down.

How I wish I could see them from below, Margaret thinks giddily.

To Troy, she says, "She loves you, you know."

To Mr. Striker: "You simply must join us for dinner."

Finally, Tinker Bell stands before her.

"Are you still angry with me for dying?" Margaret asks.

Wanda holds out her hands, like she is waiting to be given something.

"What?" Margaret is afraid she'll go without saying anything. "What is it, Tink?"

Wanda smiles. "The flag," she says. "Don't you want to get rid of the skull and crossbones?"

Margaret looks down and sees that she is holding a pirate flag. "Oh! Of course!" She hands it over. Wanda casts it over the edge. They watch it billow earthward.

"Be happy," Margaret says, taking her hands. "We're worth more broken."

Wanda answers, "I love you, too."

She goes. Her parachute is pure white.

Margaret turns. The compartment is almost empty now, smaller, too, and oddly shadowed. *Has there been a weather change?* Margaret wonders, vaguely concerned. She squints upward and tries to see around the side of the balloon. *Are there clouds moving in? Is there a storm coming?*

And then he steps forward, out of the shadows: the withered, haunted man who came to her father's shop. He wears his yarmulke and black coat; pinned to the lapel is the yellow cloth star with the word "Juif."

She is terrified. But as he draws near, she sees that his face is kind, soft. He takes off his yarmulke, reaches inside, and flings a handful of splintered glass into the air; it transforms into glitter as it descends. Bowing low, he takes Margaret's hand and kisses it. He backs away from her, grinning, until he reaches the low wall of the compartment. Then, with great dignity, he pushes himself up to sit on the edge. *"Mazel tov!"* he shouts happily, laughs, and leans backward.

Margaret gazes over the edge. She sees all the parachutes fluttering down. Most have already arrived. Everyone has landed safely. They are tugging their parachutes toward a focal point on the ground.

Why, it's me! Margaret realizes. *They're dragging their parachutes toward me!*

From above, the parachutes start to come together, their irregular, patterned edges intersecting.

"*Au revoir!*" Margaret shouts joyfully. She waves.

They all look up at her—except the down-below Margaret, who seems to be sleeping—and wave back. "Au revoir, Margaret! Bon voyage!"

The balloon begins to rise above the level of the clouds. Margaret can no longer see the earth or the Thanksgiving Day guests. *I'm so glad no one wore black and white,* she thinks.

When she turns around, the traveling compartment has changed size again; it is no bigger than a cozy, unfurnished parlor. At one end, there is a red-haired woman and a little girl—the woman's daughter, Margaret assumes, since her hair too is the color of marigolds. They are sitting on the floor and having a tea party. When Margaret looks closer, she realizes that they are using Mrs. Kosminsky's tête-à-tête. *It's her!* Margaret realizes. *It's Mrs. K.!*

Daniel stands before her. He is dressed for bed, wearing his cowboy pajamas.

"Mom, come read to me." He hands her an opened book.

"What did you pick for bedtime?" Margaret says. "Oh! I love this one!" She sits down and puts an arm around him.

"'The festivities are over,'" Margaret reads, "'night has fallen, the stars have risen in the sky, King Babar and Queen Celeste are indeed very happy.'" Daniel yawns. He snuggles deeper into Margaret's arms. Mrs. Kosminsky's daughter comes to sit on Margaret's other side.

"'Now the world is asleep. The guests have gone home, happy, though tired from too much dancing. And now King Babar and Queen Celeste sail away in their gorgeous yellow balloon, in search of further adventures.'"

Margaret looks down. Both of the children are sound asleep in her arms.

"Hello, Magpie."

"Hello, Mother."

She wears a simple cotton 1930s housedress with a Peter Pan collar. On her head is a tricorner pirate hat. "Would you like a nap too?"

"I do feel just a little sleepy."

"Why don't you rest then, sweetheart. I can pilot us from here."

"All right, Mother," Margaret says. "Wake me when we get there." She closes her eyes. "You know, you needn't wear that hat. We've unloaded all the booty."

"Oh, Margaret," Margaret's mother says, "now that you're dead, I'm really going to have to teach you how to have a little fun."

Cassandra takes the helm. Margaret sleeps with the children in her arms. The balloon arcs up forever, into the night sky, past millions of glittering stars.

When Wanda came out of the carriage house with Mr. Striker, she knew at once. She took up one of Margaret's cool hands, leaned close, and whispered the words she'd meant to say so many times and long before this. She tucked a comforter around Margaret's body, poured them each a glass of wine, and then settled on the patio floor at Margaret's feet.

Troy came and kneeled before her. "It's too cold on the ground, babe," he said. "Wear my coat." Wanda burrowed into his arms, and they wept.

The family had dinner outside as planned, with Margaret there. It wasn't difficult to get Mr. Striker to join them.

The turkey baster got a private and unusual use. None of the men slumbered in front of a television set. Nobody spent hours washing dishes; they broke them, of course.

It was, they all agreed, the Thanksgiving she would have wanted.

Thirty-four

❧

Detective Lorenzini
Makes the Collar

The broken are not always gathered together, of course, and not all mysteries of the flesh are solved. We speak of "senseless tragedies," but really: Is there any other kind? Mothers and wives disappear without a trace. Children are killed. Madmen ravage the world, leaving wounds immeasurably deep, and endlessly mourned. Loved ones whose presence once filled us move into the distance; our eyes follow them as long as possible as they recede from view. Maybe we chase them—clumsily, across railroad tracks and trafficked streets; over roads new-printed with their footsteps, the dust still whirling in the wake of them; through impossibly big cities peopled with strangers whose faces and bodies carry fragments of their faces and bodies, whose laughter, steadiness, pluck, stubbornness remind us of the beloved we seek. Maybe we stay put, left behind, and look for them in our dreams. But we never stop looking, not even after those we love become part of the unreachable horizon. We can never stop carrying the heavy weight of love on this pilgrimage; we can only transfigure what we carry. We can only shatter it and send it whirling into the world so that it can take shape in some new way.

Margaret's ashes, as she wished, were divided and placed in several lidded teapots for the members of the household to do with as they wished. Wanda came into the studio after the wake and found Troy there, listening to music, pouring a bag of dry grout into one of the large mixing buckets. His teapot was on the floor next to him.

"What are you doing?" she asked.

He took the lid off his teapot, lifted out some of Margaret's ashes, and let them sift through his fingers onto the grout. Then he reached in with his beautiful, muscled arms, elbow-deep, and started mixing. "They don't feel like what you'd expect," he said. "They're light. Like down."

Margaret had taken the money household members had paid in rent over the past two years and invested it; each of them now had an individually tailored, lucrative investment portfolio. She also willed them many of her financial and stock assets. A substantial gift had been made to the Crazy Plate Academy—enough to pay for the purchase of a separate facility—and a foundation had been formed, with Mrs. Barbara Cohen designated as chairwoman of the board, to support the work of recovering Jewish possessions and reuniting them with their original owners or their owners' kin. None of Margaret's adopted family would be facing financial impediments in pursuit of their dreams—or in the stewardship and maintenance of hers.

She left her collection and the carriage house to Wanda; she left the main house and its furnishings to Gus.

Wanda, Troy, and the volunteers continued their work on *Family Recreation;* given the size and complexity of the project, the grant monies were to extend over a period of several years.

Troy continued to meet the technical challenges of executing Wanda's artistic visions, constructing the various substrates to which the tesserae were adhered, and designing the installation so that it could be assembled and taken apart—much like a touring theatre set—when it was moved from one gallery to another. He supervised the work of the volunteers, who were now participating in the adhering process as well. They were currently gluing pieces to one of the 60-foot, $10^{3/16}$-inch lengths of substrate which would duplicate a single bowling alley lane.

Wanda broke, sorted, and adhered millions of pieces to the underlying structures that she imagined and Troy made sound.

Mr. Striker moved in. He took the Inkstand Room after receiving permission to bring a cat into the household. It was Gus's decision. He was well aware of Margaret's opposition to keeping house pets: she believed that animals subjected to indoor living could never be happy. She didn't know cats. Besides, given this particular creature's sweet nature, peculiarities, and advanced age, Gus was sure that Margaret would never have objected.

Maurice's clumsiness—rare in a cat, but understandable given his handicap—might have been an issue in another household with so many fragile items; in this family, it was a boon. Things could be heard falling off tables and shelves at all hours of the day and night. Since Mr. Striker's room was on the third floor, and stairs were challenging for a geriatric, three-legged cat, they kept the escalator in use. Maurice accompanied Mr. Striker to work; he fit comfortably into a bowling bag.

Susan and Bruce became parents of the Leo baby they'd dreamed about. His birth—witnessed by the entire household—was a sudden, dramatic event which occurred during the dessert course and on the dining room table. They named him August.

Shortly after, Mr. Striker announced his desire to take on the responsibilities of household gardener.

"It's a mighty big job," Gus cautioned as he, Mr. Striker, and Wanda toured the property. "I know Margaret felt grieved about the condition of the grounds. She had plenty of plans, but never enough time."

"That's all right," Mr. Striker said. "I've got nothin' but."

"Are you qualified?" Wanda demanded. "Have you ever done this kind of thing before?"

"No," Mr. Striker admitted. "Never."

"Well," Gus intervened, "all we really need is someone who's got the patience for it, someone who's willing to learn, isn't that right?"

"And someone who's going to stay," Wanda emphasized. "See it through."

Mr. Striker shrugged. "No problem. I'm not going anywhere."

"Great!" Gus exclaimed. "You're hired, then! Oh, our Margaret would be ever so pleased."

Wanda didn't entirely trust Mr. Striker, although she didn't know why. He seemed honest enough, and it wasn't as if anyone else had volunteered to rescue their three untended acres from blackberry canes, bindweed, and Scotch broom. There was something about him, though. Maybe it was just that—even after all this time—they didn't know anything about him, not really, other than the fact that he worked part-time at a bowling alley in North Seattle, got letters from a "J. Gallagher" in Moscow, Idaho, and was the beneficiary of a Holocaust survivor's estate. That was fishy too, in Wanda's opinion. Who was he? Where did he come from? He was a strange person, Mr. Striker. Gruff and laconic, with a deep-fissured face that made him look perpetually pissed. He certainly didn't talk much. About himself, he talked not at all.

At first he didn't do anything besides basic maintenance: mowing, weeding, a bit of light pruning—which was more than anyone else had done for years, and which certainly made for improvement. Mostly, though, he planned.

Wanda often saw him walking the grounds at different times of the day, studying the way the light changed, taking notes, making sketches. At night after dinner was done and they'd finished clearing up, he'd stay downstairs at the dining room table, studying stacks of library books on gardening. Sometimes—even late at night, after she'd finished in the carriage house and come in to go to bed—she'd find him and Troy still down there, working. She didn't like the idea that there were people in the house who worked harder than she did; on those nights she'd make fresh coffee and go back out to the studio.

Sometimes she'd hear Troy and Mr. Striker talking together. She wondered what they talked about. Not that it was any of her business.

He started showing them crude landscape designs: plans for an herb bed, a perennial flower garden, a vegetable patch. Plans that would be executed in stages and surely range years into the future: a play area for Augie when he was older; a site for outdoor dining, with a pergola, ter-race, and cooking hearth; a grassed area for lawn bowling.

When it came time to start implementing these proposed changes, he took on the back corner of the property first, near the carriage house, clearing tangled overgrowth, blackberry canes, and weeds, pruning the deadwood from red osier dogwoods and flowering currants, cutting in beds, planting bulbs, shrubs, and ground covers. It was an odd place to begin, Wanda thought, since nobody but she and Troy worked in that area of the grounds. Wouldn't his time be better spent working where more people could appreciate his efforts—in the front of the house? Or even around the patio?

Still, after a while she found it pleasant, having him nearby. She liked coming outside and joining him when she needed a break from her own labors, whether she was spending a day in the main house with the volunteers or working out in the carriage house studio on the more complex sculptural forms.

Mr. Striker was an easy person to be silent with; he was like Troy that way. As much as Wanda appreciated the volunteers, they loved to chat, nonstop. She often missed the restful, meditative quiet of working alone. When sequestered in the carriage house studio, she could work in relative quiet next to Troy, or Mr. Striker.

"My parents were bowlers," she mentioned one day. It was late October, and she'd been helping him divide and plant bulbs in a bed he'd cut in around the carriage house.

"Is that right?"

"The piece we're working on, it's kind of about them."

"I see."

"We're going to need some bowling sounds, you know. For the installation."

"Troy told me. He's coming to the Aloha next week to make recordings."

"He is?"

"You could come too, if you want. I'll introduce you around. Maybe give you a lesson. I do that, you know. Give lessons."

"No thanks." Wanda grabbed a bulb planter and started digging a hole. The ground was hard here, and catacombed with old dead roots. She twisted and burrowed and pushed until her wrist started to ache. "One of my first memories is of being in a bowling alley."

He reached over with a hand fork and helped her loosen the dirt. "What's another one?"

Before she could answer, Troy walked by. "I'm headed to the hardware store," he said. "You need anything?"

"Thin-set," Wanda said.

"Hyacinths, please," Mr. Striker added. "Some of those tulips we got the other day, and more daffies, too, if they have 'em."

"Will do."

"Thanks."

Troy moved on. Wanda paused, her hands in the dirt. She closed her eyes and breathed in the pungent, spicy-sweet smell Troy always left in his wake. Fall was the worst. It was never harder to keep from wanting him than now, when the days were growing short, the weather was turning, and she felt a need for fires.

"He'd take a bullet for you, that one, you know," Mr. Striker said, lightly. He rarely spoke about other people in the household. He'd certainly never broached any kind of personal subject with her before. "He'd follow you to the ends of the earth."

"How do you know?"

"I can see it. Anyone with eyes could see it."

He was right, she knew—the fact that the volunteers assumed she and Troy were a couple was a source of shame and embarrassment. But she didn't like hearing it, especially from someone who knew nothing about her.

Mr. Striker went on. "And whether you end up choosin' him or not, you don't wanna be settlin' for anything less."

"What do you know about it?"

"I loved somebody like that once, a long time ago." He fell silent again, and she did nothing to resurrect the conversation.

In November, the weather turned cold and rainy. The anniversary of Margaret's death was marked with a smaller gathering and held indoors.

Augie was unusually fussy that day. Mr. Striker offered to hold him so that Susan and Bruce could sit with the others and enjoy the holiday meal. Wanda could tell by the confident way he scooped Augie into his arms and the sureness with which he held him that Mr. Striker had experience with babies; he was good with them, the way some people are. He walked Augie up and down the stairs and around the house—letting him caterwaul, singing to him—until the baby finally fell asleep.

Mr. Striker's mysterious Idaho correspondent came by the house the day after Thanksgiving and was introduced to all the members of the household. Her name was Joyce. They'd met in Hawaii. Mr. Striker was noticeably absent for the next two days and nights.

"Where have you been?" Wanda demanded when he showed up late Sunday evening. She'd been greatly unnerved by his unexplained disappearance and was furious with him. She didn't like it when people suddenly up and took off. Everybody knew that. Even the volunteers notified her well in advance if they weren't going to be around, told her why they'd be gone and when they'd be coming back. As a member of this household, Mr. Striker was as accountable as the rest of them for his actions, his whereabouts. "How could you just disappear like that?" Wanda asked, surprising herself with her strident tone and intensity of feeling. "How could you leave for three days without telling anyone where you'd be? Didn't it occur to you that we might wonder where you were?"

Mr. Striker studied her. "Joyce and I took a trip to the coast," he said quietly. "Troy knew where to reach me." Then he added, "I'm sorry you were worried. I won't do it again."

By winter, he was concentrating his efforts on another part of the property, but Wanda saw him frequently as he passed by the carriage house windows. She'd invite him in sometimes to take a rest, warm up, have a cup of coffee. He didn't like breaking things, she discovered, but he enjoyed learning about techniques and studying her drawings. He never stayed long.

"Aren't you freezing out there?" she asked.

He shrugged. "I'm the gardener. There's a lot to tend to here. A person can't always do their work in the sun."

He brought his coffee to the worktable and watched her. She was buttering bits of tesserae with thin-set and then applying them to a child-sized valise. "What do you think about, when you're doin' that?" he asked. His eyes were downcast and focused in the direction of the valise, but he seemed to be looking elsewhere.

"I try to think as little as possible," she said. "Why?"

He shrugged again and wandered to another part of the studio.

"That woman you loved," she ventured. "Did you follow her to the ends of the earth?"

"You could say that."

"Did you find her?"

"No."

"What happened?"

He didn't answer right away. "I followed her until somebody else found me."

Something in his tone made her look up. He was staring at her in a way that made her think he'd been staring for a while. She didn't like being under such scrutiny.

Troy came back from the main house, where he'd been working with the volunteers. "They've got about two-thirds of one of the lanes done," he said excitedly. "You wanna see it?"

Wanda scowled and returned to her work. "Maybe later."

"It would mean a lot if you'd come by, is all. They're working really hard and they could use some encouragement."

"I said I will," Wanda answered testily. "Just not right this minute."

"Fine," Troy barked back. "Don't thank them then. Jesus, Wanda." He slammed the door and left.

A moment passed before Mr. Striker muttered, "It's a bloody wonder that boyo puts up with you. He's not gonna hang around forever, you know."

Wanda was incensed. "He can leave anytime he wants! If he's not happy, he can just go." Then she mumbled with a pinched, bitter mouth, "I hope he does. I hope to Christ he gets out, for his own sake."

"You'd better not hope that." Mr. Striker's expression was sharp now, his tone stern and biting. "You know what your problem is, girl? You're like one of those people who get their house broken into. They spend a fortune putting bars on all the windows and doors, and their property never gets violated again. And there they are, lookin' at the world from behind bars for all bloody eternity." He slurped down the last of his coffee and slammed his mug on the table. "Not every man is a fuckin' burglar, you know."

Wanda was working late in the studio. The deadline for *Family Recreation* was fast approaching, and she was often awake past the time when everyone else—even Troy and Mr. Striker—had gone upstairs to bed.

She had just gone into the kitchen of the main house to get coffee from the pantry when the phone rang.

"Hello?" said a timid voice. "I'm supposed to ask for Wanda."

"That's me."

The caller whispered, "Is this Detective Lorenzini?"

Wanda's mouth went dry. "Yes, it is," she whispered back.

"This is Dermot. From Blissed on Bop? You came in a couple of years ago, in pursuit of a B&E suspect. Do you remember?"

"Yes, I do."

"Is the investigation still on?"

"Yes," she answered, without hesitation.

"That's good," citizen Dermot hissed urgently, "because I think he's here! It was the music he asked for that made me think it was him. That, and his physical appearance, of course. I still have my notes—and that really awesome drawing. It looks just like him."

"Describe the suspect."

"Long hair, big nose—"

"Does it look like a boxer's nose? Like it's been punched a few times?"

"Yeah! Exactly like that! His face is kinda puffy, too."

"What music has he been looking at?"

"Parker. Rassan Roland Kirk. Baker. The rare recordings, like you said."

"What does he smell like?"

Dermot paused. "I don't know. I'm not that close. Would you like me to—"

"Never mind." Wanda started getting out of her work clothes. "Stall him. Find something really rare. Do you have the live Mingus recordings from Paris in '57?"

"Yeah."

"Get 'em out. Put 'em on. I'll be right over."

"Ten-four, Detective."

Wanda wanted to race up the stairs; but of course, she couldn't— her bones wouldn't let her. It seemed like an eternity before she could get to her room. She struggled into her black skirt and peplum-edged jacket. She slipped into her flat-heeled shoes. With shaking hands, she applied some lipstick. By the time she got to Troy's door and knocked, she was breathing hard. Her joints ached. Her head sizzled. She heard a recording of piano and vibes playing quietly in his room, something lyrical and smooth.

Troy opened the door. He must have been awake, reading. He wasn't wearing a shirt.

"I have to go somewhere," she said. "Can I borrow the truck?"

"Sure, but . . ." He rubbed his eyes. "Is there something wrong with the Volvo?"

"Oh," she said, dully. What was she thinking? Why was she here? "No. There's nothing wrong with the car. I don't know why I . . ." She paused. Someone sang, "*It's not the pale moon that excites me, that thrills and delights me, oh no . . .*"

"You want to come in?"

Wanda stared at his chest and chewed her lip. "What is this? What are you listening to?"

"Nancy Wilson. George Shearing."

"You don't like jazz."

"Yes I do. I just don't like the stuff you listen to."

"Why not?"

"It makes me nervous. It makes me feel like the world is coming apart."

Wanda listened to a few more phrases. "*It isn't your sweet conversation that brings this sensation . . .*" It was very nice music, but not what she should be listening to at this moment. It was not the music that would keep Detective Lorenzini in uniform.

"What's wrong?" He came closer. He took her hand.

"Can't sleep," she mumbled, feeling dazed. "I'm going for a drive. Or maybe to get something to eat."

"Let me come with you."

"No!" she cried. "I have to go alone. I'll be back in a few hours."

"You're pretty dressed up for the I-Hop."

"Oh, well, I . . ."

"Okay," he said, letting go of her hand and backing away. "Do whatever you have to do. Just be careful."

He closed the door. She leaned against the wall outside, listening to the last few bars of the song, breathing in the lingering scent of him, safe again from the dangers of being too near the one person who made her feel like something more than damaged goods.

*   *   *

From Margaret's house, it took only a few minutes to get to Blissed on Bop. She fairly flew along the crest of Capitol Hill and then careened down Denny Way, heading due west. From there it was a straight shot across town to Queen Anne and the Seattle Center, where the Space Needle was silhouetted against the glittering night sky, appearing just as it did in the postcard that brought her here almost five years ago.

She parked across the street from the store. The place looked busy. She put the finishing touches on her lipstick, her hair.

She walked in. Dermot did a double take, then signaled her to the counter.

"You look different," he whispered. "What happened? Were you injured in the line of duty?"

"Something like that," she answered. "Where is he?"

Dermot jerked his head toward the back of the store. "He came in about an hour ago, with that girl in the sundress, the one who's wearing the headphones. I gave them the Mingus recording to listen to."

Wanda wandered closer. With her back to them, she pretended to examine some LP recordings from the "Easy Listening" section. She felt Peter's voice even before she heard it: the low, fuzzy tones and slurred diction that had always given her the feeling of being wrapped in a mohair sweater. He was chuckling in a way she knew too.

"Isn't that incredible?" he was saying. "Isn't he a genius?"

He was drunk, Wanda could tell. He'd always been a nice drunk. She couldn't get a good look at him yet.

The girl smiling up at him looked like she was maybe in her early to late twenties. She was small and pert and pretty. Peter liked little women, she remembered. He'd told her that on more than one occasion.

This girl, however, differed physically from Wanda in one striking way. "It's fantastic," she cooed, her 38-D chest fully inflated with admiration. "Unbelievable."

"Isn't it?" Peter said. "People like that, they're real artists. They're like angels. They're evolved. The rest of us, we're like . . ."—he gave a muffled belch—". . . nothing."

Listening to his voice, she could feel the texture of him in a way that she hadn't before. She could feel, too, what her own texture must have been when she'd loved him—her briskness, her edginess, her competence. He'd needed that. Apparently, he needed it still. He hadn't changed. Not one bit.

She walked up behind him. He still had long hair, but it was streaked with gray now, and had an ill-nourished, desiccated look, as if it were sprinkled with road dust. She touched him on the shoulder. Beyond him, the pert, adoring girl with headphones and cantaloupe breasts turned her radiant smile down a few notches.

"Peter," Wanda said.

He turned around. She saw at once everything he was, everything she knew him to be and had loved fiercely for so many years: a depressed, brilliant drunk, not unkind, but unable to function in the real world of enduring bread-and-butter love. Who he was had taken its toll on his face and body. She hadn't saved him. No one else had, either, but anyone who wasn't careful could spend a lifetime chasing after a dream of him, healed and whole and capable of loving back. And they'd be all right, too, as long as they never lost sight of him or changed. As long as they never woke up.

"Wanda?" he said, pleasantly, sluggishly. "Is that you?" He laughed expansively, like a guiltless, inebriated Saint Nick.

They chatted for a while. Or rather, he chatted. He pontificated. Did he ask what she was doing? Why she was here? What had brought her to Seattle? How she was doing? Why her face was off-kilter? Why she walked with a limp? She didn't know. She didn't think so. But then, she wasn't really paying attention. The diffuse, sonorous quality of his voice—which had once soothed and aroused her—she now found merely slurred and bloated, the voice of the last drunk in the bar at closing time. Peter's girl stared at him with undisguised admiration, adoration, and lust. As he droned on, Wanda nodded mechanically, forgetting their exchange even as it was occurring. Forgetting him.

"Good-bye," Peter said. He kissed her lightly on the cheek, leaving a residue of breath that was part vinegar, part cigarette smoke.

"Good-bye," Wanda answered.

"Who was that?" asked the pert, doomed girl with the market-produce tits.

Wanda didn't wait to hear his answer. She approached the front counter, where poor, loyal citizen Dermot awaited some kind of reward. On the way, she picked up an early live club recording by Nat King Cole.

"Well?" he asked eagerly. "Is that the perp? Is that the guy you've been trying to find?"

She shook her head and paid for her record. Dermot looked crushed. She gave him a brusque but appreciative handshake. "Thank you for your help, Dermot, but you can throw away your notes. The case is cold."

She drove for the rest of the night, along the old routes she'd taken when she'd been looking for him, through this city she'd come to know, where streets curved, intersected, and broke off in response to unruly hills and unexpected bodies of water. Her prayers had been answered, but there was nothing at the end of them. No sense of relief or redemption. No softening or warming of that old, cold fossil, her heart. The heat of what she'd felt for him, that marvel of love which had burned like a dengue fever, could not be relit.

She arrived home about an hour after sunrise. She got out of the car and started inside. She needed to change clothes, make coffee, get to work. She'd go through the patio entrance.

Someone was whistling. The tune was familiar. As she walked toward the house, she spied Mr. Striker and Maurice, up and about, early as usual. Maurice was lolling in a patch of catnip; Mr. Striker was kneeling in the herb bed, facing away from her. He usually had his hair tucked up in a hat, but this morning it was pulled into a neat ponytail and hung down his back. The picture had a startling potency, as if she'd seen Mr. Striker from this perspective before.

She stopped, stared, listened. What was that music? She started toward him as if he were some rare, wild thing that might take flight. His jacket was off—it was already warm outside—and he was wearing one of his signature Hawaiian shirts, the pink and lime one that was especially gaudy.

Mr. Striker started to sing: "'My mama done told me, when I was in knee pants, my mama done told me, Son . . .'"

I am going to find him, she thought, and here he was singing, his voice no longer in disguise, but rich with soft wooly vowels and corkscrew punch consonants—the unmistakable paradoxes of a native Dubliner's speech. She could feel the universe laughing. She almost laughed herself.

"'A woman'll sweet-talk, and give you the big eye, but when the sweet talkin's done . . .'"

Wanda hadn't been entirely truthful on the day they christened the carriage house. Of course, she always strove for reverence and detachment when breaking Margaret's things, but sometimes her work incited—and over the years, she realized now, purged—a very personal anger. It was perhaps for that reason she was able to approach the man before her with an unclouded heart and an absence of malice, and speak to him as she was about to.

"'A woman's a two-face,'" he was singing, "'a worrisome thing who'll leave you to sing the blues in the night. . . .'"

Wanda uttered a single, quiet syllable. Mr. Striker turned around.

"Jesus fuckin' Christ!" he said. "You gave me a helluva start!" He wiped his face with a handkerchief. "You're awfully dressed-up, girl. Where have you been?"

She couldn't ask him, not yet.

"Wanda?" he said. "What is it?"

She inhaled shoe leather, paste wax, percolated coffee, remembered smells of bubble bath and Old Spice aftershave. She lowered herself slowly to kneel next to him.

"What are you doin'? You'll be gettin' your lovely dress all dirty."

"Do you remember asking me about my first memories?" she said.

He nodded, puzzled. "In a bowling alley. They weren't good ones, I take it."

She paused again. "There's no chance you'll be leaving, is there?"

"I'm not scheduled to work at the Aloha till Monday. Why?"

"What I'm asking is . . . *here*. Will you be leaving *here*?"

"Wanda, what are you talkin' about?"

She marveled at her stupidity. Looking into his eyes—the eyes of a tortured poet, a brawler, an atheist, lit up with love as pure and good and sacrificial as God's own—she couldn't imagine how she hadn't known him at once.

"I broke my arm when I was four," she began. "I remember my father . . . Da . . . giving me a bath, and singing to me, that song that you were singing just now. I wasn't supposed to get my cast wet," she went on. "He laid out a towel on the side of the tub so it would be soft for me. It was such a little thing, for him to do that, but I've never forgotten. So, you see, my memories, they aren't all bad."

Mr. Striker had started to cry.

"She was the great love of your life," Wanda said. "I understood why you left."

"There was great love where I was," he answered firmly. "I wish to God I'd stayed."

Her sclerosed heart was softening, finding its pulse, filling with blood. The dam behind her eyes was in danger of giving way.

"There's nothing wrong with you," he said, looking at her now with an unequivocal steadiness. "Never was. Never will be. You have to know that." He took her by the shoulders, moored her to his chest, and the storm of tides came then—blood to her heart, saltwater to her eyes— and he held her tight and would not let go.

"Is everything okay, Mike?"

It was Troy, coming out of the main house.

M.J. nodded. Troy smiled and went on his way.

Wanda watched him go, and then looked to her father. "How long has he known?"

M.J. cupped the precious, marred face of his only child in his hands. "He's on his way to the hardware store," he said. "You can probably just catch him, if you run."

Wanda kissed her da. She struggled to her feet. "Troy!" she called. "Wait!" She started running, as fast as she was able.

Michael O'Casey stood up and took inventory of his life to this point. He turned over a few memories, considered some of the things that were part of who he was: Gina, laughing; Maureen holding one of the babies; Irma throwing a strike; Mr. Kosminsky singing the *hamotzi;* his daughter, a newborn asleep in his arms and a million other memories of her right up to this moment; her faithful boyo's face in the street that night, and now, turning to see her as she stumbled toward him; the tangle of their bodies as they joined and kissed. He'd never seen two happier souls in his life.

And as for him, it was a sure thing that no man living was luckier.

"There's different ideas about that particular custom!" Bruce yelled. With him in the kitchen were Susan, Augie, and several Crazy Plate

Academy volunteers. The adults were scrambling to finish assembling numerous artistic hors d'oeuvre platters before the ceremony began. Augie, the ring-bearer, had given up trying to hold a pillow and walk at the same time; he was lying on his back under the kitchen table, eating a cracker and trying to pull off his new shoes. A shlemozzl of violins, clarinets, saxophones, trumpets, trombones, cymbals, drums, and singing came from the dining room, where the musicians were practicing, while upstairs Wanda, M.J., Troy, and Gus were getting dressed.

"Technically," Bruce went on, hollering over the hubbub, "it's supposed to remind us of the desecration of the Temple."

Susan called out in cheering tones, "However! Feminists insist that it symbolizes the breaking of the hymen on the couple's wedding night."

"Personally," Bruce continued, "I think it's just another one of those Jewish guilt things. I mean, God forbid there should be one day in your life when you're happy! God forbid we shouldn't be suffering! It's supposed to remind us that happiness is transient."

"Oh, God!" Susan yipped suddenly. "Where's Augie?"

"Under the table. Relax, Susie-Q."

Susan squatted, extracted Augie from his hiding place, and hoisted him onto her hip. "You are being such a big boy about all this. But me? Utterly terrified. Mummy's never been in a wedding. What do you think? Do I look all right?"

Augie popped a fig in her mouth and giggled. "Dance, Mama!" he said. "Daddy too! Do boom-boom-boom!"

Bruce put down the serving tongs and held out his arms, ballroom style. "Assume the position, Mama."

Susan joined him and started to sing: "*Shall we dance?*"

"Boom-boom-boom!"

"*On a bright cloud of music shall we fly?*"

"Boom-boom-boom!"

Within moments, the musicians took up the cue and began improvising a raucous accompaniment; they plunged single file into the kitchen, where they were greeted by a small village of people dancing the polka and booming. Augie laughed and clapped and gleefully plundered the platters of hors d'oeuvres.

Suddenly one of the Crooning Clansmen bustled in, his brow as crimson as his kilt, his garters askew. He grabbed an enormous metal funnel, banged on it several times with a slotted spoon, and then spoke into it as if it were a megaphone: "I think Wanda's relatives from Chicago just arrived," he announced. "All of them!" He patted at his flushed brow with a handkerchief as everyone caught their breath. "Step lively, people! We're gonna need a helluva lot more chairs out there."

Look now. Look at what you value, what you hold dear. Objects, first. And not necessarily because of their innate value (although that might figure into it), but because they are endowed—by your mind and imagination, by your memories—with what is known as "sentimental value."

Sentiment has been defined as ascribing a value to something above and beyond what its value is to God. This presumes a belief in God, and furthermore a belief in a kind of God that passes judgment on the inexplicable fondnesses of the human heart; there is an expression, isn't there: "the object of my affections." But perhaps you do not believe in that kind of God, or any other, for that matter.

Look then at the faces and bodies of people you love. The explicit beauty that comes not from smoothness of skin or neutrality of expression, but from the web of experience that has left its mark. Each face, each body is its own living fossilized record. A record of cats, combatants, difficult births; of accidents, cruelties, blessings. Reminders of folly, greed, indiscretion, impatience. A moment of time, of memory, preserved, internalized, and enshrined within and upon the body. You need not be told that these records are what render your beloved beautiful. If God exists, He is there, in the small, cast-off pieces, rough and random and no two alike.

Wanda and Troy celebrated their wedding in the backyard of Margaret's house under a billowing white canopy. It was a very big wedding, with the volunteers, Aloha Lanes staff and clientele, Babara Cohen, students of the Crazy Plate Academy, the Crooning Clansmen, Troy's mother and sisters, M.J.'s lady friend Joyce, and the entire Schultz clan all in attendance.

Augie, the fledgling toddler, tripped several times, but persevered with lionesque courage until he successfully delivered his pillow to the groom. Wanda's ring was lost somewhere along the way, but they recovered it later. Susan was maid of honor; Gus, in kilt and garters, stood up with Troy. A solo violin played "The Nearness of You" as Wanda walked down the aisle arm in arm with her father.

As a blessing, M.J. read from "A Prayer for My Daughter" by William Butler Yeats: "O may she live like some green laurel rooted in one dear perpetual place."

And at the end of the service, in a gesture mirroring Jewish ritual but reflecting traditions entirely their own, they smashed Irma and Lucie's tête-à-tête. The crowd huzzahed and clapped, and the festivities and dancing began.

Upstairs, dreaming, Maurice stirred, rolled over, and jostled an eighteenth-century tripod table, sending a trio of Worcester inkstands—circa 1830 and valued at roughly three thousand dollars each—careening over the edge and onto the floor.

Being deaf as a post, the crash did not wake him.

Acknowledgments

❧

It would not have been possible to sustain the seven-year effort required to write this book without the unflagging help of many kind, generous, funny, smart, loving, and infinitely patient people. It gives me great pleasure to finally recognize their efforts and express my gratitude.

I am thankful to the following authors, whose books were tremendously helpful during my research: JoAnn Locktov and Leslie Plummer Clagett (*The Art of Mosaic Design*), Richard Chesnoff (*Pack of Thieves*), and Seattle artist Gizel Berman and her husband, Nick (*My Three Lives*).

For giving me an inside look at two of Seattle's wonderful Capitol Hill mansions, I am grateful to the Shafer-Baillie staff, and to Sylvia Jones and the residents of PRAG house.

For directing me to the best of bebop, thanks go to poet, DJ, and activist Paul Nelson.

Catherine Walton graciously agreed to check my French; Erin McCarger Schilling and Jennevieve Schlemmer shared their vast knowledge of the artistic and technical aspects of mosaic-making, and gave me the courage to grout.

I owe Stephen Sandweiss for introducing me to the concept of Tikun Olam, and Deborah Frockt for illuminating the *real* reason behind the glass-breaking at the end of a Jewish wedding!

Thanks to Jerry Hahn for taking the time to answer all my questions about bowling, and to the staff of the Leilani Lanes for throwing the best birthday parties ever.

I'm indebted to the many people who ushered me into the larger writing community: Nancy Rawles, Joan Rabinowitz, Anita Montgomery, and the Jack Straw Foundation; Nancy Nordoff, the staff of Hedgebrook Farm, and my "sisters" in residence: Lynne, Anju, Jourdan, Roberta, and Merlie.

Thanks also to the Group Health Radiologists who were so generous with their time and knowledge: Dr. Daniel Winder, Dr. Maurice Miller, and Dr. David Hillier.

Miriam Greenbaum and Jennifer Wood of the Washington State Holocaust Education and Resource Center were enormously helpful in sharing their remarkable knowledge and extensive resources. Their contribution to this book was vital.

I am deeply grateful to Sheri Holman, who so graciously consented to read an early draft. Her keen insights into the craft of novel writing were invaluable; her kindness and encouragement meant so much. Sheri, you will always be my "Hero!"

To the members of my writing group, The Commoners: Craig English, Ellen Parker, Michael Maschinot, ChiChi Singler, and Ron Pellegrino. Thank you for having faith in me, and for making me a better writer than I ever could have been on my own. This book wouldn't have seen the light of day without your constant support. I love you all.

Melvin Sterne, editor of *Carve* magazine, was the first person to publish my work; I will always owe him a special debt for his early support and encouragement.

Thanks to Tom Cherwin, my copy editor, for his careful eye and kind words, and to all the folks at Grove/Atlantic for taking a risk on this fledgling novelist.

Shary Kopyt, survivor, was one of the unseen angels who made sure that Irma's story was told. Her granddaughter, Lauren Wein, edited the book with marvelous intelligence, grace, and affection. She guided me through the process of rewriting with respect and utter clarity; I learned so much from our collaboration.

To the fabulous Daniel Lazar, who found me, and my agent, Simon Lipskar of Writers House: you boychik geniuses are the best. The serendipity that brought us together is enough to make a person believe in miracles. Thank you for your Talmudic scholarship, wisdom, jokes, recipes, music, and Yiddish lessons. I am one lucky writer.

My deepest thanks go to my family: my mother, Dorie, who instilled in me my love of books and reading; my father, Gregory, who always encouraged me to reach for my dreams; my husband, Bill (the nicest little old Jewish man I know) for reading all my rough drafts and staying married to me anyway; and finally, to my beauties, Noah and Sam, for giving Mommy time to work on her "big book," for carrying my laptop, supplying me with peeps and jokes and Hot Wheels cars, for being my most valued teachers and greatest sources of inspiration. Now you'll always know where to find me: in the library, under "K."